PRIZE STORIES 1963:
THE O. HENRY AWARDS

PRIZE STORIES 1963: THE O. HENRY AWARDS

EDITED AND WITH AN INTRODUCTION BY

RICHARD POIRIER

DOUBLEDAY & COMPANY, INC., GARDEN CITY, NEW YORK, 1963

CONTENTS ..

LIBRARY OF CONGRESS CATALOG CARD NUMBER 21–9372

COPYRIGHT © 1963 BY DOUBLEDAY & COMPANY, INC.

PRINTED IN THE UNITED STATES OF AMERICA. FIRST EDITION

PUBLISHER'S NOTE

The present volume is the forty-third in the O. Henry Memorial Award series. No collections appeared in 1952 and 1953, when the continuity of the series was interrupted by the death of Herschel Brickell, who had been the editor for ten years.

In 1918 the Society of Arts and Sciences met to vote upon a monument to the American master of the short story, O. Henry. They decided that this memorial should be in the form of two prizes for the best short stories published by American authors in American magazines during the year 1919. From this beginning, the memorial developed into an annual anthology of the best American short stories, published, with the exception of the years mentioned above, by Doubleday & Company, Inc. Blanche Colton Williams, one of the founders of the awards, was editor from 1919 to 1932; Harry Hansen took over from 1933 to 1940; Herschel Brickell from 1941 to 1951; Paul Engle from 1954 to 1959; Mary Stegner in 1960; and Richard Poirier from 1961 until now.

The stories chosen for this volume were published in the period from the winter of 1961 to the summer of 1962. A list of the magazines consulted appears at the back of the book. The choice of stories and the selection of prize winners are exclusively the responsibility of the editor.

INTRODUCTION

First Prize: FLANNERY O'CONNOR, for "Everything That Rises Must Converge"
Second Prize: ERVIN D. KRAUSE, for "The Snake"
Third Prize: THALIA SELZ, for "The Education of a Queen"

Most of the stories in this volume illustrate a prevalent characteristic in current American fiction—an intense, sometimes affectionate, almost always personally involved relationship between the writer and one of the various coteries that abound in American society. Everyone is aware of the succession of stories about Jewish family life, of which Tillie Olsen's "Tell Me a Riddle," awarded first prize in the 1961 volume, is a most distinguished example, of the vogue of novels and stories about army life, of the continuing devotion of writers to characters and scenes that are representative of the South and often of the Negro's situation in it—or, in James Baldwin's work, of the Negro in a cosmopolitan white society which accepts him in ways as damaging as the Southern forms of rejection. There were at least five novels during the past year, and over twenty stories published in reputable magazines, which are wholly or in part about the academic community, including Bernard Malamud's *A New Life*. And perhaps most significant is the more frequent use than heretofore, in fiction of all kinds, of characters that are made representative of these and other identifiable social, cultural, and racial groupings.

In the present volume there are two stories of academic life, Norma Klein's "The Burglar" and "The Rise of the Proletariat" by J. G. McClure; a story about a Quaker family during the Civil War, Jessamyn West's "The Picnickers"; two stories that involve significant relations of Negroes to whites, J. C. Oates' "The Fine White Mist of Winter" and one by Ellen Douglas, "On the Lake"; two stories in which the central characters belong, in effect, to the theatrical world, Ben Maddow's "In a Cold Hotel" and James Cox's "That Golden Crane"; and Terry Southern, whose style in

"The Road Out of Axotle" expresses an essentially "beat" reaction to fantastic occurrences. Naturally, not all the stories in this volume can be categorized, even when the categories are as inclusive as those I have mentioned. Sylvia Berkman's "Pontifex," with its poignant reluctance to give more finality of shape to the experiences of the characters than they, in their frailty of memory, are able to sustain, Helen Ansell's "The Threesome," William Saroyan's "Gaston," which does, however, include dialogue between parents and child that has been made "typical" by Salinger, and the brilliant story by Ervin Krause which receives second prize—none of these encourage us to speak of the coteries to which the characters belong or to which the author's style alludes by its rhythms and idiom. But the inclination to write in a style that reflects various coteries is apparent in such a large body of fiction, and by so much in this collection, that it deserves attention as a relatively new development.

It could be argued that what I am describing is not very "new" at all, and that important American fiction has always found its location in "that theater a little removed," as Hawthorne puts it, "from the highway of ordinary travel." The "theater" may be the woods, a raft on the Mississippi, a whaling ship, or even, in James, a group of initiates who share a kind of superior consciousness. In its taste for what I call coteries, recent fiction might, then, be doing nothing more than carrying on an old tradition in American writing that is strong also in Hemingway and Faulkner. There is this important difference, however—that in giving attention less to general aspects of American life than to some particular groupings in it, American writers are now showing a more avid but selective appetite for details of social life and manners than ever before. A very good young writer like Philip Roth has written a volume of short stories mostly about Jewish family life and a more recent novel, *Letting Go*, which is concerned also with academic life, because in his relations to both of these communities he is more emotionally entangled in the stuff of daily living than he is in relation to American society at large. In fact, it is difficult to imagine how a writer or anyone else can articulate a detailed relationship to anything as vast, changing, and diversified as American society. In its appeals to our interest, its mere surface is dominated now by this, now by another of various highly vocal and powerful groups. Perhaps only Fitzgerald, in *The Great Gatsby*, has managed to write a great novel about "America" in the general sense of that term. Feeling the difficulty, even perhaps the impossibility now of achieving anything similarly general without also being simple minded or platitudinous about American life, our writers have become increasingly immersed in particular areas of it, often those to which they belonged as children or young adults.

The consequence in style and form has been to immerse the reader as well in the details and sounds that make these areas distinct and interesting within an otherwise homogenized culture. In order to give us a sense of this uniqueness, the social texture of current fiction is thus often made extraordinarily thick. By furnishing patterns and even rituals to daily life, by encouraging unusual styles in language and dress, and by giving authority to idiosyncrasies of behavior, these coteries are naturally attractive to American writers. They discover in them a sanction for style in a broad sense, for theatricalities of expression, and a license for certain intensities and complications not granted by our mass culture. It is not surprising that there is a great deal of mimicry in the style of nearly all the stories I am describing, with characters becoming exaggerations of the "types" that presumably exist in these coteries. Such mimicry can be heard in the stories of Flannery O'Connor, Thalia Selz, and Ben Maddow, in the opening of Norma Klein's story and throughout J. G. McClure. Perhaps the most engaging mimicry—a mixture of satire and affection—is in James Cox's story of middle-aged lovers awaiting the permission of a revivalist preacher, who happens also to be the eleven-year-old son of the woman ("Sometimes Mr. Gellespie thought him a little willful too. And jealous, terrible jealous"). That one has to *listen* carefully to such stories is a measure of the difference in kind between the renderings of social life which we find in them and what we are offered in most earlier American fiction of social manners.

This is not the proper occasion, however, for any preferential distinction between the kinds of attention to social manners in current fiction and the sort given by earlier American writers. For one thing, the short stories of any given year are not weighty enough to sustain such a comparison. I mean only to suggest, therefore, that within the past several years most of our writers of shorter fiction and many of our novelists have been creating a society in their works which is at once less extensive and more particularized than that found, say, even in the early novels of Saul Bellow. As a literary consequence, writers like Philip Roth or Bernard Malamud or, in the present instance, Flannery O'Connor and Thalia Selz, devote much of their stylistic energy initiating us into the scenic and conversational features of the coteries about which they are writing. They seem to be exhilarated by what is normally considered detrimental—that they are dealing with characters who are essentially stock figures or types, and who often speak in some highly formulaic way.

Exhilaration of style under these circumstances is hardly to be taken for granted. In some of the stories in this collection, there is evidence not of excitement or critical activity in the handling of representative types or situations, but rather of a limp dependence on them, as if the author felt no obligation to create these things in the mind of the reader. Presumably they are already there. Consider, for example, the phrasing by which Ellen Douglas presents the Negro woman in "On the Lake"—"like an amiable golden giantess." Being introduced by literary cliches of this kind, the Negro woman comes to life only for those whose suburban fantasies are slow a-dying. This particular deficiency exists, it should be added, in a comparison made only to the other best stories of the year and does not substantially diminish the dramatic power of the central episodes. Nor is it a condemnation of Jessamyn West's story to say that she too uses characters that belong to a coterie or type only for flatly schematic purposes and that they call forth none of her considerable inventiveness. The Quaker forms of address are tiresomely mechanical as she uses them and give an unintended obliquity of tone to many of the conversations. They contribute little to that particular social ordering which is being disrupted by the violence of war. The household is an effective place for such disruptions to occur not because the author makes it Quaker, but rather because in her details and style she so much more effectively makes it into a dying soldier's dream of home and maternal care.

Each reader will discover moments when, in almost all these stories, the author is deriving inspiration from working in specialized social areas and with figures who are representative of them. In doing so, it will be noticed that many of the writers here are in a peculiar way critical of their own practices. Most of these stories manage to express dissatisfaction with characters who treat one another the way the authors seem to treat them, who think about one another as types and who react to situations with an extravagance that takes no account of very particular human feelings. For example, while Ben Maddow's story is full of loudly satiric stock phrases and comic exaggerations, it draws from these an ultimately melancholy conclusion. The magician in relation to his son conducts himself in the way his own girl friend acts, so he claims, on all occasions: "She's practicing in real life what she might be called upon to perform on stage." His character is wholly absorbed into his theatrical egotism. In like manner, Flannery O'Connor shows, here and elsewhere, the comic surface of people who have made stereotypes of themselves, be they shiftless intellectual theorizers or Southern ladies of great illusion and small means. And yet the story is finally about the humiliations that come to both mother and son because in their different ways they treat Negroes and each other as types. Only violence, in her fiction, can break down false theories of relationship and expose the human mixtures of hate, guilt, and love that exist beneath the categories which her people mistake for reality. The stories by Thalia Selz, Norma Klein, and J. G. McClure are all comic, but each of them offers an implicit criticism of people who live by dependence on the manners and roles of some particular in-group, even while the author takes pleasure from the mannered self-assurance with which they express themselves.

The attitudes that belong to any given coterie in these stories is never the same as the authors', never as free, inquisitive, or critical. Terry Southern, in "The Road Out of Axotle," is an example of a writer who insists on his almost total hospitality of mind even while comically indulging in various constricted postures and attitudes. His story has no inherent principles for selection or economy of material—it could be twice or half as long as it is—and there is no accumulation of intensity, such as one finds in more conventional short stories. It neglects these features, which some critics treat as necessary virtues in fiction, with a full and exuberant intention. Despite the hallucinatory quality of the incidents in which he is involved, the narrator remains steadily cool and dispassionately curious about what is going on. He is without presuppositions about how he should be responding even when being attacked by wild dogs, his tone registering that independence of reaction *within* the experience which is often apparent in Mr. Southern's humor—"The dissimilarity between them and ordinary dogs is remarkable." Like Ben Maddow, Southern can play with a mixture of idioms, including the sometimes urbane, sometimes "beat" syntax and language of the narrator. He can do so because he takes any given conversational style as merely an effort on the part of the character to play a part or assume a role that he has imagined for himself. More importantly, he suggests, as have some of his contemporaries, that there need be no necessary connection between the internal states of a character (or a writer) and the events of the physical and social world around him. As Jack Ludwig points out in his study of *Recent American Novelists* (University of Minnesota Press), this acceptance of the possible foreignness of sights and sounds and events, this "letting go" of life is the reverse of those feelings of alienation, based on the sentimental assumption that these things *should* be relevant, which is characteristic of American fiction of the immediate period after World War II.

In Southern's story we have an exorbitant version of what we can notice in the other stories so far discussed—a delight in stylistically exploiting coterie behavior that verges on the theatrical, and a corresponding critical awareness of the necessary limitations or absurdities of such behavior. Perhaps this awareness will obviate some of the inherent dangers of coterie fiction, particularly of the formulaic repetition that follows whenever writers of small talent take advantage of the taste that has been created by earlier and more adventurous ones. Coterie fiction tends to a debilitating fashionableness precisely because the emphatic and energetic styles needed to create it are extremely easy to imitate. One can already see the process at work. But rarely in the stories printed here is there anything that is imitative of literary fashions without also being satiric. And, again, some of the stories are in no important way referrable to any of the identifiable social types or groups that have been made available to fiction.

The story most remarkable for avoiding any appeal to social coterie or the use of the mannerisms that accompany it is Ervin Krause's "The Snake." Here, and in the story published in the volume for 1961, "The Quick and the Dead," Mr. Krause writes in none of the fashions now admired in the literary journals or in the more commercial magazines. More than anyone in this volume he turns to the works of earlier writers and gives correspondingly less attention to social manners or to any observable social groups. Faulkner, Hemingway, Stephen Crane, and especially Lawrence are active in his style without ever taking control of it. He is a writer with great meditative dignity of address, quite unlike Thalia Selz, who lets her narrator speak from the couch, as it were, to listeners already sophisticated about lying there themselves. Her story manages with remarkable deftness in variations of style and emphasis to evoke the intellectual fashions of the twenties, in Daphne's parents, and to give us in the narrator's reminiscences some of the quality of the three succeeding decades. The story has the effect of social history, embodied in the life of the family, while being sharply slanted in its point of view. By contrast, Mr. Krause's characters are of no particular time or place, and unlike the richly identified characters in Miss Selz's story, his are given no names. The narrator in her story addresses an audience meant to catch all her slangy, time-ridden allusions and psychoanalytical jokes; she is "with it," meaning, it might be said, that she is "with" the readers of *Partisan Review*. The narrator of "The Snake," on the other hand, gives no indication in his language that he is aware of belonging to any generation that can be characterized by historical or social circumstances. Indeed, the point of the story is that what happens does not belong exclusively to any time or generation, even to any particular person. The poignancy of Miss Selz's heroine is that she is trapped by the very obstinacy of viewpoint which lends vitality to her narration, that at the end she is miserable because she is the kind of person that she is. At the end of "The Snake," the pathos of the situation is mythic in its generality: the man is guilty and the child in terror because of a benumbed recognition in themselves that they are inheritors of Eve. It is therefore not surprising that while the images and symbols of Miss Selz's story are created from scratch out of contemporary happenings, Mr. Krause's are necessarily the most obvious he could borrow from literature and the Bible. He is not in the least complacent about this symbolism, however, making of its contemporary relevance more a mystery than an assumption and showing how it comes into being within the blood stream of people who are not aware of the Biblical analogies for what they are doing.

"The Snake" is stylistically powerful in a way few stories ever are—by being wondrous before circumstances rather than operatically contentious with them. And here again the reason is perhaps that Mr. Krause's fictional circumstances are inseparable from human nature regardless of changes and varieties of social institutions. The narrator is allowed to speak of the "fierce smile of brutality frightening my face" with an awe not dissipated by any Freudian explanations or by the disposition to self-accusation—as if there could be some self that could never be guilty. To conclude with a comparison of two different kinds of stories—Miss Selz's story being what we might call coterie, Mr. Krause's what we can call mythic—is to reveal the extent to which "The Snake" is not at all typical of the good fiction now being written. It is not for that reason necessarily better, whatever that would mean, but it is worth celebrating as a rare and beautiful demonstration that fiction is not under any obligation, however good the results, to give us a preview of the various societies that constitute American society.

—RICHARD POIRIER

PRIZE STORIES 1963:
THE O. HENRY AWARDS

FLANNERY O'CONNOR was educated in the parochial schools of Savannah, the Georgia State College for Women, and the State University of Iowa. Her first novel, *Wise Blood*, was published by Harcourt, Brace in 1952. Her stories have appeared in such magazines as *Harper's Bazaar* and *The Kenyon Review*; and she has contributed to four previous O. Henry volumes—as second prize winner in 1954, and first prize winner in 1957. A collection of short stories, *A Good Man Is Hard to Find*, was published by Harcourt, Brace in 1955. Miss O'Connor lives in Milledgeville, Georgia.

Everything That Rises Must Converge

Her doctor had told Julian's mother that she must lose twenty pounds on account of her blood pressure, so on Wednesday nights Julian had to take her downtown on the bus for a reducing class at the Y. The reducing class was designed for working girls over fifty, who weighed from 165 to 200 pounds. His mother was one of the slimmer ones, but she said ladies did not tell their age or weight. She would not ride on the buses by herself at night since they had been integrated, and because the reducing class was one of her few pleasures, necessary for her health, and *free*, she said Julian could at least put himself out to take her, considering all she did for him. Julian did not like to consider all did for him, but every Wednesday night he braced himself and took her.

She was almost ready to go, standing before the hall mirror, putting on her hat, while he, his hands behind him, appeared pinned to the door frame, waiting like Saint Sebastian for the arrows to begin piercing him. The hat was new and had cost her seven dollars and a half. She kept saying, "Maybe I shouldn't have paid that for it. No, I shouldn't have. I'll take it off and return it tomorrow. I shouldn't have bought it."

Julian raised his eyes to heaven. "Yes, you should have bought it," he said. "Put it on and let's go." It was a hideous hat. A purple velvet flap came down on one side of it and stood up on the other; the rest of it was green and looked like a cushion with the stuffing out. He decided it was less comical than jaunty and pathetic. Everything that gave her pleasure was small and depressed him.

She lifted the hat one more time and set it down slowly on top of her head. Two wings of gray hair protruded on either side of her florid face, but her eyes, sky-blue, were as innocent and untouched by experience as they must have been when she was ten. Were it not that she was a widow who had struggled fiercely to feed and clothe and put him through school and who was supporting him still, "until he got on his feet," she might have been a little girl that he had to take to town.

"It's all right, it's all right," he said. "Let's go." He opened the door himself and started down the walk to get her going. The sky was a dying violet and the houses stood out darkly against it, bulbous liver-colored monstrosities of a uniform ugliness though no two were alike. Since this had been a fashionable neighborhood forty years ago, his mother persisted in thinking they did well to have an apartment in it. Each house had a narrow collar of dirt around it in which sat, usually, a grubby child. Julian walked with his hands in his pockets, his head down and thrust forward and his eyes glazed with the determination to make himself completely numb during the time he would be sacrificed to her pleasure.

The door closed and he turned to find the dumpy figure, surmounted by the atrocious hat, coming toward him. "Well," she said, "you only live once and paying a little more for it, I at least won't meet myself coming and going."

"Some day I'll start making money," Julian said gloomily—he knew he never would—"and you can have one of those jokes whenever you take the fit." But first they would move. He visualized a place where the nearest neighbors would be three miles away on either side.

"I think you're doing fine," she said, drawing on her gloves. "You've only been out of school a year. Rome wasn't built in a day."

She was one of the few members of the Y reducing class who arrived in hat and gloves and who had a son who had been to college. "It takes time," she said, "and the world is in such a mess. This hat looked better on me than any of the others, though when she brought it out I said, 'Take that thing back. I wouldn't have it on my head,' and she said, 'Now wait till you see it on,' and when she put it on me, I said, 'We-ull,' and she said, 'If you ask me, that hat does something for you and you do something for the hat, and besides,' she said, 'with that hat, you won't meet yourself coming and going.' "

Julian thought he could have stood his lot better if she had been selfish, if she had been an old hag who drank and screamed at him. He walked along, saturated in depression, as if in the midst of his martyrdom he had lost his faith. Catching sight of his long, hopeless, irritated face, she stopped suddenly with a grief-stricken look, and pulled back on his arm. "Wait on me," she said. "I'm going back to the house and take this thing off and tomorrow I'm going to return it. I was out of my head. I can pay the gas bill with that seven-fifty."

He caught her arm in a vicious grip. "You are not going to take it back," he said. "I like it."

"Well," she said, "I don't think I ought . . ."

"Shut up and enjoy it," he muttered, more depressed than ever.

"With the world in the mess it's in," she said, "it's a wonder we can enjoy anything. I tell you, the bottom rail is on the top."

Julian sighed.

"Of course," she said, "if you know who you are, you can go anywhere." She said this every time he took her to the reducing class. "Most of them in it are not our kind of people," she said, "but I can be gracious to anybody. I know who I am."

"They don't give a damn for your graciousness," Julian said savagely. "Knowing who you are is good for one generation only. You haven't the foggiest idea where you stand now or who you are."

She stopped and allowed her eyes to flash at him. "I most certainly do know who I am," she said, "and if you don't know who you are, I'm ashamed of you."

"Oh hell," Julian said.

"Your great-grandfather was a former governor of this state," she said. "Your grandfather was a prosperous landowner. Your grandmother was a Godhigh."

"Will you look around you," he said tensely, "and see where you are now?" and he swept his arm jerkily out to indicate the neighborhood, which the growing darkness at least made less dingy.

"You remain what you are," she said. "Your great-grandfather had a plantation and two hundred slaves."

"There are no more slaves," he said irritably.

"They were better off when they were," she said. He groaned to see that she was off on that topic. She rolled onto it every few days like a train on an open track. He knew every stop, every junction, every swamp along the way, and knew the exact point at which her conclusion would roll majestically into the station: "It's ridiculous. It's simply not realistic. They should rise, yes, but on their own side of the fence."

"Let's skip it," Julian said.

"The ones I feel sorry for," she said, "are the ones that are half white. They're tragic."

"Will you skip it?"

"Suppose we were half white. We would certainly have mixed feelings."

"I have mixed feelings now," he groaned.

"Well let's talk about something pleasant," she said. "I remember going to Grandpa's when I was a little girl. Then the house had double stairways that went up to what was really the second floor— all the cooking was done on the first. I used to like to stay down in the kitchen on account of the way the walls smelled. I would sit with my nose pressed against the plaster and take deep breaths. Actually the place belonged to the Godhighs but your grandfather Chestny paid the mortgage and saved it for them. They were in reduced circumstances," she said, "but reduced or not, they never forgot who they were."

"Doubtless that decayed mansion reminded them," Julian muttered. He never spoke of it without contempt or thought of it without longing. He had seen it once when he was a child before it had been sold. The double stairways had rotted and been torn down. Negroes were living in it. But it remained in his mind as his mother had known it. It appeared in his dreams regularly. He would stand on the wide porch, listening to the rustle of oak leaves, then wander through the high-ceilinged hall into the parlor that opened onto it and gaze at the worn rugs and faded draperies. It occurred to him that it was he, not she, who could have appreciated it. He preferred its threadbare elegance to anything he could name and it was because of it that all the neighborhoods they had lived in had been a torment to him—whereas she had hardly known the difference. She called her insensitivity "being adjustable."

"And I remember the old darky who was my nurse, Caroline. There was no better person in the world. I've always had a great respect for my colored friends," she said. "I'd do anything in the world for them and they'd . . ."

"Will you for God's sake get off that subject?" Julian said. When he got on a bus by himself, he made it a point to sit down beside a Negro, in reparation as it were for his mother's sins.

"You're mighty touchy tonight," she said. "Do you feel all right?"

"Yes I feel all right," he said. "Now lay off."

She pursed her lips. "Well, you certainly are in a vile humor," she observed. "I just won't speak to you at all."

They had reached the bus stop. There was no bus in sight and Julian, his hands still jammed in his pockets and his head thrust forward, scowled down the empty street. The frustration of having to wait on the bus as well as ride on it began to creep up his neck like a hot hand. The presence of his mother was borne in upon him as she gave a pained sigh. He looked at her bleakly. She was holding herself very erect under the preposterous hat, wearing it like a banner of her imaginary dignity. There was in him an evil urge to break her spirit. He suddenly unloosened his tie and pulled it off and put it in his pocket.

She stiffened. "Why must you look like *that* when you take me to town?" she said. "Why must you deliberately embarrass me?"

"If you'll never learn where you are," he said, "you can at least learn where I am."

"You look like a—thug," she said.

"Then I must be one," he murmured.

"I'll just go home," she said. "I will not bother you. If you can't do a little thing like that for me . . ."

Rolling his eyes upward, he put his tie back on. "Restored to my class," he muttered. He thrust his face toward her and hissed, "True culture is in the mind, the *mind*," he said, and tapped his head, "the mind."

"It's in the heart," she said, "and in how you do things and how you do things is because of who you *are*."

"Nobody in the damn bus cares who you are."

"I care who I am," she said icily.

The lighted bus appeared on top of the next hill and as it approached, they moved out into the street to meet it. He put his hand under her elbow and hoisted her up on the creaking step. She entered with a little smile, as if she were going into a drawing room where everyone had been waiting for her. While he put in the tokens, she sat down on one of the broad front seats for three which faced the aisle. A thin woman with protruding teeth and long yellow hair was sitting on the end of it. His mother moved up beside her and left room for Julian beside herself. He sat down and looked at the floor across the aisle where a pair of thin feet in red and white canvas sandals were planted.

His mother immediately began a general conversation meant to attract anyone who felt like talking. "Can it get any hotter?" she said and removed from her purse a folding fan, black with a Japanese scene on it, which she began to flutter before her.

"I reckon it might could," the woman with the protruding teeth said, "but I know for a fact my apartment couldn't get no hotter."

"It must get the afternoon sun," his mother said. She sat forward and looked up and down the bus. It was half filled. Everybody was white. "I see we have the bus to ourselves," she said. Julian cringed.

"For a change," said the woman across the aisle, the owner of the red and white canvas sandals. "I come on one the other day and they were thick as fleas—up front and all through."

"The world is in a mess everywhere," his mother said. "I don't know how we've let it get in this fix."

"What gets my goat is all those boys from good families stealing automobile tires," the woman with the protruding teeth said. "I told my boy, I said you may not be rich but you been raised right and if I ever catch you in any such mess, they can send you on to the reformatory. Be exactly where you belong."

"Training tells," his mother said. "Is your boy in high school?"

"Ninth grade," the woman said.

"My son just finished college last year. He wants to write but he's selling typewriters until he gets started," his mother said.

The woman leaned forward and peered at Julian. He threw her such a malevolent look that she subsided against the seat. On the floor across the aisle there was an abandoned newspaper. He got up and got it and opened it out in front of him. His mother discreetly continued the conversation in a lower tone but the woman across the aisle said in a loud voice, "Well that's nice. Selling typewriters is close to writing. He can go right from one to the other."

"I tell him," his mother said, "that Rome wasn't built in a day."

Behind the newspaper Julian was withdrawing into the inner compartment of his mind where he spent most of his time. This was a kind of mental bubble in which he established himself when he could not bear to be a part of what was going on around him. From it he could see out and judge but in it he was safe from any kind of penetration from without. It was the only place where he felt free of the general idiocy of his fellows. His mother had never entered it but from it he could see her with absolute clarity.

The old lady was clever enough and he thought that if she had started from any of the right premises, more might have been expected of her. She lived according to the laws of her own fantasy world, outside of which he had never seen her set foot. The law of it was to sacrifice herself for him after she had first created the necessity to do so by making a mess of things. If he had permitted her sacrifices, it was only because her lack of foresight had made them necessary. All of her life had been a struggle to act like a Chestny without the Chestny goods, and to give him everything she thought a Chestny ought to have; but since, said she, it was fun to struggle, why complain? And when you had won, as she had won, what fun to look back on the hard times! He could not forgive her that she had enjoyed the struggle and that she thought *she* had won.

What she meant when she said she had won was that she had brought him up successfully and had sent him to college and that he had turned out so well—good looking (her teeth had gone unfilled so that his could be straightened), intelligent (he realized he was too intelligent to be a success), and with a future ahead of him (there was of course no future ahead of him). She excused his gloominess on the grounds that he was still growing up and his radical ideas on his lack of practical experience. She said he didn't yet know a thing about "life," that he hadn't even entered the real world—when already he was as disenchanted with it as a man of fifty.

The further irony of all this was that in spite of her, he had turned out so well. In spite of going to only a third-rate college, he had, on his own initiative, come out with a first-rate education; in spite of growing up dominated by a small mind, he had ended up with a large one; in spite of all her foolish views, he was free of prejudice and unafraid to face facts. Most miraculous of all, instead of being blinded by love for her as she was for him, he had cut himself emotionally free of her and could see her with complete objectivity. He was not dominated by mother.

The bus stopped with a sudden jerk and shook him from his meditation. A woman from the back lurched forward with little steps and barely escaped falling in his newspaper as she righted herself. She got off and a large Negro got on. Julian kept his paper lowered to watch. It gave him a certain satisfaction to see injustice in daily operation. It confirmed his view that with a few exceptions there was no one worth knowing within a radius of three hundred miles. The Negro was well dressed and carried a briefcase. He looked around and then sat down on the other end of the seat where the woman with the red and white canvas sandals was sitting. He immediately unfolded a newspaper and obscured himself behind it. Julian's mother's elbow at once prodded insistently into his ribs. "Now you see why I won't ride on these buses by myself," she whispered.

The woman with the red and white canvas sandals had risen at the same time the Negro sat down and had gone further back in the bus and taken the seat of the woman who had got off. His mother leaned forward and cast her an approving look.

Julian rose, crossed the aisle, and sat down in the place of the woman with the canvas sandals. From this position, he looked serenely across at his mother. Her face had turned an angry red. He stared at her, making his eyes the eyes of a stranger. He felt his tension suddenly lift as if he had openly declared war on her.

He would have liked to get in conversation with the Negro and to talk with him about art or politics or any subject that would be above the comprehension of those around them, but the man remained entrenched behind his paper. He was either ignoring the change of seating or had never noticed it. There was no way for Julian to convey his sympathy.

His mother kept her eyes fixed reproachfully on his face. The

woman with the protruding teeth was looking at him avidly as if
he were a type of monster new to her.

"Do you have a light?" he asked the Negro.

Without looking away from his paper, the man reached in his
pocket and handed him a packet of matches.

"Thanks," Julian said. For a moment he held the matches
foolishly. A No SMOKING sign looked down upon him from over
the door. This alone would not have deterred him; he had no cigarettes. He had quit smoking some months before because he could
not afford it. "Sorry," he muttered and handed back the matches.
The Negro lowered the paper and gave him an annoyed look. He
took the matches and raised the paper again.

His mother continued to gaze at him but she did not take advantage of his momentary discomfort. Her eyes retained their battered look. Her face seemed to be unnaturally red, as if her blood
pressure had risen. Julian allowed no glimmer of sympathy to show
on his face. Having got the advantage, he wanted desperately to
keep it and carry it through. He would have liked to teach her a
lesson that would last her a while, but there seemed no way to
continue the point. The Negro refused to come out from behind
his paper.

Julian folded his arms and looked stolidly before him, facing her
but as if he did not see her, as if he had ceased to recognize her
existence. He visualized a scene in which, the bus having reached
their stop, he would remain in his seat and when she said, "Aren't
you going to get off?" he would look at her as at a stranger who had
rashly addressed him. The corner they got off on was usually deserted, but it was well lighted and it would not hurt her to walk by
herself the four blocks to the Y. He decided to wait until the time
came and then decide whether or not he would let her get off by
herself. He would have to be at the Y at ten to bring her back, but
he could leave her wondering if he was going to show up. There
was no reason for her to think she could always depend on him.

He retired again into the high-ceilinged room sparsely settled
with large pieces of antique furniture. His soul expanded momentarily but then he became aware of his mother across from him and
the vision shriveled. He studied her coldly. Her feet in little pumps
dangled like a child's and did not quite reach the floor. She was
training on him an exaggerated look of reproach. He felt com-

pletely detached from her. At that moment he could with pleasure
have slapped her as he would have slapped a particularly obnoxious
child in his charge.

He began to imagine various unlikely ways by which he could
teach her a lesson. He might make friends with some distinguished
Negro professor or lawyer and bring him home to spend the evening. He would be entirely justified but her blood pressure would
rise to 300. He could not push her to the extent of making her have
a stroke, and moreover, he had never been successful at making any
Negro friends. He had tried to strike up an acquaintance on the
bus with some of the better types, with ones that looked like pro-
fessors or ministers or lawyers. One morning he had sat down next
to a distinguished-looking dark brown man who had answered his
questions with a sonorous solemnity but who had turned out to be
an undertaker. Another day he had sat down beside a cigar-smoking
Negro with a diamond ring on his finger, but after a few stilted
pleasantries, the Negro had rung the buzzer and risen, slipping two
lottery tickets into Julian's hand as he climbed over him to leave.

He imagined his mother lying desperately ill and his being able
to secure only a Negro doctor for her. He toyed with that idea for a
few minutes and then dropped it for a momentary vision of himself
participating as a sympathizer in a sit-in demonstration. This was
possible but he did not linger with it. Instead, he approached the
ultimate horror. He brought home a beautiful suspiciously Negroid
woman. Prepare yourself, he said. There is nothing you can do
about it. This is the woman I've chosen. She's intelligent, dignified, even good, and she's suffered and she hasn't thought it *fun*.
Now persecute us, go ahead and persecute us. Drive her out of
here, but remember, you're driving me too. His eyes were narrowed and through the indignation he had generated, he saw his
mother across the aisle, purple-faced, shrunken to the dwarflike
proportions of her moral nature, sitting like a mummy beneath the
ridiculous banner of her hat.

He was tilted out of his fantasy again as the bus stopped. The
door opened with a sucking hiss and out of the dark a large, gaily
dressed, sullen-looking colored woman got on with a little boy. The
child, who might have been four, had on a short plaid suit and a
Tyrolean hat with a blue feather in it. Julian hoped that he would

sit down beside him and that the woman would push in beside his
mother. He could think of no better arrangement.

As she waited for her tokens, the woman was surveying the seating possibilities—he hoped with the idea of sitting where she was
least wanted. There was something familiar-looking about her but
Julian could not place what it was. She was a giant of a woman.
Her face was set not only to meet opposition but to seek it out. The
downward tilt of her large lower lip was like a warning sign: DON'T
TAMPER WITH ME. Her bulging figure was encased in a green crepe
dress and her feet overflowed in red shoes. She had on a hideous
hat. A purple velvet flap came down on one side of it and stood up
on the other; the rest of it was green and looked like a cushion
with the stuffing out. She carried a mammoth red pocketbook that
bulged throughout as if it were stuffed with rocks.

To Julian's disappointment, the little boy climbed up on the
empty seat beside his mother. His mother lumped all children,
black and white, into the common category, "cute," and she
thought little Negroes were on the whole cuter than little white
children. She smiled at the little boy as he climbed on the seat.

Meanwhile the woman was bearing down upon the empty seat
beside Julian. To his annoyance, she squeezed herself into it. He
saw his mother's face change as the woman settled herself next to
him and he realized with satisfaction that this was more objec-
tionable to her than it was to him. Her face seemed almost gray
and there was a look of dull recognition in her eyes, as if suddenly
she had sickened at some awful confrontation. Julian saw that it
was because she and the woman had, in a sense, swapped sons.
Though his mother would not realize the symbolic significance of
this, she would feel it. His amusement showed plainly on his face.

The woman next to him muttered something unintelligible to
herself. He was conscious of a kind of bristling next to him, a
muted growling like that of an angry cat. He could not see anything
but the red pocketbook upright on the bulging green thighs. He
visualized the woman as she had stood waiting for her tokens—the
ponderous figure, rising from the red shoes upward over the solid
hips, the mammoth bosom, the haughty face, to the green and
purple hat.

His eyes widened.

The vision of the two hats, identical, broke upon him with the radiance of a brilliant sunrise. His face was suddenly lit with joy. He could not believe that Fate had thrust upon his mother such a lesson. He gave a loud chuckle so that she would look at him and see that he saw. She turned her eyes on him slowly. The blue in them seemed to have turned a bruised purple. For a moment he had an uncomfortable sense of her innocence, but it lasted only a second before principle rescued him. Justice entitled him to laugh. His grin hardened until it said to her as plainly as if he were saying aloud: Your punishment exactly fits your pettiness. This should teach you a permanent lesson.

Her eyes shifted to the woman. She seemed unable to bear looking at him and to find the woman preferable. He became conscious again of the bristling presence at his side. The woman was rumbling like a volcano about to become active. His mother's mouth began to twitch slightly at one corner. With a sinking heart, he saw incipient signs of recovery on her face and realized that this was going to strike her suddenly as funny and was going to be no lesson at all. She kept her eyes on the woman and an amused smile came over her face as if the woman were a monkey that had stolen her hat. The little Negro was looking up at her with large fascinated eyes. He had been trying to attract her attention for some time.

"Carver!" the woman said suddenly. "Come heah!"

When he saw that the spotlight was on him at last, Carver drew his feet up and turned himself toward Julian's mother and giggled.

"Carver!" the woman said. "You heah me? Come heah!"

Carver slid down from the seat but remained squatting with his back against the base of it, his head turned slyly around toward Julian's mother, who was smiling at him. The woman reached a hand across the aisle and snatched him to her. He righted himself and hung backwards on her knees, grinning at Julian's mother. "Isn't he cute?" Julian's mother said to the woman with the protruding teeth.

"I reckon he is," the woman said without conviction.

The Negress yanked him upright but he eased out of her grip and shot across the aisle and scrambled, giggling wildly, onto the seat beside his love.

"I think he likes me," Julian's mother said, and smiled at the woman. It was the smile she used when she was being particularly gracious to an inferior. Julian saw everything lost. The lesson had rolled off her like rain on a roof.

The woman stood up and yanked the little boy off the seat as if she were snatching him from contagion. Julian could feel the rage in her at having no weapon like his mother's smile. She gave the child a sharp slap across his leg. He howled once and then thrust his head into her stomach and kicked his feet against her shins. "Be-have," she said vehemently.

The bus stopped and the Negro who had been reading the newspaper got off. The woman moved over and set the little boy down with a thump between herself and Julian. She held him firmly by the knee. In a moment he put his hands in front of his face and peeped at Julian's mother through his fingers.

"I see yoooooooo!" she said and put her hand in front of her face and peeped at him.

The woman slapped his hand down. "Quit yo' foolishness," she said, "before I knock the living Jesus out of you!"

Julian was thankful that the next stop was theirs. He reached up and pulled the cord. The woman reached up and pulled it at the same time. Oh my God, he thought. He had the terrible intuition that when they got off the bus together, his mother would open her purse and give the little boy a nickel. The gesture would be as natural to her as breathing. The bus stopped and the woman got up and lunged to the front, dragging the child, who wished to stay on, after her. Julian and his mother got up and followed. As they neared the door, Julian tried to relieve her of her pocketbook.

"No," she murmured, "I want to give the little boy a nickel."

"No!" Julian hissed. "No!"

She smiled down at the child and opened her bag. The bus door opened and the woman picked him up by the arm and descended with him, hanging at her hip. Once in the street she set him down and shook him.

Julian's mother had to close her purse while she got down the bus step but as soon as her feet were on the ground, she opened it again and began to rummage inside. "I can't find but a penny," she whispered, "but it looks like a new one."

"Don't do it!" Julian said fiercely between his teeth. There was a streetlight on the corner and she hurried to get under it so that she could better see into her pocketbook. The woman was heading off rapidly down the street with the child still hanging backward on her hand.

"Oh little boy!" Julian's mother called and took a few quick steps and caught up with them just beyond the lamppost. "Here's a bright new penny for you," and she held out the coin, which shone bronze in the dim light.

The huge woman turned and for a moment stood, her shoulders lifted and her face frozen with frustrated rage, and stared at Julian's mother. Then all at once she seemed to explode like a piece of machinery that had been given one ounce of pressure too much. Julian saw the black fist swing out with the red pocketbook. He shut his eyes and cringed as he heard the woman shout, "He don't take nobody's pennies!" When he opened his eyes, the woman was disappearing down the street with the little boy staring wide-eyed over her shoulder. Julian's mother was sitting on the sidewalk.

"I told you not to do that," Julian said angrily. "I told you not to do that!"

He stood over her for a minute, gritting his teeth. Her legs were stretched out in front of her and her hat was on her lap. He squatted down and looked her in the face. It was totally expressionless. "You got exactly what you deserved," he said. "Now get up."

He picked up her pocketbook and put what had fallen out back in it. He picked the hat up off her lap. The penny caught his eye on the sidewalk and he picked that up and let it drop before her eyes into the purse. Then he stood up and leaned over and held his hand out to pull her up. She remained immobile. He sighed. Rising above them on either side were black apartment buildings, marked with irregular rectangles of light. At the end of the block a man came out of a door and walked off in the opposite direction. "All right," he said, "suppose somebody happens by and wants to know why you're sitting on the sidewalk?"

She took the hand and, breathing hard, pulled heavily up on it and then stood for a moment, swaying slightly as if the spots of light in the darkness were circling around her. Her eyes, shadowed and confused, finally settled on his face. He did not try to conceal his irritation. "I hope this teaches you a lesson," he said. She leaned forward and her eyes raked his face. She seemed trying to determine his identity. Then, as if she found nothing familiar about him, she started off with a headlong movement in the wrong direction.

"Aren't you going on to the Y?" he asked.

"Home," she muttered.

"Well, are we walking?"

For answer she kept going. Julian followed along, his hands behind him. He saw no reason to let the lesson she had had go without backing it up with an explanation of its meaning. She might as well be made to understand what had happened to her. "Don't think that was just an uppity Negro woman," he said. "That was the whole colored race which will no longer take your condescending pennies. That was your black double. She can wear the same hat as you, and to be sure," he added gratuitously (because he thought it was funny), "it looked better on her than it did on you. What all this means," he said, "is that the old world is gone. The old manners are obsolete and your graciousness is not worth a damn." He thought bitterly of the house that had been lost for him. "You aren't who you think you are," he said.

She continued to plow ahead, paying no attention to him. Her hair had come undone on one side. She dropped her pocketbook and took no notice. He stooped and picked it up and handed it to her but she did not take it.

"You needn't act as if the world has come to an end," he said, "because it hasn't. From now on you've got to live in a new world and face a few realities for a change. Buck up," he said, "it won't kill you."

She was breathing fast.

"Let's wait on the bus," he said.

"Home," she said thickly.

"I hate to see you behave like this," he said. "Just like a child. I should be able to expect more of you." He decided to stop where he was and make her stop and wait for a bus. "I'm not going any farther," he said, stopping. "We're going on the bus."

She continued to go on as if she had not heard him. He took a few steps and caught her arm and stopped her. He looked into her face and caught his breath. He was looking into a face he had never seen before. "Tell Grandpapa to come get me," she said.

He stared, stricken.

"Tell Caroline to come get me," she said.

Stunned, he let her go and she lurched forward again, walking as if one leg were shorter than the other. A tide of darkness seemed to be sweeping her from him. "Mother!" he cried. "Darling, sweetheart, wait!" Crumpling, she fell to the pavement. He dashed forward and fell at her side, crying, "Mamma, Mamma!" He turned her over. Her face was fiercely distorted. One eye, large and staring, moved slightly to the left as if it had become unmoored. The other remained fixed on him, raked his face again, found nothing and closed.

"Wait here, wait here!" he cried and jumped up and began to run for help toward a cluster of lights he saw in the distance ahead of him. "Help, help!" he shouted, but his voice was thin, scarcely a thread of sound. The lights drifted farther away the faster he ran and his feet moved numbly as if they carried him nowhere. The tide of darkness seemed to sweep him back to her, postponing from moment to moment his entry into the world of guilt and sorrow.

ERVIN D. KRAUSE lived on Nebraska and Iowa farms as a youth, attended Iowa State College, has worked for an aircraft company, and taught English at the universities of Nebraska and Wyoming. He is now teaching in Honolulu. An earlier story of his, "The Quick and the Dead," was published in the 1961 O. Henry Awards volume.

The Snake

I was thinking of the heat and of water that morning when I was plowing the stubble field far across the hill from the farm buildings. It had grown hot early that day, and I hoped that the boy, my brother's son, would soon come across the broad black area of plowed ground, carrying the jar of cool water. The boy usually was sent out at about that time with the water, and he always dragged an old snow-fence lath or a stick along, to play with. He pretended that the lath was a tractor and he would drag it through the dirt and make buzzing, tractor sounds with his lips.

I almost ran over the snake before I could stop the tractor in time. I had turned at the corner of the field and I had to look back to raise the plow and then to drop it again into the earth, and I was thinking of the boy and the water anyway, and when I looked again down the furrow, the snake was there. It lay half in the furrow and half out, and the front wheels had rolled nearly up to it when I put in the clutch. The tractor was heavily loaded with the weight of the plow turning the earth, and the tractor stopped instantly.

The snake slid slowly and with great care from the new ridge the plow had made, into the furrow and did not go any further. I had never liked snakes much, I still had that kind of quick panic that I'd had as a child whenever I saw one, but this snake was clean and bright and very beautiful. He was multi-colored and graceful and he lay in the furrow and moved his arched and tapered head only so slightly. Go out of the furrow, snake, I said, but he did not move at all. I pulled the throttle of the tractor in and out, hoping to frighten him with the noise, but the snake only flicked its black, forked tongue and faced the huge tractor wheel, without fright or concern.

I let the engine idle then, and I got down and went around the wheel and stood beside it. My movement did frighten the snake and it raised its head and trailed delicately a couple of feet and stopped again, and its tongue was working very rapidly. I followed it, looking at the brilliant colors on its tubular back, the colors clear and sharp and perfect, in orange and green and brown diamonds the size of a baby's fist down its back, and the diamonds were set one within the other and interlaced with glistening jet-black. The colors were astonishing, clear and bright, and it was as if the body held a fire of its own, and the colors came through that transparent flesh and skin, vivid and alive and warm. The eyes were clear and black and the slender body was arched slightly. His flat and gracefully tapered head lifted as I looked at him and the black tongue slipped in and out of that solemn mouth.

You beauty, I said, I couldn't kill you. You are much too beautiful. I had killed snakes before, when I was younger, but there had been no animal like this one, and I knew it was unthinkable that an animal such as that should die. I picked him up, and the length of him arched very carefully and gracefully and only a little wildly, and I could feel the coolness of that radiant, fire-colored body, like splendid ice, and I knew that he had eaten only recently because there were two whole and solid little lumps in the forepart of him, like fieldmice swallowed whole might make.

The body caressed through my hands like cool satin, and my hands, usually tanned and dark, were pale beside it, and I asked it where the fire colors could come from the coolness of that body. I lowered him so he would not fall and his body slid out onto the cool, newly-plowed earth, from between my pale hands. The snake worked away very slowly and delicately and with a gorgeous kind of dignity and beauty, and he carried his head a little above the rolled clods. The sharp, burning colors of his body stood brilliant and plain against the black soil, like a target.

I felt good and satisfied, looking at the snake. It shone in its bright diamond color against the sun-burned stubble and the crumbled black clods of soil and against the paleness of myself. The color and beauty of it were strange and wonderful and somehow alien, too, in that dry and dusty and uncolored field.

I got on the tractor again and I had to watch the plow closely because the field was drawn across the long hillside and even in that good soil there was a danger of rocks. I had my back to the corner of the triangular field that pointed towards the house. The earth was a little heavy and I had to stop once and clean the plowshares because they were not scouring properly, and I did not look back towards the place until I had turned the corner and was plowing across the upper line of the large field, a long way from where I had stopped because of the snake.

I saw it all at a glance. The boy was there at the lower corner of the field, and he was in the plowed earth, stamping with ferocity and a kind of frenzied impatience. Even at that distance, with no sound but the sound of the tractor, I could tell the fierce mark of brutality on the boy. I could see the hunched-up shoulders, the savage determination, the dance of his feet as he ground the snake with his heels, and the pirouette of his arms as he whipped at it with the stick.

Stop it, I shouted, but the lumbering and mighty tractor roared on, above anything I could say. I stopped the tractor and I shouted down to the boy, and I knew he could hear me, for the morning was clear and still, but he did not even hesitate in that brutal, murdering dance. It was no use. I felt myself tremble, thinking of the diamond light of that beauty I had held a few moments before, and I wanted to run down there and halt, if I could, that frenetic pirouette, catch the boy in the moment of his savagery, and save a glimmer, a remnant, of that which I remembered, but I knew it was already too late. I drove the tractor on, not looking down there; I was afraid to look for fear the evil might still be going on. My head began to ache, and the fumes of the tractor began to bother my eyes, and I hated the job suddenly, and I thought, there are only moments when one sees beautiful things, and these are soon crushed, or they vanish. I felt the anger mount within me.

The boy waited at the corner, with the jar of water held up to me in his hands, and the water had grown bubbly in the heat of the morning. I knew the boy well. He was eleven and we had done many things together. He was a beautiful boy, really, with finely-spun blonde hair and a smooth and still effeminate face, and his eyelashes were long and dark and brushlike, and his eyes were blue. He waited there and he smiled as the tractor came up, as he would smile on any other day. He was my nephew, my brother's son, handsome and warm and newly-scrubbed, with happiness upon his face and his face resembled my brother's and mine as well.

I saw then, too, the stake driven straight and hard into the plowed soil, through something there where I had been not long before.

I stopped the tractor and climbed down and the boy came eagerly up to me. "Can I ride around with you?" he asked, as he often did, and I had as often let him be on the tractor beside me. I looked closely at his eyes, and he was already innocent; the killing was already forgotten in that clear mind of his.

"No, you cannot," I said, pushing aside the water jar he offered to me. I pointed to the splintered, upright stake. "Did you do that?" I asked.

"Yes," he said, eagerly, beginning a kind of dance of excitement. "I killed a snake; it was a big one." He tried to take my hand to show me.

"Why did you kill it?"

"Snakes are ugly and bad."

"This snake was very beautiful. Didn't you see how beautiful it was?"

"Snakes are ugly," he said again.

"You saw the colors of it, didn't you? Have you ever seen anything like it around here?"

"Snakes are ugly and bad, and it might have bitten somebody, and they would have died."

"You know there are no poisonous snakes in this area. This snake could not harm anything."

"They eat chickens sometimes," the boy said. "They are ugly and they eat chickens and I hate snakes."

"You are talking foolishly," I said. "You killed it because you wanted to kill it, for no other reason."

"They're ugly and I hate them," the boy insisted. "Nobody likes snakes."

"It was beautiful," I said, half to myself.

The boy skipped along beside me, and he was contented with what he had done.

The fire of the colors was gone; there was a contorted ugliness now; the colors of its back were dull and gray-looking, torn and smashed in, and dirty from the boy's shoes. The beautifully-tapered head, so delicate and so cool, had been flattened as if in a vise, and the forked tongue splayed out of the twisted, torn mouth. The snake was hideous, and I remembered, even then, the cool, bright fire of it only a little while before, and I thought perhaps the boy had always seen it dead and hideous like that, and had not even stopped to see the beauty of it in its life.

I wrenched the stake out, that the boy had driven through it in the thickest part of its body, between the colored diamond crystals. I touched it and the coolness, the ice-feeling, was gone, and even then it moved a little, perhaps a tiny spasm of the dead muscles, and I hoped that it was truly dead, so that I would not have to kill it. And then it moved a little more, and I knew the snake was dying, and I would have to kill it there. The boy stood off a few feet and he had the stake again and he was racing innocently in circles, making the buzzing tractor sound with his lips.

I'm sorry, I thought to the snake, for you were beautiful. I took the broken length of it around the tractor and I took one of the wrenches from the tool-kit and I struck its head, not looking at it, to kill it at last, for it could never live.

The boy came around behind me, dragging the stake. "It's a big snake, isn't it?" he said. "I'm going to tell everybody how big a snake I killed."

"Don't you see what you have done?" I said. "Don't you see the difference now?"

"It's an ugly, terrible snake," he said. He came up and was going to push at it with his heavy shoes. I could see the happiness in the boy's eyes, the gleeful brutality.

"Don't," I said. I could have slapped the boy. He looked up at me, puzzled, and he swayed his head from side to side. I thought, you little brute, you nasty, selfish, little beast, with brutality already developed within that brain and in those eyes. I wanted to slap his face, to wipe forever the insolence and brutal glee from his mouth, and I decided then, very suddenly, what I would do.

I drew the snake up and I saw the blue eyes of the boy open

wide and change and fright, and I stepped towards him as he cringed back, and I shouted, "It's alive, it's alive!" and I looped the tube of the snake's body around the boy's neck.

The boy shrieked and turned in his terror and ran, and I followed a few steps, shouting after him, "It's alive, it's alive, alive!"

The boy gasped and cried out in his terror and he fled towards the distant house, stumbling and falling and rising to run again, and the dead snake hung on him, looped around his neck, and the boy tore at it, but it would not fall off.

The little brute, I thought, the little cruel brute, to hurt and seek to kill something so beautiful and clean, and I couldn't help smiling and feeling satisfied because the boy, too, had suffered a little for his savageness, and I felt my mouth trying to smile about it. And I stopped suddenly and I said, oh God, with the fierce smile of brutality frightening my face, and I thought, oh God, oh God. I climbed quickly onto the tractor and I started it and pulled the throttle open to drown the echoes of the boy shrieking down there in the long valley. I was trembling and I could not steer the tractor well, and I saw that my hands were suffused and flushed, red with a hot blood color.

THALIA SELZ grew up in the Midwest, attended Oberlin and the University of Chicago, and has taught English at Pomona College and the Illinois Institute of Technology. She has had stories published in *Partisan Review*, the *Virginia Quarterly*, the *Chicago Review*, and film quarterlies. She, her husband and two children live in New York.

The Education of a Queen

Where is that green iron gate, swinging to with an easy clang, hurled carelessly backward by my young hand as if batted by an Amazon?

I woke precipitously last night, teetering back from the dizzy lip of tuinal sleep, hearing that pipe-stem gate creak and slam, and the sleeping pill stuck in my throat like a chip of blue and red ceramic tile. For no reason I was as afraid as if I were a girl again—an adolescent girl whose periods have just begun and who is panic-struck by the magnitude of her sins.

I did not get up and fling open the French windows to inspect my charming Tyrolean wooden balcony, my geranium-box, my compulsive *Seebach* rushing pell-mell and churning up foamy spittle and make-believe racket like a mountain brook in the movies. Or the soft, midnight walls of my valley—in the daytime cropped, domesticated slopes: tilting, hummocky mattresses for cows to lie on. At night cradled in wood—intimate, old-fashioned wooden fences; wooden turnstiles, the spokes crossed with stiff ceremony like arms in a folk-dance or children's games (". . . take the key and lock her up, my fair lay-dee-e-e!"); or long, cumbersome wooden gates, slow as a cow.

I knew it was not a cow gate. With a damp, mossy fear born of guilt and drugs I fixed that swift, ominous, metallic *clank* as an intrusion from another world. I curled up icily, trying this gate and that, poking and prying through the rubbish-heap of childhood,

floating over games and lawns, deep-sea swimming among side-
walks, collie dogs, secret huts, dried skin from once-young faces,
old people's coffins. The young never die.

I switched on the bedside lamp. I was clammy-nosed, drunk on
sedative, and absurdly terrified because I had abruptly remembered
and could not cry for my childhood acquaintance ("friend" is too
strong a word), Aggie, whom I had not seen for at least twenty
years, who was still in the fifth grade when she was fourteen years
old, and who was the simplest, most absolute and apocalyptic
Catholic it has ever been my misfortune to meet. A few months
before my mother had mentioned in a moment of brisk reminis-
cence that Aggie's aunt had told Norbert Leinfelder who had told
her that Aggie had died of uterine cancer last summer, having
given birth to three living children and one stillborn.

"German Catholic!" snorted my mother. "You'd think they'd
learn, but they never do!"

My first thought then and last night, too, was thank—well, just
thank—for all the children, even the stillborn, for the husband who
infused them into that treacherous womb, and even for the mythic
Lord who eased Aggie's end by promising her cherubs with pan-
cake makeup on their puffing cheeks to take the places of her children—not to mention of course forgiveness of her awful sins.

I lay on my pillow, seeing her face dying on her dying pillow,
not as it really must have looked: clayey and nook-cheeked, puff-
eyed, sour-breathed, sweating out her imbecilic immortal soul at
the pores. But twenty years ago, smooth-skinned, innocently boyish
and square-jawed, fearsomely stupid under her miracle-spinning
eyebrows.

I tried to weep, but she was so evil. She was the most evil girl
under heaven. She was dumb. Often she smelled of pee, because
she was apt to wet herself when her mother hit her with the razor
strap or locked her into her room for two days at a time. She cried
every passing-time when she did not pass and the others filed
proudly, banners blaring, brasses flying, into the next home-room.

What's Aggie to me or me to she, that I should weep for her?
"Come on in," said Aggie's loving ma, "and recite to my guests.
Aggie don't have no memory at all, but now *her*, she's *fabulous*—"
indicating me in my lank pig-tails, horrid scarred knees, and scuffed
Buster Browns.

With a fierce pride, ignoring the reproach of poor Aggie's ashamed, admiring eyes, I dove with flawless form:

Up from the meadows rich with corn,
Clear in the cool September morn,
The clustered spires of Frederick stand
Green-walled by the hills of Maryland.

Sixty lines complete with dramatic modulations of tone, inspired gestures, and bell-like enunciation. I had had no other teacher than my mother with her beautifully controlled, schoolmarm voice and her untamed, gothic imagination. Aggie, asking nothing from life, congratulated me solemnly:

"Gee, you sure got a fabalus memry, all right . . ."

Except for Oliver Twist, she had the most wretched childhood I have ever heard of.

"Weep, damn you," I plead into my frozen featherbed, in the guilt-lit hotel room. And *reeeeek* I hear it once more out on the flowering Tyrolean meadows, the light swing on the Gary, Indiana-manufactured hinges, opening to the gentle, firm touch of Mr. Doom with his soft death's eyes, coming to claim me once and for all.

It was Aggie's gate. No, it was mine—it was Mary Melowski's (*Polish*-Catholic) next door!

I am crying now, without effort, without guilt, into my fragrant pillow smelling sweetly of straw, crying for Mary's lessons in wickedness under her back porch, for her brothers' further lessons in the secret hut, for calling and yodeling at front and back doors, for the drunken Mexicans up by the tracks, for running in the ozone-smelling sunshine—a sudden, mindless, breast-bursting sprint toward the train-whistle miles away, for the Dirty Dozen with their flies open, for Aggie's idiot countenance—sorrow and doom dimly smeared across it like a double-exposure, for my thirty-four years and the refuse of all our pasts and my own death, for the beautiful, simmering, chocolate eyes of Mr. X.—his sweet smile madly calm—his timid, pale, long girl-fingers insanely sure as he delicately places the green pipe-stem gate in the wooden box and matter-of-factly swings it to.

I first met Mr. Joshua X. the way I met anyone worthwhile or peculiar at all—through my family. I loathed my family, of course, but I was shrewd enough even then (I was twelve) to know that rather than sneak off to Hollywood to be adopted by Jeanette Mac-Donald, I'd better hang around the house and see the world come by.

It was 1937 and the war hadn't yet jerked us up out of the Depression. My father was still piping home strays—usually Greek, but sometimes Negro or Jewish: anybody with a real or manufactured right to pity. We had a table with food on it, even if it was in the kitchen. We had a rusty iron cot in the basement, but the blankets were still warm in spite of great age, and they bore our proud, mad, double-family crest like a brand, branding with our mixed blood, irrational phobias, and rash hopes anyone who slept under them. 1833 said the red, white, and pink "Lemon Star" quilt: the year Oberlin was founded and my great-great grandmother Otis drove a wagon, all alone, from Barnstable on the Cape to the new one-room farmhouse in north-central Ohio. But the harsh, iron-woven blanket with its queer, lowering, iconic colors and its surface like John the Baptist's hair shirt was dated in stilted, twisted, gothic numerals 1897: my father's mother, Anastasia Karamoulis, had woven it with thumb-pricks, tears, and hate for her husband to keep himself warm and uncomfortable with in steerage on his way to make a million grass-green dollars in the States. Green fell for the parched, tawny hills of *Griechenland.* (Not that many of his few hundreds ever traveled back home. The barren slope, the empty pot were all that Anastasia got, which is why I tend to sneer at that Lawrencian image of the sturdy Peasant Woman: poor and sexually satisfied!) Together, these blankets were enough to endow any two-dimensional stray with all the length, breadth, depth, and momentous history he could use, and by god we were there to see that he didn't shirk. All of us, dead and alive, whooping him on. No chance to let go and die happy!

I offer as proof that in all those years from the crash till the war we had only three cases of theft and one instance of bedbugs.

But Mr. X. is no ordinary stray. At first, indeed, he looks like one of many usual types of strays. I see him tread hesitantly in the back door after my father, and because he is sure of his shabbiness and unsure of his welcome he sets the heel of one shoe awkwardly down on the toe of the other. This makes him collapse almost to his knees at the next step, and my cruel, insensitive, unfeeling

eight-year-old brother laughs. But Jason has a soul like an arma-
dillo's back, anyhow. I am twelve and have not laughed in six
months. It is unlikely that anything will ever be able to make me
laugh again. I am setting plates for dinner, and I look gravely across
the kitchen into those rich, innocent, madman's eyes, as they wash
over me without seeing me at all really, only feeling Watchers,
Warm, Food, Place.

"This is Joshua X.," says my father; "he is an artist." Simple
declarative, like a royal sentence of death.

At once I am in love. Without transition, conscious memory, or
anticipation. But this has happened so often before that uncon-
sciously I am quite used to it. Gently I set his place between my
mother's and mine; deliberately I single out the best piece of every-
day California Friarware: without chip or crack, an heraldic orange.
My mother and I of necessity—by *rights*—get the two unmatched,
most nicked plates. I am subtly aware that my little brother is beginning to be on to me, but I would no more think of setting at his
place, and in revenge, my chipped plate with its brown stains along
the cracks than I would of letting him ride my new bicycle.

"How do you do," says my mother's mellifluous, slightly strained
voice. She is neither tired nor haughty. Her voice is simply stretching to make a place for him, too. "Will you eat with us?" (As if
he'd been dragged in here for any other reason!) "Are you Greek
perhaps? If you are, you'll like our lamb stew I'm sure."

She is impossible, I am thinking. Our lamb stew! She's as prissy
as a New England preacher (I have met no preachers and only a
few priests: Greek Orthodox), and I *hate* those clothes. Years before they become chic on women's campuses she is wearing tight,
worn Levis and one of my father's castoff shirts. She wears this
costume to make her other clothes last, and I know this, but its
shabby unwomanliness and the ludicrous contrast of the long, gray
hair piled in loose coils and old-fashioned silvery puffs on her
stately head fill me with distaste. She is a walking anachronism,
and I have grown sensitive to the artistic verities. Also, I consider
her abused and either too proud or too stupid to fight back—for
pretty clothes or fewer free guests.

But most of all I detest the Greek routine. She thinks *any*-thing
Greek is peerless though among peers. At least I think she thinks
so.

"But I'm not Greek," Mr. X. says helplessly. Like Aladdin, he sees it vanishing—whoosh! the cast-iron kettle of stew, the dinner plates, the whole table fly out the window in a twinkling and skim away, up, up, to take their place with Orion's Belt.

"I'm not either," says my mother comfortingly.

"Never mind!" shouts my father. "You're an artist. You belong to the world!"

He always shouts, indoors or out in the back lot. Parlors or bedrooms or kitchens. I hate it.

"Where will you seat our guest, Daphne?" my mother asks, with this habitual loftiness that is not hauteur so much as the result of her persistent romanticism.

At twelve I consider my mother absolutely the creature of her dreams. She must make a ritual even of our simple, monotonous meals! But faced with exposure I feel my stomach curling up to tap startlingly at my palate. I swallow it back down again, and Jason sniggers the dirty snot-eyed pig behind his smelly paw. I am contemplating him being run over by a railroad train, when my mother quite simply puts Joshua X. down beside me, places a napkin between his transparent fingers, ladles stew onto his sunset-colored plate, and tells him not to wait . . .

"We are never *polite* with each other in the family circle." She makes politeness sound like B.O.

Joshua X. did not get to sleep on the iron maiden in the basement. (Oh, honor those harsh spikes, corners, and springs smelling of rust and, deliciously, of moist cement; they've pierced courage into many a poor stumblebum!) Mother put him on the parlor couch, but the next morning she would not allow Jason or me to touch anything in the room until he returned with a pink OK slip from the chest X-ray unit in the neighborhood clinic. Then she carefully made up the couch herself, tenderly folding her ancestors and my father's and laying them away in the coat closet till evening.

"Anyhow, I *won't* have him sleeping in the basement. He is *much* too frail! Daphne, see that he gets fresh bedding every week, like the rest of us."

"How long is he going to stay, Mother?" My love was already blooming in bleeding stigmata on my underdeveloped bosom, but she didn't notice.

"Daphne, we never ask a guest how long he is going to stay."
She was embarrassed for me: with the Otis and Karamoulis blood
in my veins I should have known better *instinctively* than to
breathe the vaguest suggestion of a termination to his visit.

At the dinnertable, she once said to Jason and me: "Hospitality
is the *strongest* of the Greek traditions."

"In Homeric times," roared my father, "we would even send our
wives to bed with the guests!" My mother bent over the Brussels
sprouts and pursed her lips, but I saw the corners of her mouth
twitch.

At one time I had found my father's steady harping on the
means and functions of the procreative organs very amusing, indeed. There was an embarrassing family legend that Daphne, aged
five, glimpsing her papa making drunken (let us give him the
benefit of the doubt) passes at a girl during one of the intermina-
ble Karamoulis parties had tripped up to him, crying, "Go to it,
Daddy!"

What do you suppose he did then? Coughed, got up, and strode
off, looking well over the bridge of his nose—suddenly very much
the dignified Mediterranean *paterfamilias*. Probably it cramped his
style for the rest of the evening. At any rate, the "bohemian parties," as my mother chose to call them, stopped a few years later.
She put an end to them herself, of course. She said, "no more or I
walk out." Since no Otis ever uttered a threat without being willing
to back it up (the Lord of the Atheists at our right hand), there
were no more bohemian parties.

But there continued to be a certain strain, like dangerously
stretched rubber-bands, in and around the subject of sex. When I
was nine or so my father made some sexual smart crack at which I
laughed broadly.

"Mother," I cried, "isn't he funny? Don't you think he's funny,
Mother?"

"Daphne," said my mother, "it is my hope that someday you too
will grow beyond Rudolph Valentino!"

"Oh Mother," I said, "you're no fun."

My parents belonged to the progressive school of child-rearing,
and I was not reproved, but sometime later—I must have been ten
or eleven—Mother clarified the subject slightly.

"Grown-ups, even mothers and fathers, do not always agree about everything."

"When I grow up," said Jason, "I'll always agree with Daphne."

Mother quickly seized his pawn. "When you grow up, I hope, children, that you will no longer kick and scratch like animals—"

"Oh no-o!" We shook our heads. We should live to see the day!

"But you won't *always* agree either. Your father and I don't always agree. . . ."

Jason and I sidled glances. Damn right they didn't!

"But we *resolve* our differences for the sake of the family." Jason was looking puzzled, but Mother bellied on triumphantly down the wind. "Because our family is more important than any one of us, isn't it? Try to remember this, children . . ."

We nodded solemnly.

"And Daphne, never forget that a woman's first duty—her *privilege*—is to keep her family together."

I sighed. How horrid and prissy it all was!

But of course, in spite of our united family, I found myself making choices. Probably it *wasn't* good to blurt sex-sex-sex all over the place, all the time. I didn't realize that Mother did it, too, that it was the almost ineradicable hallmark of the 'twenties when she and my father had come to maturity and found their gods (Nature, Freedom, Passion).

"You have the most beautiful young *body!*" she would exclaim, gazing rapturously after the bath at my pipe-stem shanks, my almost concave belly, and poor funny little breasts. I could have cried, but because I loved her I forgave her and glozed over these unseemly comments.

I did not forgive my father.

It is Sunday and I have on a new pink rayon blouse. My first that clings. I am standing beside the Victrola, winding it up to play the "Anvil Chorus," my favorite piece of music at this time next to "Juanita." I want to play it for Marianne, whom I admire and who, together with her boyfriend, Dr. Digger, is having Sunday dinner with us. I don't admire Dr. Digger one bit and he has just tumbled himself into limbo by drunkenly catching me behind the bathroom door, screwing his satyr's grin up to his eyebrows, ecstatically touching his tongue to the tip of his long nose, and whimpering,

"*Oh* what cute little boobies! Jus' like inverted tea-cups—makes a fella wanna drink out of 'em, I tell *you!*"

I am disgusted and indignant with the outrage that only an adolescent can muster, but I am also strangely flattered. In addition, my mother is bringing me up to be a lady, and I am damn well going to make it up to Marianne.

At just this moment, as I am leaning down to wind the Victrola, I am sent catapulting against it with a stupendous WHAM! on the back that slams the breath through my lips, and my father strides by, bellowing jovially,

"Stop slumping! Stick 'em out and show us what you've got! It may not be much now, but you'll get more someday . . ."

Dr. Digger snickers.

I try to smile. I could set a tiger on my father.

I really didn't love my father in those days. I adored him, which meant that I fervently hated him too. But I loved Joshua.

I loved him, insufficient body and puerile soul. I loved him tenderly—and hopelessly, except in raging fantasies when he would rescue me from the brink of Niagara or from a burning hotel and press his clean, hard, all-American lips to mine. He really had a wide, thick-lipped mouth—out of place in that otherwise delicate landscape. His face was square, but the pale skin was stretched so tightly over it that the bones looked ready to tear right through. Indeed, the teeth had already burst it and his lips were the swollen flanks of the wound. I used to fancy that in the night they bled of their own accord.

A horrid notion. My periods had come on almost two years before, and though I was used to them I was much taken up with thoughts of bleeding. Was sap tree-blood? (I knew better.) Was fish-blood warm or cold? Did bleeding begin *right* under the skin, or how far down did you have to go? I would take these problems to my mother, and when she couldn't answer she would shoo me on to my father.

I took neither of them the night and the prayers. The long, unsteady nights without sleep—several times I lay dizzily awake till breakfast, my ears growing funnels, my heart plopping, my lips in mounds. What was the matter? At times I couldn't imagine. At others I knew at once, with implacable self-judgment, absolute horror:

"Oh God, forgive me for doing dirty things at night and with Mary and Steven and Junior when I was six and eight years old but that was a long time ago and they taught me. Oh gran'ma *please* . . ."

This last was addressed to Grandma Otis whose Christian Science martyrdom I trusted to get me in right again with God. (She had died of cancer of the stomach, refusing to see a doctor—"I'm perfectly well in Science, dear." . . . "B'lieve I'll just stick to my Spirit, thank you! And don't you forget, Daphne, we wouldn't have a speck of pain if t'weren't for Mortal Mind." But oh what horror at the end, the mindless maggots of the eyes crawling in the sockets, the pretty old lady mouth screaming for *aspirin* to ease the pain.)

There was no help to be had by invoking my immediate family: they didn't believe in God. Even Jason would declare self-righteously, if asked by an unwary neighbor: "I'm an atheist, like my whole family."

Whereas these days I hedged. "Well, I was *bap*tized Greek Orthodox . . ." And when hard-pressed: "I don't really think we ought to discuss religion; it's more private, like politics, don't you think?"

Then at night, heavily weighted down with my lippy passion for Joshua X., I would plead God's pardon for evading Him. But what were these slender filaments of lips that drove me crazy morning to night and to morning again? Why *there*? I knew—I knew, well enough, without knowing. My parents singly and together (with Jason lately wise-guying it behind the door) had explained to me the whole process of sexual love (oh, the 'twenties), mating (oh, the 'thirties), and having babies blah blah blah! I persisted in imagining that babies emerged from the rectum, though when asked directly (as I often was by mates—like poor Aggie—with less progressive parents) I would reply dutifully that of course they came out of your you-know-what, whatja think goofy cross-eyes? Huh, goofy?

Aggie said she didn't think so. Why not? "Our Sister in Cath'lic school says babies come from Heaven."

Aggie, did they come from Heaven when your man stuck them in you and they ripped out again, swollen with life—even that putrid stillborn—leaving placentas and blood and cancer behind them? In you? In your torn, bleeding, pulpous, lippy box?

At night, in foreign quaint-garden Tyrol, I know no better. I have such a horror of what can be put in boxes: children and dead people and cancer and garden gates and palpable, breathing, passionate fantasies.

Joshua was an artist. A story so monotonous as hardly to bear notation. He was on WPA but he had caught pneumonia and WPA could not pay his bills. He needed to live free somewhere for a brief time to save a little money. He lived with us for four months while my mother built up his health and morale and my father helped him find a steady job that left him enough time and energy to make his "objects."

They weren't paintings and they weren't sculptures and at the time and for years afterward (though I never admitted it to anyone but myself) they seemed very queer even to me. Now I know that he was a kind of Surrealist and that he was doing really very original work, though Giacommetti had made related objects a few years before—and Cornell was doing so then but quite without knowledge of Joshua's work. No one came to know Joshua's work.

Usually he used shoe-boxes without lids, or he would cut holes or little doors in the lids or sides and sheet them with cellophane so you could peek through. This was in the beginning. When he began earning a few dollars he bought scraps of lumber and hammered together boxes which he fitted with glass tops.

"What's *that?*"

"A platypus."

"What?"

"A clong. A schnoo. A fllmnp.—Daphne!"

It is impossible to *describe* a work of art (which is what these were) without driving out of it that very quality of unexpected, perfect resolution which makes it art. I said these boxes were queer, and they were, but in spite of my adolescent fears, shames, and proprieties I rather liked them. They reminded me of the dollhouse I had played with till I was ten and was ashamed (but yearned) to play with now that I approached, queenly, the years of high school.

In the boxes and in precise, painstakingly considered juxtaposition he placed all manners of madnesses: coils of thin wire and snippets of hair (one of my shorn curls went into a box labeled "Little Side-Dream": I was delighted by the curl but obscurely hurt by the title), fragments of newspaper photographs and print, toothbrush bristles and fingernail parings and empty lipstick cases, shreds of cloth and bits of broken glass or china, pebbles, the insides of watches, pencil stubs, even one of Jason's molars. My mother got to saving all the non-decayable refuse of each day for him to pick over at night.

"I don't like them or understand them," she said, "but he has the *right*, I believe." She could be very romantic about her principles.

At night Jason and I would hurtle down to the basement to watch him work till bedtime. He never complained at our presence though he talked very little while he worked. We jabbered incessantly, boomed and yakked the radio, and even tinkered with his tools and tiny toys. Occasionally Joshua would frown us away from something, and once he said to me,

"Daphne, if you were my little girl I would slam you one on your behind," which made me rush upstairs to my room weeping with humiliation and disappointment. *Little girl*, indeed! when he was the forbidden fruit of my fantasies. I wouldn't blossom forth (Elaine, the lily maid of Astalot) until he came to murmur through my keyhole, "Come on out, sweetheart; I'll make you a special box all your own. OK?"

He made us—each member of the family—several boxes, which have been flooded out or burned or lost in the way of most flotsam. I see now that his boxes were more than cute three-dimensional collages or elaborate toys. They were often playful but just as often wistful or downright sad. There was frequently a narrative or descriptive element to them, but neither simple nor temporal: they didn't tell stories like a picturebook.

"Little Side-Dream" was a wooden box almost a foot square. Under the sliding glass lid with its delicately beveled edges lay a whole nest of old-fashioned watches, perhaps a dozen, each telling a different time. He had bought them (all broken) in a lot at a rummage sale. When you slid out the glass and lifted the watch-faces you found beneath each, instead of the works, a special scene or object: a used railway ticket; a ship tumbling over the waves; a tiny effulgent city, the neon lights drops of colored enamel; a sidereal landscape; a sleeping maiden; the silky parabola of my curl. Like all his boxes, it revealed in a flash a whole fantasy or fragment of experience.

In short, it was art. If it were to be resurrected today I suppose the museums, ravenous as ever, would stick it in an Extinguished Talent or Old Americans show and then, frail creation, it'd be taken up and touted about by the best fairy gallery in New York. *Requiescat in pace*.

My friend, my secret pet, my slight gentle idol, ignorant companion of my midnight, pre-breakfast and, frequently, surreptitious naptime revels was no fairy himself, however. At first he simply seemed to pull a blank around women. Maybe he was just too tired or discouraged. Maybe he wanted to work more than to chase girls. This disturbed my father. He had not the usual over-aggressive male's fear of homosexuals; quite the opposite, in fact. He relegated to them a position as honorable as that of women, only less fortunate.

"There are three species of sexual humans in the world." He hammers his fist on the dinnertable for silence, and the knives and forks skip at our places.

"First (with a broad wink toward my mother), the least important: women who sleep with Men. Next, fairies who sleep with each other or with Men; and finally, Men who sleep preferably with women, but with fairies if there aren't any women around or if they need a free meal or a little extra cash. These—"

He stops for an instant to swallow: during his harangue he has been cramming food into his mouth with the same breathless insatiability with which he talks.

"—are called the *bulls* (*bools*); homosexuals and women we call the *cows*."

Mother is furious. She hacks her food in bits and snaps it off the fork.

Chin arched intellectually—I have recently discovered *Well of Loneliness* wedged in at the end of one of our bookshelves—I inquire where he would place Lesbians in his scale. It is one of the compensations for our peculiar childhood that he almost always considers Jason's and my questions seriously. He stops chewing, thoughtfully clears his sinuses, and replies:

"Upon reflection I can recall only two important Lesbians: Sap-

pho and Queen Elizabeth. And though I have none of the usual
prejudices—in fact, I was once in puppy-love (*poppy-lahve*) with a
beautiful Lesbian girl named Rosemary—how is it possible to
count a movement(!) which in approximately five thousand years
of recorded history has produced only two significant examples?
Whereas from Plato to Gide there have existed thousands of important fairies, only here I will distinguish further between fairies
and pederasts. . . ."

At this point even I, really interested only in sex these days—even
I weary and cease to listen while I toy with Joshua's empty coffee-
cup at my elbow.

After a quick, seemingly casual inspection my father decided
that Joshua (certainly no fairy, and probably not even a pederast)
needed nothing so tonic-y as a woman, and accordingly he began
to bring them in. It gave him a good excuse to gather pretty girls
around him, and my mother, after a grim sigh, pitched in to help
with extra meals and occasional parties, though she "would have
nothing wild" she stated, darting a menacing glance at my father.

"*Puritana!*" muttered my father, but he stopped hanging out his
tongue all the same.

At first they came and went in swift succession, frail blossoms on
the gusts of our prince's bored sighs. Grace, who helped with
dishes, and Viola who did not and smeared "I really love Jason
best" all over the bathroom mirror with Tangee lipstick. Pretty
Nanette with whom I fell briefly in love and to whom we gaily
sang all one evening, "*No, no Nanette! No, no.*" Jean—from a dull
Iowa family—who had joined the social revolution and tried earnestly to convert Joshua to socially significant art. Sarah who was
Jewish and was really having a hell of a time trying to organize the
lady garment workers in her district. He liked her best for a while,
but, I heard him tell my father, he just didn't feel like sleeping
with her.

"Why *not?*" roared my father.

"Why?" queried Joshua, and there Sarah rested.

Then my father started to round up the Greek girls. Had I
thought, had I been strong and brave and used to offering advice
to my father, I would simply have warned him, "*Don't!*" I understood this instinctively, for I had no truck with Greek girls myself,
but in those days I didn't know how to examine an intuitive re-

action for its validity as a genuine mode of conscious behavior. I was still all instinct and feeling, rushing about with my eyes tight shut and my mouth wide open—panting, greedily swallowing. By the time (very soon) I knew enough to take rational action, I didn't want to act. I wanted calamity. I hated Joshua. I stood like a fence-post and let it come down.

Joshua did not nibble at the first two or three "Greek girls" either, and my father grew really worried. But I had seen a spark light up, far back in those sweet wild eyes of his, at the very suggestion of Greekness and I was worried. With my customary self-condemnation (Daphne, you mean skinny witch, you!), I attributed this to simple female jealousy, and I tried to scour it out of my heart. I couldn't have Joshua (I still had to go to high school and college and become famous and besides, I was just his "little side-dream," wasn't I?) but that didn't mean some Woman (grown up and with breasts) couldn't gobble him up, marry him down, discharge him with babies, and make him blissful or at least quiet in the accepted manner.

It never once occurred to me—till a little later, of course—that I might be seismographically recording a very faint tremor in Joshua's crust which, intensified, could split his delicate world wide open.

That first tremor was in his eyes, but it was not, really. It was in "Little Side-Dream." Stupid Daphne!

The girl's name was *Vasiliki* (broad "a," accent on the last syllable). It is the feminine form of Basil: in Greek most of us are merely afterthoughts of the male, as it were: female appendages, like an extra set of nipples, on the male name. It means "little queen."

She was. She was small and she carried herself as if she expected to have both her hands kissed. This in a seventeen-year-old movie cashier is no minor attainment. Perhaps she was merely modeling herself after Norma Shearer or Bette Davis, but within the boundaries of her very limited world she succeeded. Her hands were kissed and fondled. She received orchids for dances at a time when few young men could afford to send orchids. She was sent presents and she took them, except for clothing. Here of course she was already approaching the dangerous no-man's land of the Greek community where no unmarried girl, not even a little queen with a diadem between her thighs, dares to walk abroad. She had been engaged twice and had kept the diamonds and the wrist-watches, for which it was already whispered that she was a *poutana* by a very few old hens. But this whisper got no breeze to travel on. Vasiliki carried about in her patent leather handbag a clear image of herself, to maintain which she was willing to make considerable sacrifices.

She gave the plainest wrist-watch to her favorite girl cousin who *needed* it, she pouted to her mother, father, aunts, uncles, and girl-friends. She had the diamond prized out of one ring and set in a gold, heart-shaped locket in which she actually wore the beefy, be-wildered countenances of mama and papa. The other ring she gave with a certain amount of ladylike publicity to St. Dimitrios during a fund-raising drive. She was even included in a group photograph of church "donors" in the *Greek Daily*. By the time Joshua came along she was forging a pretty coat-of-arms in the Greek community for a mere cook's daughter.

I see now that she used Joshua to get to us because she really believed she needed us for the construction of her private palace. I'm not contriving excuses for her; she was wrong from the moment she took it into her shiny, black-helmeted head that it was a shameful thing to be the issue of a poor restaurant cook. But oh Vasiliki, queen-bee, grubby infant of a fat, sweaty Macedonian hick who always smelled of other people's food, snorkled in his soup and wiped the grease off on the back of his hand—target for the slings and arrows of portly, be-taffeted, real gold-ed Daughters of Hera with their "teas" and their "luncheons" and their squealing Demotic "minutes" and their infernal money-raising—you with your purse-mouthed pursuit of a cell padded in real Brussels lace and imported Spanish shawls with a grand piano in the middle to play the latest Greek tangoes on (they were still tangoing in Ath-ens in 1937)—miscarriage of your environment, lost crown-jewel of Byzantium set in village mud, lemon-blossom with your soul like the withered lemon rind—let me not judge you.

My father was a lawyer and for all his mixed marriage, free talk, and derision of the church, he was a great prince in this tiny prin-cipality in the marches. I could afford to be scornful of Greek girls and go my way: I had an American mother, American girlfriends, and an American college waiting for me. My mother had graduated from the same college in 1918—my grandfather in 1892—my great-grandmother in 1860. I was a free agent.

Vasiliki was not. She lived in a box; her soul wasn't big enough to break out, so she felt she had to see that her box got furnished right.

Joshua did not appear to nibble the first time. He sat far back on the couch that was his night-time bed, with his thin legs awkwardly crossed like a boy just beginning to wear long trousers and his skinny, supple hands jammed in his pockets. Maybe he was running. Interior flight. He said little except, challengingly, that he read *PM*, voted for Roosevelt (this was no challenge, everyone Vasiliki knew voted for Roosevelt), and believed that art could best serve the social revolution by following its own organic growth in joyous freedom (hear hear!).

Vasiliki was only seventeen but she was no fool; she was a good Greek girl. She ignored him gently except for an occasional sweet, plump glance full of sisterly laughter and spent her time talking to Mother and me. She was demure with my father. Though she allowed herself, at the end of the evening, to be pinched on the behind, she quickly spatted his hand, sped to my mother, kissed her on both cheeks, slipped her arm around my waist and gave me a hug, and drew that imp Jason to her bosom with real affection.

She had a beautiful bosom. I loved it. It was high and full without being distorted like those on the calendar Petty Girls Jason was already collecting. On her second visit, a few nights later, she wore a soft white lace collar folded in a deep V across her breasts— a fichu really. There were a number of uniquely old-fashioned touches about her: she bought long earrings in the dime-store and wore them with her black hair, which had never been cut, spiraling in a sombre crown round and round the summit of her perfect little head.

What my father had failed to take into account with Viola and Sarah and even Nanette was that an artist usually demands both genuine and unusual beauty in his woman. Not just any pretty girl. But a *different, beautiful* girl. When Vasiliki bent over Joshua to offer him a snowy box of *loukoum* and a glass of *mastikaha* and her pretty breasts belled downward in her Betsy Ross bodice and her obsidian coronet tilted toward him, like gleaming, curved blades —*then* I saw him leap toward life. His hands and feet jerked, and his face lit like a Roman candle: eyes, lips, teeth, taut incandescent skin. My father saw it, too, and purred deep in his throat like a big cat—rumble of vicarious pleasure in all that fragrant female flesh. Then he sighed and drew his brows together, probably at his own denial.

But I was lost in the second act. What divine revelation was taking place in our makeshift crèche? Such pain, such pleasure! Like my father's really—pleasure in the sudden stimulus to the senses which the spectacle of those two offered us, pain in knowing that I was only in the audience.

Once Jason, who knew a Trojan horse when he saw one, said, "What's he so crazy about that glamorpuss for?"

"Oh, he thinks it's so la-dee-da, being Greek," I sneered.

Years later—only a matter of weeks ago—I saw Joshua's face again as it was at that moment. I was standing in the Uffizi before the central panel of the Portinari Altarpiece: the "Adoration of the Shepherds." And there he is. The third peasant, racing in on the tides of his need, his shepherd's crook clasped to his breast like a crucifix, like the hand of his beloved—his crazy northern face lit and wild with recognition as he stares at the Virgin. Diamond of Judah! Full, bursted melon of the House of David, spilling the secret of all creation from the cornucopia of your womb! Van der Goes, they say, ended his days as a monk in a madhouse—oh mad in that monkeyhouse—of course I stand and stand to stare and muse, why do I love it? where does it hurt so? whom have I seen him become before? It isn't till now, jerking suddenly up on my mattress of geraniums and cuckoo-clocks that I remember and am ashamed for the cruel, casual, protective loss of memory that denies us our intensest experiences so that we can go on living.

There was already some slight, subtle footwork between my mother and me on the subject of the boxes.

My father only said, "What th'hell! Let her take him as he is. She's only a woman, isn't she? Good brood mare!"

But we knew better. Their third meeting was a date, so there wasn't any danger then. He took her to see *The Garden of Allah*, and I suppose Vasiliki thenceforward incorporated Dietrich into her rogue's gallery for the composite model: the ironic queen never really possessed, even in the final close-up caress. Joshua came

home, contemplated the autographed still of Charles Boyer I had
tacked over my own fretted couch, and said cryptically,

"Wait and see."

Then he said, "If you like, Vasiliki will get you all the photos of
stars you want. For free. From the movie where she works."

Greedy little beast Daphne! It was clear what she was up to, but
I grabbed at my bribe with delight. Pride and personal autographs
to the winds! What I hungered for were pieces of Hollywood
dream-cake to nibble on. I was only twelve and I didn't hesitate
for an instant to toss away the ruby so I could take the glass chip
to dream on.

There followed in quick succession a book for my mother, a toy
watch for Jason (she favored watches), and two packs of the best
Turkish cigarettes for my father. Vasiliki had almost no extra
spending money so she had to buy shrewdly, and she bought with
taste. The volume for my mother was a stroke of genius: the *complete* poems of Browning. Enormous. Later I learned that she had
paid a special visit to her old English teacher in high school simply
to ask her what one gave an American lady who had been to college and liked to read. Of course her teacher said Browning (amaz-
ing that it wasn't "Bobby" Burns); even so, Vasiliki had the fine
good sense not to buy a "collected verse." A delicate point maybe,
but she went up fast in my mother's estimation after that.

Really, though, that was so Greek of her—the desire to impress
by amassing *all* the riches. While of course my mother mistakenly
concluded that Vasiliki had read and liked Browning and had the
true poetry lover's distrust of an anthology, "which—Daphne—de-
pends on some *other* reader's taste."

Not much later I became Vasiliki's confidante, and I never betrayed her, till now when all the marbled batter of venom and love
pushes up in me like something rising too fast in the oven. I de-
spised her sly maneuvers, but I loved her. Because Joshua wanted
her, because she was beautiful, because I longed to *be* her, because
with all my mother's brains and education she had never developed
such a skill in stratagem to teach to me so I could become a woman
like other women.

At their fourth meeting, in spite of all mother's and my delaying
tactics, Joshua took Vasiliki down into the dank basement to see
his boxes. Mother was a romantic and wanted their idyll to con-

tinue a little longer. I was afraid of what might happen to Joshua. Nervously, we traipsed downstairs together after them, peering ahead to see what was going on under the electric light bulb.

"How-do-you-like-them-aren't-they-marvelously-clever?" Mother cried all in one breath.

"Oh yes, they're so cute," said Vasiliki in her pretty, very very faintly accented syllables. "I like *that* one," pointing at random.

"Which? Which?" cried poor Joshua.

"Oh—that one, I guess." It was written all over her face: well, so you're a nut after all; I'm not going to have any nuts in *my* box, thank you!

But Joshua wasn't looking; if he had been I think even he would have understood. Instead, he said with great excitement and satisfaction: "Well, if you *really* like them and don't *mind*, of course, I'll make you one, too."

"Oh, thanks a million!"

"Unless of course you'd rather have *this* one . . ."

"Oh no, no! Thanks *ever*."

"I'm glad," said Joshua simply. "I would rather make one just for you and give it to you myself." He looked her straight in her black tip-tilted eyes, without a trace of childishness or evasive flirting. His money was plumped there on the line and she could take or leave it. Do I get my ticket or don't I?

Vasiliki's gaze actually fell; she pursed her lips, swiveled on her spike heels and marched off upstairs with her adorable rump switching and her eyes bent thoughtfully on the carpeting.

I was sweating with repressed laughter and nerves. I raced after her, ahead of Joshua and Mother, and confronted her in the parlor.

"What are you going to do?"

She gave me a long, calculating look. "Daphne, what about him? Is he . . . ?"

I stopped being twelve and became a hundred. "W*ell* . . ." I smiled compassionately.

Suddenly she slipped her arm around my waist and gave me a tight squeeze. "Daphne, you're *marv!* Why don't we have a regular hen-fest one of these days? We could go to the movies on my free pass and then to Prince Castle after. I *love* Prince Castle, with all that glop they put on top!"

Joshua came into the room. "Who's this prince you love? I'll take him on right now."

"It's like an ice cream parlor," Vasiliki said, with the faintest trace of stiffness.

"I'll take you there myself."

He's jealous of me, I thought. I could have wept to see things so turned around. But he had seen my face fall, for he walked right over and rubbed his nose in my hair—the tenderest gesture he had ever made toward me. "Don't cry, Betty Boop! You'll get your ice cream sundae; never fear."

I burst into tears and ran out of the room.

The next afternoon as I came in from school, the phone rang: Vasiliki inviting me to see *Stella Dallas* and go for a sundae afterward.

I had to ask Mother. "I think that would be *nice*," she said, rolling out cookie dough. "I guess she's interested in Joshua, after all."

I'll fix that, I thought to myself and dashed back to set the time.

I didn't actually tell any lies behind the white tiled turrets of Prince Castle; I simply let her convince herself of what she already wanted to believe.

"He's really off his rocker, isn't he?"

I blinked.

"Why do your mother and father let him hang around, then?"

I shrugged.

"I don't see how you can stand it," she said, sticking out her tongue to lick her cherry. I proffered her mine, on my spoon.

"Don't ever do that with a fellow, Daphne."

"Why not?"

She stared. Then she hissed, with her face in mine, "*Cherry!* Get it?"

"No. I don't like maraschino cherries; I don't see why I shouldn't give them to somebody who does."

"You *are* a dope. Cherry is what you've got here," gesturing toward her lap with her spoon. "Virginity. Get it?"

"Oh." I thought of all the times Joshua had taken me out for ice cream and gobbled up my cherries greedily. Probably he'd been mocking me all the time. I hated him for it. "What will you do with that box Joshua's going to make for you?"

"Turn him in."

I really don't think I heard her at first. I went on destroying my
Double Chocolate Delight until gradually the whipped cream began tasting like cheese. I laid down my spoon.

"What did you say?"

"*I'm* not taking any chances."

"You wouldn't!"

"Oh but definitely! He's probably a sexual pervert or something."

"But he hasn't done anything—"

"How do you know? You don't know anything about him before
he came to live with you. All you know is he's from Sioux Falls or
someplace. He might be a rapist, even." She paused. "You know,
I'll bet he's an Indian."

"Why?"

"Oh, I don't know. Sioux Falls or something. *I* wouldn't let an
Indian sleep in my parlor. That's why I don't understand your
folks—"

"You're *prejudiced!*" I cried hotly, my voice echoing from the
damp, tiled walls, reeking of warm milk and sugar.

She eyed me haughtily. "I don't discuss politics, myself."

I went home feeling sick in my soul and my stomach. I wanted
to tell my parents what Vasiliki had said, but they were out. Jason
was in bed though awake, of course, the little snoop. I went in and
asked him where Joshua was.

"He's in the basement making a box for Vasiliki. Ooo! Lovey-
dovey!" Then he began to sing, "Daphne lu-uvs Josh-wa! Daphne
lu-uvs Josh-wa!"

I was terrified that Joshua might hear him down the hot-air
register, so I snapped, "Shut up or I'll lock your door."

He subsided at once, and I went into the bathroom. I wanted to
go right down to warn Joshua but I was afraid of three things. One.
That Jason might hear me and set up that yodel again. Two. That
Joshua had already heard Jason and now knew my secret shame.
Three. That I was going to be horribly sick to my stomach.

I threw up everything: Double Chocolate Delight complete with
whipped cream, malt-balls from the movies, supper's lamb chop,
even the salted peanuts I'd nibbled after school.

Then I went to bed and cried for a long time.

Eventually I heard Joshua trudge upstairs. He went into the

parlor, opened the coat closet door, shut it again, and came back, poking his head in at my door.

"Daphne?"

I considered a moment and then murmured, "Mm-m—"

"I'm going out for a breath of air. Your folks should be home soon. You scared to stay alone?"

"No." This was a lie.

"I won't go far."

"OK."

"Goodnight, Betty Boop."

Now is the time. Now—now! Call him in before he gets to the kitchen, before his step crosses the threshold, before he shuts the back door. Sit him on the foot of your bed. Tell him everything in a rush, no matter how it sounds. He is your Joshua and he is in danger.

Instead I sulked silently, listening to his steps crunch down the cinder drive, because in my hideous self-consciousness I was afraid I smelled sour from the vomit and because I was even more afraid of his disbelief. He was crazy—and he was crazy about that piece of fake exoticism, Vasiliki; he wouldn't believe me. He would think I was mean and jealous and he would never call me "Betty Boop" again.

In addition, there lingered a fantastic apprehension at the back of my memory. Maybe Vasiliki was right. We knew very little about him, after all. He had said *for a breath of air*, but what if he meant something else? I shivered and wriggled farther under the covers.

Some time later my parents came home. They were arguing as they walked up the drive, and I heard them step into the basement, probably just for a look, and then come upstairs, still arguing. Briefly they were silent while my mother trotted into the parlor and quickly returned toward the kitchen, gently closing Jason's door and mine on the way.

I knew they wanted to be alone to argue so I did not summon them in to hear my troubles. Instead, I got up and quietly opened my door to listen. I heard my father say,

"You're up to your old tricks—you want to limit my freedom."

"We must all learn to live within limits," said my mother.

"Man is born free. Woman enslaves him!" He began pacing up and down the kitchen.

"Nonsense!" snapped my mother. Then she murmured something I couldn't catch.

"Look," he said, "if you want another child, I'll give you one. We can't really afford it but times are bound to get better. I'll give you a great, big, walloping belly, and then . . ."

"And then," said my mother in a voice suddenly as lean as bone, "you'll go chasing after the first pig in skirts you see. No, *thank* you. I've served my term. No more having my husband fall all over me *simply* because the mindless slut he slept with couldn't satisfy him."

I could have thought another woman had spoken, the words were so strange. She stopped and I could hear her panting sharply with anger. But when she spoke again it was in a very different voice. "I'm sorry. I shouldn't have said those things. Only once in a while I allow myself to feel bitter—I lose control . . ."

"You've made it quite clear what you think already," my father said with a sound of stiff and terrible pride.

"No," my mother said. "No.—That's only part of it."

I closed the door and slipped back into bed. I was trembling with disgust but I was puzzled, too. What did she mean, *only part of it?* Then, quite simply, the way children do, I decided to forget the whole discussion. Mother was Mother. My father was "difficult" (Mother's word) but he was "terrific," "awfully smart," and "loads of fun," too, and though I wasn't then capable of loving him, I certainly worshiped him, and the notion of any other father would have been heresy.

The next morning I went in to breakfast fully determined to make my confession to Joshua, but the sight of his red, red mouth —too red no matter what the weather—made me think of that breath of air, and I turned mute in adolescent alarm and jealousy. The more he tried to wheedle out of me what the matter was, the more I shunned him.

But that evening when he was again in the basement working, I pricked and poked up my courage and went downstairs. He was fitting a gate made out of green pipestems into a long, wooden box —Vasiliki's.

"Why did you make it green?"

"Why not?" Then, afraid perhaps that he'd been too brusque with his pet, he looked up and smiled with extraordinary sweetness.

It shredded to bits my puerile soul, and I could hardly bear the thought of letting him down by telling him the truth.

"What are you going to do now?"

"I'm going to put *her—here*." He pointed with one hand to a space behind the gate and with the other he picked up and held aloft my—*my* little porcelain mermaid.

I gave an involuntary cry. "You can't!"

"Why not?"

There she was, darling and white and nude with little softly-rounded, pink-tipped breasts. Once long long ago she had reclined, exquisitely languid, on the sandy sea-bottom of somebody's gold-fish bowl. Then oh bliss she had lost an arm (Madame Recamier undergoes surgery) and been given me for my dollhouse. I never played with it anymore of course, but the notion of giving her to Vasiliki—try to imagine this gnashing agony. The night-brown walls of the basement turn a sickly mud-yellow with the approaching hurricane. I could kill. In an instant. In the despotic obliquity of youth I perceive that I, who merit all rewards *by right*, am losing one of my possessions to a cook's spawn.

I almost spit. "She's mine!"

"Funny. I found her here on the table. Jason or your mother must have . . . Never mind; it doesn't matter. Here, sweetheart, take her back. You're my best girl of all." Then he utters the ultimate misfortune. "I'll find something better for her."

I was dumb with bitterness and shame. I stumbled back upstairs, clutching my one-armed mermaid, so long outgrown, so much a part of my myriad inadequacies.

What happened during the next two days I have to reconstruct from what my mother has told me.

During the night Joshua must have finished Vasiliki's box. What it looked like in its final form only Mother knew, for she was the only one of us to see it and she recalls a nude female figure of some kind. He was still at his job when I came home from school, and I ran eagerly across the street to call on Aggie, with whom I hadn't played for at least two months. We retired to the ping-pong table in the depths of her basement, and I let her win game after game—anything to avoid going home. At six o'clock her mother, in a rare good humor, invited me to stay for supper, and I eagerly accepted after sending Aggie back across the street to ask permission of Mother.

At seven-thirty Aggie and I wandered upstairs to her bedroom "to read library books" (Aggie read the comics). Meanwhile, Joshua cleaned himself up, put on his *other* suit, wrapped the precious box in tissue dug up somewhere by Mother, and departed to seek out Vasiliki in her cashier's box, longer than a coffin but not much wider. He hadn't called for a date, but he told Mother it didn't matter for he knew her schedule. Mother said he was perfectly at ease.

I am sure it never occurred to Joshua that Vasiliki might laugh; worse yet, might disapprove, be afraid. Why should it? We had adopted and protected him, surrounding him like a wall with our family, our love, our broad shoulders. My mother accepted his boxes as an honor and showed them to all her friends—not because she understood or even liked them, but because she loved Joshua. He can hardly be blamed for not knowing all this.

At eight o'clock my father went off to a professional meeting, and at eight-thirty while I was still buried in *The Red Fairy Book* in Aggie's bedroom, two policemen called at our house and demanded to see the "pornography" in the basement. It was a great pity my father wasn't at home then. Though he seldom handled criminal cases, he was known and respected down at City Hall, and I dare say that with a phone call he could have sent them away, at least temporarily. As it was, they put a large number of "exhibits" in the police-car and drove away, shaking their heads over "the crazy guy."

My mother finally managed to reach my father at his meeting, and he went rampaging over to the police station, bailed out Joshua, and brought him home. He did not think, however, to check on the fate of all those "exhibits," and Joshua didn't know about them.

Mother said Joshua looked very queer when he arrived back from the police station. She said he looked the way he did four months before when my father first dragged him home to supper. She saw to it that he didn't go down to the basement but gave him a sedative with orange juice (Mother didn't really approve of sedatives and thought that swallowing them with the aid of orange juice somehow made them morally acceptable), and sent him to bed on the parlor couch. When I slunk in—at ten o'clock, unheard of during the week—all she said was,

"Oh, where have *you* been?" And then, "What a time we've had!" And shut me in the kitchen with her to tell me all. I sat there on the hospital-white kitchen stool, utterly condemned by myself, but I felt it would be even worse to confess.

Joshua slept through breakfast, and Mother phoned his job to say he was sick and not coming in that day. I took one peek at him, lying there in his faded pajamas like a pauper on his slab, before running off to school and I have never been able really to gloze over that memory. I think right then I died a little without knowing that was what I was doing. I walked to school abstractedly and on the way I decided that "it would be better to forget about it." And by virtue of a prodigious effort I really forgot him off and on during the day.

While I was working at forgetting, my father went to see Vasiliki and quickly persuaded her to drop the case. She appeared eager to talk to him and took both his scolding and advice without a murmur. She said she had been "frightened" and "mistaken," and she cried "pathetically" (his word) on his shoulder. For a lawyer he could occasionally be fairly obtuse. They drove together to the police station, and my father asked for the boxes. The harassed sergeant, glad to make an end of the matter, said he would send them to the house in a patrol wagon. My father then went to his office.

By the time Joshua waked, my mother was able to tell him that everything was all right. He washed, shaved, and ate a good breakfast; he seemed cheerful enough, Mother said, though perhaps still a trifle groggy from the sedative. Then he went into the parlor to watch for the patrol wagon.

When it still had not come at noon Mother telephoned the police station. The sergeant was polite but brief: obviously he had had his fill of this case. One of his men had thrown them boxes in the incinerator, thinking they was just trash. Sorry. Mother shut the kitchen door and phoned my father at his office. I don't know what they agreed to say to Joshua, but whatever it was, wasn't enough.

He listened calmly, "only," Mother said, "tilting his head at me a little and going rather paler, *if* possible . . ." Then he left "without his coat." This fact correctly struck her as ominous, and she waited for him in great apprehension the rest of the day, not even going out into the back yard for fear of missing the telephone.

When I came home from school at three-thirty, there still hadn't been word from or about him. I wandered down to the basement, regarded the dismal scrap-heap left behind by the invading policemen, and then I recalled my new resolution to forget it all. I went across the street again to Aggie's, but she was being punished by her mother, so I took a long walk up the railroad tracks toward the country.

At dusk I ambled home to find Mother and Jason crying in the kitchen. Joshua, they said, was in the state hospital. At four he had appeared with a form for Mother to sign, admitting him for treatment. His family was dead; she must sign. In desperation she telephoned my father, and together they stormed at, argued and pleaded with Joshua. Finally, gravely, he rolls up his cuffs to show them the slightly twisted, delicate white twine scarring his skinny wrists.

This scene I have always found it impossible to visualize. My father and mother are real: they cough and move. But there is Joshua, displaying the emblems of his martyrdom as sedately as a saint. Like a schoolteacher he points to the blackboard—no! I can't see him. Once upon a time he had cut his wrists, that's all. He was my Joshua and I done him wrong deliberately and with hatred in my heart. Joshua, I summon you. I resurrect your fleshless narrow delicate most beautiful blanched cutting bones! When did you slash your wrists? Why? *You never told me.*

I was twelve. No one told me much of anything I wanted to know. My father drove Joshua to the hospital and returned, silent with gloom, to his law books. I hung about his study door. Back and forth. Aimlessly pawing the threshold.

"Whatever—why—what do you think . . . ?"

I couldn't get it out, but suddenly he shouted,

"Joshua was too damn weak, that's all! The race is to the swift, the strong, the sonuvvabitching pigs who never even take their brass knuckles off in the bathtub. He—was—too—goddam—*weak*, for Christ's sake, Daphne! Now will you leave me alone and get the hell out?"

I got: embarrassed, frightened, appalled by his tears. But shamefacedly thanking the family gods that we were never, any of us, really, in Joshua's way at least, weak.

Joshua was well-treated at the hospital. The chief resident psychiatrist was a friend of my father's law-partner and anyhow, he said, Joshua was one of the most amenable patients he had ever had. Very soon we were allowed to visit him. I was frightened the first time, but he took my arm and led me to a bench on the hospital lawn where we talked pleasantly about my school work, how they treated him, and what books I should bring him next visit. When I left he called me "Betty Boop."

My mother went to see him regularly once a week. How she found time to add these visits to all the rest of her urgent scurrying, I'll never know. My own appearances were irregular and I did not look forward to them, but once there, with him, my anxiety drained away and I was almost as happy as I had been watching him work in the basement. I no longer believed I loved him; in a way of course I didn't—I never had.

We talked about everything except the boxes. He said of Vasiliki that "it was a kind of insanity even to have fallen for her."

I worked the toe of my oxford in the gravel, feeling I was hearing something too old for me.

"Dangerously immature," he continued, like a pupil who wants to please Teacher by giving the correct answer.

"Still . . ." He paused with an expression of stunned wonder on his face. ". . . what happened to me? What a dreamer I was! What pitiful, magnificent visions they personify!"

"They?" I asked myself. "They *who?*"

On another, very different day we were walking through the gardens loosely holding hands when suddenly he turned to look closely at me, his face right up against mine—as if he were nearsighted, I remember thinking at the time.

"I should have waited for you to grow up, Daphne. But of course you wouldn't bother with someone like me. Why should you?" And he laughed deprecatingly.

I could have said right then, "Yes I *will* bother." I was thirteen now—almost a woman—but I was too startled and besides I didn't want to. The moment spilled on really unnoticed, for Joshua had from the beginning been relegated to dreamland.

As time passed I began to feel that growing up was learning not to care. I decided that in removing myself from Joshua—from my dreams—I had begun to grow up.

After Joshua was released and took a job teaching handicrafts in a trade school (work for which he was conspicuously unsuited), we continued to visit back and forth, but gradually and almost consciously I forced our relationship into a new pattern in which I was the elder, the big sister, the girl-mother. He played along with it although sometimes I used to catch him watching me with the quirk of a smile. I think that by trying to dominate him I was trying to keep my dreams under control.

We had of course to see that he didn't meet Vasiliki at our house. This was not easy, for she was always running in "just to say hello" but really to find a good husband at our hands. At first my mother would barely speak to her, but gradually even her principles were caught and enervated by Vasiliki's wiles. Vasiliki and I were quite comfortable together. We agreed about very little except the unspoken mutual tact which absolutely prohibited any mention of that conversation at Prince Castle, and this bound us together in easy familiarity.

As time went on, I was occasionally made the recipient of her discarded boyfriends, gifts which I accepted without any false pride. Sometime, I don't know exactly when, I had decided that I wasn't above taking what I could get where I could get it. By and by, one of these rejects (the dullest, of course; isn't it always that way?) made me. The seduction was mutual—both pantingly determined. The act took place in our garden hammock: no mean accomplishment. Because of the lurching, swaying hammock, he couldn't scramble out of his clothes, and I never got to see what he really looked like, but it didn't much matter. I was made, initiated, deflowered, uncherried: no longer a silly, giggling virgin like most of my friends, surreptitiously passing around dirty paragraphs about creamed bananas, but a woman, a queen, or at least a princess.

The boy, somewhat to my surprise, had got genuinely excited; he wanted to meet again. I held up my chin, gazing off into the delicious landscapes beckoning me on, and said no thank you. I was a princess, wasn't I? Casual dispenser of ladies or tigers. Sometimes ladies (myself) but quite frequently tigers, too.

I was wise enough not to sleep around. Some tatter of dream

remained around my shoulders like a leash, and I was also aware that I must protect my reputation. The world couldn't get too familiar with a princess, or she would lose her power. I learned that Vasiliki permitted the most extraordinary liberties without ever "going the whole way." I didn't despise her. She was a good Greek girl: just didn't have the soul of a princess. It wasn't her fault.

One day when I went to drop off at Joshua's a box of cookies Mother had packed for him—she was always putting up extra batches of cookies for other people: "our Joshua" or "our Marianne"—I found two small canvases propped against the sofa-back in his one-room apartment. They were still tacky: I could smell the turpentine. I was relieved that he didn't look at me as I stared at them, because I didn't like them.

But when I dropped in again, perhaps two weeks later, he was openly at work on some boxes. The top of his only table looked as if he'd just turned the waste-basket upside down on it.

I said "Joshua!" I was so excited I bent down and kissed his cheek.

Again he didn't look up, but he said with his smile—"Then this one will be for you."

He brought it round the following week, and it was "Little Side-Dream," exactly as it had been, even to the black curl.

I said, "Where did you get the hair, Joshua?" I think I was actually jealous again for the breath of an instant.

He laughed. "What did you think? That I'd kept only one of your curls?"

But there were no more good boxes. Whatever it was that had made them good was gone. Vanished. Blitzed. I think he realized this—I am sure he did from a remark he made to me sometime later about failure. But slowly he continued to turn them out. Frequently he went back to see his psychiatrist, and they held long discussions together. Perhaps they talked about his boxes. I don't know. Joshua was a very patient man, but he was no longer either talented or mad. I think his talent blew out at the same time as that lovely wildness in his eyes. This was hardly the psychiatrist's fault. Please understand that I am not repeating "artists are madmen" or "psychoanalysis removes the desire to create"—those glib catch-phrases of our blind times. Joshua was not The Artist. He was a particular human being in a special set of circumstances. I think the light in Joshua's eyes was a conviction of immortality—mistaken, maybe, but necessary to *his* continuance as an artist. That light was quenched when he realized that the striking of a match had—not *could*, but *had*—destroyed his fantasies. Killed his boxes. That his dreams had proved to be as casually ephemeral as his mere life.

At about the time I went off to college he got a much better job and moved to another city, but we corresponded with some regularity. It was 1943 and he was glad, he wrote, to be ruled 4-F (shirker! draft-evader! people said) because of those weeks in the state hospital. He had a small lath-and-plaster bungalow with a garden, and he would much prefer, he remarked in a letter to me, killing weeds than people.

I was having a rousing good time at college. There were almost no male civilians left on campus, but the air force, in its infinite wisdom, had seen fit to set up a base in the next town—eight minutes by bus, every hour on the hour. I liked the air force uniforms, and the sense of dash and urgency their lives imparted to the "boys" excited me, too.

Why was it that there was nothing so sexy as frolicsome Mr. Bones, jauntily tap dancing around the corner? Flyers were killed all the time in routine training flights, and with each crash we co-eds pursued the survivors ever more hotly. It was more than grab-pleasure-while-you-can. More than the youthful romantic desire to give ourselves to potential heroes. It was as though we were trying to get through, into the very crashes, to immolate our own young bodies on those exploding gasoline pyres. We wanted to die, too, consumed by our sex, the violence of the times, the frightful rape of flame and history. We wanted to kill and be killed in one glorious holocaust—to become both the raper and the raped in the red womb of our crazy collective suicide. And we would do strange things to express our excitement. A certain memory recurs.

I am lying flat on my back between the lectern and the altar in the Church of the Holy Trinity. I have not a stitch on and the young gentleman on top of me, pumping sweatily away, hasn't either. We have earlier in the day rejected both the Baptist and the First Congregational as not provocative enough in their imagery, and as I lie there afterward staring thoughtfully up at the medium-high church Episcopalian stars in the modest plaster firmament above me, I reflect (in that moment of awesome clarity which always follows a climax with someone you in no way love)—I *understand* that what we have really been looking for up there is a good, old-fashioned, implacable Byzantine Pancreator like those I have seen in slides of Monreale and Daphne (yes!).

Of course I am not ashamed. I use the Church of the Holy Trinity the way I use the "boys," to excite me with the spectacle of my own prodigious power. And to see if I can't get caught, somehow, and be made to die for it all. Oh, sweet death, with your infinitely wet kisses.

Even Vasiliki has got her husband (acquired, of course, through us) killed in the Battle of the Bulge, and now my family finally shuns her. Even Jason won't speak to her when he meets her on the street. It is as though they suspect she is a witch, has the Evil Eye, and so at last she can be allowed to pay (lucky Vasiliki) for what she did to Joshua.

Am I never to pay? Later my boy takes me to a forbidden roadhouse with an imitation log-cabin bar. Not beer, but whiskey, for the boys have money to squander in the quaint, rusticated antechambers of doom. I have two scotch-on-the-rocks that I remember and then probably more. Suddenly I am insisting that I must see Joshua.

"Who?"

"My uncle."

"A-a-ah!"

My boy is getting too familiar: he questions my word. I sway up the bar—has anybody got enough gas coupons to drive me to Cleveland?

"You bet I'll drive you to Cleveland, baby! Me and my buddy here—NOW?"

Since I do not believe in mass fornication (princesses are particular), I catch the ten o'clock bus alone.

I have a distant suspicion—all my suspicions are distant now—that Joshua is a little displeased by my condition when he opens his lath-and-plaster front door. But I also suspect that he is genuinely delighted to see me. He takes off my shoes, makes me coffee, and turns up the thermostat.

"Now," he says, "now, Betty Boop, what the devil have you been up to?"

I gaze over the rim of my cup into his sweet, fond, innocent, patient face, and I decide to give it to him straight. He's asking for it, isn't he? Betty Boop, indeed!

And I do. In spite of a certain drunken tendency to dump all my words into one pot, like a goulash, I begin with the hammock, progress through Uncle Sam's boys, and conclude chapters later with the Church of the Holy Trinity. I get to liking the sound of my own voice and describe actors and scenes in rapturous, epic catalogs. When I run out of true confessions, I make them up and since, in spite of everything, I am not really so wicked as I like to believe, some of the most inspired episodes in my saga are fictitious. Perhaps he understands this. I never really stop, however; I just drivel off to sleep in his armchair.

When I waken he forces more coffee on me, washes my face, and bundles me into his car for the sixty-mile drive back to college. It must use up a month's gasoline ration; he can't have a very high priority. Before letting me out at my dormitory, he takes me sternly by the shoulders. His thin fingers dig through the wool of my coat.

"Listen! Can you understand me? If your parents ever hear any of this—from *anyone*—I'll slap that stupid smirk right off your face myself! OK. Now go on up to bed and try sleeping by yourself for a change. What do you think you look like: coming to me like a slut tonight?"

In the morning I was fortunately still drunk enough to write him a letter of apology. My rhetoric was high-flown schoolgirl, but I don't remember what I said except for two things. *One*. That I would die if he didn't answer me. *Two*. P.S. That I loved him. Now this was not really true, of course, but I was still in the grip of an arsenic green hangover: the asphalt billowed puckishly as I crossed the street to the mailbox.

My answer came the next afternoon, by special delivery, and since I still have it, like all the other letters he wrote me, I'll transcribe a little of it.

"You do not disgust me. Don't say that! Nothing you ever do can disgust me, and I'm sorry if I said some hard things. I was furious. At first I felt I had failed you, somehow, for you to do these things, as I have failed in other ways. Later on I remembered that you are grown and a free agent and must make your own choices. But I think you can't really know anything about death, though you talked so much about it the other night, or you wouldn't try so hard to hurt yourself in these ways. It is simply not pleasant or sexy or even easy to die—so don't." There followed a humorous paragraph about the garden and then a

"P.S. Yes, Daphne, I love you."

By the time I got his letter I was sober, twenty years old, and yellow with embarrassment. As far as I let myself reflect on the matter, I perceived that by traipsing drunkenly into his parlor to confess I appeared to have been issuing another invitation. Probably I had only our old friendship to thank for the fact that Joshua hadn't made me right in that overstuffed armchair. Then I remembered Sarah and Nanette and Vasiliki, and scornfully concluded that nothing would have happened anyhow. For of course it never had.

Just the same, I vowed to reform and put the letter away to answer when I could face it. But I never had to. The next week he caught pneumonia hoeing in that damned garden and, even with sulfa, died in a few days. Perhaps if penicillin had been released for civilian use—but I don't think so. There is destiny.

Mother and Jason traveled three hundred and fifty miles for the funeral. I did not write them that I was in the infirmary, though I was tempted. I went with them to the funeral and forced myself to look into Joshua's box and I promised that fearsome, unnatural face . . . what? I don't know. To love, maybe. Simply to love.

I was sincere, but it is not so easy to keep promises. Love what? Whom? I like my work as an art critic very much, and I love my family. Perhaps that's enough. The promiscuity stopped, of course, and of course I quickly became a very steady character. Sometimes, I suspect, a bit of a bore.

Before leaving for Europe this summer I spent a week with all of them—my parents, Jason, his wife, their four-year-old Daphne Otis—in a cottage on one of the lakes where we go, where we've always gone.

Little Daphne said to me: "When will you be married, aunty? Will you be married tomorrow?"

"No."

"I'm very sorry," she answered with genuine regret.

"But Daphne, I don't really want to marry anyone I know."

It is true, but their obvious disbelief—all of them with apologetic eyes—unnerves me. When we fall to discussing Joshua, as we inevitably do, I can no longer sustain my objectivity. He rides up to greet me—that smiling skeleton beating time on his brass steed—and I become annoyed and questioning.

"I mean, why didn't he do good work after that?"

"Weak. He was too weak, I tell you!" My father shrugs. For him Joshua will always be a shrug. There he lost a battle, not with Joshua but with fate who leers and snatches back even from the grip of kings.

"He took himself in and out of a state institution. Singlehanded. He laid hold of his life and lived it reasonably through to the end. I don't call that *weak*," says Jason.

"Just the same, his relationships with women . . ." I proceed caustically. They have made me wince today, and I am going to kill Joshua over again if I have the chance.

"What *about* his relationships with women?"

My mother is bristling. Hands on hips, shoulders thrust forward pugnaciously, she glares at me. The white tower of her hair, still ramped and turreted like the Tower of Babel, trembles down its proud spiral with the passion of her defense. "Just because he didn't sleep with Sarah and break her *heart!* Well, Nanette was crazy about him and they had *quite* an affair together later on, I can tell you. Also, there were *several* other girls before he moved away, and then that married woman he lived with later . . . Oh, I was his confidante all right, and I used to say to him, 'Settle *down*, Joshua! Settle on *one* of them before it's too late!' And you see? I was right."

I am thunderstruck and some of it must show, for Jason roars with laughter and claps me a brother's clap on the shoulder. "Did you think he was going to carry the torch forever?"

"Carry the torch for whom?"

We are all confused and stare at one another and then off in several directions toward the somber black pines and the passive, sky-colored lake.

So that I no longer have even that leg to stand on.

Later that night I paced beside the lake, upon the round smooth pebbles the glaciers had broken and caressed down from rocks and left behind in their vast, magnificent passage, and I tried to understand and thaw that secret, hard core of my anger.

Absurd! I tossed into the charcoal dust of night, settling, like an invisible, infinitely soft fall of black snow, on the invisible, tender surface of the summer lake.

Absurd, but why not? I argue now, sitting stiffly upright in the icy sharp cold, arguing with Joshua who smiles into my eyes, as always, with an air of infinite relinquishment.

I observe him this time in earnest annoyance. My determination. My passionate nature. I am so used to getting my way because I know what I want. If he hadn't been so evasive I could have helped him do really good work again, as he did in our basement. Perhaps that's only conceit, but my mother and father seem to help each other work somehow; they still spar over sex, but as Mother said, "that is only part of it." I wouldn't really have been afraid to bear Joshua's children; I think all together we could have thrown up that magic ring of fire to protect our immortality.

I had a kind of share of immortality once. As always, my soul unwithers when I remember it. So did Joshua. Within that fiery iron ring of Family—internecine passions, false pride, bitter resentments, pointless loyalties—in that magic area we were for a while doomed to live, not to die. If we had held tightly together, I think that no one, not even Vasiliki, could have hurt him.

But I suppose it's always the oldest child who breaks the ring first. One has to get out, go beyond, become a free agent. And it's probably woman's greatest single delusion that she can save a man from his destiny.

I am not crying now in Tyrol for Aggie, but for death, the stillborn life—that monstrous foreclosure of the mortgage after nine months of hard work and promises—the cancer at the bottom of the box, my own death at twelve years of age, my murder of Joshua. After all, he could never have loved me if he had known about the Prince Castle, could he? (But I dare say, wistful ghost, you could have performed even that miracle.)

There was only one thing he couldn't do. He couldn't raise himself from the dead. The absolute, imponderable quality of extinction surrounded him all in a breath, and he just wasn't able to ignore that awful Presence. I believe that every time he lifted his hand to paste some bauble in a new box, he felt it moving slowly through the ether of final outer space, and he simply didn't have the energy to push his way through it all alone. None of us do.

But I had so much energy, and I could have helped him. Had I been older, less selfish; had I understood; had I not been me.

WILLIAM SAROYAN, the well-known story writer and play-wright, was born in 1908 in Fresno, California. His career began in 1934 with the publication of *Daring Young Man on the Flying Trapeze*, the title-story of his first volume, published the same year. He became known as a playwright in 1939 with *My Heart's in the Highlands*. Among his best-known works are *The Time of Your Life*, *The Human Comedy*, *My Name Is Aram*, and *Peace, It's Wonderful*.

Gaston

They were to eat peaches, as planned, after her nap, and now she sat across from the man who would have been a total stranger except that he was in fact her father. They had been together again (although she couldn't quite remember when they had been together before) for almost a hundred years now, or was it only since day before yesterday? Anyhow, they were together again, and he was kind of funny. First, he had the biggest mustache she had ever seen on anybody, although to her it was not a mustache at all; it was a lot of red and brown hair under his nose and around the ends of his mouth. Second, he wore a blue-and-white striped jersey instead of a shirt and tie, and no coat. His arms were covered with the same hair, only it was a little lighter and thinner. He wore blue slacks, but no shoes and socks. He was barefoot, and so was she, of course.

He was at home. She was with him in his home in Paris, if you could call it a home. He was very old, especially for a young man— thirty-six, he had told her; and she was six, just up from sleep on a very hot afternoon in August.

That morning, on a little walk in the neighborhood, she had seen peaches in a box outside a small store and she had stopped to look at them, so he had bought a kilo.

Now, the peaches were on a large plate on the card table at which they sat.

There were seven of them, but one of them was flawed. It *looked* as good as the others, almost the size of a tennis ball, nice red fading to light green, but where the stem had been there was now a break that went straight down into the heart of the seed.

He placed the biggest and best-looking peach on the small plate in front of the girl, and then took the flawed peach and began to remove the skin. When he had half the skin off the peach he ate that side, neither of them talking, both of them just being there, and not being excited or anything—no plans, that is.

The man held the half-eaten peach in his fingers and looked down into the cavity, into the open seed. The girl looked, too.

While they were looking, two feelers poked out from the cavity. They were attached to a kind of brown knob-head, which followed the feelers, and then two large legs took a strong grip on the edge of the cavity and hoisted some of the rest of whatever it was out of the seed, and stopped there a moment, as if to look around.

The man studied the seed dweller, and so, of course, did the girl.

The creature paused only a fraction of a second, and then continued to come out of the seed, to walk down the eaten side of the peach to wherever it was going.

The girl had never seen anything like it—a whole big thing made out of brown color, a knob-head, feelers, and a great many legs. It was very active, too. Almost businesslike, you might say. The man placed the peach back on the plate. The creature moved off the peach onto the surface of the white plate. There it came to a thoughtful stop.

"Who is it?" the girl said.

"Gaston."

"Where does he live?"

"Well, he *used* to live in this peach seed, but now that the peach has been harvested and sold, and I have eaten half of it, it looks as if he's out of house and home."

"Aren't you going to squash him?"

"No, of course not, why should I?"

"He's a bug. He's *ugh*."

"Not at all. He's Gaston the grand boulevardier."

"Everybody hollers when a bug comes out of an apple, but you don't holler or *anything*."

"Of course not. How would *we* like it if somebody hollered every time we came out of our house?"

"Why *would* they?"

"Precisely. So why should we holler at Gaston?"

"He's not the same as us."

"Well, not exactly, but he's the same as a lot of other occupants of peach seeds. Now, the poor fellow hasn't got a home, and there he is with all that pure design and handsome form, and nowhere to go."

"Handsome?"

"Gaston is just about the handsomest of his kind I've ever seen."

"What's he saying?"

"Well, he's a little confused. Now, inside that house of his he had everything in order. Bed here, porch there, and so forth."

"Show me."

The man picked up the peach, leaving Gaston entirely alone on the white plate. He removed the peeling and ate the rest of the peach.

"Nobody else I know would do that," the girl said. "They'd throw it away."

"I can't imagine why. It's a perfectly good peach."

He opened the seed and placed the two sides not far from Gaston. The girl studied the open halves.

"Is *that* where he lives?"

"It's where he used to live. Gaston is out in the world and on his own now. You can see for yourself how comfortable he was in there. He had everything."

"Now what has he got?"

"Not very much, I'm afraid."

"What's he going to do?"

"What are *we* going to do?"

"Well, we're not going to squash him, that's one thing we're *not* going to do," the girl said.

"What *are* we going to do, then?"

"Put him back?"

"Oh, *that* house is finished."

"Well, he can't live in our house, can he?"

"Not happily."

"Can he live in our house *at all?*"

"Well, he could *try,* I suppose. Don't you want to eat a peach?"

"Only if it's a peach with somebody in the seed."

"Well, see if you can find a peach that has an opening at the top, because if you can, that'll be a peach in which you're likeliest to find somebody."

The girl examined each of the peaches on the big plate.

"They're all shut," she said.

"Well, eat one, then."

"No. I want the same kind that you ate, with somebody in the seed."

"Well, to tell you the truth, the peach I ate would be considered a bad peach, so of course stores don't like to sell them. I was sold that one by mistake, most likely. And so now Gaston is without a home, and we've got six perfect peaches to eat."

"I don't want a perfect peach. I want a peach with people."

"Well, I'll go out and see if I can find one."

"Where will I go?"

"You'll go with me, unless you'd rather stay. I'll only be five minutes."

"If the phone rings, what shall I say?"

"I don't think it'll ring, but if it does, say hello and see who it is."

"If it's my mother, what shall I say?"

"Tell her I've gone to get you a bad peach, and anything else you want to tell her."

"If she wants me to go back, what shall I say?"

"Say yes if you want to go back."

"Do you want me to?"

"Of course not, but the important thing is what you want, not what I want."

"Why is *that* the important thing?"

"Because I want you to be where you want to be."

"I want to be here."

"I'll be right back."

He put on socks and shoes, and a jacket, and went out. She watched Gaston trying to find out what to do next. Gaston wan-

dered around the plate, but everything seemed wrong and he
didn't know what to do or where to go.

The telephone rang and her mother said she was sending the
chauffeur to pick her up because there was a little party for somebody's daughter who was also six, and then tomorrow they would
fly back to New York.

"Let me speak to your father," she said.

"He's gone to get a peach."

"*One* peach?"

"One with people."

"You haven't been with your father two days and already you
sound like him."

"There *are* peaches with people in them. I know. I saw one of
them come out."

"A *bug?*"

"Not a bug. Gaston."

"*Who?*"

"Gaston the grand something."

"Somebody else gets a peach with a bug in it, and throws it
away, but not him. He makes up a lot of foolishness about it."

"It's not foolishness."

"All right, all right, don't get angry at me about a horrible peach
bug of some kind."

"Gaston is right here, just outside his broken house, and I'm not
angry at you."

"You'll have a lot of fun at the party."

"OK."

"We'll have fun flying back to New York, too."

"OK."

"Are you glad you saw your father?"

"Of course I am."

"Is he funny?"

"Yes."

"Is he crazy?"

"Yes. I mean, no. He just doesn't holler when he sees a bug
crawling out of a peach seed or anything. He just looks at it carefully. But it *is* just a bug, isn't it, *really?*"

"That's all it is."

"And we'll *have* to squash it?"

"That's right. I can't wait to see you, darling. These two days have been like two years to me. Good-bye."

The girl watched Gaston on the plate, and she actually didn't like him. He was all *ugh*, as he had been in the first place. He didn't have a home anymore and he was wandering around on the white plate and he was silly and wrong and ridiculous and useless and all sorts of other things. She cried a little, but only inside, because long ago she had decided she didn't like crying because if you ever started to cry it seemed as if there was so much to cry about you almost couldn't stop, and she didn't like that at all. The open halves of the peach seed were wrong, too. They were ugly or something. They weren't clean.

The man bought a kilo of peaches but found no flawed peaches among them, so he bought another kilo at another store, and this time his luck was better, and there were *two* that were flawed. He hurried back to his flat and let himself in.

His daughter was in her room, in her best dress.

"My mother phoned," she said, "and she's sending the chauffeur for me because there's another birthday party."

"Another?"

"I mean, there's *always* a lot of them in New York."

"Will the chauffeur bring you back?"

"No. We're flying back to New York tomorrow."

"Oh."

"I liked being in your house."

"I liked having you here."

"Why do you live here?"

"This is my home."

"It's nice, but it's a lot different from our home."

"Yes, I suppose it is."

"It's kind of like Gaston's house."

"Where *is* Gaston?"

"I squashed him."

"Really? Why?"

"Everybody squashes bugs and worms."

"Oh. Well. I found you a peach."

"I don't want a peach anymore."

"OK."

He got her dressed, and he was packing her stuff when the chauffeur arrived. He went down the three flights of stairs with his daughter and the chauffeur, and in the street he was about to hug the girl when he decided he had better not. They shook hands instead, as if they were strangers.

He watched the huge car drive off, and then he went around the corner where he took his coffee every morning, feeling a little, he thought, like Gaston on the white plate.

BEN MADDOW is the author of a novel, *Forty-four Gravel Street*, published in 1952 by Little, Brown. He lives in California, where, as a director and writer, his motion picture credits include *The Steps of Age* and *The Savage Eye*.

In a Cold Hotel

The winter before victory, a light snow was falling along the whole Atlantic Coast from Maine to Delaware Bay. A train decorated with flags drew into a black New Jersey station. It was Sunday noon, late January of 1918. Feathers of steam from the locomotive mingled with the snow in the air, the snow in the sky, the landscape of snow piled up on either side. People in black rubbers stood up and down on these miniature hills, laughing and stamping their big, numb feet.

A famous comic of the time, bare-headed and wearing an immense coat with a fur collar, appeared on the observatory platform. The iron rail on which he leaned was iced like a cake. He smiled and waved and brushed the snowflakes out of his long eyelashes. There was a delegation from City Hall, with tall hats, upon which the snow was already piled half an inch thick. There was also a seven piece band, playing patriotic tunes in a brass cacophony that could be heard up and down the narrow factory streets.

The comedian held up a sheaf of Liberty Bonds in his thickly gloved right hand. There were ironic cheers from a dozen or so uniformed soldiers in the station, smoking cigars and drinking Red Cross coffee. All at once, the band stopped playing, but slowly, as if the spring of the victrola had run down.

The Erie Railroad tracks divided the town, like God, into right and wrong. On one side were mills and fire-escapes; on the other, lawns and curtains. A window on the third floor of the Passaic Hotel, which was definitely in the wrong, opened violently, and a

Reprinted by permission from *The Hudson Review*, Vol. XV, No. 2, Summer 1962. Copyright © 1962 by Ben Maddow.

man in a night shirt leaned out into the speckled air. His voice was
extraordinarily deep, almost flamboyant.

"Damn you," shouted the man, "finish the tune, you blasted—"
he paused, mostly for the effect, "—sons of Huns!"

The crowd turned about on its pedestal of snow, and waved
and laughed. The famous comic condescended to laugh, too. The
man in the hotel window said to the brass band, "Play! Play! Finish the tune, so's I can get back to sleep!"

Far more in concert than they had ever been before, the players
turned the mouths of their cornets, their trombones, and the great
brass tuba, all up toward him together. They stared at him from
under their misshapen hats. "Papapah, papapah!" he said to them.
At once, one of the soldiers in the station threw away his cigar,
and walked across the hillocks of snow, and toward the Passaic
Hotel. He heard the window slam down.

The young soldier went up the steps of the hotel and into the
lobby. He circled it once, spitting experimentally into one of the
cuspidors, and touching the fronds of the palm trees, potted in
enormous, shabby tubs. At last he came around to the front desk.

The clerk said, "Well, soldier boy, what is it now?"

Soldier said, "Yes sir." Then he said, "I saw him at the window,
sir. He must be awake."

The clerk rang 301 again. There was no reply. "Mr. Watkins is
dead to the world."

The soldier nodded, made another turn around the lobby, this
time kicking the cuspidor with the huge leather toe of his shoe,
and plucking a bit of palm tree as he passed. He came to a stair-
case, made a right flank turn and went up about fifteen steps. He
went past the redolent toilet, and then through two narrow corri-
dors, each of them slightly warpèd, as if the hotel had been crushed
flat, and then unfolded once more. After taking several false directions,—for some of the halls branched unexpectedly, rose by
several steps, or by passages that resembled a ramp,—he came
suddenly and directly before the thickly painted door of 301. A
voracious noise came out of it, like the sucking and rasping of an
iron pump.

"Poor man," said the soldier. He pushed the door open and
went inside. There was no sign of a man, but on the bed was a sort

of cocoon of quilts, from which there evoluted this monstrous vibration, the snore of a megalomaniac worm.

Dark roller shades had been drawn over both windows. Within the room were four steamer trunks, set up on the smaller end, on which the words THE GREAT NORMO were stencilled in white paint. The soldier said, "Sir?" Getting no civilized reply, he went and banged each green shade with his fist; they flew up like frightened birds, and winter sky light glared through filigreed panes into the room.

The cocoon slowly unrolled, and the man in the night shirt staggered out of bed, and had already pulled one of the shades down again, before he saw the intruder.

The soldier said, "Yessirree!"

The Great Normo replied, "Yessirree, what? I haven't said anything yet." He had a strange flat nose, with cavernous nostrils, hair in the ears, broad bones in his cheeks, darkly outlined and fascinating eyes, a real show business face. He said, "Great God in the morning, it's cold!" and flung the quilts around his shoulders like a cape. "Were you raised in a stable?" he asked the soldier.

The soldier appeared to be hypnotized by a black opera hat on top of one of the trunks. He advanced toward it, put the tips of his fingers to the fine silk. He said, addressing the hat, "I was raised in a two story shingle house in Davenport—"

"Whuzzat? Whuzzat?" cried the Great Normo, "Davenport—where?"

The soldier lifted the rim of the opera hat. A white pigeon, on the other side of the room, shook open the brown paper bag in which it was imprisoned, and flew to the top of the window, where it emptied itself in utter fright.

The soldier said, "Davenport, Iowa."

"What kind of a house?" said the Great Normo.

"It had a porch, front and back, sir."

"Fascinating," said the Great Normo. "Did it have any doors?"

"Oh, yes, sir! It had thirteen of them."

"What?"

"Doors, sir."

"Appalling," said the Great Normo. "Now go and shut it."

"The door, sir?"

"The door, sir."

The soldier went across the room and closed the door very carefully.

"Now," said the Great Normo, finding himself not the butt, but the mere crumb of a cigarette left in a saucer, "open it again, and get out."

The soldier would not obey. Instead, he sat down on a chair, from which at the last possible moment, he retrieved a plate which contained the skeleton of three lamb chops and some execrable home-fried potatoes. He said to the Great Normo, "Sir, you don't mind my saying so, you look terribly tired."

"What the devil!" cried the magician. "You woke me up before breakfast."

The soldier answered, "You're kind of a liar, sir. I saw you at the window, bawling out the brass band."

The Great Normo, attired in his goose-feather toga, walked around the boy, examining him from various angles. He said quietly now, and rather kindly, "In the first place, you're in the wrong room."

"No, sir," said the soldier.

"And secondly, I'm the wrong sex."

"Yes, sir," said the soldier.

"You have wonderful manners," said the Great Normo.

The soldier said, "You weren't around to teach me any worse."

"Hey? Hey?" said the Great Normo, astonished again.

"I've been told, by people who ought to know," said the soldier, "that you're my papa."

The Great Normo retreated several paces and struck his hand theatrically to his forehead.

The soldier said, once more, "Yes, sir." And then again, "Yes-sirree."

The magician had retreated backward until he reached his bed. Holding on to the brass fittings with one hand, he fished behind him with the other, and retrieved a pint of liquor secreted under the pillow. He poured himself a neat slug, gasped, groaned, belched, sucked his teeth, shuffled his feet, wiped his lips, cracked all ten knuckles of both hands, and once again scraped and shuffled the calluses of his bare feet on the bare hotel floor.

The soldier, meanwhile, had found a glass tumbler among the refuse on the dresser. He said, "This glass sanitary?"

"I haven't used it yet," said his father, "if that's what you mean."

Curiously, the boy seemed very much at ease; he was not without emotion, but it was as if he had rehearsed this emotion many times before; and had finally mastered it. He went and took the bottle out of his father's fingers and poured himself half a glass. He examined the daylight through the lens of this amber and noxious fluid. He asked, "What is it?"

"Applejack," said his father. He watched the boy fill the glass, then, to the very brim. "Applejack," he continued, "—diluted with aromatic spirits of country skunk."

The soldier drank it all at once, the bony box in his throat bobbling up and down. He looked at the empty glass and said nothing.

"Have a little more," his father said, "to kill the germs."

The soldier took another half glass, rolled it round and round in his mouth, swallowed it at last without any particular comment.

"Feeling sick?"

"No, sir."

"Not even a faint touch of mental paralysis?"

"No, sir."

The older man went and lifted the boy's face with one hand, examining it carefully, as though it were a piece of china. The boy suffered it. He had pale blue eyes and a sunburned skin. The Great Normo said, "Well, why not?" He went to the window, opened it, took a taste of snow, shut it again. "Why not? Why not? There are parts of the U.S., especially east of the Rockies, where I couldn't spit a loose tooth from a local train—without hitting one of my romantic moments."

"I'm not a romantic moment, sir."

"I doubt if you'd remember, son."

"Mama showed me the license."

The magician said, "Well, now. I've been married three times. Once in Norway. That was annulled—I was under age. And they didn't think I was capable, which was a God damn lie. And then the second time in Boston. On that occasion, I was dead drunk, beside all of which, the little woman was re-married twice herself, and is now living in sin with a Chief of Police and five naturally dull-witted daughters. And of course, there's the third and last—" he said, grinding his teeth audibly and dramatically.

"Maggie Roberts is my Mama's name," said the soldier.

"Maggie Roberts, Maggie, Maggie, damn her hide."

"Don't abuse her, Papa, if you got to mention her at all."

The Great Normo said, "I suppose you want me to go down on my prayer bones and beg to be forgiven? Well, I tell you, son, it's the other way around!" And then he added, rather softly, "How old are you, boy?"

"Nineteen. I was born on the 29th of February. So I figure I'm only five years old by birthdays. I was born on a Tuesday midnight. They said I had an exceptional head of hair."

"My congratulations."

"Don't you believe in the stars, Papa?"

"Do I have any choice?"

"It stands to reason, Papa! We're weak individuals, and the stars, every one of them, big as the sun and the moon put together. So they've got to have some influence upon us, don't they? Don't you believe that?"

His father said, "When you get my age boy, you believe nothing but the whistle of the midnight train."

"Papa, I've got to straighten you out about a lot of things."

"What the devil is your name?" asked the Great Normo irritably.

"Same as yours, Gerald Thomas Watkins."

"That Maggie Roberts had a lot of nerve," said the magician. Then he came and touched the soldier's sleeve. "What rank are you, soldier boy?"

"PFC—private first class. Only there ain't anything particularly *first class* about it, and there certainly ain't anything *private*."

"Good with the bayonet, are you boy?" said the Great Normo. He seemed a little out of breath.

"No, sir."

"Crack shot?"

"Instructor told me, he said, point that gun around at yourself for God's sakes, not at me. He was very gangoofled."

"Eh?"

"Gangoofled, it's a word I made up, which I find very useful in the Army."

"What the devil does it mean?"

"Gangoofled. Like a bird with the feathers rubbed the wrong way."

"You've got a lot of imagination. You ought to get rid of it," said his father.

The soldier said, very cheerfully, "Papa, did you see the slogan they got on the walls down at the station? *'Eat all you can, and what you can't, you can!'*"

"Miserable bureaucratic pun," muttered the Great Normo.

The pigeon came down from the window shade and sat on his shoulder. He let it twinge at his hair. The boy kept watching him, and he, in turn, the boy; each of them sidelong and surreptitious. Finally the magician said, "Son, you expect to kill the Kaiser in those puttees?"

The soldier plucked at the wrappings of his legs. One of them had come loose, and he had to stoop to rewind it. He said, "I don't expect to kill anybody whatsoever."

"Ha ha! Where's your patriotism, boy?"

"I've been worried about that, sir."

"Scared are you? I thought you had faith in your stars."

"I do!" said the soldier. "I do, sir! But it ain't the bullet with my name on it, which I'm scared of, Papa. It's the one that says, *To Whom it may concern.*"

"You got your mother's mind. What else of hers have you got?"

"I can cross my eyes at will," said the soldier. He showed his father what he meant.

The Great Normo shook his head with dramatic sadness. His cheek twitching, he sat down again on the bed, and let the quilt fall behind him. Slowly, he decided to dress, talking almost to himself all the time. "I tried to see you a thousand times," he said. "Every time my circuit passed through Davenport, I tried to track you people down. You were never there, nor that dratted woman, either."

The soldier said, "Well, sir, Mama would hear you were in town, she'd see the posters and all, and she'd take and hide me and Sister Dear—"

"Which?" His face twisted curiously around the word.

"Caroline is her name, but Mama called her Sister Dear."

"Sister Dear," said the magician. "Ah, sister dear."

"Well, sir, she'd hide the two of us, until you left."

"Where?"

"Gold Star Moving Picture Palace," said the boy.

The Great Normo uttered a foghorn pronunciamento of contempt. He pulled on his trousers, which he drew inch by inch from under the mattress, and let the braces hang down until he could find his shirt.

The soldier said, "Don't you like motion pictures, Papa?"

The Great Normo replied, biting off the words with some precision. "I have never, never, drunk or sober, set foot in a place where they debase humanity by flattening actors into two dimensions."

The soldier cried, "Oh, you're wrong, Papa. You'd love it. When I was a little bitty kid, I'd sit right close to the piano. Suspense? Why, me and Caroline,—"

"Who?" said the magician.

"Sister Caroline, like I told you."

"Ah."

"And then we couldn't hardly bear to wait until next week! Episode Nine! Don't fail to see it! Because some of these old foreigners have suspended him—"

"Him, who?"

"Why, Harry Houdini. They have got him where he is hung up by his ankles in this bicycle factory,—"

"What in kingdom come, is he doing in a bicycle factory?"

"Run by foreign spies, Papa!"

"Ha, the dogs! Spies, hey?"

"And Harry Houdini is suspended by the ankles! Over a vat of boiling acid!"

"They should drop him," said the Great Normo.

"How horrible, Papa!"

"Not at all. Harry Houdini is not a Dutchman, I believe; but he's a God-damned traitor all the same."

"Then why should they try to kill him?"

"Who?"

"The foreigners! With the black mustachios!"

"What are you yelling about, son?"

"The episode, the episode, Papa!"

"Harry Houdini has sold out his profession for a mere $1000 per picture."

"A thousand dollar bill buys a lot of pickles, Papa."

"Are you fond of pickles?"

"Crazy about them."

"I'm not. They give me flatulent eructations."

"What in the heck is that, Papa?"

"Gas."

"Well, I never felt no gas."

"So much for heredity."

"Mama said I was born under Mars and Jupiter, and that's why I favor these little sour mash pickles."

"Mars and Jupiter! You were born in a Yakima, Washington, apple-box."

"I know. But—" he said sadly, "Mama would never tell me the details."

The Great Normo was squeezing his broad, small feet into long, narrow oxblood shoes. "More to the point—" he said, "did she ever tell you about me?"

The boy said, "Many a time, sir."

"Well?"

"Well, she kind of admired you."

"Did she indeed?"

"Yes sir. She called you a handsome, generous, nice-mannered," he held back the rest, rather theatrically—"pig."

"What?"

"She said you were a pig, Papa."

The Great Normo stamped his feet into his shoes. "If I was a pig, she was a butcher," he said.

The boy came and helped his father put the mother-of-pearl stud into the back of his collar, where it was thick and glossy with starch. The soldier said, as flatly as he could, "She's died, Papa."

"Died?" said the Great Normo at last. He put both hands out and touched his son, then retreated and sat down into an arm chair, stunned and sad, crushing a package of round collars which he now drew out from under him, one by one. He asked the soldier for a cigarette, and sat smoking it greedily, inhaling as if it were food. "Died," he said.

"Yes, Papa."

"Finished."

"Yes, Papa. Last year. In the month of July."

The Great Normo went to find his tie. He fumbled everywhere, but found nothing. With his fist closed around this emptiness, he walked about and pounded against the four walls of the room. His son found a tie for him under a hat. "Died? Finished? Before me?" said the magician. "I never thought that would happen. Died? No! She wasn't that old, son. She had natural hair, the color of roses. Extraordinary effect!—Finished? Kaput? It ain't possible." He sat down, got up again at once. "How did it happen?"

The soldier said, "She died going up the stairs in the old house."

"No, don't tell me," said the Great Normo. "All death is nasty." Then he added bitterly and violently, "What kind of coffin would you prefer for the dear departed? We have the deluxe for thirty-seven dollars cash."

"It was heart trouble," said the soldier.

"How can you lock up a lifetime,"—he glared wildly about him, as if to an audience,—"into a box with silver-plated handles? How is it possible?" He stopped moving; he panted as if he had been running.

The soldier went on, "It was a consequence of double pneumonia, Papa."

The Great Normo leaned on a trunk. Tears began to roll down from the corners of his eyes. The soldier scuffled about the room.

"I lost my partner!" cried the Great Normo.

"She hadn't seen you in nineteen years, Papa," said the soldier.

"She was with me—mentally."

A long while passed. The soldier found a woman's slipper on the floor, and dusted it off. It had a pink pompom over the instep. He blew at it as if it were a dandelion.

The soldier said, "Pneumonia is a killing disease. And it was a particular hard winter. Even for Iowa. You remember the back stairs in the old house?"

"I was never there, son," the Great Normo answered. "I was the dirty part of her life."

"Well, Papa, I'll say this. You're nowhere as bad as she made out."

"Think so, boy?"

"You do people good, Papa."

"I try not to."

"You perform with magic—"

"There is no such thing, boy."

"Why, now, look here! You take a silk hat, don't you, Papa?

And abbakadabba, a bunny, a bird and a glass of cold champagne."

"Cheapest trick in the world."

"You bring fun and pleasure to thousands, Papa."

"So does a whore."

The soldier said, "I have read my Bible and I don't cast no stones, Papa."

"May God bless you," said the magician.

He turned then, and made as if to embrace his son; his silk-striped shirt scraped against the khaki uniform and the brass buttons. Both men were terribly awkward in this embrace. The Great Normo said, "Would you like to see a piece of my act, son?"

The soldier said, "I'd be proud, Papa."

The Great Normo turned to the wall opposite to the windows, and yelled as loud as he could, "Girlie! Girlie!" The soldier thought his father had gone mad; in a moment the magician took hold of one of the upright trunks and shouldered it up out of the way. There was a door behind it. The Great Normo shouted through this panel, "You come in now, girlie! I got a soldier in here," and turned and grinned at his son.

The door, through which several nails had been driven, on one of which hung a tinted photograph of General Pershing, was pushed open about two inches. A girl's voice said, "Go away. You're nothing but a dirty old man."

At this insult, the Great Normo seemed to regain all his gaiety. "I resent one of those adjectives," he said. "I don't know which."

The girl's voice said, "I hate you, Mr. Smarty-Wisenheimer, from the bottom of my heart."

The soldier took up the slipper again and handed it through the crack in the door.

"That's only one of them," said the girl. "Where's the other?"

The Great Normo cackled with laughter.

The door moved open another six inches and the girl moved slowly and sullenly into the room. She had a long black skirt and a white blouse with lace at the wrists; her face was an odd mixture of sensitivity and stupidity. She inspected the soldier from head to shoes, and then slowly back again. It made him feel extremely warm.

"Who is this? Don't tell me. Just go away. I already bought my Liberty Bond."

"My name's Gerald Watkins, the same as my Papa."

The girl swung her slow eyes over to the Great Normo, who was tightening his tie to within a hair of strangulation.

The Great Normo said, "That's right, girlie, he's my son, by george and by jimminy."

The soldier said, "Are you his daughter, ma'am?"

The girl said in a loud voice, "Ha, ha, ha, ha, ha!"

"This piece of luscious femininity," said the magician, "is poisoning my life."

The girl said, "You're not just whistling Dixie."

The Great Normo pulled the trunk down on its side. He opened the lid, and spanked the lining to remove some of the dust. Inside was a pink pillow and a tufted pink lining. The Great Normo said, "Would you mind? I'd like to show my boy how it's done."

The girl said, "Some joke. Really. He's big enough, but is he old enough?"

The soldier said, "I've got to be, ma'am." He smiled with instinctive charm. "I'm going to Paris, France, as soon as I finish my training."

The girl was intrigued with this reply. She shuffled her stockinged feet over to where he was standing and stood on her tiptoes and looked into his eyes. "There's a Paris, Pennsylvania. Did you know that?"

"Why, no. Is that a fact?"

She went on, "And a Paris, Michigan. Also a Paris, Wyoming."

"Ain't that something?" said the soldier.

The Great Normo thought things were going too far. He said, "Will you get into the trunk, or do I got to beat you up again?"

The girl said, putting up her little finger to rub the soldier's shave the wrong way, "I can't. Not without my costume."

"Well, come on, get into your costume," said the Great Normo.

"My costume is downstairs getting washed, starched, dried, dampened again, and ironed. And even then, I doubt if it'll ever get itself clean."

"What the devil, fuss, fuss," said the Great Normo.

The girl said, pointing to the Great Normo with the same little pinky, "He don't even remember."

"Remember what, ma'am?" said the soldier.

"Spilled ketchup all over it last night."

"I call that criminal," said the soldier.

"I love you dearly," said the girl. "I truly do. I wish there was one million of you wherever I may be."

"There is," the soldier said, "that's the heck of it."

"Heck, heck! What is that word? Can't you say hell?"

"No ma'am. I took the pledge."

The girl gave him a dazzling smile of pure adoration. The Great Normo said, "She'll corrupt you, son." The girl hissed at him. He went on, "I found her in the five-and-dime. She was selling stove polish. Bored? She was yawning so profoundly, all you could see of her face was her little pink tonsils."

For some reason, this description annoyed the girl. She moved back and kicked him as hard as she could, forgetting she had no shoes on. The girl said, "I can go straight back to Forty-Second Street in New York City and get into the toe shoe ballet, which was just about dying to have me."

"Ballet! Ballet!" roared the magician, "On those feet?"

"Yes! Yes! Yes! Yes!" The girl was shouting back at him. "They adored my feet! The manager told me so! He did! Mr. Ebenstein did! He did, he did, did, did!"

The Great Normo said, "And what else did that greasy little manager admire?"

The girl began to cry; she sank down and twisted herself over the nearest trunk.

The soldier said, "Oh, gosh, don't cry, please don't cry!" At the same time he noticed with some astonishment that she was inclined to be plump.

The Great Normo drummed on his own skull, upset in spite of himself. "She's not crying, she's doing a scene," he muttered. "She's an actress, not a woman. She's practicing in real life, what she might be called upon to perform on stage. And she's overdoing it."

The soldier said, "Now, Papa, don't be mean." And he said to the girl, "Are you really an actress?"

The girl stopped snuffling, bent down, straightened out, and without any further announcement, walked on her hands. Her head, with mouth reversed, began to sing "*K-K-K-Katy, Beautiful Katy.*"

The soldier applauded. Her legs, thick, smooth and white, danced upside down all around him.

"If only she could do that in bed," said the Great Normo, with a certain melancholy.

The soldier turned his own head upside down, so as to speak to the girl more comfortably. "Is this gentleman an acquaintance of yours?"

"He'd like to be," said the girl, her eyelashes flickering, upside down. "Oh, he'd like to be! He's just spoiling out of his mind to be my friend."

"Ain't he a little bit old?"

"No, he's not. Which is unfortunate," said the Great Normo.

At this interruption the girl leaped back into a spiral arch; the arch straightened itself and delivered the magician a stunning slap. Pained, astonished, and over-balanced, he fell back among the trunks. At once the girl became meek and agreeable; opened the cover of the trunk, and squeezed herself inside, curling to fit inside the pink satin padding.

"Close it, soldier boy."

The soldier came and put the lid down carefully upon her. Immediately her feet popped out of an orifice at the bottom of the trunk, fully clad in the net stockings known in the trade as "kinky." At the other end, her head reappeared through a second aperture. She smiled sweetly at the soldier. The Great Normo rose up out of his corner. He had a carpenter's saw in his two hands, which he bent back and forth to show the savage flexibility of the steel.

He said to his son, "Watch, now. I'm going to saw that bitch in half, thus making two bitches where there was purely one before."

He knelt down upon one knee and began to saw through the lid of the trunk. The noise was horrible.

The soldier said, "Papa, I don't think I care to—"

"Of course you don't!" cried the magician, sawing madly away. "That's the whole point! It's repulsive!" He paused and blew away the not quite imaginary sawdust. "Sickening! And universal! And intellectual!"—(sawing away again)—"Eclectic! Vibrations of the psyche! Animal magnetism!" And then, with theatrical horror, "It brings out the insane doctor in all of us."

He had sawed almost half way down the trunk.

The soldier said in a sickly voice, "It's beautiful, Papa, just a beautiful trick."

"He wishes it wasn't," said the girl.

"Don't it tickle at all?" asked the soldier, anxiously.

"I got her hypnotized to where she feels no pain," said the magician. "The only one time it genuinely hurts, is when it cuts through the spine."

The girl uttered a horrific, unearthly scream.

"Please, please don't improvise," said the Great Normo. He was half an inch from the floor. A few strokes of the saw, and he scraped bottom.

"There, see that," he told his son. "Women are particularly fond of this trick. In fact, that's how I met your mother."

The soldier was staring at the two halves of the trunk, now separated by a quarter inch of air. "May I have a cigarette?" said the upper half of the girl.

"Do you smoke, too?" he said, utterly astonished at this lack of virtue. But he got her a cigarette, put it between her lips, lit it for her with a kitchen match, of which he had several dozen in the upper left hand pocket of his uniform.

The Great Normo had gone to the window, breathing upon it to create a fine mist. "Middle of January," he said with tragic intonation, "and still no goddam heat in these places." He went and kicked at the radiator. It was invisible behind one of the trunks. "Wake up, janitor! Wake up, this is the twentieth century!" he cried to the mythological person in the masonry far below.

Then, exhausted by emotion, he sat on the lower half of the girl in the trunk. He said "Son, soldier boy, you know if the Proctor Theatre in Davenport is still there?"

"No, sir."

The Great Normo struck his palm to the region of his heart, "What happened?"

"It's a warehouse, Papa. For the Red Cross!"

"My God, couldn't they find any other place to roll their God damned bandages? The Proctor Theatre! It had solid gold-plated cupids on the balconies. And acoustics? If you scratched your head on stage, it could be heard way up in Nigger Heaven."

"Mama told me all about it," his son said.

"How I asked for volunteers in the audience?"

"Yes, sir."

"And she stepped forward, a fine big woman, peace to her soul?"

He backed away into the room, and was reenacting the scene with mock sincerity. "How I sawed her in half? And took the two halves out to dinner—to Spanner's Chinese Restaurant?"

"Papa, I really don't—"

The Great Normo said fiercely, "How she borrowed my Waterman pen,—never gave it back, by the way—and drew a little heart on the lampshade? And do you know what she wrote inside?"

"No, sir," said the soldier.

"Well, if she didn't tell you, I'm not, either. I don't want her leaning down out of heaven and calling me a cad."

"Heaven!" said the upper girl, snorting smoke like a dragon, "What makes you think she's in heaven?"

The Great Normo said, "She was determined upon it, kiddo. And what she was determined to do, she did. Me, for instance. I never asked her, but I woke up the next morning and found her sitting in a straight-back chair, watching over me. She'd gone and packed her six valises, and taken her daughter Caroline, who was all of a ripe sixteen, and these two ardent females then prepared to follow me all over these United God damned States.—Infatuation? No. It was idolatry."

"Then why did she leave you, Papa?"

The magician smiled, "The sin of pride?" he suggested.

"Hippity-hoppity, ha ha," said the girl in the trunk.

The soldier said to his father, "What about love? Didn't she love you anymore, Papa?"

The Great Normo answered him, rather slowly, "She left me a note, which she attached with stickum on to the mirror in my dressing room. It said, and I quote, *Happy hunting, buffalo!*— There was also a bunch of pink rosebuds. But those were from Caroline."

He unlocked the girl in the trunk. She uncoiled and lay upon the floor, stretching herself fore and aft, as if each vertebra had to be wiggled separately.

His son came and took hold of him. "Papa, papa! You loved her, didn't you, Papa? Did you love her, Papa? Or didn't you?"

"There's degrees and qualifications to love," said the magician.

"No, sir. There ain't," said the soldier passionately.

"He's young, oh he's so young, the boy is painful," said the girl. She got up off the floor and examined the bottom of her left foot.

"About the only thing I've learned so far," she said, "is that the world is full of splinters."

The soldier pointed to her. "Papa,—what about this little girl right here?"

He turned to the girl and said, "What do you say? Do you want me to lie?"

"Not for my sake, no."

"You must love somebody, Papa. It's not natural."

"I do, desperately." The Great Normo went and cleared a space in front of the mirror, which was part of a birdseye maplewood dresser; so he could see himself, unencumbered and unadorned. "And I will reveal to you the name of the person by whom I am so enslaved and so enchanted." He pointed to himself in the mirror, at a spot where his left eye was distorted by a defect in the glass. "Him! Him! I love that ignorant slob from the bottom of my heart! Got a lifelong attachment to the man! Perverse, if you want to go so far! And why not? If he dies, I die. What about that, eh? What about that, boy?" He picked up a comb, ran it through his hair, threw it down as if in anger and disgust. "Not to change the subject, but when my elderly mother," he said, "moved into New York City from the wilds of Jersey, she discovered they had inside toilets. Toilets *inside?* She was profoundly shocked." He went to the hall door, picking up a pink turkish towel as he departed.

The boy called after him, "Papa, you want me to stay, or you want me to go?"

"Suit yourself, son," cried the Great Normo, going down and away through the twisted hall.

The soldier sat looking at the girl. There were bright tears in his eyes.

"Stay for a while," she said.

He nodded his acquiescence.

She said, "You've got a pretty uniform."

He said, "Itches like all get out."

She laughed at him. He went and slammed the door shut with his foot.

"Why do you stay with him?" he asked the girl.

"It's a job."

"That's not what I mean."

"Last week he borrowed a beautiful ten dollar bill off of me," said the girl.

"And never paid it back."

"How did you know?" said the girl.

"I know, I just know."

"Well, then, he took and bought me a two dollar box of brandied chocolates. With my own money! And you know what? It brought tears to my eyes! The same as you! Sincerely!"

"He won't trick me," said the soldier.

"He will if he can."

"He won't! I'm tougher than he is! You'll see! I've got my Mama's character! I'm going to crack him open like a cockroach! And when I'm done, and the yellow's run out of him—I'm going to walk away, same as my Mama did!"

"He won't crack."

The door was shoved open, and the Great Normo flung the pink Turkish towel somewhere away from him. "No need to lock the door, was there?" he said.

"If it was locked, Papa, how would you get in?" he answered in sudden fury.

The Great Normo turned around to the girl and scratched his face slowly; at last he said, "Go get me some hot coffee. With a cup around it."

The girl didn't move. Still angry, the soldier said, "Go on! Do what he says!"

"I don't have the money."

"Money, money. People are mad about money," said the magician mildly.

The soldier found a half dollar in his pocket, tossed it in the air, caught it back-hand, and gave it to the girl. As she took it, she softly closed her hand on his before she left.

"He won't, you'll see," she said to the soldier, and closed the door. The soldier remained standing where he was.

"Won't what?" said the Great Normo. "Never mind, unimportant," he added at once. "Son, son, son!—Will you go into business with me?"

"No," said the boy. "What for?"

The Great Normo pointed to one of the walls, on which there was a rusty stain from the sink upstairs. "Look there: imagine: a darkness full of people. I can't see them, but I can feel them. Like you can feel a cat or a woodchuck watching to see you move. There's no feeling like that in the world! None! None whatsoever! That feeling! That's what I live for! The rest is nothing!"

The soldier stared at the wall with its enigmatic stain. He sprang up, as his father had done, and addressed the circle of the imaginary theatre. "It's over!" he told them. "It's all there is! The act is over! Go on home! Go on. Get out! We want a little privacy! Him and me! Father and son!"

"They won't go," said his father, going along with this double play. "We've got 'em fascinated, boy! Hooked by the balls of their eyes—!"

The soldier still looked through the soiled and magical wall; then all at once he turned his back on the ghostly audience, in a sweat and a fury, and began to dismember the steamer trunks. He pulled them ajar, and jerked out the small wooden drawers of which they were composed, and from these he drew contraption after contraption: a trick deck, with the cards sewn together with fine silk; a glass pitcher full of solid wine; then the silk flags of all nations, that could be pulled out one by one from a thimble; and hats that were hats inside out as well; and a saber that collapsed into its impotent handle; then three colored balls, which fell rolling to the floor, and which the soldier retrieved and began to juggle amazingly into the air: red, violet, yellow-green.

The Great Normo said, "How the devil did you learn that?"

"Houdini," said the boy. "In the moving pictures. I watched it twenty-three times."

But the trick made him sweat; it was not the physical exertion, but the three-part splitting of his brain: one ball leaving his left hand, another reaching his right hand, the third rising and falling, in the winter of this cold hotel room, his breath coming and going in fine white puffs of mist. Then he had enough; tossed the red, the yellow-green and the violet into the empty silk hat on the farthest trunk; and turned and drew, link by link, a two-foot length of galvanized bicycle chain out of his pants pocket. He said to his father, "Harry Houdini is able to tear this apart in three minutes flat. Can you?" He tossed the iron to his father, who caught it strongly and gracefully, and then bit the chain as though it were a false coin.

"Welll! Pure steel. Expensive trick!" he said, contemptuously.

"It's not a trick, Papa!" said the soldier. "It's a demonstration of manly strength."

"Episode thirteen," said the magician, but he looped the chain around each hand. He said, "Watch closely, folks. I learned this demonstration of manly strength from my dear son Gerald, who learned it by pure osmosis from a Yiddish-Wop named Harry Houdini."

The magician then pulled the chain violently between his left and his right hand. Sweat began to run down into his collar. Under the moisture, the blue veins stood out thick and swollen under his powdered skin.

The soldier stood up as he watched. Slowly his anger was going, going; he wanted it back, but now it was gone. His father had bent double in the agony of his effort.

The soldier said, "Papa, quit."

The magician kneeled to the floor, straining, his face grown dark, almost monstrous; he sank down on his side, on the floor, grappling the chain as if it were alive and poisonous.

The soldier bent down, too. "Papa, Papa, please, you'll tear yourself into a heck of a rupture. Papa, Papa! Please,—please, Papa!"

The chain slipped out of the magician's left hand; knotted and cramped beyond endurance. All his visible skin looked as though he had doused it in water. The soldier seized the iron and threw it across the room until it rang against the audience wall. The soldier said, "Papa, I can't do it either."

The magician got to his knees, pulled himself to his feet near one of the trunks, and gasping, panting, opened the drawer and found a pair of very large blue steel scissors. "Want to join the act, do you, son?" He was ferocious.

"Why, no, Papa. I told you that."

"You told me, but you don't mean it!"

He grabbed the boy by the thick brass buttons of his jacket. "Come on! It'll only hurt for a day or two. Give me your trigger finger. I'll have you out of the Army in two seconds flat."

The soldier shoved him back as hard as he could. "Papa! Now you're acting cuckoo!"

The Great Normo said, brandishing the scissors, "I was never more sincere in all my life. I got one son, do I want him slaughtered? Do I give a hoot in hell for little Belgium? The Kaiser has got guns, boy, which if they're aimed in your approximate direction, can turn a man into a raspberry jelly!" The scissors slashed through the bloodless air.

"Pa, will you stop?"

"We're fragile, son," said the magician. "Do you realize the human skin is no more than one-thirty-secondth of an inch thick? I don't know how we survived all this long, to tell the God's gospel! And then—and then!—What?—They urge you to collect peach pits! Peach pits!—Why? So they can charcoal 'em black and put 'em into the canister of your gas mask." He inhaled, exhaled, twice, dramatically. "Fifty thousand years of slow civilization! *Per aspera ad astra!* Upward and onward! Excelsior! Charles Darwin! Mary Baker Eddy! And what's the crown and culmination of it all? Poison gas!"

He pretended, scissors gaping in his hands, to stagger about, to gasp, and choke like an alligator. "Ga-a-as! Ga-a-as!" he said hoarsely, "Ding-a-ling-a-ling! Sound the alarm!"

The soldier got hold of his sleeve and tried to pull away the brandishing blades.

"Don't do it, boy!" cried the magician. "Don't go to war! Stay with me! Join the act!—I'll show you the secrets of the visible world. Not the way—" pulling himself out of his son's grasp,— "you think it is! But," recoiling and recovering himself, "the way it really is!"

He plunged the two points of the scissors into his own shirt. They bent double; they were made of painted rubber. But his eyes glared, as though he had been genuinely stabbed. He said, "Lesson number one. As follows: there's nothing in the whole wide world that's sincerely genuine."

The soldier sat down resentfully. He felt obscurely taken and cheated. "I disagree with you, Papa!" he said at last.

"You won't quit the Army?"

"I can't!"

"Why not? Scared of Woodrow Wilson? I didn't vote for him, so you got no obligation."

"Don't be stupid, Papa!"

The boy wanted desperately to leave. Instead, he sat perfectly still. At last, neither of them spoke or looked at each other. The short afternoon was darkening; a low sky, and snowflakes heavy as crumbs from a crust.

The girl came back, carrying a steaming white cup, a cloth napkin, and a large round spoon. The Great Normo took them from her in silence. The girl looked at the soldier, and said, "You're still here, poor boy?"

"Oh, I'm going."

"Go on, then!" said the magician; and put the spoon in his pocket and the cup to his lips. "What are all these lumps?" he complained.

"Noodle soup," said the girl.

"What are you trying to do, nourish me?" He went to the window, shoved it open and threw out the cup and the napkin. Neither made a sound, falling or fallen. The snow was growing deep and soft outside, on the hills, the marshes, the Jersey canals with their iron bridges, and the long curving right-of-way of the railroad tracks.

The Great Normo shut the window hard and tight. "He's turned us down, girl. He won't come with us."

The soldier was unwrapping and wrapping the puttee on his right leg. "I want me an honorable discharge. And a pension to go 'long with it. I'm nobody's dern fool—"

"Nineteen years of age," interrupted the magician, "and already he's turned sensible." He no longer addressed his son. He talked to the window, the wall, even to the girl. "Gumption! His mother fed him—Iowa mush and mama's milk. Big bones, big head. Take a look at him, girl! The uniform is busting out with muscles! But not the gumption to go with them. Hup, tup, trip, fuh! You don't have a brass button that ain't shined up like a star in the sky."

The soldier swallowed the bitter taste in his mouth. He said, "Don't run down the stars, Papa, they're mighty important."

"The stars, ha!" cried the magician. "Ever swim in the Ohio River by night in the month of April?"

"Never had the time, sir."

"And flat on your back, and look up at the Milky Way?"

"I can't swim," said the soldier.

"Son, son, there's no hup, tup, trip, fuh—up there. It's all wildness, son. Wildness beyond belief! Those stars drink applejack together and make love in the sight of the One Eternal.—"

The girl said, very coldly, "Oh, shut up, heaven's sake. There's more to life than making love."

The Great Normo said, "That's true, and that's sad, girl!" He sat down on the bed. All at once he seemed completely exhausted. He hadn't shaved at all, and now he plucked at the grey bristles along his neck. The soldier was putting on his long overcoat at last. The girl helped him with the button holes.

"Papa," he said, "I got one hour left, Papa. The New York train leaves at three sharp."

The magician made some sort of affirmative growl. His son said, "Want to walk with me to the station, Papa?"

"Station?"

"Erie Railroad Station."

"Don't believe I will, son." He looked to the icy window. It was strange outside, and growing stranger still; all above was the darkness of winter afternoon, but glowing with the white inner fire of crystalline snow. And all the traffic went rolling silently by, iron rims on the wagons, iron shoes on the horses, and iron mudguards on the big, square automobiles. "Don't believe I will," he said, forgetting, like an old man, he had said it once before.

"Well, then," said the boy. He looked for his hat among the furniture and the confusion. The girl found it for him and put it affectionately on his head. He took it off at once; out of politeness, perhaps; and held it in his hand. "It was nice to talk to you, Papa. I'll just mosey along now."

"Son," said the magician.

"Yes, sir?"

"Care of yourself."

"You know me, Papa."

"And boy—?"

"Yes, sir, Papa."

The Great Normo said, without a trace of enthusiasm, "Catch the Kaiser for me, will you? Do that little thing. Bring him home in a chicken-wire cage."

"Not me, Papa," said the soldier. "You got the wrong boy." He went to the door. He was half-way out when he thought to turn and say, "Girlie," in a tone much like his father's, "Care to walk me along to the station?"

"Not right now," she said.

"I'm going to have a meal over to the station restaurant. I got my mind on flap-jacks."

"I have to rehearse, love-bird," said the girl sweetly.

"Go on, walk him to Paris, France," said the magician.

The girl shook her head. The boy tossed his hat in the air, caught it on his head, squinted out the window, and said at last, "Well, folks, see you in the funny papers."

"Katzenjammer Kids," said the girl.

"Happy Hooligan," he replied. He went out and down the cold and creaky hall.

His father got up then, found a bit of cracker in the ash-tray, ate it, and went back and sank into the bed. Some time passed. He pointed to the row of thumb-sized marks on the wall. "Just look here, would you? Chaps too lazy to get out of bed, have snuffed out their cigarettes on this wall.—Now, ain't that the saddest thing you ever saw? Ain't it, girlie?"

The girl had begun to put the room to rights. She took off the pillow case and stuffed the Great Normo's laundry into it. She moved about very swiftly and softly.

"Steal a couple of towels while you're about it," the magician said.

The girl said, almost in a whisper, "That was no way to say goodbye. It was awful. Awful."

"What did you want me to do, kiss him?" Fully clothed as he was, he shucked off his shoes and pulled the quilts around him.

The girl was at one of the windows, and with a corner of the laundry she wiped a circle on the glass so she could look down. She said, "He's coming down the steps of the hotel. Oooh! Oooh! He walks so straight. Honestly, he's so handsome."

"From that angle, anybody's handsome."

"Wave to him. He's looking up here."

The magician rolled over in bed to where his stubborn back was to the windows. Nevertheless, he was shivering.

"He got on my nerves," he said. "Had he stayed one minute longer, I'd have told him the truth. Maggie Roberts! She wasn't his mother at all."

The girl, guessing what he was about to say, put both hands over her mouth.

The magician said, "His sister Caroline, that was his Mama! Not Maggie—that old churchified sinner. I did it for revenge! And so did little Caroline, believe you me. She never told him, and Maggie never told him, and that's how it is. Should I have told him? No! It's the truth! But what's so sacred about the truth?"

The girl said, "Oh God, he'd just about die!"

"Ha, ha!" said the magician. He got up, draped in the quilt, and twisted the heavy trunks about, to have something equal to himself to struggle with, heavily and forcibly.

"When pretty Caroline began to get sick of a morning, Maggie Roberts brought in a man about six feet tall. Face like John L. Sullivan. I thought he'd come to assassinate me. Until he took off his scarf and I saw his collar reversed. She married me, Maggie Roberts, and took the midnight to Davenport. All three of them gone. Should I have told my son that? Should I, girlie?" he shouted at her.

She shook her head, her fingers still over her mouth, but woven together like a mesh. He looked through the frosted, fanciful window. Snow fell past his glance, like worlds going by. Quite suddenly, he shoved open the window as high as he could; he leaned into the snowstorm, and yelled, "Soldier! Soldier!" There was an indistinct answer, as if someone were shouting back from the shaft of a mine.

"Don't!" cried the girl. "Don't tell him! Don't ever tell him!" She clasped him round the waist.

"I'm too late, anyway. Good or bad. Poor boy,—he's turned the corner and gone," he said. And freeing himself from the girl, "You should have gone along with him."

"No!—No, no, no."

"Why not?" said the magician. "What's the big attraction here? Hey?"

"If you don't know why," answered the girl, "I can't tell you!"

"Look now, girlie," said the magician, his voice smoking in the cold, "No! Turn around and look at me!—You see? I lock the door every Thursday at twelve noon. Have you noticed that? Have you?" his voice became driving, harsh, and unnaturally precise. "I lock the door, and fill the sink, and dye my hair back to what it was

twenty years ago. Well, girl—some Thursday I won't do it. I'll let
you see my natural color. It'll make you just as sick as it makes me.
Which I hate to get old! I hate it!—All right. Why stick? What's
your reason?"

"It's personal," she said.

"Well, for sure, it isn't the money! I see to that, don't I?"

"I stay for sentimental reasons," she said.

"Well, don't! Don't. I've known a million so-called women, and
don't remember even a one. Nothing! Except, of course, they all
had something wrong with them!"

The girl leaned on a chair, looking away. His voice was so cruel
and loud; she thought, suddenly, how much she disliked his fits
of truth.

"—Wrong with them," he was saying. "Ears too big, or poor thin
hair. Big nose, little hips. Or unhappy with their miserable hus-
bands. Or choked up inside. Or busted loose. Wild nerves. Nerve
tonic by the quart bottle. Or some damn screw loose rattling
around in their heads. Oh, girlie, girl, I've lived a life of careless
love! By picking on cripples."

"What kind of a cripple am I?" said the girl, very quietly.

She came and put both hands on the corrupted knobby brass
of the magician's bed. "What kind of a cripple, will you tell me,
please? I'm not angry. Just tell me."

The Great Normo said, "You always think I'm talking about
you. I'm not. I'm talking about history."

"What kind of a cripple?" she screamed at him suddenly.

The Great Normo lifted her hands from the brass bed, and
kissed them in the innermost palms. She drew back as far as she
could, but not so far that he had to let go. "What kind of a cripple
do you believe I am?" she said softly.

"Peg O' My Heart, I Love You So," he said; he had a fine smile;
different from his professional one. He kissed her. "You've got an
ugly heart, that's why."

The girl said, "That's true."

Then he turned once more to the window, the girl leaning
against him, and cried out, "Soldier! Goodbye, soldier! Goodbye,
boy!" And after a moment, still in the huge tones that carried
easily to the railroad station, and made people turn around, to

stare upward in their snow-shaped clothes, "Kill the Kaiser, kill him, boy!"

He waited. Someone too far away to see, a soldier to judge by his stance, unlikely by now to have been his son, waved both arms and uttered a faint, far-off Indian whoop. The magician reared back and laughed. "Unreal, unreal," he said to himself. All at once, his misery was gone. He did a time-step, neatly, among the trunks.

"Girlie, girlie-girl," he told her, "we've got a great year coming up. Bookings clear up into April, which is in Ogden, Utah.—Tara-tarata-tum."

"I know."

He found his spotted scarf, and wrapped it clownishly around her neck. "Ever see an Injun, girlie?"

"No."

"There's real live buckaroos on the main stem of Ogden, Utah. Ugh! Ugh! How! How!"

The girl pulled off the scarf, but she found herself smiling. Snow blew in over the gritty, coal-sooty sill.

The Great Normo turned again, entranced by the window. At the far end of the station, the brass band strangled a tune that might once have been patriotic.

"Oh, Jesus, God, this is a wonderful country!" the magician said. "America! The U. S. of A.! Niagara Falls! Grand Canyon! The Coney Island Boardwalk! Sea breeze and steeplechase! Grand, just grand! Be there by August, girlie!—You smell the snow? It gets colder every year."

"Does it?" she said.

"When I was young, we used to have summers where we have winters and vice versa."

"Did you really?"

"We did, dear, really we did."

"But I mean, really?"

When he had no answer, she said, as if it was part of the same query, "And that was all a lie about the boy and his sister, wasn't it?"

"Whatever you say, dear," he told her.

"But was it?"

"Sure."

The train began to chug and strain into a switchback, turning itself around to go back to Jersey City, and to the lighters, the barges, and the ferries; the transports, the four-stack steamers, shouldering through chunks of Hudson River ice, toward the chances of the open ocean; and then to Paris, and the first of the impossible Wars. Was it his son's train? Most likely not.

"Girlie, girlie," he said. "Don't go marching off to fight."

"If you want me to stay, I'll stay."

"Let the Kaiser live to a ripe old age, girlie."

"I hear his left arm's all small and shrivelled up," she said.

"Stay with me," said the Great Normo, "you'll have good times. I mean it, woman."

"Can I shut the window?"

"No."

"Shall I get us some hot coffee?"

"Why not?" he said, "We only live once."

She went to the door, and came back and shook the Great Normo's coat; it jingled, and she fetched out a quarter from the left hand pocket.

"Bring change," he said to her.

She leaned against the open door. "If I thought I knew how to make you happy," she told him, "but I don't." He grinned at her. He began to do knee bends before the open window. She went on, "Oh, I love you. I love you very much. But why? Can you tell me one good reason why?"

"It's the stars, girlie. The stars!"

The exercise made him breathe deeply; the air had the sour-apple taste of falling snow.

The girl looked back at him fondly as she left. She would leave and abandon him long before Ogden; but the time was not yet.

SYLVIA BERKMAN grew up in a hamlet in eastern Massachusetts. She attended the local schools, received her A.B. degree from Pembroke College, Brown University, and her Ph.D. degree from Radcliffe College. She is currently a lecturer in English at Wellesley. She has written *Katherine Mansfield: A Critical Study*; *Blackberry Wilderness* (a collection of short stories); and several short stories that have appeared in various magazines. Miss Berkman was also a prize winner of the O. Henry Awards in 1960. She hopes to have a second collection of short stories soon.

Pontifex

The late afternoon sunlight fell pure and clear upon the cove, a rarefied still quintessence of light in which the pale yellow buildings on the opposite shore stood aloof, remote, meeting their own concentrated image in the level mirror below. On the wide porch running the eastern length of his house, overlooking the cove from a stubby hill, Octavius Benedict sat upright, a copy of Shakespeare's *Tempest* in his hand, watching the slow renewal of the tide as imperceptibly the waters swelled. The noisy speedboats with their frenzied buzz saw crescendo churning the cove in unnatural waves—*thrrrummmm brrrummmm brrrummmm*: how he hated the sound!—were gone now; the plague of locusts had departed for another year. But at least he had kept his bit of road, he thought with a faint dry smile. Let the big summer automobiles come blundering along the ruts; they were not so clever when the road dwindled out among scratchy juniper and pine, and they found nowhere to turn. The whole point, from the causeway linking it to the village to the irregular spear of marshland running into the sea, belonged to him. Pensive, he sat motionless: a big gaunt man clothed in a soft corduroy suit and white shirt open at the throat; the long head oval, with perfectly brushed silver hair; the eyes set deep within their caverned sockets gazing afar at a perspective beyond this actual horizon of sky and sea. When Mrs. Holcomb joined him, hitching her wooden rocker into place, he did not speak.

"Well, whatever's keeping her!" Mrs. Holcomb exclaimed. "Not an accident I hope. Scarcely a day you don't read of some terrible accident. It's the speed people drive at. Fast! Lickety-split, and rake the pieces up." She drew her handwork from its bag and began to push the steel crochet hook in and out. "Didn't you say she said at four? It's way after that now." Just at that moment the bells in the Methodist church steeple clanged the first of five strokes. Both listened, counting, looking across the cove at the slender white spire thrusting upward from its lacy circlet of trees. "Not that it matters much," Mrs. Holcomb resumed; "except that I do hate to serve a warmed-over meal, everything stringy and scorched, none of the good juices left. Even so, you'd better have your supper at the regular time, whether your daughter's come or not."

Mr. Benedict let his eyelids fall. Under the creased parchment of his skin the bony modeling of his face was strong, the nose and chin firm, the wedge of the cheekbones distinct. It was a measured, introspective face, touched now with a solemn frailty through extreme old age. He had directed the local high school English classes for thirty-five years, until his retirement over a decade before. It pleased him now to sit idle holding a book, clasping this solid kernel of experience compact within his hand. Other certainties could prove uncertain. He had himself never written the books he had once believed he would write. Yet curiously, in this declension of his life, fragmentary notions, seedling poems, often floated through his mind: the image of the pale houses opposite, brilliant in the limpid waters of the cove, something might flower from that, given adequate soil.

"Well, let's hope for better luck this time," Mrs. Holcomb remarked, with a click of tartness in her voice. "It's a free country. You can always hope."

Mr. Benedict felt a faint stirring of surprise. It was not like Mrs. Holcomb to allude to his personal affairs. In the seven months that had passed since Lorraine had stalked out of the house, shouting back a last vituperative insult above the racing motor of her car, Mrs. Holcomb had maintained a studied reticence, not so much through tact as through a natural conviction that it was unseemly to pry. Yet she had hovered close behind the curtains of the kitchen window, shadowy through the mesh, while Lorraine had flung both locked hands to her temples, tugged at her wild short hair, and hurtled off grinding pebbles and grass beneath the wheels —as he stood wordless in the yard he had noted that. This had been her first encounter with Lorraine. It had left her obviously alarmed. "Hmmmmmmmmm," he answered, slowly turning his head.

Mrs. Holcomb's cheeks were flushed; she wielded the sharp crochet hook with attentive force. "I mean," she went on, "this time I hope your daughter'll think better of the meal I've prepared."

Mr. Benedict watched the quick stabs of the hook draw one taut loop from out another, forming a neat design. This live ember of resentment suddenly disclosed bewildered him. It had never once brushed against his thought that in his own stormy collision with Lorraine that night Mrs. Holcomb had been somehow nicked.

"Did Lorraine criticize your meal?" he asked.

Mrs. Holcomb's round face flushed brighter. "Not criticize in words. I won't say that. I know she lived her married life in Italy, and I don't hold with all those condiments and oils; but it was a good nourishing supper, and tasty too."

Mr. Benedict sighed, restive before the bundle of thorns she had proffered him. Lorraine's marriage to that flashy no-good Bevilaqua, after the war, had failed, as he had known that it must fail, though it had never been his habit to preach. How could it not, with that conceited cinema novice a dozen years younger than she, dedicated only to arranging for himself an easy passage to New York? But Lorraine had merely paraded him before her friends, and hauled him back to the studios of Rome. Had she actually believed that she could prod that slippery lollipop into a career? And now Mrs. Holcomb beside him pursing self-righteous lips, widowed, children grown and scattered, surely equipped with common sense, harboring a secret grudge for months because Lorraine in her wild fury had flouted her nourishing meal. Mr. Benedict turned to the cove again, rubbing one hand along his cheek. The petty vanities of human nature were even more chastening to consider than the major defects.

"Just pushed back her plate and never touched a mite." Mrs.

Holcomb continued as though parched for sympathy. "I couldn't help but notice when I cleared up. I'm not stone blind yet."

Mr. Benedict wished he could find a neutral word in answer; but he shrank from touching upon a subject which, like the chain of loops meshing from Mrs. Holcomb's hands, might form a pattern visible but incomplete. Lorraine had acted as his adversary now for more than thirty years, ever since her mother had died, probably earlier than that if he should probe. After the funeral in the snow-filled graveyard—was it the same week, or was it even the same year?—he had come upon her one morning in the attic tumbling through Victoria's clothes. What did she expect to find? What did she intend? Blazing above the garments she clutched, she flashed him a furious hot blue glare, suspicion and defiance mixed, with her bold nose thrust high. He had hung Victoria's dresses back in the wardrobe again, and closed the door. Not a word uttered: he had never believed in meeting rage with rage. Cool water always tempered hot; Lorraine would learn that elementary lesson in time. For all her hasty passions the edge of her intelligence was keen. But it wearied him to grapple with the idea of Lorraine. In her periods of absence she receded from his mind, as her mother had receded, and his vanished friends: dispersed into a pale approximation, or by a mercurial change turned brilliantly intensified; in either case, unreal.

"Even so," Mrs. Holcomb said, "she must have been very handsome in her youth, your daughter I mean, tall and athletic like that."

He swung his gaze toward Mrs. Holcomb again, a plump little figure in her crisp cotton dress with pinkish cheeks and trim graceful ankles of which she was modestly proud. She smelled always of fresh ironing and the geranium lotion she used, an unobtrusive comfortable smell. She chattered, it was true, more than there was need; she walked with quick sharp steps; but he had come to value her presence in his house, like the familiar varnished pictures on the wall or the steady background clicking of the clocks, especially after the frightening confusion of poor Miss Osgood's failing days. She was herself not many years older than Lorraine, eight or nine perhaps. Yet the equation seemed absurd. Lorraine would never lapse into middle age; she refused the part. She still flaunted the extravagant colors she had affected as a girl—violet, emerald, coral

—like the shimmer of a wild fantastic bird. Even when she stood before him, long limbs turning angular and somehow harsh, beyond the actual flesh he saw the reckless hoyden rushing in late at night daring him with her eyes to utter a reprimand. She had driven to Bristol, forty miles off, through pelting sleet, in somebody's borrowed car? The locks of springy chestnut hair framing her face quivered; the fierce blue eyes gleamed. Why should he scold? Lorraine must measure out and prove her own experience.

The clear light bathing the waters had turned more luminous, September light steeped crystalline. Already the brambles trailed a skein of scarlet through the grass, and the golden crab apples clustered along the bough showed one polished rosy cheek. This was the season he had most loved as a boy—clambering over the old stone wall to the place where the big butternut tree grew: hard nuts they were, with rough green coats running a bitter juice but pure and mellow in the fruit. Mr. Benedict glanced down at his hands. It took days of scrubbing before the dark stain of that juice began to bleach. And his mother in her long percale apron buttoned close, her hair caught high with combs, threatening to paint his nose with the juice if he didn't watch out. What good had that done? He had himself daubed his nose one afternoon and, stinging in every freckle, swaggered home. How his mother had shrieked! Mr. Benedict gave his thin frail laugh. Some day, he must try to venture out to the butternut tree again.

"Carl" Mrs. Holcomb exclaimed: her hearing was sharper than his. She rose from her chair. But the sound of the vehicle rattling along the bumpy ruts was careful and slow. An old-fashioned station wagon appeared, groaning in every joint, and stopped at the foot of the hill. Andrew Wrentham swung open the door. "Afternoon, folks," he called.

Mr. Benedict watched him climb the irregular slope leading to the house. Andrew was grizzled now, shambly too, as though the chief controlling cord on which his limbs were strung had lost its pull. For a moment he seemed decked out for a Hallowe'en prank, with a bleak knobby likeness imposed on the features Mr. Benedict used to know.

"Now you just visit with Mr. Wrentham here for a while," Mrs. Holcomb said, stowing her needlework away. "I'll go tend to things inside. Remember, Mr. Benedict, supper's at the regular time. No matter what, we can't take chances with your health."

"No," Mr. Benedict answered, "I'll wait—" He broke off before he added "for Lorraine." The pointless delicacy made his lips twitch; or was he merely, in a minor fashion, perverse?

"I was just down the road a piece on an errand," Andrew offered, taking Mrs. Holcomb's chair.

He sat with his hands outspread upon his knees, laconic and stiff, as he used to sit in the parlor all those years ago watching the doorway for Lorraine. He had seemed promising as a boy; never spectacular, but observant, alert, with a sensitive dramatic gift surprising in one whose customary talk was so reduced. Now he was lodged for life running the village general store. Mr. Benedict turned his gaze to the pale houses across the cove. Somewhere amidst the subterranean levels of the earth there must lie hidden a still dark glassy reservoir composed of all the human promise that had drained away, gathering in silence year by year. Had he achieved much more than Andrew had, himself? He tapped the cover of *The Tempest* lying on the round wicker table at his side. "Remember Prospero's famous speech?" he asked.

Andrew blinked his lids. Leaning forward, he plucked a dry leaf from the woodbine threading through the spokes of the porch railing and began drawing it against one palm. "Well, I can't say that I've put my mind to it lately," he returned.

To his own embarrassment, Mr. Benedict's voice took on a deepened histrionic note: " 'Our revels now are ended . . .' "

In the way that often happened now, as though a colored slide kept in some vast uncatalogued dispensary had shot itself upon his brain, he saw Andrew in his blue serge knickerbockers and black ribbed stockings firmly planted on the auditorium stage, copper hair gleaming, scrubbed face bright, rolling out the mystic cadences:

> "And like that insubstantial pageant faded
> Leave not a rack behind . . ."

It was not true for the mortal world at any rate, Mr. Benedict thought. There was always a last gritty particle of feeling charred out of any serious experience, submerged, forgotten perhaps, but destined in its proper season to enter the bloodstream again. Why,

otherwise, had Andrew come this afternoon? But what should he
say of himself? What, out of serious experience, did he retain of
Lorraine's mother, of Victoria his wife? Who had those two young
creatures been? What was it he had perceived, that distant summer
they had met? Could he now even summon up Victoria's face? A
misty oval outline, a smudge of dark eyes; then—so vividly as to
make him catch his breath—a fling of frail pale bluets swaying on
delicate stems, under thin descending rain, in a field of cold grass.
Where had that vision taken place?

He shook his head uneasily, flipping the covers of his book.
That was the worst of Lorraine's invasions, the period before in
which all matter of settled residue was stirred. He felt his nerve
ends coiling taut, waiting, waiting, ready to quiver at the slightest
twang. If she must come, let her come. Then she would stride into
the house—critical, ironic, mordantly amused—until the sudden
quarrel struck, and she strode off again. What had been the reason that last time, when she had shoved back Mrs. Holcomb's
plate, blue eyes flaring, bony nose high, raging in a thickened
voice: "All right! All right! I'm finished, I tell you! I'm through!"
Some scheme about opening a travel bureau in New York, for
which he was to furnish the funds. He didn't begrudge her the
money, for any reasonable cause; he never had. He had bailed her
out of the Bevilaqua affair, and a dozen lesser scrapes. But he knew
her caprices; he doubted that she'd persist.

Andrew cleared his throat with a rasp and shifted his feet.
"Cove's pretty," he said. Both watched the water washing in faster
and higher now, with a quick skimming ripple at the surface scattering the reflection of the pale buildings opposite. A fresh breeze
had sprung up; the little pine trees bordering the road tossed flexi-
ble soft needles back, like silvery brushes in the air.

"Funny what you remember," Andrew said. "I was just thinking
of that first fur coat she had."

Mr. Benedict waited. Lorraine's first fur coat? He had no certain recollection. Lorraine had chosen to buy her clothes herself
after Victoria had died, taking the commuter's train to Portland
alone. She had turned strident and sarcastic as she left childhood
behind, shockingly rude to poor Miss Osgood, who was subject
to confusion even then. She still kept the trick of jerking back her
head, an upthrust of dismissal, which she had adopted at this time.

It was at this time, also, that she had formed the habit of calling him by a series of derisive names—Maximus, Caesar, Augustus— a silly habit which, though it annoyed him, he thought it best to disregard. Frowning, he stroked the covers of his book. What was it he had felt, when he was forced to realize that he was the single authority in charge of a girl of seventeen, the winter Victoria had died? Shrouded, sullen days, a dense blank sky, the cove running a crest of frosty foam along the waves—that might apply to any winter in his life. What had they talked about, together in the chilly house? He could not think. That was the winter he had tried to put his strictest grasp of knowledge into ordered words; and had failed; and had never tried to write again. Sitting at his desk, staring through the window, with the dry snow scratching against the panes, and the powdery little heaps rustling along the ledge. No sound in the world at all except the thin white whisper of snow smothering headstones and hills.

"We went to a dance, over at Bristol, at the Grange," Andrew continued. Andrew had never been hindered by a pause. "There was a big blizzard, five or six inches piled up, but it'd stopped by then. There were a lot of stars out. That was just before Judgment Day."

He meant the stock market crash of 1929, Mr. Benedict supposed, which had cheated him of further education and consigned him to the store. He cast a look at the silent profile, the knobby cheekbone, the gaunt mandible clamped hard. What quality had Andrew lacked—some necessary drive, some central thrust? He had moped about the village after Lorraine had left for college aimless and forlorn. Actually, Lorraine had never come home to live again; merely to swoop in and out. At length Andrew had married, had fathered children, had developed a mild ailment of the chest. Was that a just summation of his life? No: there was still the sensitive, declamatory boy to reckon with. Was it he who, in some obscure compartment of the brain, had kept the image of a heavy fall of snow, a spray of stars, a quick bright obstinate girl vaunting the rich apparel of a first fur coat?

"Funny what you remember," Andrew said again. "It had a silk lining. I guess my hands were kind of chapped. I remember the feel when I hung it up."

The mirrored houses in the cove wavered in broken patches as the breeze gathered strength, dispersing in watery streaks. Suddenly Mr. Benedict wished that Andrew would go. He was tired; too old, too spent, to acknowledge that grazing shot. It edged against his mind with pain, how long and deep and ineradicable the memory of the physical senses is. He could wander through the chambers of the past to discover only random pictures and fragmentary scenes, a specter uninvolved; yet this trivial detail rising out of Andrew's youth brought a sharp ache to his eyes. Irritated, he rubbed his hand along his cheek.

Andrew cleared his throat again. "She really through with that Italian fellow for good?" he asked.

Mr. Benedict nodded, uttering his cracked dry laugh. He knew that in the village every available droplet of Lorraine's personal affairs had been garnered, debated, assessed. Where the secret pipelines ran he was never altogether sure; but he never for a moment doubted that they ran.

"Just as well." Andrew flipped the leaf he still held up in an arc, over the porch railing and onto the grass. "She was always choosy. That way, your judgment can go soft."

"Or hard," Mr. Benedict returned. Bevilaqua was a shadow, a mummer in the stage scenery Lorraine had knocked together for herself after the war. He had never wondered that Lorraine had seized upon the war as her first great chance; she had leaped into her little Red Cross commissary niche like Anita Garibaldi, firing pistols, on her horse. Nor had he wondered at her subsequent escapades, in Europe after the war. She had a belated garden row to till. "Lorraine was born into a sorry time," he said, with a rueful quirk of his lips.

Andrew swung his chair back on its rockers, as though balancing between silence and speech. When he spoke at last his voice, though deferential, was firm. "I shouldn't lay it to the time, myself, I guess. Not the whole of it anyway."

Mr. Benedict glanced at him in surprise. Very few people troubled to differ with him now, except of course Lorraine. Andrew gave hard, considered thought, he knew, to any subject he was willing to broach. Oddly, through the petulance he felt, a flicker of gratification ran—that Andrew had opposed a statement he had made. Before he could take up the challenge the bells in the church steeple began to ring. They sat silent while the six slow lingering strokes shook their echo through the air.

"She never was a whiz at being punctual," Andrew said. "I thought myself she was due about four."

With brisk sharp footsteps tapping, as though operated by the same mechanism as the clocks, Mrs. Holcomb emerged on the porch. She had changed into another immaculate cotton dress and wore obviously new high-heeled beige shoes.

"You'd think she'd telephone if she's put it off," she said, again with a snap of rancor in her voice. "They have all those little out-door phone booths everywhere now—you know what I mean, all painted blue and white?" She fixed on Andrew an oblique signifi-cant look. "At any rate, Mr. Benedict, supper'll be on the table in half an hour."

Mr. Benedict gazed far off, severe and dignified. The wind had fallen to a vagrant breeze. The cove brimmed full, glittering through its high strong amethyst a streak of purple, a streak of shifting green. At the under edge of a soft billow of cloud, motion-less in the pure blue sky, a luminous faint rose appeared. Solitary, becalmed, the houses on the opposite shore met their own bril-liant reflection again, in a strange marriage of the semblance and the real.

"Well, I'm counting on you then," Mrs. Holcomb said. She gave a nervous laugh. "Maybe your daughter can wait until doomsday to eat, but I know better than to think you can."

"Mrs. Holcomb! If you please!" Mr. Benedict exclaimed. In-stantly he was contrite as a hot stricken flush mottled Mrs. Hol-comb's cheeks.

"Well, I'm sure!" she mumbled, scurrying toward the door.

Mr. Benedict sat more rigidly in his chair, bracing his hands against the arms. What claim had Mrs. Holcomb on his life, to evoke his snubs and fling off in a huff? Why should she disrupt his peace with the spit of her resentment jabbing against his mind? What concern of hers was Lorraine? He was weary of this buzz of questions like a swirl of gnats about his ears. But as Andrew began to struggle to his feet he turned.

"No, don't go yet, Andrew," he said. "There's something I want to get clear. What was that remark of yours, just before Mrs. Hol-comb came out?"

Andrew considered, standing loose-limbed and lank. From below him looking up Mr. Benedict observed again how bleak and worn his features had become.

"Well," Andrew replied, "it's a good long while back."

"I don't like evasions and confusions," Mr. Benedict rapped out, as though Andrew were a high school student still. "Now what's this mystery you were hinting at?"

"Well . . ." Andrew stopped to think. "As I said, it's a good while back. Like that line you mentioned from the play." Surprisingly, he smiled. " 'Our revels now are ended.' Not that I'd call them revels exactly, myself."

"I suppose you know what you're getting at."

"Let's put it this way then." Again Andrew paused, searching for accurate words. "We don't always choose what the game's going to be, or even know the score sometimes. We've all played it blind, I guess."

"We?" Mr. Benedict asked, bewildered. "You and Lorraine?"

Andrew met his look firmly, and Mr. Benedict was startled to see how keen and tolerant his dark eyes were. "All of us. Not just Lorraine and me. You too."

Mr. Benedict stared up at him. A strange echo rang within his head. That Andrew—Andrew!—should stand before him in judgment leveling this cryptic charge; and worse, as though it were a simpleton's commonplace. His voice came dry, displeased. "I don't know what you mean."

"About Lorraine." Andrew lapsed into meditation, blinking his lids. "You could say, maybe," he went on at last, "that Lorraine's been making a hullabaloo all her life because she was scared to be still. She had a time to listen once—I happened to be there; and she couldn't hear anything."

"I don't know what you mean," Mr. Benedict said again. "I got tired of bothering with riddles long ago."

"That's what I mean, maybe," Andrew replied.

With a screech and a roar Lorraine's car shot into view. "By golly!" Andrew said. Straight up the hill she swept, chestnut hair flying, and stopped with a grinding jerk. Andrew pretended to shudder; Mr. Benedict watched.

"Well, Pontifex!" Lorraine called. She strode toward them swiftly, brilliant in her scarlet coat and peacock-colored scarf. "And

Andrew. And a perfect high tide. What more could anybody ask?"

She mounted the porch steps with a rapid swing and paused at the top, regarding the two with a quizzical smile; then she moved purposefully toward Mr. Benedict's chair. In such matters, he knew, she wasted no time. Immediately after the brisk swooping kiss she pulled her handkerchief from her pocket and scrubbed the lipstick from his cheek.

"Well, Lorraine," he said. During the first moments of her appearance he always found it hard to fuse this figure with the remembered figure of his mind. Had he and Andrew been arguing about this stranger, with her look of whittled elegance?

"Old Ander," Lorraine said, mocking. She tapped two fingers against Andrew's arm; the cluster of jewels in her ring flashed, shimmering toward the flash of jeweled buttons on her blouse. "Old Ander the Gander. Hi."

A slow sheepish grin lighted Andrew's face, spreading even to his ears. "You know better than to take the road like that," he told her severely. "Have you gone soft in the brain? First thing you know you'll go crashing straight off the causey into the cove."

"I'd rather crash than crawl, any day."

Andrew continued to grin. "Well, you'll do both in the end, driving that car like a hopped-up maniac. What good'll those fancy buttons do you then? What are they anyway, polished-down carbuncles or what?"

Lorraine laughed, and immediately began to cough. "Poor Ander," she said in a roughened voice. "You still try, don't you?— though you never do seem to improve. You're mistaking me for Job."

Mr. Benedict sat a little huddled in his chair. What was all this foolish talk of buttons and Job? They chattered in a language which he could not understand, confederate, conjoined. Absently, he reached for his book, resting it gently against his knee. By what magnetic spell must Lorraine always return? For she always did return, to bestir his bones and disoblige his house. He could hear Mrs. Holcomb's irritable footsteps clicking up and down before the porch door even now. Let them talk, Lorraine and Andrew, in their old complicity. What could they really know of one another after thirty years? What could they know of him? He had paid wholly in his life span for whatever he had lost. What outrageous implication had Andrew tried to make, buried within his cryptic words? They were all what they had become. Vision distant, he gazed across the shore at the thin transcendent spire of the church. The light was beginning to wane; the cove was turning blank, draining swiftly as it did these nights from blue to pallid gray; the little trees stood somber along the empty road. Rising, he loomed stiff and frail. He felt hollow, diffused, and suddenly cold.

NORMA KLEIN was born in New York in 1938, graduated from Barnard in 1960, having won the Elizabeth Janeway Prize for Prose for two consecutive years. She is in her third year of graduate study in Russian at Columbia. Her stories have appeared in *Grecourt Review, Southwest Review, Nimrod, Ivy Magazine, Northwest Review, Mademoiselle, Canadian Forum* and *MSS*. "The Burglar" was written during Miss Klein's senior year at Barnard.

The Burglar

They were hot and tired from driving all day. As they walked into the drive-in, Louise said sullenly, "That's what I should have done this summer—been a car hop."

"Why?" Marty said. "You just would've met all kinds of crummy guys who would've tried to pick you up."

"Ya, but you get experience," Louise said. "You see what life is really like."

"Yes," Marty said. "But so what?"

"I don't know."

Inside they sat down and looked at the menu. Marty ordered chicken pot pie on the dinner and Louise ordered fruit salad. Then they went into the restrooms and washed up. When they came back, the food was on the table. The fruit salad consisted of a bowl of lettuce, two prunes, and a peach half. Louise peered at it and quickly ate the two prunes. Then she poked around in the bowl.

"It's all lettuce," she said.

Marty looked up. He was eating hungrily. "Yes," he said.

"That's not worth $1.10," said Louise. "It's nothing but lettuce." She stared at Marty's dish of hot chicken and then buried her face in her arms, her eyes closed. She lay there a long time. Marty looked at her and went on eating. He reached over and touched her shoulder.

"Hey, come on, Lou," he said.

MSS 1962.

Louise remained with her face down.

"Come on," Marty said. "What's wrong?"

Louise sat up.

"You have to eat more than that," Marty said. "You have to eat something."

"It's all lettuce," Louise said. She covered the salad with a napkin. "I guess I should have gotten the dinner," she said.

"Yes," Marty said. "Why don't you get something else?"

Louise said nothing for a long time. She looked down. Then she said, "I don't like their food."

Marty stopped eating and looked at her incredulously. "Well, why didn't you say that before?" he said. "God, I only came here because I thought you liked it. Why didn't you say something?"

Louise said nothing.

"Look, don't you remember?" Marty said. "In the car—you were the one who mentioned it. Don't you remember? You should've said something. You know it doesn't make any difference to me where we eat."

Louise said nothing.

"Well, I wish you'd mention these things," Marty said.

The waitress came over. "Will that be all, sir? Will you have dessert?"

"What is there?"

"Jello, cherry cobbler, sherbet."

"Cobbler, please."

Louise had lain down again and was eyeing Marty. "Hi," she said loudly in a deadpan voice. "Hi there."

"Hi," Marty said quietly.

"I can get something to eat somewhere else," Louise said. "It's okay."

"Okay."

The waitress brought the cobbler. It had whipped cream on top. Marty removed the round of crust and began eating it.

"Cobbler mit schlag," Louise said. "Why don't you put some in your coffee?"

"I don't know."

"Then you could have coffee mit schlag."

"Yes," Marty said.

"Don't you want that?" Louise said. "Don't you like coffee mit schlag?"

"Sure, I love it."

They left the restaurant. Marty paid the check while Louise waited in the parking lot. It had begun to rain.

"There's some place across the street," Louise said. "It's some barbeque place. Let's go there."

They crossed the street and looked into the restaurant.

"I could get spareribs," Louise said.

"Yes, why don't you?" Marty said.

Louise poked her head in the door and looked around. "It looks grimy," she said.

They walked down the street to another restaurant. It was dark and quiet. In the corner was a very large airconditioner. It was so strong that when Marty blew smoke from his cigarette, it instantly whirled away and disappeared.

"This is airconditioning," Marty said.

"This is airconditioning with a vengeance," Louise said.

They sat down. The restaurant was deserted. Near the airconditioner was a sign: Eat our Dorfer's Cheesecake: It's different and delicious. Outside it was raining heavily. In silence they watched the rain pouring off the awning. While they were waiting for the menu, Louise picked up her fork and began poking at Marty's hands with it.

He laughed. "Hey, come on," he said.

"You know, I feel an overwhelming desire to be drivingly mean," Louise said. She prodded the palm of Marty's hand with the fork. He picked up his fork and lightly poked her arm.

"What are you doing?" Louise said sharply. "What are you doing to me?"

"Just the same thing you were doing to me," Marty said.

"Well, stop it," Louise said, enraged.

"Good God!" Marty said. "I give up. For Christ's sake. Do you mean to say that hurt you? God!"

"You have no right to do it," Louise said. "I just did it because I feel put upon. You're not put upon."

"The hell I'm not."

"What are you put upon about? What have you got to be put upon about?"

"Plenty," Marty said.

"Well, I'm sorry to hear that," Louise said. "That's really sad." She looked away. Marty said nothing. The waiter came over.

"I'll have the steak," Louise said.

"Will you have something to drink?"

"Does it come with it?"

The waiter smiled. "No."

"No, then."

"Oh, come on—get a cup of coffee, for God's sake," Marty said.

"No," Louise said stubbornly.

"I'll have the cheesecake," Marty said, "and a cup of coffee."

"That's a pretty expensive steak," Louise said with a grieved expression. "If you count that other dollar for the fruit salad."

"Well, you couldn't help it," Marty said. "Forget it."

Louise looked at the grill which the man was wiping off with a cloth. "I think I deserve a steak," she said.

The steak came.

"This is good," Louise said. She pushed aside a pile of French fried onions. "You want some?"

"No."

"How's the cheesecake?"

"It's terrific."

"Is it different and delicious?"

"It's very creamy."

"I'm going to get some coffee."

"Okay."

"Why don't you get some schlag with it? You could have cheese-cake mit schlag."

When they had finished eating, Louise wiped her face with a napkin. "Boy, that was really good," she said.

Outside the rain had stopped and the air was hot and humid again. Already the streets had dried and only the wet leaves on the trees showed it had rained. They walked back to Marty's apartment, still feeling irritable and tired. Neither spoke for most of the way.

"Look, there's a Jewish church," Marty said.

"It's not called a Jewish church," Louise said in an annoyed voice. "It's a synagogue."

"Okay—a synagogue."

Finally they reached the apartment, three rented rooms in a

large white house. Marty took out the key and opened the door. "Wow, it's hot in here," he said. He went into the bedroom and opened the window. Then he clicked on the radio and flopped down on the bed on his stomach, his face buried on his arms. The bed wasn't made and clothes were scattered on the floor and chairs.

Louise went over and clicked off the radio.

"What's wrong?" said Marty, looking up. "Don't you like Beethoven?"

Louise said nothing.

"Don't you like classical music?" Marty said.

"I hate all art," Louise snapped sarcastically. "Didn't you know that?" She sat down in a chair. "I just don't like music on all the time," she said. "I like peace and quiet . . . What's wrong? I listen to that damn breakfast program every morning. Can't I have a little peace and quiet?"

"I thought you liked it," Marty said, closing his eyes again.

There was a long pause. Then Louise got up and lay down next to him. She looked up at the ceiling. "I know why I feel like this," she said.

"Why? Because you haven't gotten your period?"

"No."

"So why then?"

"Because I don't respect you."

"Oh."

"You're supposed to respect the man you love. You're supposed to be in awe of him."

Marty snorted. "Aren't you in awe of me?" he said.

"Ya, it's very funny. Ha ha."

"Okay, it's tragic."

"It's your fault too."

"Okay, so it's tragic and it's my fault. Everything's my fault. I take all the blame."

"Stop being so sarcastic."

"Okay."

"You haven't even read that much," Louise said. "That's one reason I can't respect you. I bet I've read more than you."

"Oh cut it out. That's not true by a long shot."

"It is."

"It is not. I've read more Jane Austen than you."

"Well, I've read more Dostoevsky. Have you read all his novels?"

"No, and I wouldn't want to."

"Well, I wouldn't want to read all of Jane Austen. In fact, there's nothing I'd want to do less."

"Well, that's too bad," Marty said. There was a moment's pause. Then he added, "God, this is incredible! How can you be so egotistical?"

"Egotistical! What's so egotistical? When you do it, it's fine, it's nothing, and when I do it, it's egotistical."

"But it's entirely different. Obviously at nineteen you can't have read as much as I have at thirty-four. That's absurd."

"Why not? You said you didn't even start reading things 'til you were twenty-three . . . Anyhow, you can't help it. I'm not saying it's your fault. It's just the kind of background you come from."

"Incredible."

"There's nothing so damn incredible about it. Why don't you find another word?"

"I consider that you've read almost nothing," Marty said. "You haven't read the 18th century, you haven't read Conrad, you—"

"So—you never read Proust."

"I did."

"The whole thing?"

"No—the first volume."

"Well—see!"

"Okay, you're perfect. I give up."

Louise sat up and abruptly crawled over Marty. "Now, that's really stupid," she said furiously. "Why don't you go sleep with Jane Austen if you're so damn crazy about her?" She marched out of the room, slamming the door.

For ten minutes neither of them opened the door. Marty turned over on his back and muttered, "Oh hell." On the bed he saw a cockroach and reached over and squashed it between the sheets. At once he felt a strange repulsion, not of the bug or of killing it, but—yes, he remembered. It was during their last really ferocious argument. It had been last week, just after he had heard about not passing the Latin exam. "God, what did your father do to you?" Louise had said. "He must have squashed you—like a bug—to make you like this. It's unbelievable." Her face was contorted with rage and her voice hoarse and cracked as it always was when she was upset. She seemed in a kind of unnatural fury, so much so that he was afraid of her. She had been unpacking something. She kept carrying the same dress back and forth from one room to the other without noticing it. "You're crazy," she said finally. "It's crazy." He broke down and began shaking all over, almost weeping, but ashamed to let her see it. Overwhelmed with guilt, she had stopped abruptly and begged him to forgive her. "Please," she had said. "I only do it because I love you. Otherwise I wouldn't care. I didn't say you were crazy. I said this whole idea was. That's all. Please—believe me."

For nearly a year he had kept repeating to himself over and over —it's necessary to be free, and the word Freedom became an incantation for him. He had probably read it somewhere, but in fact, whatever meaning it had had for him at first was gone. Often, impatiently, he tried to stop himself as he was saying it. What does it mean? What're you talking about? But all he could think of were isolated moments of seeing someone he loved laugh or waiting for a bus at night, alone, when it was cold, and he could see the lights of the other buildings, the lights on the river from the electric signs, the red traffic light reflected on a tree. And what were these things? No, mainly it was just a negative sense that most of the time he was surrounded by a kind of veil or film and that if he could tear through it, beyond this would be clarity and whatever freedom meant.

Louise in the other room got a book out of a carton in the corner and, sitting down at the kitchen table, began reading it with a flashlight. She used the flashlight because Marty had once cautioned her about wasting electricity, and at the moment she wanted to feel herself a martyr to his poverty. She knew she had been acting nervous, disagreeable, and she tried to puzzle it out carefully, logically. First there was not getting her period, which meant either getting married to Marty, which she did not want, or an abortion, which her father would have to pay for. In the back of her mind she recalled a remark Marty had made the first night she had stayed with him. It had been two months ago, the first week they had met. "You could be doing this with anyone," he said. "It's not because of me." She had protested. "That's horrible, then," she had said. "I shouldn't stay, if that's so." But she had stayed anyway, though she had never succeeded in ridding herself of the thought that he was partly right, that it could have been with anyone that she had set up this first "experiment with love." She was convinced by now that he loved her, that there was nothing vicious or degrading she could do to herself or him that would change the way he felt toward her, and in some way she looked down on him for this. She wanted him to be strong enough to humiliate her and yet she knew that he wouldn't or couldn't. He was thirty-four. He had spent ten years working for his Ph.D. in English and was no closer to getting it now than he had been ten years ago. She thought of his diary which he hid in a drawer (he would never let her see it and said mysteriously: "It's more honest than Rousseau!"). She had pawed through it in frantic curiosity one day when he was out, curiously disappointed (what miracles of crimes had she expected to find?) What had amazed her was that he kept referring to himself as a genius in all seriousness, comparing himself to Cezanne and Van Gogh. And should she have brought it up at all? She had brought it up, partly at least, to show him that it made no difference to her if he was a genius or not, but as she discussed it, the fantastic idea of the whole thing had overwhelmed her. "Lots of people have said I'm a genius," he had said stubbornly. "Look, please," she said. "It doesn't matter. To have some talent in anything—that's enough. It's more than enough." "How do you know I'm not a genius?" he said. How do I know? How do I know anything? she wondered. And suddenly a line flashed through her mind from the diary: "Women are either to have sexual relations with or to avoid." Had he known she had seen it, he would have said, as he had said about other things, "But that was earlier, before I knew you." But she hated this. She hated his blank lonely shiftless past. She wanted him to have had affairs with other women. She hated his inward timidity and fears, hated his family whom she had never met, all of them Protestants, Midwesterners ("My sister says she's known lots of nice people who were Jews," he had told her consolingly), hated it until each day it seemed to her that every action was only an attempt to smother her hatred, to drive it into some petty minor argument until the day when she would finally bring herself to leave for good.

Finally Marty walked in and sat down beside Louise. There was no light except for the long beam the flashlight cast on the wall.

"Lou?"

"Ya, what?" Louise looked up. "Listen—did Hamlet love Ophelia?" she said.

"God, I don't know. Why?"

"I want to know," Louise said, leaning intently forward. "I'm serious. Tell me."

"Well, you're not in a mood to talk about it objectively," Marty said. "We'll talk about it some other time."

"No, I want to know now," Louise said, her voice rising. "Tell me."

Marty sighed. "Yes, of course he did," he said quickly.

Louise sat back, calmer. "Oh," she said.

"Look, Lou—I feel closer to you than I ever have to anyone. You know that."

Louise looked at him and then smiled mockingly. "Oh," she drawled. "Well, that's strange."

Marty turned away. "Why do you kill everything?" he said. "You kill everything I say."

Louise frowned. "I'm sorry," she said.

They sat there mournfully, their faces pale and shadowy in the dark room.

" 'Two people of different ethnic backgrounds come together for one summer of happiness,' " Louise recited in a monotone.

Marty made a face. "God! Where's that from?"

"I don't know. I read it somewhere."

"God!"

"Well, it's true, isn't it?"

"I don't know. No, I don't think so . . . But, then, only time will tell, to coin a phrase."

"Ya."

They both laughed, embarrassed.

"Why don't we take a shower?" Marty said.

"You want to take one together?"

"Yes, don't you?"

"Ya, sure."

"Are you sure you want to?"

"I said I did."

"You're not just saying it to please me?"

Louise laughed. "You know I never say anything to please you," she said.

The shower was out on the porch. They got into it.

"God, it's boiling," Marty said. He turned on more cold.

"This isn't hot," Louise said.

"Yeah?" Marty said. "It's hot enough for me."

"It's not so hot," Louise said.

They began washing.

"Let me wash your back, okay?" Louise said.

"Sure." Marty turned so his back would get wet. With the bar of soap Louise rubbed his back. "Boy, that feels good," Marty said. "You know, there're some parts of my back that've never been washed. I can't reach them."

"Oh, you mean these little mossy patches here?"

"Yeah, that's them."

They sponged each other with the soft soapy sponge. Louise, her eyes squinting with water, looked up at Marty, who was grinning broadly. "Well, *you* seem to be having a good time," she said.

"Aren't you?"

"Ya, sure." She laughed. "I was just joking."

He began sponging her breasts again.

"Hey," Louise said. "I didn't know they were *that* dirty."

"Umm," said Marty, ignoring her. "Does that feel good?"

Louise smiled. "I'll say."

They got out of the shower and rubbed themselves dry with towels. The porch was chilly, but in the kitchen it was warm. The light was clicked on. Outside it was dark now. Louise stood in front of the stove, warming herself. Her shower cap was still on so she pulled it off, letting her hair fall loose down her back. Marty came over, drying his ears with the towel.

"Better not stay near the window," he said.

"Why not?" Louise said.

"I don't know. People might look in."

"Oh."

They stood a moment in silence. They felt relaxed from the shower, pleasantly exhausted. But they were suspicious of being relaxed. Each was aware of the effort it took them to joke this way, to pretend that everything could be simple and unthinking. Their awareness s   it for them, though they tried to ignore it, to   ght.

    ung her arms, Louise turned around and said, "May I have

this waltz?" She laughed and Marty, confused, got into a dance position. Naked, in the warm dim light of the kitchen, they danced around and around. Then they began to jitterbug. Marty kicked his feet out while Louise danced wildly, her hair flying, her breasts shaking.

"Let's go to bed," Marty said, grinning.

Louise stopped short, embarrassed, her face flushed. "Oh," she said, panting. She smiled half shyly. In the warmth of the room their bodies were dry already with the markings of tan on their shoulders and legs.

"We might as well," Marty said.

"Ya, okay."

They got into bed and made love quickly. Afterward they lay there in a warm silence, half asleep. It was too painful to question things now, too easy to accept the peaceful satisfaction of physical enjoyment they knew they could depend on. They lay there, willing to be content, to believe they had conjured up something resembling love. Almost involuntarily their minds strayed to other people they knew, to other hopes of relationships in the past or ones that were purely imaginary, composed of daydreams. Marty thought of a woman he had had a long talk with that week. She was married and it had been clear that she was unhappy but far from the point of being able to admit it to herself. She had confided in him openly, warmly, for three hours pouring out the secrets of her heart. It had amazed him for he scarcely knew her, but he had been touched and pleased as well. He was attracted to her and felt she was to him and perhaps because there seemed something impossible about their ever getting together, he had felt happy with her. In his mind this incident, sitting in that park among the trees and talking, had taken on a holy quality, isolated from what he knew as painful and therefore real. Thinking of it in bed a dozen memories awakened in Marty's mind, memories of beautiful women he had seen and desired but never spoken to, of gifts he had wanted and never received, of words he had waited to hear spoken and had never heard. Louise, too, was lost in thought. She was thinking of a card she had gotten in the mail that morning from a boy she was once close to. Perhaps she would see him that winter, she thought, once she was back in New York, a thousand miles from here, from Marty. But what she thought of was not what would happen when she saw the boy, but of the first time he had kissed her. He had said: May I kiss you goodnight? And she thought of what Marty had said: Let me kiss you. And of other boys she had known who had said nothing or who had merely commanded her: Kiss me. And what would she say if she were a boy? She felt that, strangely, she would be like Marty, too timid to command or demand things. And if she was like him (for it was so and she knew, too, it was his resemblance to her that had attracted her to him at first), how had she come to hate him now for these very things? Why was it so?

Outside, a dog barked. A moment later there was a faint sound of footsteps and again barking, subsiding in a growl. Neither wanted to mention it because they weren't sure the other had heard it. Marty lifted his head slightly to hear better. He wondered if it might be a burglar coming up the steps. Had he locked the door? He couldn't remember. There—those steps again. He began imagining what he would do if the burglar got in. He would hide Louise under the bed. Then he would throw things at him— stones, books. He could throw that Modern Library Giant of Jane Austen. But then the burglar might hear something in the next room. He might suspect that there was someone else there and come in to search. He would find Louise, attack her—involuntarily Marty tightened his hold on Louise. She was crouched down, her head pressed on his shoulder, her feet entangled with his. Sleepily she imagined the burglar creeping around in the yard and coming up to the room. She would open the window and jump out and run. Marty would stay behind to defend her, fighting off the burglar. But another one would rush up the stairs, push her out of the way and together they would surround him so that—again a growl. Then gradually the sounds were stilled. It was probably a cat, each decided. That's all it was—just a cat or, if not a cat, a dog, prowling around somewhere in the garbage. Each of them knew it. Yet they could not quite free themselves from a feeling of fear, of dread even. Tensely they lay there together, neither daring to move, listening.

TERRY SOUTHERN'S work has appeared in many magazines in America and Europe. He is the author of *Flash and Filigree*, *The Magic Christian*, and co-author (with Mason Hoffenberg) of *Candy*. He is presently writing a novel entitled *The Hipsters*.

The Road Out of Axotle

There's an interesting road leading south out of Axotle, Mexico, that you might like to try sometime. It isn't on the Good Gulf Map, and it isn't on those issued by the Mexican Government. It is on one map—I wonder if you've seen it?—a map of very soft colors, scroll-edged, like some great exotic banknote; and the imprint of the publisher is in small black script along the lower left, "Ryder H. Raven and Son—San Jose, California." I came across it about a year ago.

The way it happened, I was with these two friends of mine in Mexico City—I say friends of mine though actually we'd met only a few days before, but anyway we were together this particular night, in their car—and the idea was to pick a town, such as the one we were in, and then to sort of drive away from it, in the opposite direction, so to speak. I knew what they had in mind, more or less, but it did seem that in being this strong on just-wanting-to-get-away-from, we might simply end up in the sea or desert. Then, too, at one point there was a kind of indecision as to the actual direction to take, like left or right—so I suggested that we look at a map. I knew there was a map in the car, because I had been with them earlier in the day when one of them, Emmanuel, bought a secondhand guidebook, of the kind that has folding maps in it.

"That is good, man," said the other one, who was driving, Pablo.

That was the way they talked, "That is good, man"; "This is bad, man." They were from Havana, and they spoke a fine, foppish sort of Spanish, but their English wasn't the greatest. Still, they insisted on speaking it, despite the fact that my own Spanish was good—in fact, the Mexican dialect part of it was so good that they preferred me to speak, whenever it was necessary, to the Mexicans —and it pleased their vanity to argue that, if *I* spoke, it was less obvious we were tourists.

Emmanuel got the guidebook from the glove compartment now and handed it to me in the backseat. We were at a corner southwest of the town, out beyond the stockyards and the slaughterhouse—at a crossroads. There was nothing happening here, only the yellow light from an arc lamp above, the yellow light that came dying down through the dead gauze of red dust which slowly rose and wound, or so it seemed, and bled around the car. That was the setting.

I had some trouble finding the right map and finally in seeing it, distracted, too, by the blast of California mambo from the radio; and it was then, while I was trying to hold the book up in a way to get more light, that something fell out of it.

"Let me see your lighter a minute, Pablo."

"What? What is?" He turned the radio down, just a bit. Sometimes he got quite excited if he heard his name.

What had fallen from the book was a map of Mexico, a map which had evidently been put there by the book's previous owner. One may say this because it was obvious the map was not a part of the guidebook; it was not of the same school of map making as were the maps in the guidebook. It was like something from another era, not handmade but somehow in that spirit: highly individual. It was large, but not as large as the ones given out by the gasoline stations—nor was it square; when op ed, it was about eighteen by twenty-four inches, and was scaled 1:100.

The paper was extraordinarily thin—Bible paper, but much stronger, like rice paper or bamboo—and it was hazed with the slightest coloration of age which seemed to give a faint iridescence to those soft colors. They were Marie Laurencin colors, and it was like that as well, a map for a child, or a very nice woman.

"Where we are at this time?" asked Emmanuel, in a shout above the radio. Emmanuel was a year or two older than Pablo, and about one degree less self-centered.

I had looked at the map a few minutes without attempting the analogy, just tracing electric-blue rivers to cerulean seas, as they

say, but I did know where we were, of course; and, almost at the
same time, I saw where it might be interesting to go.

"Make a right," I said.

"A right, man," said Emmanuel. "Make a right." They had a
habit of repeating and relaying things to each other for no apparent
reason.

Pablo gave a sigh, as of pain, as though he had known all along
that's how it would be, and he lurched the car around the corner,
sliding it like a top over the soft red dust, and up went the radio.

I continued to look at the map. We were going due west, and
the map showed that about twenty miles ahead, on this same
road, was a little town called Axotle. The road ran through the
town east-west and then joined a highway, and this seemed to be
all there was to it. But holding the lighter quite close, I had seen
another road, a narrow, winding road, as thin as the blood vein of
an eye, leading south out of the town. It seemed to go for about
twenty-five miles, and on it there were two other towns, Corpus
Christi and San Luiz, and there the road stopped. A blood-vein,
dead-end road, with a town at the end of it; that was the place to
go all right.

Pablo drove like a madman, except that he was quite a good
driver actually. He was supposed to be upset, though, about not
having found the kind of car he wanted to drive in Mexico. His
story—or rather, his-story-through-Emmanuel, since Pablo himself
didn't do much talking—was that he had a Mercedes at home and
had been looking for a certain kind of car to drive in Mexico, a
Pegaso, perhaps, but had finally bought this car we were in now,
a '55 Oldsmobile, which had three carburetors and was supposed
to do 145 on a straightaway, though, of course, there weren't too
many of those.

"Man, this old wagon," he kept saying, "I dunt dig it."

But he drove it like the veritable wind, making funny little comments to himself and frowning, while Emmanuel sat beside him,
wagging his closed-eyes head, shaking his shoulders and drumming
his fingers along with the radio, or else was all hunched over in
twisting up sticks of tea and lighting them. Sometimes he would
sing along with the radio, too; not overdoing it, just a couple of
shouts or a grunt.

We pulled in then at a Gulf station for gas. We were about halfway to Axotle now, and I was looking at the map again, outside the car, standing under the light of the station, when it suddenly occurred to me to check with the more recent map of the guide-book to see if perhaps the town had been built up in the last few years; it would put me in an embarrassing position with my new friends if we drove to the end of the line, only to smash headlong into a hot-dog stand. So I got out the guidebook and found a map of the corresponding region—quite detailed it was—and that was when the initial crevice of mystery appeared, because on this map there was *no* road leading south out of Axotle; there was only the east-west road which joined the highway. No road south and nei-ther of the towns. I got a map then from the service station. It was a regular road map about two feet square, and was supposed to show every town with a population of 250 or more . . . and the crevice became the proverbial fissure.

"This is bad, man," said Emmanuel, when I told him. Pablo didn't say anything, just stood there, scowling at the side of the car. Emmanuel and Pablo were both wearing dark prescription glasses, as they always did, even at night.

"No, man," I said, "this is *good*. They're ghost towns . . . you dig? That will be interesting for you."

Emmanuel shrugged. Pablo was still frowning at the car.

"Ghost towns," I said, getting into the backseat again. "Sure, that's very good."

Then, as we got under way, Emmanuel turned to sit half-facing me, his back against the door, and he began to warm to-ward the idea, or was perhaps beginning to understand it.

"Yeah, man, that is very *good*." He nodded seriously. "Ghost town. *Crazy*."

"It is very good, man," he told Pablo, while the radio wailed and the car whined and floated over the long black road.

"What is this, man," Pablo demanded then in his abrupt irate way, half-turning around to me, "this goat town?"

"Goat town! Goat town!" shouted Emmanuel, laughing. "That's too much, man!"

"Man, I dunt dig it!" said Pablo, but he was already lost again, guiding his big rocket to the moon. And I lay back on the seat and dozed off for a while.

When I woke up, it was as though I had been on the edge of

waking for a long time; the car was pitching about oddly, and I
had half-fallen from the seat. The radio was still blasting, but behind it now was the rasping drone of Pablo's cursing. And I lay
there, listening to that sound; it was like a dispassionate chant, a
steady and unlinked inventory of all the profane images in Spanish. I assumed we had gotten off the road, except we seemed to be
going unduly fast for that. Then I saw that Emmanuel had his
hands up to his mouth and was shaking with laughter, and I realized that this had been going on for some time, with him saying
softly over and over, "Man, dig this . . . *road!* Dig this . . . *road!*"

So I raised up to have a look, and it was pretty incredible all
right. It was more of a creek bed than a road, but occasionally
there would be an open place to the side . . . a gaping, torn-off
place that suggested we were on something like a Greek mountain
pass. And then I saw as well, dishearteningly so, why we were going fast; it was because every now and then one of the side pockets
stretched right up to the middle of the road, so that the back
wheels would pull to that side, spinning a bit, as we passed over it.
And, as we passed over it, you could see down . . . for quite a long
way.

"What do you think it's like to the side?" I asked.

Emmanuel finally controlled his curious mirth long enough to
turn around. "What do *I* think it's like?" he asked. "Man, it's *lions
and tigers! And . . . big . . . pointy rocks!* Why? What do *you*
think it's like?" And fairly shouting with laughter, he handed me
another joint.

"*Goats,*" said Pablo with a grotesque snicker. "There are the
goats there."

"All right, man," I said, and lay back with a groan to express my
disquiet.

Pablo snorted. "Man, I'm swingin'!" he said, reassuringly.

Emmanuel broke up completely now and laid his head down
laughing. "Pablo's swingin'!" he cried. He could hardly speak. He
had to hold onto the rocking dashboard to keep from falling to the
floorboards. "Ma-a-an, Pablo is . . . too . . . much!"

It was too much all right. I lay there smoking, my thoughts as
bleak as the black rolling top I stared at, though gradually I did
discern, or so it seemed, a certain rhythm and control taking hold

of the erratic pitching of the car, and the next time I sat up the
road, too, seemed in fairly good shape.

The moon had come out and you would get glimpses now and
then of things alongside—strange dwarf trees and great round
rocks, with patches of misty landscape beyond. It was just about
then that the headlight caught a road sign in the distance, a rickety
post akimbo with a board nailed to it (or maybe tied with a strand
of vine) across which was painted, crudely to be sure, "*Puente*,"
which, in these circumstances, would mean toll bridge.

"Crazy road," I heard Pablo say.

There was a bend in it just after the sign, and the glow of a kerosene lamp ahead—which proved to be from the window of an old
tin shack; and in front of the shack there was a barrier across the
road: a large, fairly straight tree limb. Beyond it, vaguely seen, was
the small, strange bridge.

When we had stopped by the shack, we could see that there
was someone inside, sitting at a table; and, after waiting a minute
while nothing happened, Pablo jerked his head around at me.

"You make it, man," he said, handing me his billfold, "I can't
make these greaser."

"Very well," I said, "you rotten little Fascist spic." And as I got
out of the car I heard him explaining it again to Emmanuel:
"Man, I can't make these greaser."

Inside the shack, the lamp was full up; but, with the chimney
as jagged and black as a crater, I couldn't see too much of the
room's appointments—only a shotgun leaning against the wall near
the door, the barrel so worn and rust-scraped that it caught the
yellow light in glints harder than brass. But I could see him all
right—bigger than life, you might say, very fat, his sleeves twisted
up, playing with cards. There was a bottle half filled with tequila
on the table. I remember this because it occurred to me then, in a
naïve, drug-crazed way, that we might have a pleasant exchange
and finish off with a drink.

"Good evening," I said (with easy formality), then followed it
up with something colloquial like, "What's the damage?"

He was squinting at me, and then beyond, to the car. And I
recall first thinking that here was a man who had half lost his sight
playing solitaire by a kerosene lamp; but he was something else as
well, I realized, when I took it all in: he was a man with a *very*

sinister look to him. He was smoking a homemade cigar, gnarled
and knotted enough to have been comic, except that he kept bar-
ing his teeth around it, teeth which appeared to have been filed—
and by humanity at large, one might presume, from the snarl with
which he spoke, as he finally did:

"Where are you trying to go?"

"Corpus Christi," I said.

It occurred to me that it might be less involved, not to say
cheaper, if I didn't divulge our full itinerary.

"Corpus Christi, eh?" He smiled, or it was something like a
smile; then he got up, walked to the door, glanced at the car, spat
out some of his cigar, and walked back to the table. "Five dollars
a head," he said, sitting down again.

"Five dollars," I said, more in a thought aloud than a question,
"Mexican dollars."

He made a sound, not unlike a laugh, and took up the cards
again.

"You think you're Mexican?" he asked after a minute, without
raising his head.

I had to consider it briefly. "Oh, I see—you mean, 'a-fool-and-
his-money . . .' that sort of thing."

"You said it, my friend, I didn't."

"Yes. Well, you'll give me a receipt, of course."

"Receipt?" He laughed, spitting and wiping his mouth on his
arm. "This isn't Monterrey, you know."

I hesitated, determined for the moment, in the responsibility to
the rest of my party, not to be so misused; then I put my hands
on the edge of the table and leaned forward a little. "I think you've
probably picked the *wrong* crowd this time, Pancho," I said.

Whereas, actually, it was *I* who had picked the wrong party, for
he laid his head back laughing with this—and an unpleasant laugh
it was, as we know.

"Pancho," he said, getting up, "that's funny." Still laughing and
wiping his hand across his mouth, his eyes half shut so that I
couldn't quite see where he was looking, he walked around the
table. "That's very funny," he said.

And you can appreciate how for a moment it was like a se-
quence in a film, where someone is supposed to be laughing or
scratching his ear, and suddenly does something very aggressive

to you—except that I stepped back a little then, and he walked on past me to the door . . . where it seemed my show of apprehension had given him not so much a fresh lease as a veritable deed on confidence.

"*You* don't need a receipt," he said, turning from the door, his eyes still two smoked slits, "you can trust me." Then he flicked his cigar with an air and gave his short, wild laugh, or cough, as it were. But when he faced the car again, he sobered quickly enough. And Emmanuel and Pablo were sitting there, peering out, frowning terribly.

"What have you got inside?" he asked, and his tone indicated this might be the first of several rare cards he intended.

Somehow I felt it would not do to involve my friends, so I started reaching for the money.

He kept a cold, smoky silence as he watched me count it out. Then he took it, leaning back in the smug, smiling, closed-eyes strain against cigar smoke and the effort of pressing the loot deep into his tight trousers.

"Yes," I said. "Well, thanks for everything."

He grunted, then stepped out and raised the barrier. I started to get into the car, but he said something and turned back into the shack, motioning me with him.

"Wait," he said, as a quick afterthought, and from one dark side of the room he came up holding a cigar box.

"You want to buy some good marijuana?"

"What?"

"Marijuana," he said, letting the word out again like a coil of wet rope, and proffering the lid-raised box for my inspection.

"Very good," he said, "the best."

I leaned forward for a look and a sniff. It didn't appear to be the greatest; in fact, it didn't appear to be Mexican—and it looked like it was about fifteen years old.

"What is it, a spice of some kind?"

"Very good," he said.

"How much?"

"How much will you give?"

I took a pinch and tasted it.

He nodded toward the car. "Perhaps your friends. . . . I'll make you a good price. You tell me your price, I'll make you a good price. Okay?"

I stared at the box for a minute, then made an eccentric grimace. "You don't mean . . . you don't mean marijuana . . . the loco weed? What, to smoke?" I shook my head vigorously, backing away. "No, thanks!" I said, while his face went even more sour than one might have expected.

"Come back when you grow up!" he snarled, shutting the box; and for the first time, as he turned into the shadow of the shack, he seemed slightly drunk.

The bridge itself was noteworthy. A bit longer than the car, but not a foot wider, it consisted of oil drums held together with barbed wire and covered with wooden planks, only the outer two of which seemed at all stationary. The device was secured at each bank by a rope attached to stakes driven into the ground.

We held back a few seconds before embarking, taking it all in. Then, as we crossed over, the whole thing sank about two feet, completely out of sight, swaying absurdly, as the black water rose up in swirls just above the running boards.

Nobody commented on the bridge; though once we were across, onto the road, and I was resting on the seat again, Emmanuel said:

"What happened back with the greaser, man?"

"Five dollars a head."

"That swine."

"That rotten greaser swine," said Pablo.

"You said it," I said, closing my eyes. I had not gotten to bed the night before; I was thinking, too, of a certain time-honored arrangement in Mexico whereby a cigar box full of marijuana is sold to a foreigner and then retrieved by the merchant at customs. I once heard that the amount of annual foreign revenue so gained in the consequent fines is second only to that from the tax on the shade-and-barrier seats at the bullfight. And I soon began to wonder, here on the soft-focus margin of sleep, how many, many times that particular box I just looked at had been sold. Ten? Twenty? How many miles? How many missions? Fifty missions to Laredo, and they would decorate the box and retire it. And smoke it. But, of course, it was no good. Why would they use anything good for a scheme like that? No, it would be like those bundles of newspaper money left for kidnapers; I suppose they send to New Jersey for it. Anyway, I decided not to mention the incident to my friends; it would only excite them unduly.

I must have been asleep when we reached Corpus Christi, because when I came up again to have a look, the car was already stopped. We were in the middle of the square, and Emmanuel was saying: "Man, dig this . . . *scene*. Dig this . . . *scene*," while Pablo was just sitting there, leaning forward over the wheel, his arms hanging to each side of it.

The town, if it may so be called, is simply this square of one-story frame buildings, fronted all around by a raised, wooden, sidewalk arcade. Besides the car we were in, there were two or three others parked in the square along with several small wagons that had mules or donkeys hitched to them.

"Now, this is your true Old West, Pablo," I began. "Notice the attempt at a rather formal—" But what *I* had failed to notice was that the shadowed arcades, all around the square, were lined with people. They were leaning against the storefronts, and lying on the wooden sidewalk, or sitting on the raised edge of it—not just grown people, but children as well; children, a number of whom were to be seen crawling about, in the manner of the very young indeed. This struck me as odd because it was now about two o'clock in the morning. But what was really more odd was the pure, unbroken torpor which seemed to overhang the crowd. For a large group of people—perhaps 200—their inactivity was marvelous to look upon like an oil painting. It seemed that all of them were leaning, sitting, or lying down; and it was not apparent that they were even talking to each other. And here and there was someone with a guitar, his head down, as though playing for only himself to hear.

As I was speculating about the possible reasons for this, my attention was suddenly caught by something that was happening to a wall nearby, the side of one of the buildings—it seemed to be soundlessly crumbling, and I thought now I must be out of my skull entirely. But it was not crumbling, it was simply oozing and changing color all over, *green*, and shades of green, changing from one instant to the next, from bottle-dark to shimmering-Nile; and this, in a strange and undulating way. Had we been in Rockefeller

Plaza or the Gilbert Hall of Science . . . but here there was no
accounting for it. But while I was assuring myself that first-rate
hallucinations are only doubted in retrospect . . . Emmanuel saw
it too. I knew he had seen it because he quickly leaned forward
and began changing the radio stations. Then he turned around
with an odd look on his face.

"Man, what is that? On that wall."

"Well," I said, "it must be *oil* . . . or something like that."

"Oil? Man, that's not oil. What's happening? That wall is *alive*."

"Listen, let me get out of the car for a minute," I said, perhaps
because of his tone. "I'm . . . curious, as a matter of fact, to see
what it is myself."

As I got out of the car, I felt that if I took my eyes off the wall
for a second, when I looked back it would have become just an
ordinary wall—so I kept looking at it, and walked toward it then,
very deliberately until I was there, leaning forward from two feet
away to peer at it; and while I must have known before, it was
not until my face was six inches from the wall that the field finally
did narrow to the truth, a single moving inch: a green roach. For,
true enough, that's how it was: alive—with a hundred thousand
green-winged flying roaches, ever moving, back and forth, sideways
and around, the wings in constant tremulous motion.

I looked around at the people then, sitting and leaning nearby.
I started to say something—but I was distracted to see that they
as well were covered with the roaches . . . not in quite the profu-
sion of the wall, but only for the reason that from time to time
they passed a hand in front of their faces, or shrugged. So I was
not too surprised when I looked down at myself and saw that *I*,
too, even as they and the immobile wall . . . and then I heard the
sound, that which had been in the air all along—a heavy ceaseless
whirling sound—and it was a sound which deepened intensely in
the dark distance of the night above and around, and it seemed to
say: '*You think there are quite a few of us down there—but if you
only knew how many of us are out here!*'

I thought I understood why the people weren't talking: because
the roaches would get in their mouths; or sleeping: because they
would crawl up their noses. But I may have really felt that it was
not so much because of this, but because of something else, past
or impending.

I stuck my trousers into my socks, and my hands into my pockets, and started back to the car. I had heard about the green flying roaches, how they settle on a town like locusts, and now I felt a gleeful anticipation, like the first of a party to swim an icy stream— toward springing the phenomenon on Pablo and Emmanuel. I thought it might be good to pretend to have scarcely noticed: 'What, those? Why, those are bugs, man. Didn't you ever see a bug before?'

When I got back to the car, however, I saw they had already surmised. Indeed, half the car was covered: the windshield wipers were sweeping, and inside, Pablo and Emmanuel were thumping wildly against the side-glass in trying to jar the creatures off.

"You finicky spics!" I shouted, snatching the door open and pretending to scoop and fan great armfuls in on them. Emmanuel jerked the door closed, and locked it; then he rolled the window a crack, and raised his mouth to it: "Man, what's happening?" he asked and quickly closed the glass.

I stood outside gesticulating them out and pretending to shout some emergency information. Pablo had started the car, and was racing the engine, sitting all hunched over the wheel; I got a glimpse of his maniacal frown and it occurred to me that an experience like this might be enough to snap his brain.

After a second, Emmanuel rolled down the window just a bit again.

"Listen, man," he said, "we are going to drive over nearer to the bar, so we can make it into the bar—you know?"

I looked around the square. So they had already found the bar. None of the buildings had signs on them, but I suppose it wasn't too difficult to tell. I saw it then, too, on the side we had come in, and next to it, a café.

"Let's go to the café first," I said, "that would be much cooler."

Emmanuel nodded, and as I turned away, I knew he would be relaying it to Pablo: 'The café first, man, that's much cooler.'

We reached the door of the café at the same time, and went right in.

It was an oblong room, with a hard dirt floor and raw-wood walls; there were about ten tables, set two by two the length of the place—bare boards they were, nailed to four sticks, and accompanied by benches. We sat at the first one, near the door.

The place was not quite empty. There was a man, who was evidently the proprietor, sitting at a table at the end of the room, and a man who was evidently drunk, sitting at a table on the opposite side. The man who was drunk had his head down on the table, resting it there as in sleep; his head kept sliding off the table, causing him to shake and curse it, and then to replace it carefully, while the proprietor sat across the room, watching him. I construed the situation as this: that the proprietor was ready to close, and was waiting for the drunk to leave; this possibility seemed strengthened by the way he simply remained seated when we came in, staring at us until we ordered some coffee. When he had brought it, he went directly back to his table and sat down, there to resume watch on the drunk. There seemed to be a point of genuine interest for him in watching the drunk's head slide off the table. I noticed that it did, in fact, drop lower each time.

There were fewer roaches here, though still enough so that you might want to keep your hand over the coffee, or, in drinking it, hold it as though you were lighting a cigarette in the wind. Pablo didn't drink his coffee, however, and didn't bother to protect it, so that after a minute there were four roaches in it, thrashing about, not unlike tiny birds at bath. Whenever one of the roaches was scooped out to the rim of the cup, it would crawl along for an instant, fluttering like a thing possessed, and then jump back in. Pablo was poking about in the cup with a matchstick, and both he and Emmanuel regarded the roaches with manifest concern. Pretty soon they were talking about them as though they could distinguish one from another. "Dig this one, man, he's swinging!"

"Don't hold him under, man, he can't make it like that!"

For my own part, I was content to watch the drunk and the proprietor, and this was as well, for, very soon, there was a bit of action. The drunk straightened up and started looking around the room. When his eyes reached our party they stopped, and after a minute, he leaned toward us and vomited.

I turned to get the proprietor's reaction to this, he who was sitting, somewhat more stiffly in his chair now, still staring at the drunk, and frowning. Then he gave a short humorless laugh, and said in measured tones:

"Let's-see-you-do-that-again."

This caused the drunk to stop looking at us, and to turn around to the proprietor as though he hadn't seen him before; and after staring straight at him, he laid his head back down on the table.

The proprietor slapped the table and gave several short, barking laughs, then resumed his scrutinous vigil.

During this vignette, Pablo and Emmanuel had abandoned their cups, which, I saw now, was crowded with the drowned.

"Well, that seems to be that," I said, "shall we go to the bar?"

"Man, let's cut out of this place," said Emmanuel.

Pablo, with deeply furrowed brow, was staring at where the man had been sick. Finally he shook his shoulders violently.

"Man, I dunt dig . . . *vomit!*"

"Are you kidding?" I said, "I happen to know that you *do* dig good greaser vomit."

The remark amused Emmanuel. "Ha-ha-ha! Good greaser vomit! Pablo digs good greaser vomit! That's too much, man!"

"Listen," said Pablo, leaning forward in serious confidence, "let's go to the bar now, I think there are groovy chicks there."

Like the café, the bar was unpretentious; but, where the café had been sparse and fairly lighted, the bar was close and steeped in shadow—sinister enough, as dark places go, but there wasn't much happening, at least not to meet the eye. A few men at the tables, a few beat hustlers at the bar.

My friends, being at the head of our party now, chose a table in the very heart of things, and we ordered tequila.

Emmanuel nodded toward the bar, straightening his tie.

"See, man," he said, giving me a little nudge, "dig the chicks."

"Sure," I said, "you're swinging." Pablo kept involuntarily clearing his throat and making sporadic little adjustments to his person and attire, even touching his hair once or twice. But after a moment or two, this fidgeting turned into annoyance that the girls, though they had seen us come in, had not made a play; so very soon, he and Emmanuel got up and took their drinks to the bar.

The girls, there were four of them, appeared to be extremely beat—two, by way of example, not wearing shoes—and were each holding a glass, untouched it seemed, of dark brown drink.

It was interesting to see them and my friends at a distance, not hearing, only seeing the gestures of hands and mouth, the flash of teeth and the tilted glass—man at an ancient disadvantage.

Sipping my tequila, I began to pretend I had settled down around here—quite near the toll bridge, actually. And a few days after my arrival, there had been a nasty run-in with the fat road-block greaser, who, it developed, was loathed and feared throughout the region, and was known as "Pigman." I heard the hushed whispers of the gathering crowd:

'Good Lord! The stranger's smashed his face away!'

'Did you see *that*—a single blow from the stranger sent the Pigman reeling!'

'Smashed his face entirely away! Good Lord! Etc., etc.'

I was going along with variations on this, when Pablo and Emmanuel came back to the table, sullen now and unrequited.

"Man, those chicks are the *worst*," Emmanuel said, as they sat down, "Let's cut out of this place."

Pablo was looking as though he might black out momentarily.

When I asked what had happened, it was to learn that the girls had said they weren't working tonight, that they *never* worked on Tuesday night (or whatever night it was—it wasn't Sunday) and to come back tomorrow.

I took another look at them, and whatever rationale was behind their refusal, they were evidently satisfied with it, though it was obvious they could have made their entire month off my madcap friends.

As we rose in leaving though, one of them raised her dark glass in a toast of promise, and tomorrow.

Now we were off for the second lost city: San Luiz. It would be ten or twelve miles along the road that had brought us, so we re-crossed the square and drove out on the opposite side we had come in.

The road here was just two tracks across a flat, rock-strewn plain. In five minutes we were in wilderness again, and after ten miles or so, when we finally reached the place where the town was supposed to be, the road stopped dead, at an extraordinary wire fence —a fence about 17 feet high and made of wire mesh the size of quarter-inch rope. We got out to have a look.

The fence was topped by four running strands of an odd-looking barbed wire, jutting outward, and along this, at intervals, was a large, white, professional sign which said in Spanish:

KEEP OUT
VERY HIGH VOLTAGE
DANGER OF DEATH

Beyond the fence, a trace of the old road's continuation was visible in our headlights for about fifty feet, before it disappeared into the night. On our side of the fence the road branched out left and right, and it ran alongside the fence in both directions for as far as one could see.

With the idea now of driving *around* the fence and picking up the road again, we got back into the car and took the right branch, following it until, shortly, at a ravine, it turned away from the fence and back toward the town. Retracing our route, we took the other branch of the road; again, after an eighth of a mile or so, the road turned away from the fence and back to the town, while the fence itself disappeared in the heavy growth.

Here it seemed to me that one might follow the fence on foot, and while I didn't think we could actually do it, having no flashlight, I was eager to try. So we left the car and walked alongside the fence, on a field of rock and stubble, but it was immediately so dense as to be almost impassable. The thicket grew right into the fence, and the fence had evidently been there for quite a while. Emmanuel soon turned back toward the car.

"It's a drag, man," he said.

Pablo, who had wandered off to the left, kept stopping and brushing at his clothes.

"Man, what is this? This is all scratch."

Finally he stopped completely and began striking matches; he seemed to be examining something in his hand. I beat my way through the brush to him.

"Man, this is bad," he said, "this is all scratch."

He was examining what appeared to be an invisible scratch on his hand.

"I couldn't see it," I said as the match died, "is it bleeding?"

"*Bleeding?*" He struck another match. "Man, is it *bleeding? Where?*"

We both peered at his hand.

"It looks all right," I said, "doesn't it?"

"Man, I dunt *dig* this place? What is this?"

I suggested that he go back to the car and I would try to follow the fence a little farther.

I had become obsessed by the mystery of it. What was it behind this fence, in the vast area where one town used to exist and no town was supposed to? The fabulous estate of a mad billionaire? The testing ground for some fantastic weapon? Why had not the sign proclaimed the source of its authority? Why had it not strengthened itself with 'Private Property,' or 'Government Property'? No, here was a case of security so elaborate, so resolved upon, that even the power behind it would remain secret. Whatever it was—was so dreadful it was not supposed to exist.

Many are familiar with the story that infant-mortality (in childbirth) is not the figure it is represented to be—and that the discrepancy between the actual figure and the statistics are teratological cases—with the consequence that in every Christian country there is a monster-home, wholly secret, maintained by permanent appropriation, in the form of a "hidden-rider," self-perpetuating, and never revealed by the breakdown of any budget.

As I mused on this, moving cautiously along the edge of the black fence, and now at a considerable distance from the car, I stumbled against a rock and fell; I grabbed at the dry brush, but the terrain had changed, dropping away sharply from the fence, as did I with it now, about 15 feet down into a small gully. Here there was even less light than above, and as I sat there in pitch blackness, momentarily rubbing my forehead, I had a sudden uneasiness of something very menacing nearby and moving closer. And, as suddenly, I knew what it was.

Wild dogs have existed in Mexico for so long that they are a breed apart; the dissimilarity between them and ordinary dogs is remarkable. Wild dogs do not bark; the sound they produce comes from the uppermost part of the throat—a frantic and sustained snarl, and the strangeness of it is accentuated by its being directed *down*, for the reason that they run with their heads very low, nose almost touching the ground. Even in a pack, with blood dripping hot from their muzzles, they keep their backs arched and their tails between their legs. Their resemblance, in many ways, is less to the dog than to the hyena; they do not spring—their instinct is to chase a thing, biting at it, until it falls to break a leg . . . where-upon they hit it like piranha fish, taking bites at random, not going for the throat, but flailing it alive. It is improbable that wild dogs will attack a person who holds his ground—at least, so I was told later—so that it was a rather serious mistake that I began to run.

Through the snarls, before they caught me, I could hear the teeth snapping, as though they were so possessed by rage as to bite even the air itself. I half stumbled and turned when the first one bit the back of my leg and clung to it, in a loathsome knot, like a tarantula; I kicked it away violently, but so much more in a fit of repulsion than in adroitness that I took a nifty pratfall, there to grope for a frantic second or two for a rock or stick of defense, before scrambling to my feet again while being bitten again on the same leg. Exactly how many there were I don't know—at least six. I was bitten two or three times more, on the legs, before I fell again; and the bites, having come at just the moment before I fell, gave me the strong impression that they were now *closing in.*

But abruptly the scene was flooded with white light and the scream of twisting mambo, as our car came lurching and crashing down the ravine, headlights bouncing; then it suddenly stalled.

For an instant the action became a frozen tableau, the dogs petrified in strange attitudes of attack, and myself crouching at bay—a tableau at which my friends in the car simply sat and stared.

'Man, what's he doing?' I imagined Emmanuel saying, 'dig those weird *dogs.*'

And by the interior light of the car I could see Pablo's expres-sion of exasperated amazement.

I was on the verge of shouting urgent instructions about com-pleting my rescue, when Pablo, apparently at the end of his tether, began honking the horn wildly and lunged the car forward with a terrible roar, lights flashing—and the dogs scattered into the night.

"Come, man," said Pablo, gesturing impatiently, "we cut out now."

There was no sign of life as we crossed the square at Corpus Christi, so we drove on to the outskirts of Mexico City where we managed to rouse a doctor. He gave me a shot of tetanus, a cou-ple of sutures, and some morphia tablets—which I had to share with Pablo and Emmanuel, after the doctor indignantly refused

to sell them a hundred goofballs. Pablo was more indignant about
it than the doctor, and as we drove away, he leaned out the window and shook his fist at the dark building:

"Go to devil, you greaser quack!" This broke Emmanuel up, but
we got home without further incident.

My friends left the pension a few days after that, on a Sunday.
I came out to the car and we shook hands lightly.

"You ought to make it," Emmanuel said. He had a thin, unlit
cigar in his mouth. "Swinging chicks in Guadalajara, man."

"Guadalajara? I thought you were going to Acapulco."

"No, man, I don't think we'll go there. I don't think anything's
happening there. Why? *You* want to go to *Acapulco?*"

"No," I said.

"How about Guadalajara? Crazy town, man."

"No, thanks."

Emmanuel nodded.

"Okay, man," he said.

Pablo raced the engine and leaned over the wheel, turning his
head toward me; he looked like a progressive young missionary in
his white linen suit and dark glasses.

"Later, man," he said.

"Yeah, man," said Emmanuel, "later."

"Later," I said.

They took off with a roar. At the corner, a very old woman with
a great black shawl over her head, started across the street without
looking. Pablo didn't slow down or perceptibly alter his course,
and as she passed in front of the car, it looked like he missed
her by the length of a matchstick. She hardly seemed to notice it
though, only slowly turned her head after them, but by then they
were almost out of sight.

So that was that; and the point of it all is, they left me the map
—that is, should anyone ever care to make it, I mean, down to the
big fence on that road out of Axotle.

JESSAMYN WEST was born in Indiana in 1907, and has studied at Whittier College and in England. She is the author of *Mirror for the Sky*, an opera based on an original conception of Raoul Pène DuBois for portraying the life of Audubon; *To See a Dream*, a book of reminiscences; and novels, *Cress Delahanty*, *The Witch Diggers*, and *The Friendly Persuasion*, for which she also wrote the screen play.

The Picnickers

In their bedroom under the roof, where Jess and Eliza slept, the July morning was already warm at 5.30. Though he hadn't roused her when he got up, Eliza knew before she opened her eyes that her husband was no longer beside her. She awakened slowly, listening . . . "What do I expect to hear?" she asked herself sleepily. The answer brought her awake with a start: gunfire. She had been listening, even in her sleep, for gunfire. Why, on a farm in southern Indiana . . . Then she remembered, all at once, not piece by piece. The whole of the day before crowded her mind. Yesterday there *had* been gunfire . . . and she and Jess had listened with their very veins . . . not out of any fear for themselves but because their eldest was off with the Home Guard, every one of his Quaker principles thrown to the wind, trying to save Vernon from Morgan, the raider.

As her memory of Josh and their fear for him came to her, Eliza threw back the already too warm sheet and hurried across the rag carpet to the windows. She felt thirsty for the reassurance of the known landscape, parched for it. The air outside the window was cooler than that inside the room and she leaned as far out as she dared, grateful for the freshness. Rolling summer fields, wheat yellow, corn green. Cows, already milked, standing switchtail in the sycamore shade. Summer haze in the hollows mingling with morning mist off the Muscatatuck. Crows flapping by, early to work. An old hen, deceived by early warmth, letting off a premature mid-morning cackle. A few Juneberries, escaped the children by some miracle, hanging drawn and dried like summer raisins on the June-berry tree. Nothing changed. Nothing bearing the signs of disaster. And there had been a disaster yesterday, had there not?

It was odd for Eliza to ask herself such a question. It showed what the day before had done to her. You do not bear five chil-dren, become a recorded Quaker minister, and survive twenty years as Jess Birdwell's wife without knowing a disaster when you see it. Yet she was uncertain as to the proper name for yesterday's hap-penings; yesterday, toward the end of the day, "picnic," instead of "disaster," had seemed as good a name as any. Labe had found his brother Josh, who, except for a head cracked in a fall over a cliff, was none the worse for the wear. None the worse physically, anyway. Spiritually was another matter, for Josh was convinced that by his warlike valor he had single-handed saved Vernon from the enemy. And for any outward indication Jess believed the same. Jess had welcomed his prodigal home with a few prayers and many helpings of food. When she had rebuked Jess for giving Josh his best horse to ride off to war on, Jess had quoted George Fox to her. When Penn asked Fox what he should do, now that he had become a Quaker, with the sword he was accustomed to wear, Fox had replied, "Wear it as long as thee can."

That quotation had been a mistake on Jess's part. "Fox didn't," Eliza reminded Jess, "*give* Penn the sword. Nor let him go off to a real war with it, telling him to lop off heads and arms as long as he could. That's what thee did, sending Josh off armed, on thy fast horse."

This conversation had taken place before Josh's return. And it had reminded both Jess and Eliza that lopping off was a two-way street. What Josh could do, he could also suffer. And being the boy he was, to suffer would more likely be his fate. Jess had turned away, sick at heart, she knew. But she had let him go without a word of comfort. There was no honest way for a Quaker to let his son go off to fight, and at the same time be comfortable—and she wasn't the woman to try to deceive any man, let alone Jess.

But after Josh's safe return Jess had become more and more comfortable; and, when the children had finally gone to bed, every one of them was in a war fever of some kind: Mattie, proud of

Gardiner Bent, her Methodist beau, who was a full-time soldier; Labe, resisting soldiering but banged up from a private fistfight he had won; Josh, with his cracked skull, evidence of his warlike courage; Little Jess, only eight, but in a swivet to land a blow somewhere on someone himself.

After the children were all asleep, she and Jess had stood on the back porch, breathing the cool and the peace of the evening. She, with two minds about the day's events: rejoicing in Josh's return, but downcast that he had gone at all; and Jess, for all of his talk of how bright the stars were and how well the peaches were ripening, was not, she could tell, completely easy in his mind either. Jess, when happy, never lacked for a subject for conversation, particularly late at night when everyone else was ready for sleep. But last night he had finally found nothing to say. And it was in this silence that he had heard the sounds down by the springhouse, and, investigating, had found the poor Southern boy.

Jess had carried him into the kitchen. The boy had been hurt several days earlier at Dutch Ford and since then had been hiding, living off the country and trying to catch up with Morgan. He had been trying to find something to eat in the springhouse when he had fallen down the steps and reopened his wound. It was this fall and the moans he had tried to stifle which Jess had heard. In the beginning the boy was in too much pain and too hungry to worry about being caught by the enemy. And after Jess had bound up his leg, and she had fed him, he was too worn out and too sleepy to care. They had half led, half carried him to the spare room, and, before Jess could get him undressed, he was already sound asleep.

The arrival of the rebel boy had done wonders for Jess's peace of mind. After he had put him to bed, Jess had become as talkative as ever, his qualms about the day's events washed away in the flood of his happiness at being able to care for one of the enemy. That proved, didn't it, that he was free of hate? Eliza didn't know what it proved. But Jess, cleaning up the kitchen after the bandaging and feeding, had hummed as carefree as if the morning's gunfire had been nothing more than the sounds of an Independence Day celebration. Or real gunfire, but of no consequence, because he *didn't* hate.

He had stuffed the last of the soiled bandages into the cookstove, and had momentarily paused in his humming. "I'll set some buckwheat batter for breakfast," he said. "We'll have a hungry crew on our hands in the morning. How about my bringing up a crock of sausage meat from the springhouse? Buckwheat cakes and sausage gravy? How's that strike thee, Eliza?"

It struck Eliza as something she had no heart for. If Jess was in a picnic mood, she couldn't stop him. But she couldn't pretend to share it, either. She went upstairs to bed leaving all the breakfast preparation to him.

These were the events of the day before. Thinking about them, it took her a half hour instead of ten minutes to dress. It was 6.00 when she came downstairs. When she opened the kitchen door she saw that the picnic mood of the day before was still in full swing. Jess, in one of her checkered aprons, motioned to her with the griddle cake turner to come in and to be quiet. When she had closed the door behind her, he said, "No use rousing up all the others. Jimmy and Little Jess are keeping me busy as it is."

"Jimmy?" she asked, and Jess, like a schoolmaster with a backward pupil, pointed to the soldier boy.

Little Jess and Jimmy were seated at the end of the table next to the stove. The gravy bowl was already half empty and the sorghum molasses pitcher needed refilling.

"Good morning, boys," Eliza said.

Little Jess, who was in his own home, and besides had a mouthful of buckwheat cake and gravy, didn't reply. The boy, Jimmy, said, "Good morning, ma'am."

He looked worse to Eliza than he had the night before. In morning light she could see that the rising above his left temple was big as a turkey egg, but less solid, discolored and wobbly. She looked away quickly.

"I thought thee'd like to sleep late this morning," she told him.

"I'm out of the habit of sleeping after daylight." He appeared to think this over. "Out of the habit of sleeping, you might say. Anyway, I was hungrier than I was sleepy this morning, ma'am."

"Thee could've had thy breakfast in bed."

The boy looked at Eliza, amazed. "I ain't sick, ma'am." He had lifted his head quickly and the rising on his head trembled.

Eliza, courteously ignoring the ugly rising, motioned to his leg. "I been hit," he said, "but I ain't sick."

"Doesn't thy head hurt?" she couldn't help asking.

"I know that bump don't look nice, ma'am," he said, "but it's a real good sign. I got a shell splinter in there and it's working its way out. It's just like a splinter in your thumb you can't dig out. It's got to fester its way out. Don't cause me no pain. It did at first, but it don't any more. My leg hurts. That's a good sign too," he said. "It's beginning to draw. That's a sign of healing."

"Did a doctor tell thee all this . . . about your head and leg?" Eliza asked.

"Doctor?" He repeated what she had said as if she had spoken in a foreign language. Then he understood. "I was with Morgan, ma'am, and we been riding real hard. If you get hit, Morgan don't get off his horse and fetch you to a doctor." Jimmy laughed, and in spite of herself Eliza looked again at that soft-shelled, egg-shaped rising. "No, not Morgan," he said quietly. "No, ma'am, you ain't with Morgan for your health. That's a dead sure cinch."

Eliza didn't need any argument to convince her of that. If Jimmy had ever had any health, he had lost it a long time ago. He was rawboned, though the bones he had were small. Under his tan was the yellow of fever. His blue eyes were back in his head like an old man's. His hair, which in health had been black, was as dingy and matted as an old worn-out buffalo robe. Eliza didn't know where he got the energy to eat and talk as he was doing. From fever, probably. But back of the courtesy and the conversation, the "yes, ma'ams," and the apparent willingness to answer all questions, Eliza saw a constant wariness. He was practising half-forgotten parlor tricks. A sudden sound or movement and his sunken blue eyes were hard as stones. The skin would tighten across his sharp little jaws. Then he would go back to his eating, spooning sausage gravy onto buckwheat cakes, like a mannerly fox or stoat.

"How old is thee, Jimmy?" Eliza asked.

"Nineteen." He saw her surprise. "I know I'm kind of runty," he admitted. "Two years with Morgan's kind of shook me down in the saddle. A good thing. You ain't such a good target down low." Then he laughed again and touched his forehead. "Sat up too high once, though. I sure did."

"We'll get thee to a doctor this afternoon, Jimmy."

Jimmy, all fox now, put down his fork quickly. "No," he said.

"I don't need any doctor. I'll stay right here if it's all the same to you."

Jess, who had been keeping the supply of griddle cakes coming, intervened. "Eliza, I've got a cake here for thee."

"I'm not hungry," she said. "I'll bake while thee eats." She poured herself a cup of black coffee and managed it with one hand, the cake turner with the other.

At the table Jess began, and Jimmy unbelievably continued, to eat. Little Jess, a knife and fork winner himself in lesser company, gave up, pushed back his plate, and settled down to a steady stare at the Johnny Reb . . . a man, Eliza knew, Little Jess had expected to carry some sign of the nether regions upon him: a brimstone smell, or even horns. Maybe he thought that Jimmy's rising was horns beginning to sprout.

"Can thee give a Rebel yell?" Little Jess asked.

For a minute Eliza saw the boy thought Little Jess was making fun of him. Then he said, "Is that what you Yankees call it?"

"What do you Rebels call it?"

"We don't call ourselves Rebels."

Little Jess wasn't interested in the names for things. "Can thee give the yell?" he persisted.

"Sure," Jimmy said.

"Will thee give it now?"

"Now? No, it wouldn't be right, here in the house."

"Couldn't thee give a quiet Rebel yell?"

"You can't give that yell quiet . . . any more than you can shoot a quiet cannon."

This gave Little Jess ideas about an even more interesting subject. "Did thee ever . . ." he began; but Eliza stopped that question before he could finish it.

"Fill up the woodbox, Little Jess," she said. "Now, this minute."

Little Jess, no soldier, still knew a command when he heard it. He left the table promptly. Eliza, when Jimmy had finally pushed back his plate, urged him, if he wouldn't see a doctor, to go back to bed. But he refused to budge, too proud perhaps to show any weakness before his enemies. All his signs were good, he said again, head easy, wound drawing, belly tight as a drum. He tilted his chair against the wall and looked at her and Jess and the room: house, furniture, and civilians—all curious and faintly ridiculous to him after two years on a horse's back. He answered Jess's questions, though plainly puzzled by many, without hesitation. Jess wasn't as simple as Little Jess. Rebel yells didn't interest him, but Rebels did. Where was he from? What was he fighting for? He was from Plum Tree, South Carolina. And as to what he was fighting for, Eliza had heard the same story word for word from Josh a dozen times in the last two months: honor and freedom and self-preservation. The Mason-Dixon line hadn't changed that story a whit.

She cleared the table, washed the dishes, swept the floor around the two men. Jess lifted his feet to make way for the broom, but didn't pause in his talk. By midmorning she had fresh peach pies in the oven. The heat from the cookstove, which she was keeping fired up, would surely drive them out, she thought. Jess gave no sign of feeling it. He was making a day of it, celebrating something, peace or victory or Josh's return or the enemy made welcome. He was waiting for the surprise the children would have when they finally got up and saw who had spent the night with them. He was anticipating the love feast they'd all celebrate at dinner, North and South united around his table. Eliza, stringing green beans for a mess of succotash, listened to the talk and, through the opened window, to the summer sounds: the regular creak of the windmill and the papery ruffle of the big-leafed maples. Over the smell of the baking pies, she caught whiffs from the Prairie Rose now in full bloom, and, over that, all the mingling of scents of fruity ripenings from Jess's orchards. She could see the big cannon-ball clouds at the horizon and above them the arch of deep summer blue. Stretch her senses in every direction, there was nothing but felicity; nevertheless she could not manage happiness. Children at home and in health; enemy routed; Jess in high fettle. She counted her blessings; and, like women at weddings, had to squeeze back her tears, for at the heart of the tulle and the orange blossoms there is a core of sadness: and the fairer the bride, the higher the wedding cake, the greater the cause for sorrow; for life, which is going to contradict these things, will be, by contrast, the darker.

As if to tell her how silly tears were on such a day, she heard singing. The trees hid arrivals from her sight, but Little Jess brought in the news with his armload of wood.

"Enoch," he announced in great excitement, "is bringing home a prisoner."

Enoch was the Birdwell hired man and hadn't been, insofar as Eliza knew, mixed up with the fighting.

Jimmy, at the word "prisoner," brought his chair down on all four legs. Jess, stopping his talking to listen, said, "Mighty happy prisoner, sounds like."

Eliza, who could see the porch, said, "It's no prisoner. It's Clate Henry."

Eliza often thought Jess could have a hired hand a little less talkative and self-assured than Enoch. But Enoch came in now, meechin as you please, holding Clate Henry up with one hand and quieting him down with the other.

"You folks know Clate Henry, don't you?" Enoch asked. "From over Sand Creek way? He's been in the Guard for the last couple of days."

Clate Henry was a straw-colored, pudgy little man. Eliza didn't know a thing about guard duty, but she'd think twice before she'd give Clate a job of egg-hunting after dark. Clate sat down suddenly and looked surprised.

"What's the matter with him?" Eliza asked Enoch.

"He's a little under the weather at the minute," Enoch, as slick with words as Jess when he wanted to be, answered.

Clate, as if embarrassed by the silence which followed this, lifted his round face, shut his round eyes, and began to sing.

> "Oh Lily up and Lily down,
> And lay them on the side wheels."

He delivered the two lines loudly but plaintively, then stopped suddenly as if he'd received an order.

There followed another silence, which Little Jess finally took care of. "That don't make sense," he said.

Ordinarily, Eliza would have rebuked Little Jess for such discourtesy. Under the circumstances it seemed a mild observation. She, herself, said, "Enoch, Clate Henry is drunk."

At the sound of his name Clate Henry roused up for an encore.

> "Oh Lily up and Lily down
> And lay them on the side wheels."

He kept his eyes shut; for a man as small, round, and pale as he was, he had resounding voice.

"Is that all he knows?" Little Jess asked Enoch.

"No," Enoch said shortly, "it ain't." He turned, as if fearful that the question would refresh Clate's memory, to Clate himself. "Hush up, Clate," he said. "Hush up your noise."

Clate opened his eyes and looked at his friend as if he couldn't believe his ears. Eliza looked at Jess, waiting for him to take charge. Jess didn't say a word, he didn't make a sign. So she herself spoke.

"Enoch," she said, "thee knows I won't have a drunkard in the house."

"Clate ain't a drunkard, ma'am," Enoch protested. "He's a farmer and not used to fighting—or drinking either. If I turn him loose he'll just do himself harm. He was lost for the last two nights as it was."

"Lost? How could he be lost? He's lived around here all of his life."

Clate roused himself to answer Eliza. "The first night," he said, "I was lost because I was scared and running and hiding. Then somebody offered me a jug of corn likker to get me over being scared. From then on I was drunk *and* scared. But I was lost both nights. Where am I now?" he asked, looking around wildly.

Eliza would have nothing to do with such play acting. "Thee knows where thee is, Clate Henry. This isn't the first time thee's been here. Thee's drunk."

There was no arguing with such a man. He agreed with, then enlarged upon, her accusation. "Drunk," he repeated. "Dead drunk and sick to boot. I ain't real stout, ma'am. Fleshy, but that's not the same. I've never slept out of my own bed a night in my life— let alone on the ground. There was a heavy dew the last two nights. I've got a weak chest. They say summer nights are short. They're long. Longer than any winter night I ever knowed."

Eliza didn't feel melted by his story. Her boy had been out those nights too; one of them spent at the bottom of a cliff with a cracked skull. *He* hadn't taken to corn likker.

"Why did thee join the Guard," she asked, "in the first place?"

"I didn't know my own nature, ma'am," Clate said sadly. "I wasn't prepared for what I'd see and hear. I wasn't prepared for the screeching."

"Screeching?" Eliza asked. "Josh didn't mention any screeching."

"He's deef then. Or calloused. Them Rebs kept up a-screeching like hoot owls fresh from hell. Excuse the bad language, ma'am. But they're bloodthirsty. They're white Comanches."

Without warning Clate Henry cut loose with a couple of terrible screeches. Hoot owls and Comanches would've turned tail at the racket he made. Eliza would never have guessed the pursy little fellow had such sounds in him. She felt as stunned as though he had struck her a blow.

Clate appeared well satisfied. "Bloodcurdling, ain't it?"

But Jimmy wasn't stunned and his blood wasn't curdled. He leaned forward in his chair, his rising livid. "That's no Rebel yell," he said.

"How do you know?" Clate asked.

"He's a Rebel," Little Jess said. "That's how he knows."

Clate stared at Jimmy for a few seconds; then he closed his eyes and began once again to sing.

> "Oh Lily up and Lily down
> And lay them on the side wheels
> And everytime the wheel goes round . . ."

Enoch took his friend by the shoulders and shook him out of harmonizing. "What he needs," he told Eliza, "is a pot of strong coffee, hot and black. Hush up," he told Clate, who was showing signs of continued melody.

Before Eliza could get the pot on the stove, Clate had collapsed, head on his arms and arms on the table. At that minute Labe, still tucking his shirt in his pants, appeared in the doorway, blinking around at everyone sleepily.

"A diller-a-dollar, a ten o'clock scholar," Jess greeted him.

Labe smiled. It was no trick to make Labe smile. He had a mop of curly tow-colored hair, a black eye, and a dingy unwashed look. He was big-framed, man-sized, but his seventeen-year-old face showed that he hadn't met any man-sized troubles yet.

"I thought I heard something," he said.

"If thee's up," Jess said, "thee heard something."

"It was a Rebel yell," Little Jess said.

"No," said Jimmy.

"Who's he?" Labe asked, staring at Jimmy.

"A Rebel," Little Jess said proudly.

"He give that yell?"

"No," said Jimmy.

"Where'd he *come* from?"

"He come from falling down our springhouse steps."

Labe was much too polite a boy to say, "What was he doing on our springhouse steps?" Instead, taking in head and leg, he said, "Must've been a pretty bad fall."

"He got *them* in the war," Little Jess explained. "He's one of Morgan's men."

"*Was* one of them," Enoch corrected him.

"Am," Jimmy said. "I'll catch up with him. Men are away a month and catch up. I've only been away a week."

"And every time the wheels go round . . ." Clate muttered.

Labe turned his attention to Clate's collapsed figure. "Who's he?"

"Home Guard," Little Jess replied promptly.

"That's Clate Henry from out Sand Creek way," Jess told him. "You've seen him before."

Clate moaned or snored. "What's the matter with him?" Labe asked. "He hurt too?"

Little Jess was happy to give him the answer. "He's soused," he said.

With that word Eliza ended the picnic. Picnic was one thing, but circus was another. She was not going to have a circus in her kitchen. Drunkenness was no subject for fun. Wars, simply because they had moved from your neighborhood to someone else's, were no cause for rejoicing. Under her roof were three men who had been ready to kill: Josh, spared that evil by falling over a cliff; Clate saved by cowardice; and Jimmy maybe not saved at all. If you wanted a picture of war and death, she thought, take Jimmy. His own mother, like as not, wouldn't recognize him. He had shed his humanness. He was shrunk down to bullet size. He carried a thing on his head that looked like the grave. The bones of his head were saved by the thinnest of coverings from being a skull. Yet he was a boy. She tried to find in the back of his sunken eyes the boy he had been, before he rode off with Morgan. She turned on him every bit of motherliness and love she had. She had as well said "son" to a rock. She was an enemy, a part of a household whose people had been out to kill him and who called him "Reb."

"Get out of my kitchen," she said to all of them but Jimmy. Jess turned to her in surprise, but she cut him off before he could say a word. "I need the room for cooking."

It wasn't true. She could cook in a nest of them. Rebelling against ugliness and blindness, she had lied. So far as she knew, none of them was a liar.

"It's not true," she said. "You're not in my way."

But Jess herded them out. She and Jess were as divided as the states, and she let him go without attempting to explain. Jimmy rose with the rest of them, but some weakness in head or leg made him hang onto the chairback. Outside, Eliza could see the others settling down in the side garden where there was a lawn-swing and a hammock slung between two cedars. There, on the hottest days, the air in the clumps of cedar needles moved with a mountainy sound and smell. Clate was singing again. The picnic was not much interrupted.

Eliza did not make the mistake of saying "bed" again to Jimmy. "If thee stayed inside, thee might help me later," she told him. "Come on into the dining room. Thee'll be out of my way and handy for table setting later."

She went to him but didn't offer to help him. A pulse was beating in his rising like a misplaced heart.

"This way," she said, and went, without looking behind her, into the dining room which opened out of the kitchen. It was a long narrow room, papered green, and dark now with blinds pulled to keep out the sun and discourage flies.

She turned and Jimmy was on her heels. "Thee can sit there," she said, pointing to a narrow black leather lounge with a built-in hump at one end to support the head. She said "sit," but no one could sit on that narrow leather thing and Jimmy, once seated, lay back against the bulge of the built-in pillow.

"You let me know if there's anything I can do to help you," Jimmy said, as if this readiness excused his stretching out.

"I will," Eliza said.

The voices of the picnickers could be heard. "I hope you didn't think that yipping was the real thing," Jimmy called to her.

"It scared me," Eliza said. "I suppose that's what it's supposed to do."

"No," Jimmy said. "We ain't trying to scare anybody." In the gloom Eliza could see the little fox skull part at the mouth, and yellow teeth, whiter than yellow skin, show in a smile. "We don't need to, once they know Morgan's around."

"Why do you do it, then?" Eliza asked.

"We do it," Jimmy said, "because it's what we feel like doing. We feel better doing it."

He would've talked more about it; Eliza, however, didn't want to hear any more about it. She went back to her work, but Jimmy called after her, "That's why I wouldn't do it. You can't do it except *then*."

"Then" was what Eliza wanted to forget. She went upstairs and wakened Josh and Mattie. Josh came down to breakfast, his shame at blundering over a cliff less, and his pride in being one of the defenders greater. Fear had sent Josh toward the enemy and Clate Henry away from them. But fear was the master of both. Mattie came downstairs, hung uneating over her cakes, her throat too thick with worry about Gardiner Bent to swallow.

"There's a wounded Southern boy in the dining room," Eliza told her children. "He's lost from Morgan. He stumbled in here last night. Maybe you'd like to talk to him."

Neither one wanted to. Josh felt embarrassed at the idea of sitting down and talking to someone he'd spent a couple of months screwing up his courage to take a shot at. He felt funny enough already, falling over a cliff, without finding out that he'd taken all of his trouble and done all of his shaking because of some poor, starved, done-in, bunged-up Johnny. This was the very reason Eliza wanted him to see the boy. It would take some of the false pride out of his sails; make him see how big Goliath really was, this poor boy of bones and festerings. But Josh wouldn't budge. He didn't want to see any Rebs who weren't fire-eaters. And Mattie wouldn't go either.

"If Gard gets home safe," she said, "I'll see him."

"All right," Eliza said. "Outside, both of you. Out with the pic-nickers."

"Picnickers?" Mattie asked.

"Look," Eliza said, and she pointed to the side garden. There they were, spread around under the cedars amid the phlox and the snowball bushes, the lawn-swing creaking, the hammock swaying. "What's thy name for them?"

Josh looked at his mother and left. Mattie put a hand on her mother's arm. "Come on out, Mama," she urged. "Isn't thee glad Josh is home? And that Vernon's saved from Morgan?"

"Morgan's in some other town today."

"But, Mama, thee can't be sad for every town in the county."

"I don't know why not," Eliza said.

There was sorrow in her, though whether enough for every town in the county she wasn't sure. But she didn't want to make any big claims. Mattie made a pitcher of lemonade and took it outside, but Eliza stayed in her kitchen working, halfway between Jimmy and the picnic—able to see one and talk to the other. She took her pies out of the oven and put her light bread in. She scoured the case knives with brick dust and scalded all the milk pans and put them in the sun to sweeten. Blackbirds were at the cherries. White butterflies hovered over the little cabbage heads. The Dominique rooster's colors were faded in the heat. She picked enough Summer Sweetings for a dish of applesauce.

Little Jess came in for more lemonade. When she made it, he said, "Can I take a glass to Jimmy?"

Eliza poured the glass. "If he's asleep, let him sleep. He needs that more than lemonade."

Little Jess tiptoed in and Jimmy must have been awake.

"I brought thee a glass of lemonade."

There was a silence followed by, "Does thee want another?"

"Why do you folks say 'thee'?" Jimmy asked.

"We're Quakers."

"What's Quakers?"

"A church."

"Like Baptists?"

"Is thee a Baptist?"

"Yes."

"We don't believe in being baptized."

"What do you believe in?"

Eliza waited.

"God."

"So do Baptists. You're no different from us."

"We're different," Little Jess said. "We don't believe in fighting."

Jimmy hooted. "Who don't? Your Mama?"

"Father don't."

"He didn't keep his son home from fighting."

"Labe don't believe in it."

"How'd he get that black eye?"

"That was a private fight, not war."

"What was your hired man doing?"

"Saving Vernon from Morgan."

"Same as me. Saving the South from the Yanks. If I say 'thee' I reckon I'll be a Quaker. Little Jess, will thee bring me some more lemonade?"

Little Jess brought the glass out to Eliza to be refilled. "He said 'thee' to me," he complained.

Eliza was short with him. "He can if he wants to," she said.

After Little Jess went outside with his lemonade, Eliza took a piece of warm peach pie into Jimmy. The boy was lying back, flat as the hump would let him, one hand picking at the nub of the rag carpet. "I'm too full of lemonade—to eat any more right now," he said.

Eliza shooed a couple of big black flies away from him.

"Those buzzards have smelled me out," he said.

"It's my pie they smell," Eliza said. She apologized to him. "I'm sorry thee had to get in a house that's so mixed up with the war."

"That's what you got to expect in wartime, ma'am."

"Not in a Quaker house," she said.

She decided to give the family their dinner outside. It was hotter out there and succotash, light bread, and peach pie could've been served easier at a table. But if she set the table Jimmy would get up and she didn't want to disturb him. Besides, in serving the meal picnic style there'd be so much running back and forth and waiting on, she'd have an excuse not to sit down with them—and no excuses to make, either, for not doing so. She was disturbed by her reluctance to break bread with her own family—but she had it; and once they were attended to she sat down with Jimmy.

"You got some kind of an old rag I could have?" Jimmy asked. "This here thing's begun to run."

She brought him clean cloths, saved from worn-out pillow shams, and would've brought him a basin and water too, but he wouldn't hear to it. "Don't want to get in the habit of washing again," he said. "I'd just have to break it. I'll be well in no time now, soon as the corruption drains off. That's what's been making me dauncey. It's been poisoning my system."

There was a smell now and Eliza would've liked to shut it away from her kitchen. "Does my clattering out here bother thee, Jimmy? Could thee doze, if I closed the door?"

"No, ma'am," he said. "Leave it open. It sounds good. I ain't heard anybody stirring around in a kitchen for quite a spell."

After a while he called to her, "What's that click-clack I hear?"

Eliza went to the dining room door. "That's the windmill," she said.

"I don't feel any wind moving."

"The windmill catches it when we can't feel it."

As they listened to the windmill, the voices of those on the side lawn came through the opened window—still eager and rejoicing in midafternoon, recalling each incident, real or reported, of Morgan's routing.

"They sound happy," Jimmy said. "All safe at home and happy."

"Yes," Eliza said.

"Like a party."

"That's what it sounds like."

"I could watch your cooking if you want to set outside for a spell."

She felt more at home with Jimmy, with his wounds and dirt and bad smell, than with those high-spirited ones out there.

"No," she said. "I feel like cooking this afternoon."

"What's for supper?" Jimmy asked.

"What strikes thy fancy?"

"Corn bread," Jimmy said, "greens, and custard pie."

"This time of year, I can't manage greens, but the corn bread and custard pie I can."

"I forgot what time of year it was," Jimmy said.

She was glad for the need of cooking, of keeping the stove going, of stirring and peeling, mixing and washing. Sometimes she stood at the back door and looked at the view which for twenty years had sustained her as much as food. Jess was in it. Jess had made it, except for the rise and dip of hills beyond the farm's boundaries. Apple orchard, berry patch, vegetable garden, snowball bushes and syringa, and a graveled path edged with bleeding heart and sweet alyssum. She couldn't joy in what she saw without taking joy in Jess too. Maybe what made Jess such a good nurseryman made him a man not easily separated from the joy of others—even when they were wrong. When she wasn't with Jess, she imagined conversations with him. Now she could hear him in defense of himself quoting more George Fox to her; reminding her of the time when George, no smoker, had put a proffered pipe in his mouth to show "he had unity with all creation." "That's all I'm doing, Eliza," she could hear him say, "out here with the returned warriors showing them I have unity with all creation." In her imagined conversation she was able to have, what wasn't always so easy when she was face to face with Jess, the last word. "What thee's showing them thee has, Jess Birdwell, is unity with all destruction."

She felt better after that, the way Jimmy said he did after he gave the yell. It wasn't said to put Jess in his place; but it did tell her something about hers. Behind her, the kitchen clock struck 5.00. The afternoon was ending. A wind out of the southeast had sprung up, changing the windmill's tune and spattering the pathway with the green-white litter of broken snowball blossoms. Away off westward past Jess's handiwork, where the joining of Sand Creek and the Muscatatuck showed in a thicker mounding of sycamore green, the sky was murky, gray-yellow, like some old fire-opal in need of a cleaning. The wind which was turning the windmill, scattering the petals, banking the clouds was strong enough to feel now. Eliza turned back the collar of her gray dress—but there was no refreshment in warm sultry air.

It must've been around 5.30 when Gardiner Bent trotted into the yard, tied his lathered horse at the upping block, and got a hero's welcome from everyone on the side lawn.

Mattie flew into the house for more lemonade and to ask if Gard could stay for supper.

"Won't he want to go home to his own folks?"

"He's been there already."

"It'll make quite a crowd."

"That Clate Henry won't want anything to eat. He's been sick and now he's asleep."

"He'll wake up the hungriest of all."

"Please, Mama. I'll help."

"I don't need help," Eliza said. "Tell Gard he's welcome. Everyone else is. I don't see why we should draw the line at him."

Mattie turned to go, then stopped. "How's the boy?"

"Don't pretend thee's given him a thought all afternoon."

"I haven't," Mattie said. "I'm not pretending. It was Gard I was thinking about. This boy might take it in his head that he ought to keep on fighting."

"No matter what he takes in his head," Eliza said, "he's too sick to fight. Thee just see to it that Gard stays peaceable and we'll have nothing to worry about."

One outdoor meal a day, Eliza decided, was enough. She was not going to carry fried chicken, mashed potatoes, corn bread, and custard pie outdoors. She'd have a sit-down meal at the table. But instead of moving Jimmy upstairs to the spare room—where he'd be shut away from everything (and refuse to go, anyway, probably) —she'd move him out to Enoch's room. That was only a step away, off the kitchen, a part of the porch roofed over and sided up. It was nothing but a hired man's room. Nothing fancy, but Jimmy wasn't in shape or practice for enjoying anything fancy.

He surprised her by being perfectly willing to move. He sat up, holding the cloths she had given him wadded against his head.

"Who was that rode in a while back?"

"A neighbor boy," Eliza told him.

"He had on a uniform."

"He's a soldier," Eliza admitted.

"He's a Quaker, too?"

"No," Eliza said, "he's a Methodist."

"I reckon it don't make much difference," Jimmy said.

Jimmy followed through the kitchen, across the back porch, and into Enoch's room. He walked as if the floor under his feet were uneven, and as if Enoch's door shifted from left to right. But he was in good spirits. When he saw the custard pies lined up to cool he said, "If some of them turn up missing you'll know where to look for them."

Eliza, after she had settled him unresisting on to Enoch's bed, brought him a half-pie on a plate, and a supply of clean rags.

"Thank you, Mama," he said.

Eliza was at first pleased; then, after she went back to her work in the kitchen, puzzled. Had he spoken jokingly—or in a minute of lightheadedness did he think he was back in Plum Tree with his own mother? But she was too busy frying chicken with one hand and mixing a batch of corn bread with the other to worry about it.

Jimmy asked to be excused from going to the supper table. "I ain't a very pretty sight for eaters. Besides, I spoiled my appetite with pie."

Eliza was glad he felt that way. Apart from his looks and his smell, something might be said he would take exception to.

She got them all down to the supper table before lamplighting time, all hungry after the pick-up dinner, the fighting, and the talk of fighting; and Clate Henry, just as she'd guessed, was the hungriest of them all. Eliza served them like a woman working in a stranger's house. She knew that this day of estrangement would pass; that it signified nothing but the dying down in her of a spirit of perfect sympathy which would rise again and would embrace them all. But she accepted the lull and the separation, fought neither it nor them—and moved back and forth silently with platters and pitchers to be refilled.

She had brought the supper plates from the table and gone to the porch for the pies when she saw Jimmy—who had seen her first—standing on the steps below her, immovable. He had the rations-bag he'd arrived with over his shoulder, and one side of his face, for all that he had tied up his head with a bandage torn from one of her pillow shams, was covered with the bloody outpouring from his rising.

"Jimmy," she said, "what's thee doing?"

Jimmy didn't stop to argue. He hurried down the step in his hobbling, stiff-legged gait.

"Jimmy, thee's not fit to travel."

Fit or not, he traveled, his gait uneven, his hands to his head as if afraid it might, in spite of the bandage, split open. He took off down the pathway littered with the false snow, under the green-yellow Summer Sweetings, heading for the main road. He was running, but weaving and stumbling as he ran.

"Jimmy," Eliza called, "Jimmy, let me help thee."

With skirts lifted she was far fleeter footed than he. He barely missed trees, stumbled over hummocks of grass, lost his bandage and kept going.

At last Eliza understood that he was running away from *her* and stopped. "Jimmy," she called. "I'm not following."

It was too late. The boy tripped, fell over, and lay where he had fallen. When Eliza reached him, he struggled to sit up and Eliza, kneeling beside him, supported him. Half of his head seemed to have fallen away. From the brain-deep cavity where his rising had been, blood and pus covered his face. Eliza cradled his head against her shoulder and rocked him a little before it occurred to her that this might be bad for him.

He appeared to be trying to say something. An indistinguishable sound filled his throat and Eliza thought, when no words took shape, that he might be trying to give that yell, the one he believed the others had mismanaged and that made him feel good. She hoped he could do it. But it wasn't a yell he had in mind. He said perfectly clear and quiet, "Be good to Jimmy," and underneath the blood he closed his own eyes.

Eliza sat flat on the ground under the apple trees with the boy in her arms. She felt guilty, as if she had killed him herself. Not by running after him, which might have hurried things—but no more than that. But because when the others came down from the house, as they would in a few minutes, and found her here with the boy dead in her arms, he would say to them what she had been saying all day, "Don't rejoice so much." And they would listen to him as they hadn't to her. He would be her "I told you so." With all her heart she wished him a live boy and no sign. But he was both: a boy and a sign and she couldn't separate them—and shouldn't try. Whatever message he had for those who found him, he had earned the right to say.

J. G. McCLURE was born in Michigan in 1931. He has worked as a hospital orderly, radio operator, supervisor in an egg processing plant, technical editor, and has an M.A. degree from the University of Michigan. Since 1958 he has been writing in California. "The Rise of the Proletariat" is his second published story.

The Rise of the Proletariat

While eating lunch with her room-mate she spoke of the strange telephone conversation she had had a couple of hours earlier with a young man named Morris Holmes. He had needed a tutor and, on someone's advice, had called the seminar room. She happened to be the only one there at the time. "He thinks he can learn everything there is to know about the Expressionists in an hour or two. But I don't think he even understands the terminology of art."

"What's he trying to do," her room-mate asked, "pass a course?"

"*Whose* course? I mean, the questions he asked prove he doesn't understand what it's all about. 'What motivates Goto to sculpt the way he does?'"

"Goto! Who's he?"

"*I* don't know. I said, I thought you wanted to know about the Expressionists. And he says, well I have to know about Goto, too."

"What did you tell him?"

"Tell him? What could I tell him? That's no art historical question. How would I know what motivates Goto? I told him to go ask a psychologist."

"What did he say to that?"

"He said he has no confidence in them."

"How weird."

"I promised I'd meet him in the library at one o'clock. He says he'll pay me two dollars an hour."

"I think you'd better get it in advance."

"That's impossible. He's already admitted he hasn't any money."

"I wouldn't go then."

"Do you think I shouldn't?"

"How old is he?"

"I'll see you later," she said, glancing at the kitchenette clock as she rose.

From the apartment it was about a ten minute walk to the corner of the campus. Phylis was a brisk walker. She quite often did the distance in seven minutes. That day she might have reduced her time to six minutes—she believed it but could not determine it because she had left her watch in the ashtray beside the sink—yet arrived late for the meeting with Holmes. This was Frank Nestor's fault. He stopped her as she was passing the student union. He asked her to join him for a cup of coffee and it took her just long enough to give a satisfactory explanation for her refusal—an explanation sufficiently loaded with pejorative reference to the individual responsible for her obligations as not to raise any question in Frank's mind of her interest in him—that she did not arrive within the library until five after one. She was annoyed to find that Morris Holmes was not there.

While thus far her only contact with him had been the telephone conversation, she felt she would know him if she saw him. "I look like Martin Luther," he had said, "with long hair." And she knew which engraving he meant, though his knowledge of art seemed, to say the least, capricious and haphazard. There was nothing for her to do but sit and wait for him.

At one-thirty she saw a multi-colored cardigan enter the reference room. Like Joseph's coat, it bore all the colors of the spectrum. Instantly she coveted it and instantly she knew the owner was he. He was not as homely as Martin Luther. Of moderate height and girth and about twenty-eight years of age, he walked with the heavy tread of a man twice his size. This, in spite of the fact that he was wearing sandals. He also wore a beard.

"You're late," she said. She stood as he approached the table where she'd been seated with a few other students. The boy across from her glanced at her, at him, at her again and returned to his geometry book.

"Sorry," he said, "I met a friend and was persuaded to have coffee." Everyone at the table looked up; he had not whispered. She walked toward the entrance and he followed. In the hallway, without another word exchanged between them, he loped beside her, held the double doors and, apparently having forgot her, dashed ahead of her up the stairway to the third floor. But he was waiting for her there. She led him into a small classroom next to the art history seminar room, closed the door and placed her books on one of the chairs.

She sat and wrote in her small brown notebook: Morris Holmes; instruction Tues. Jan. 17, 3:00 P.M.—— "We can just work until you get tired," she said.

He smiled with a smirk of embarrassment. "I suppose I should ask what your qualifications are," he said.

"I thought we discussed that over the phone."

"Well, you started talking about Woodrow Wilson and then I lost you. The only Woodrow Wilson I ever heard of was president, I don't know any painter, and then . . ."

"It *is* the president. I have a Woodrow Wilson fellowship. For graduate study. I'm a graduate student in art history." Usually it made her feel fairly well to say all this. He just looked at her blankly for a moment.

"Ohhhh. Oh, I see. A fellowship. They give you money or something."

"You're not a student, are you?"

He laughed lightly and scratched the side of his beard.

"Would you please explain?" she said a little irritably. "This whole project is so preposterous I really don't know what you want me to teach you." As he squinted out the window she had an insight. "Are you trying to pass a board of examiners, is that it?"

"Yes. Yes, that's it."

"Then it's the *art* department, not the art *history* department you want to get into."

He shrugged. "I don't know." He sat on the edge of a chair and sighed. "It's like this. I met a guy at a show in Chicago. He says I should come out here. I came." His eye seemed to be caught by the Skira book she had brought along and, somewhat tentatively, he began to page through it. "You should see the equipment they got in their shop. Materials. They don't even use much scrap iron here. Tremendous."

"I don't know what you're talking about."

"What?"

"You're trying to get into the art graduate school. Where did you get your B.A.?"

"My what?"

"Don't you even have a degree?"

He shrugged again. "I'm afraid I don't dig you either. What do I need a degree for?"

"*That's* why the board of examiners. I see."

"I'm glad somebody does. Look. Bert said I better learn all I can at least about the expressionists before Thursday. Can you teach me anything or can't you?"

"Thursday! Oh my God, this is worse than I thought. Who is Bert?"

"Fellow I met at the show. Cockle or Cuckold or Conkshell or something."

"Professor Conklin? You know him?"

He shrugged, a little impatient now. "I just told you. I met him in Chicago. He says come here, they'll give me a job—all I have to do is teach the guys techniques. So here I am, so now they tell me they thought I knew about these other things."

"Holy mackerel."

"That doesn't express it."

Her antagonism faded. "That's a terrible thing for them to do to you," she said. He only shrugged again. She was still puzzled. "But I mean, really, how *can't* you know about art? If you're an artist."

He looked at her. He smiled, again with embarrassment. "Wellll," he said, and he gazed at his hands as he folded them. She followed his gaze and started at sight of the hands. They were grotesque. Unlike the rest of him, his face for example, taut and quite without blemish under a deep tan, his hands were scarred and calloused, even blistered in places. "Good heavens, what did . . ." But she did not know him that well.

"I know this," he said, pointing at a Grosz in another of her art books. He turned rapidly through the pages. "Why, I know all these guys. Sure. Him. He's good." He flipped a mass of pages. "Christ yes. I know him, too, real well."

"He really doesn't belong there," she said, "but that's splendid."

"What do you mean, he doesn't belong here?"

"The way he paints."

"What's wrong with it? I think he's pretty good."

"Yes, he's all right. But that's not the point. Chagall, you see, he's much different from Grosz."

"No shit."

She reddened. "Another school," she mumbled, "or rather not a school actually but . . ."

"So?"

"Well . . ." Then she grew angry again. "Listen, do you want to learn about the Ex*press*ionists or don't you?" She was highly flushed now.

He raised his hands palms outward, ugly, calloused, burnt palms, to placate her, and smiled. "Yes. Yes. By all means. Let us be taught."

And off they went.

Much, much later—he was indefatigable; she drilled him for three hours, grew hungry, realized with consternation that he meant expressionists in general, not the German Expressionists, drilled him another two hours, was famished, but could not seem to reach *his* point of physical-emotional-intellectual saturation—she described the session to her room-mate. "He has *no* historical sense. None, none, none. It's the most exasperating encounter I've ever had. Do you know how he learned about these people? He *looked* at the *pictures*. He has *never* read a *word* about *any* of them. He can't read."

"What? You're kidding."

"It's true! He can't read. He just *goes* where it is, and looks. Looks. He spent two years bumming around Europe, looking. He speaks three languages, Dutch, French and Italian and can't read or write a word of them. He's a sculptor. He's even been to the Orient on his own."

"A sculptor. I thought he was a painter. How come he can't read?"

"Well, actually I guess he can. He said he *used* to read. He *must* still be able to."

"How weird. Can I meet him?"

"No."

"Wh . . . ?"

"I mean, I don't think you'd want to be seen with him. He's very unkempt."

"Oh. He sounds interesting."

"But it's so strange. Imagine thinking of Bernini and Frank Lloyd Wright as contemporaries? He just doesn't bother with dates."

"He must be good, though, or they wouldn't have invited him here."

"If you ask me, I think Professor Conklin made a mistake this time."

"I'd still like to meet him."

"Isn't dinner ready?" Phylis asked. "I'm starving."

After dinner Frank Nestor called. She didn't mention Holmes to him. Frank asked her to a movie. She had used up the entire afternoon instructing the sculptor and was behind in her study schedule, but she had already declined one invitation from Frank that day and felt she ought not refuse him a second time. "I'd love to," she said.

At seven-thirty she heard him roar up before the apartment in his TR3. She pulled on her coat and met him at the door. The top was down on the sportscar, she tied a scarf about her hair and they moved off in the evening breeze.

"How was your student?" Frank asked.

"Impossible," she replied. But she didn't feel like speaking of him to Frank. She left the subject hanging.

"Guess what," Frank said.

"What?"

"I was going to tell you this afternoon but you ran off. I've got an appointment."

"Oh, Frank, that's wonderful! Where?"

"UCLA."

"Golly. Well, that's certainly better than the Midwest."

"Better! I should say it's better. They've got a great econ school there."

"Of course it's a little smoggy."

"Oh, come on."

She laughed gaily.

"Well, how about it; will you marry me now?"

"What?"

"I said, would you care to be a faculty wife?"

"My goodness, Frank, I . . ." She had been about to say: I had no idea. But that would have been a little corny; also false, for she *had* had an idea. A fair one. For over a month now. "Gee," she said.

"Shall we go to a movie or shall we celebrate?" he said.

"Let's celebrate by going to a movie. I'm all confused." Though she was gazing straight ahead, she knew that he peered at her oddly. Evidently he, too, felt there ought to be a foregone conclusion here somewhere. Suddenly, laughing, she turned and put her hand on his arm that was resting on the gearshift and kissed him on the cheek. He beamed at her. They wheeled sharply around a corner, parked at a meter and walked to the Esquire Theatre.

For an hour and a half she watched a film about an advertising executive and a model in New York and then, briefly, saw President Kennedy talk about this country's determination. They stayed for the cartoon—Mr. Magoo at the Circus—and walked back to the car. Dew had settled on the tonneau cover.

"As soon as my thesis is accepted we could leave," he said.

"All right," she said. She felt rather apprehensive and held him tightly when he kissed her goodnight. Her room-mate was asleep and the apartment was dark.

"Are you tired?" Holmes asked her the next day. "Shall we stop for a while and go have a cup of coffee?" He was dressed the same. Except for his hair his appearance was unaltered. He had combed his hair.

She smiled wanly. "I'd love to," she said. As they left the library she said: "Why don't we cross the street; I don't feel like going to the student union." He nodded.

They waited in silence for the traffic light. "You look tired yourself," she said. "Were you up late?"

"That shop they've got," he said. "What a great shop."

"Oh, you were sculpting."

"No, no." He laughed. "No. Metalwork. Brass, for Christ sake. They let me have a whole mess of brass. For nothing. That boy Conklin's not bad. The rest of those creeps . . ." he hesitated. She thought he hesitated as if he were not sure she weren't also a creep, but as if he knew *she* must know and could therefore possibly be offended. He was far too polite a person to be deliberately offensive, even to a creep.

They had coffee in the Old German restaurant. He ignored the bad cartoons on the walls. She brought his attention to them, as if apologetically, but he did not even care to scorn them. That they were not good evidently provided enough excuse for him not to talk about them and he would not talk about them. Somewhat perversely, she wanted to keep talking.

"I'd like to see some of your work sometime," she said. And it will have to be soon, she thought.

"Anytime," he said.

This offended her, for he said it as he might have answered to the vapid curiosity of—of—someone like Silvia, her room-mate. "I mean it," she said, "sincerely." This was worse. He just looked at her. Trying to shift her mental stance, her pose, she said: "Will you tell me something? How did you get started sculpting?" Yet nothing came unstiltedly off her tongue; her voice seemed a trifle too crisp, its tone too high. She saw that she was embarrassing him again. He attempted to answer.

"I . . ." he said. Both his hands were clasped about his cup. He released his left hand to gesture, opening it merely; an ineffectual movement of which it was ashamed and sought to retract by closing itself once more about the cup.

"Oh," she said, glimpsing that hand. Without thinking, she grasped it with her own two hands and re-opened it. "Oh, how awful." The palm was more raw and blistered than it had been before. "How did you *do* that, Morris?" She probed gently. Although the skin looked very tender, he seemed to feel nothing.

He shrugged. "I forget the gloves sometimes and, uh," he shook his head, "the metal gets hot."

"Come on," she said, "we'd better put something on that."

"Sit down," he said. "I haven't finished my . . ."

"You'll get infected," she said sternly.

". . . my coffee. Not within the next five minutes. Sit down."

She glanced about. People were watching her. The old proprietor at his cash register, no doubt fearing Holmes had cut himself on something at the table, was stretching to see. She sat. Blushing, she had deliberately to prevent herself from bowing her head.

When she looked at him she saw that he, out of politeness, was watching his spoon.

"What were we saying?" he said. "About Chicago." He stretched his back a moment and then rubbed his spoon against the saucer. "There was this guy Tony Barrolo. I met him when I was working at the Helmlick Drop Forge. I didn't meet him *there*. He came into Smiley's Bar one night after the second shift looking for a welder. Well, I was a welder; I welded over the flaws in crankshafts. You know? And, uh, he said if I'd show him how to work metals he'd pay me. Well, of course welding hasn't much to do with metal work, but I happened to know quite a lot about metal work from the time I was working for Minnesota Mining, except sheet metal but he didn't care about that. So I took the job. And, that was the funny thing. When I saw what *he* was doing; I mean, Tony isn't *real* good, but there were these terracotta things and it was the idea, you see?"

She nodded.

"And I started making things. I had a lot of friends at the shop and they'd filch the alloys I wanted; you should have seen that, that was really funny, these guys walking out the gate with their pants down to their knees, their pockets full of iron scraps, like kids. Until some foreman raised hell. Well. And, uh, Tony told me about the stuff other guys had done and I looked at that. It was sort of a brand new life. I . . ." he shrugged. "This isn't a bad place here, is it?" he said, meaning the university.

"Oh, if that board doesn't pass you tomorrow it will be a crime," she said, "an absolute crime. You're brilliant. You're really very, very bright. If we had only a month, I know . . ."

"Forget it," he said. "Tony told me a long time ago that wasn't important anyway."

"Oh, but it is!" She flushed again. "I mean, relatively."

He stood. "Shall we have another go at it, then?"

She rose with him. There followed a minute's chagrin before the German proprietor because it happened Holmes hadn't all the money needed to pay the bill. She contributed a nickel. But the chagrin was hers alone. Holmes was like a duck in the rain.

"You're going to get married!" Silvia exclaimed. "How marvelous. Frank of course." They were eating dinner.

"We're going to live in Southern California."

"Ugh."

"I'm sure it's not all vulgar."

"No, I suppose not." Silvia poured tea. "I'd probably like it myself, after I got used to it."

"It's always sunny, and he'll be teaching at UCLA."

"Oh, fine."

"I think so. It will be a wonderful opportunity for me, too; there are so many galleries in Los Angeles. We might even start a collection."

"I'd love that. Milt is such a boor when it comes to art, if we ever do get married I'll probably wind up with Norman Rockwell on the wall."

"You can't have everything."

"True. He has a marvelous personality."

"I wasn't thinking of that."

"Oh, now, *your* boy isn't exactly *poor* either."

"His father didn't want him to go into teaching, though."

"I'm sure he'll cut him off without a cent."

Phylis, with her fork, fumbled through her salad.

"Tell me," Silvia said, "has he, eh . . ."

"Oh, Silvia, don't be so middle class."

"I just wondered if he'd given you a ring."

Phylis studied most of the evening but went out with Frank at eleven for a late snack at the student union. Afterward he asked her to his apartment. She went. He put Debussy's *La Mer* on his hi-fi and they sat on the hide-a-bed and listened for a while and talked about their plans. He asked if he should pull out the bed, could she stay with him that night? She said no. He asked why. The answer she gave, had it been true, might have caused her a good deal of unconscious shame, but the shame she felt was in having lied. So she admitted to him she'd lied. She said she was afraid. Another lie. He decided to be a gentleman. He said it wasn't that important anyway. Which was not the right thing for him to have said.

When she awoke the next morning she immediately thought of Holmes. He was to go before the board at ten o'clock. She had slept late, it was nine-thirty, she had a class at eleven and she reflected disappointedly that she would probably not see him now until after twelve. For breakfast she could eat nothing but coffee and toast. At nine fifty-five she thought of Silvia's bicycle and, gathering her books together quickly, she dashed downstairs and peddled off to the campus in a last minute effort to intercept Holmes before he met his examiners. On arriving before the Art and Architecture Building, she dropped the bike in a heap, dashed inside and caught the sculptor as he was about to enter the office of the art department. He turned at her call. And for the first time since she'd known him she saw him blush. "I wanted," she said, hesitating, out of breath, "I wanted . . . to wish you good luck."

"Thank you, Phylis," he said.

She watched him go into the office, still wearing his multicolored cardigan.

Feeling very dejected then, obscurely guilty, illogically remiss, she walked slowly, carrying her books, leaving the bike, across the campus to the student union. Too late, she remembered that she had forgot to ask him to meet her somewhere after the examination. But she had his phone number; he lived with an art student.

I haven't even seen if he's really good, she thought. He must be. He must be.

While she sat at the table alone eating a bowl of chili—she had suddenly become very hungry—pondering why he must be, Frank Nestor entered the snack bar with a couple of friends, spotted her and left his friends to come and sit with her.

"That was kind of a bad night," he said.

"I'm sorry," she said. "I am sorry. I feel terrible for acting so badly."

"No," he said, "I came on too fast. I'm sorry."

So they both were sorry. What now, she wondered. Was he still interested in a girl who might prove to be frigid? But you're not frigid, she thought. He is frigid, ah . . . impotent. Where was his spirit?

"There's a play tomorrow night," he said, folding a straw wrapper. "*Endgame.* Would you like to see it?"

"No," she said, a little too vehemently. "No," she said, more softly. "I think I'd rather just drink beer with you or something."

"Fine. Fine," he said.

All her life she would have a husband whose principal interests would serve her own interests. The course of his life would circle back upon hers as hers would revolve about his; they would get along excellently, accumulate nice things and enjoy a mature way of life in an advanced society. What had been but an unattainable ideal of numerous men for centuries actually for them was a possibility. She pushed away her bowl emptied of chili.

"I met Silvia a while ago," Frank said. "We were talking about your beatnik friend."

"Who?"

"The guy you've been teaching."

"Beatnik? He's no beatnik. At least he doesn't act like one. In fact he's not at all depressed."

"Well. I mean Silvia said he ran around in a beard and sandals."

"Because he travels a lot hitch-hiking and often can't find a place to shave he wears a beard so he won't look completely disreputable. He wears sandals whenever he can in order to save his socks for other occasions. He's quite poor."

"Yes, and she said he wasn't paying you either. I think you're crazy."

"Why?"

"Well, it's his own fault he hasn't got any money, isn't it? He can't expect people always to be giving him something for nothing. You're just encouraging him."

"Encouraging him!"

"To be a sponge. I'm sure he could get a job if he wanted to."

"You don't understand, Frank."

He laughed. "I know a fraud when I see one."

"That's not fair. You've never met him."

"That's true. I take that back. But just the same I get kind of fed up with these guys. They criticize society and other people's standards all the time, but in actuality they're the biggest parasites around. If a guy wants to be an artist, fine, but that doesn't make him better than anybody else and I don't see why he shouldn't meet his obligations like everyone else."

"Oh, let's talk about the weather," she said. She looked at her watch. "What time do you have anyway?"

"Ten forty-five."

"My watch is slow. I have to go to class."

"Okay." He started to rise. "Are you sore about something?"

She shook her head. "I'm just tired," she said as she gathered her books. "Will I see you later?"

"How about tonight?"

"I absolutely *have* to study tonight."

"We can meet for coffee."

"All right. Bye."

On reaching the glass doors she glanced behind and saw that he had walked over to his friends. She went on to her class.

After the class she hurried back to the Art and Architecture Building. Holmes' examination had been concluded. She asked the secretary if she knew how well he had done. Not too well, the secretary thought, judging by a remark she'd heard dropped by Mr. Sinel. "Somebody should have told him not to come dressed that way," the secretary said.

"What did his clothes have to do with it?" Phylis asked. Of course she knew; she was simply indignant for the moment toward a human bias she normally accepted.

"He obviously didn't make much of an impression on Sinel. And, you know yourself Sinel isn't too fond of Conklin."

"Oh, them and their damned rivalries." Phylis turned. She stopped. "You don't happen to know where he went?"

"Why, yes. He left a message for you. He's in the workshop."

"Of course," Phylis said. "He would be. Thank you, Angie."

"I'm sorry," the secretary said. "But then, I could be wrong."

Phylis rode Silvia's bicycle to the workshop, which was in a far corner of the campus. The day had opened cloudily, but now the sun shone through a blue-white sky. Outside the workshop—a small, wood-framed building—two students sat on a porch rail eating lunches. She asked if they knew or had seen Morris Holmes. One of the boys jerked his thumb. "He's inside, straight through to your right." They both looked at her. She walked in.

Morris almost collided with her. He paid no attention, pushed by her, out the door and stopped. "Hand it over," he said to the two students.

They gazed at him in surprise. "What?" the blond boy asked.

"You know damn well what," Morris said, and advanced upon him. Instantly, the boy reached behind and pulled a rat-tail file from his pocket. He laughed as he held it out. "Take it easy, Holmes."

Without a word, Morris grabbed the file and re-entered the building, once more brushing past her without seeing her. She followed him. He seemed not to hear her footsteps. "Morris," she called. He stopped. "Morris?"

Turning, seeing her, the frown promptly left his face. "Oh," he said. "How are you?"

"How am *I!* I came to ask you that. What were those boys doing?"

He giggled self-consciously and looked at the file. "Ah, they're kids," he said. "They like to play hide and seek with the tools. It's a little annoying." He laughed and shifted the file to his left hand.

"Let me see your hand," she said.

"Hm?"

"You're hiding something yourself," she said. "Let me see it. Oh, heavens, Morris, you're bleeding."

Impatiently, he pulled the hand away. "Never mind my damn hands," he said. "Come here, I want to show you something."

She followed him. "How did it go, Morris?" she asked.

"The inquisition? I lost. They're going to burn me at the stake at sun-up." He led her behind a partition. He had been given his own work-space within the shop. It was littered with debris; scraps of mis-shapen iron, broken drill bits, brass filings, shreds of wire and discarded metal brushes. A tank each of oxygen and acetylene stood in a corner behind the bench and several files and worn strips of emery paper were scattered over the surface of the bench. On a small, round, waist-high table pocked with cuts and burns rose a brass image about a foot and a half high. She stared at it. He had not only shaped the brass; he had apparently attempted to alter its metallic qualities. Staring at it, she felt as if either some machine were in process of changing into animal or some formerly exquisite creature were being grotesquely reduced to a mechanism. The object repelled her, and on impulse she decided she did not believe it, that it was not valid. "Is this," she asked, "what you call zoomorphic expressionism?"

"It's, uh, you," he said, rubbing a stain on his elbow. Then something in the figure caught his attention and he turned to it.

"No," she said. But he had already turned his back to her. He placed a hand over what she might have assumed to be the shoulder of the figure, to steady it, and with several heavy thrusts of the file he had just retrieved worked a change the effect of which seemed imperceptible. He rubbed the raw spot with emery paper, blew on it and, grasping the figure with both hands, rotated it a few degrees. "Now of course it doesn't actually have sides," he said, "but if you were to see it from only one particular angle I suppose . . ."

A smear of his blood stained the figure and as he lifted his sleeve to rub it off she caught the hand and put it to her cheek. "Morris," she said, "it's not me."

That afternoon they went for a long walk. She talked about herself, about matters she had resolved a couple of years earlier never again to discuss with anyone, and he listened. He looked everywhere while she talked, at a bird taking a drink of water, at a dog waiting outside a grocery, even noticed and probed with his toe a snail lying some distance from the walk, yet listened with an attention she was not accustomed to receiving. With any one else she would have been ashamed, at her age, to speak with bitterness of her parents—"radicals; they *thought* they were radicals because when they were young they knew a few socialists and went to Greenwich Village parties occasionally, but that didn't stop my father from accumulating real estate or prevent my mother from turning into a social climber. They're fakes."—but he listened thoughtfully and, to her relief, made no attempt whatever to analyze her attitudes. Perhaps he knew nothing of Freudian theory. "It's a shame it was so lousy," he said.

And they strolled finally toward her apartment, arriving about three, when she knew Silvia would be gone. He observed that she lived rather sumptuously, a circumstance of which she had not been at all aware; but while he made no effort to conceal his enthusiasm for the idea of eating steak three times a week he seemed to regard the practice as he might regard a piece of architecture, as something quite outside and apart from *him*, not anything he would or should hope to possess.

And it occurred to her that his art required only that he be fed, clothed and sheltered, not fed well, clothed well or sheltered well;

still, a kind of indignation tainted her inclination to admire him
for his devotion to his work.

Even his muscles were not such as she was accustomed to seeing
on men. Clearly, they were the muscles developed by work, not by
athletics. Yet he seemed too thin, almost emaciated, and the whiteness of his skin when he pushed his shirtsleeves past his elbows in
a nervous gesture shocked her as, when a small girl, she had once
been shocked by the deeply burned arms, necks and faces and utterly pale trunks and legs of a couple of farm hands she had
glimpsed bathing in a creek near her summercamp.

Before Silvia returned they were out again, walking up toward
the campus. She suspected she would have been ill at ease had he
held her hand, but he was quite diffident. Or sensitive. Still shy
perhaps. She thought she saw Frank Nestor strolling toward them
and, suddenly confused, she pulled Morris into the recessed entrance of a shop. It happened to be a jewelry shop. Further confused, she instantly drew him out again, saw that the man
approaching was not Frank, and then realized she could easily have
explained Morris' presence with her anyway. She began to despise
herself for all the second thoughts coating the core of her good
will.

At five-thirty she left him outside the workshop; kissed him on
the cheek and rode off on Silvia's bicycle.

"So what now?" Silvia asked.

"He won't know until he's spoken to Mr. Conklin."

"Poor guy."

She had not told Silvia about the brass image; absurdly, it
seemed to her that to mention its existence would be like betraying
a secret. "He's not as poor as you might think."

"Oh? He's paid you?"

"No, I mean . . . well, spiritually."

"Pfffft."

"Psychologically then, dammit. He has a great deal of calm and
confidence."

"So has Milt."

"Milt is an engineer."

"That's right. And he doesn't have to go around dressed like a
clown to show how individualistic he is."

"That again. I don't feel like arguing about it." They ate in silence for a minute.

"I saw Frank this morning."

"Yes, he told me."

"I think secretly he wants to meet your beatnik."

"I doubt if Morris would be the least interested in meeting Frank." In the space of silence that followed this remark she was conscious of Silvia's eyes upon her.

"Has, uh, has Frank given you a ring or anything yet?"

"An engagement ring? Really, Silvia."

"He could afford it, couldn't he?"

"That isn't the point. Can you imagine me running around with a semi-transparent rock attached to my finger? I'd feel vulgar."

"You could *always* put it in a box."

"Silvia! For heaven's sake."

Silvia shrugged.

Phylis was now so far behind in her reading she decided the only way she could catch up, what with all the daytime distractions, was by staying up very late. When Frank called she begged off the usual coffee date. Frank was displeased. He told her to relax; why all the drive, drive, drive; did she really think what she was doing was that important? He had a singular knack for saying all the wrong things at the wrong times. Poor Frank. Very sweetly, she tried to explain, all the time hinting that this might be a wifely virtue, that one had an obligation to get one's money's worth, didn't one, mustn't she? Laughing, he wanted to know if *she* was trying to teach *him* a socio-economic principle.

The conversation grew a bit tense. She said that at any rate she would meet him for coffee tomorrow and she bade him goodnight. She stayed up very late studying, shutting from her thoughts the problem that seemed to be growing thick about her even as it remained indefinable.

The next day Frank informed her that his parents were coming up for the weekend to visit him and meet her. He hoped she didn't mind the short notice, but his father's business was such that he could never be sure when he might get away for a few days. She said she would love to meet them.

But, naturally, she was quite anxious that they should like her.

Although she gave some thought to Holmes that afternoon, she was much too busy between classes with small tasks preparatory to the weekend to choose an opportunity to meet him. She wondered if he had talked to the professor yet and she felt a little selfish at being involved with private social matters when, for him, such a great deal was at stake. But probably, objective as he was, he did not see it that way.

On returning to the apartment late in the afternoon she asked Silvia if there had been any calls.

"Yes, one, your beatnik friend. Wooie, does he sound sexy."

"Did he leave a message?"

"Nope."

And she felt as if she had offended him. She called his number twice but no one answered and by seven-thirty she and Silvia had both left the apartment so she had no way of knowing whether he had called her again.

"You'll like them," Frank told her.

"I'm sure I will."

"Dad's a real smoothie, an old pro."

She smiled. The passengers disembarked from the plane. Frank pointed out the couple that were his parents. She watched them approach. Frank's father, contrary to her expectations, was slightly obese. His hair was such a pure silver-grey it seemed to be tinted and he came toward them smiling, right hand extended, carrying a Homburg in his left hand. Mrs. Nestor tended to stomp as she walked. A head shorter than her husband, but equally heavy, she clutched the strap of her purse tightly with a small, plump fist.

"So you're the girl," Frank's father said, taking Phylis' hand while his wife took the other. Phylis smiled charmingly. Mrs. Nestor, the black purse dangling from her forearm, whispered something in Phylis' ear and giggled. Phylis did not catch the remark but laughed all the same. As they waited for the bags they chatted about rough air, the lovely day and the breakfast aboard plane. Frank's parents were hungry and Mr. Nestor expressed a desire to spend lavishly, so they drove directly into the city to a French restaurant for lunch.

Phylis watched the crepe suzette flaming and listened to Mrs. Nestor's analysis of the trend in waist lengths and suddenly recalled something Holmes had said about his friends in Singapore eating—what was it?—some awful mixture "once a day; it's the only place I've ever been I didn't feel skinny."

She then had asked him how *he* managed to survive, since he never seemed to have much money; and, as she might have guessed, Tony Barrolo had taught him how: beef heart, peanut butter, spinach and whole wheat bread.

She watched Mrs. Nestor consume a dish of strawberries with her French pancakes.

The afternoon passed, for the most part, uneventfully. She strolled about the campus in high-heeled shoes with Frank and his parents. Although the Nestors tried gamely not to be bored, they were disappointed by their inability to sense the university through sight and betrayed themselves to the most casual observers as the tourists that they were. And Phylis noted with some satisfaction Frank's discomfort in his role of guide to this mammoth unattraction.

The sole interesting incident of the day arose from Mrs. Nestor's spying a bearded individual. With a jolt of self-consciousness, Phylis recognized the multi-colored cardigan. Mrs. Nestor giggled as Holmes, head high, empty handed and besandaled, strode swiftly down a walk at some distance from them. Mr. Nestor, pausing to wipe his sunglasses, remarked that he supposed that fellow thought he was a rebel or a communist or something and Frank replied that there were always a few of those around; once they left college and found they had to earn a living they gave up the beard and sloppy clothes and you never saw them again.

"One thing about Frank at least," Mr. Nestor said, more or less at large but for Phylis' edification, "we never had to drum any nonsense out of his head." Frank reddened and Phylis smiled graciously.

That evening they all saw the play that Frank had wanted to see Friday night. Afterward Frank lit a cigarette and lamented the amateurish performance. Mr. Nestor agreed the writer was a little far out and had overdone it. Mrs. Nestor, however, commended the parts she thought she had understood—she giggled repeatedly over the people in the garbage cans—and Phylis could think of nothing to say.

An hour later Frank kissed her quickly and left her at her door because his parents were waiting in the car. When she entered the apartment to find a note lying on the floor, from Holmes—"I asked Cecil to write this for me because my own writing is poor, but he can be trusted. I have thought about you all day yesterday and today. Conklin has arranged a job for me, not the one we tried to get but a job, only it's in a different town. May I see you before I leave?"—she sat in a canvas chair and wiped her eyes.

"Are you going to be here today?"

"I don't know. Why?"

"If Morris Holmes calls, tell him to leave a number when I can get in touch with him."

"I thought you had his number."

"No cracks, please."

"Anyway, Milt is coming over for lunch. We may go out for a while."

"Every time I call this number nobody answers."

"Why don't you stay here?"

"I have to help entertain Frank's parents."

"Well, don't get excited. Holmes will probably be there tomorrow. Or are you afraid he'll skip out without paying?"

"Yes."

"Calm down then. There's nothing you could do anyway."

Only she did not care to leave Holmes' question unanswered. While waiting for Frank to come she dialed Holmes' number fourteen times. On the last call she heard a busy buzz. She was about to dial again when Frank arrived.

"Darling I don't feel very well," she said. "Do you think your parents would be very upset if I didn't go with you today?"

"Certainly not. What's wrong? Do you have a fever?"

"It's my stomach. I'm afraid if I went to dinner I'd vomit in the middle of it."

He winced. "You're sure you'll be all right, though?"

"Oh, yes, I'll probably feel fine tomorrow."

"Maybe it's psychosomatic. My parents?"

"I don't think so. I'm only afraid they might be offended if I don't come."

"Don't worry, they're not that subtle. Maybe we could drop back later and see how you feel."

"I'd hate to spoil their day. Oh, maybe I should go anyway. I'll just not eat."

"No, you'd only be miserable." He stroked his brow with his thumb. "I'll tell you what; I'll entertain them and see them off this afternoon and then call you, okay? Maybe by this evening you'll feel better and we can go out, the two of us. But go to bed now."

"All right," she said. She kissed him goodbye. Before closing the door she waved to him again as he skipped down the stairs.

"Now what in hell," Silvia said, advancing from the kitchen, "was all that about?"

"Nothing. I really don't feel well."

"Hah."

Phylis peered through the curtains and saw Frank climb into the car.

"Pretty clever," Silvia said.

The car drove off. As if to prove she weren't clever, Phylis rushed into the bathroom and vomited.

She walked swiftly across the campus. She felt much better, had brushed her teeth thrice, removed much of the make-up she had been wearing when Frank came and for the suit and high heels has substituted a corduroy skirt, tan blouse and Capezios.

She met with some difficulty in her search for Holmes' apartment, or rather Cecil Abrams' apartment. A considerable distance from campus, in the opposite direction from her own apartment, it was not one among dozens in a large building, but apparently one of three or four in a two story house in a semi-residential section. After several inquiries she was advised that the number she was seeking was perhaps not 1347 but 1347½. This was true. They lived above a two-stall garage. She climbed the steps, knocked on the door and was greeted by Holmes. He was wearing only a pair of Levis.

"Cecil," he called back, "put on a shirt, we have a lady visitor. Cecil," he said to her, "has discovered that paint comes off his skin more easily than out of his clothes, so he works almost naked."

"I called earlier," she said, "and no one answered."

"I just got back," he said. "I was about to take a bath. Cecil was here, but he won't answer the phone when he's painting. Once ev-

ery two months he can afford a canvas and a few tubes and he
plain refuses to let anything interrupt him. I'm sorry."

"I can understand," she said.

"You can come in now."

She stepped inside. Immediately she perceived that she was not
welcome. Cecil, a short, skinny, long-haired, dark-skinned and
sweaty boy of about twenty, dressed now in a perfectly clean
smock, sat on a stool glowering at her. But after a quick glance
about the room she felt she did not care to linger anyway. Wads
of paper, wood shavings, broken crayons and discarded tool handles were scattered over the floor, while tacked to paint-smeared,
finger-printed walls and propped against chair legs drawings in
various stages of incompletion contributed to the disorder. An oilcloth had been rippled to the back of the single table to make room
for a pile of clay, beside which sat a box of Rice Krispies, a plastic
bowl and a spoon. On an olive-drab cot in the corner lay a bag
of laundry and a grey cat. The cat, for the way it stared at her,
might have been Cecil's familiar. "Pardon the scene," Holmes said.
"If you'll wait a minute I'll get a shirt and we can go up on the
roof."

"The roof?" she asked. But he disappeared into the other room.
Cecil, waiting patiently now, observed her. Knowing he would not
like it, she tried to see what he was painting. He rose and turned
the easel away from her. Holmes reappeared wearing his cardigan.
"There are a couple of lawn chairs on the roof," he said. "I've
been taking your advice and getting a tan."

"I'm afraid I didn't bring my sun suit," she said. Nobody
laughed. She followed him out and up a step-ladder onto a flat,
tar and gravel roof. Accepting the chair he offered, she sat and
waited for him to speak. But after seating himself he said nothing.

"I came because of your note," she said awkwardly.

"Yes. Well." He squinted at the sun. "There isn't much to say,
really, but I hoped I could say it under better circumstances."

"Is this so impropitious?"

"What? Yes. Well, yes, it is. Old Bert has arranged a job for me
in New York and all I have to do is go there."

"Oh, you need money?"

"No, no, no, no." He laughed. "But I'm leaving tomorrow, see?"

"Oh."

"And I haven't the money to pay you."

"Oh."

"And I love you."

"What?"

"I love you."

She stared at him. "I'm engaged," she said stupidly.

"I know. Your room-mate told me."

"She did!"

"I asked her. It doesn't matter. I couldn't top that. The point is I hate to go away loving you and owing you money too, so I wondered if you would accept the thing I made of you."

When she gathered what he meant she thought first of what the figure might be worth and of what it might be worth in the future. She couldn't help this, though she reprimanded herself for it. "Of course," she said, "but it's so valuable, I mean it's . . ."

"Yes, it came off pretty well." But she could tell that he had detected the greed in her language. "Accept it as a wedding present," he said, as though a wedding were a quaint tribal custom to which he, an anthropologist, was contributing a picture of himself. He rose.

"You're unspeakably egotistical," she said.

He looked at her.

"What right have you to say that to a woman? It isn't fair. What have *you* to offer? If a woman accepted you she would do nothing but work for you. And you'd let her. You wouldn't care. You'd let her live in a pig pen and go without decent clothes or even a decent meal, just so you could do your sculpting. What makes you think you're worth so much? How can you *dare* say that you love me?"

He did not reply. He left her there, climbed down the ladder. She heard the door open and close. After swallowing several times, she stood, descended and walked home.

There was not a cloud in the sky. Birds sang vigorously in the tree tops and when she passed the tennis courts all were occupied; young men in white trunks, a few girls, batted balls back and forth.

"Well, did he pay you?" Silvia asked, coming out of the kitchen as Phylis was removing her sweater. But she was angry with Silvia and did not answer. She studied that afternoon until Frank called. On Tuesday Cecil brought the brass image.

HELEN ESSARY ANSELL was born in 1940 in Washington, D.C., lived for a time in Japan, and traveled around the world in a freighter in 1950. She is a senior this year at Sarah Lawrence College. "The Threesome" won second prize in the *Story* college contest which was sponsored by the Book-of-the-Month Club in 1961.

The Threesome

Clover and Joey met one morning on the hotel beach. The sand lay in the shape of a giant cuticle, enclosed on the inside by a wall of palms and on the outside by a submerged wall of coral. The bay between the beach and the reef reflected the stone porches and white awnings of the hotel perched like Noah's Ark on the rocks above.

The waiters had been flapping out white breakfast cloths over the round iron tables on the dining porch when Clover, in her bathing suit, ran down the hewn steps to the sand. She stopped abruptly, her face pinched tight with disappointment. Someone was there before her. She looked unkindly at him as he knelt with his diving hoses by the hem of the water. She had thought she would be alone on the beach and here was this boy, foolishly squatting there with his apparatus. She walked down to the edge of the water, and ignoring his bent, busy form, scooped up a shimmering handful of sea and wet her legs with it. He stopped what he was doing and examined her from under his bleached brows, then he said, "Hi," in a cheerful voice that grated on the soft morning like the metal screws he was untwisting.

Every morning after that she went down before breakfast and every morning he was there before her. She would stand still and frown at him, her close cap of curls burning red-gold in the sun, and her white skin, which never tanned, glowing peach-colored on her straight narrow back. Once she came an hour earlier than usual, but from the railing on the dining porch she saw him below on the sand, a single dark bug in a bin of sugar. He never failed to say good morning and she could not arm herself against his friendliness. Soon she was greeting him first, and one morning she filled a cup with drinking water from a table pitcher, carried it down and poured it on his hot back. After that they were friends; and with the clinks of the silverware being placed and the spurts of native voices coming down over the ledge, they worked together on his air hoses. He taught her to dive in the clear bay where the shallow coral caves held bright waving plants, and where vast sheets of tiny fish flashed through the filtered sun that pierced far into the water; shattering into fragments on the sandy bottom. Sometimes they spent whole mornings and afternoons together and the days were somehow spoiled if one of them did not appear.

Then Margaret came and everything was changed.

Everyone knew Margaret Few and sought her out for her witty conversation. Yet everyone was a little afraid of her. Her smile was beautiful and quick but it always rose with the same uplift of the mouth and always fell into the same hard mold, where her features lay trapped and immovable. She danced and drank with all the young men but the music could not loosen her and the wine could not flush her cheeks. Of all the men who had tried to kiss her none had succeeded more than once, and of the women who had tried to speak intimately with her none had succeeded at all.

One morning Margaret swung unexpectedly onto the dining porch to a table near the rail, and ordered breakfast. She sat upright and reserved on her chair, her face smooth, expressionless, her large, hard-muscled body moving slowly and deliberately as she turned the sheets of the morning paper. Over the open sheets she looked down to the beach that glowed pink in the early light.

She saw the figures of Joey and Clover as they moved together and she watched their two bodies as they stood and gestured and bumped together, the one very white, the other a dark cherry-brown. They were wet and the light shone off them as they raised their arms and bent their backs. The boy and the girl looked very much alike, curly brown head next to curly white head; and she watched them, her own head tilting toward them. Her eyes, plain brown eyes with brows like short crayon marks, eagerly took them in; Margaret was outspoken and confident, but she had eyes as timid and darting as little mice. Like small creatures that play dead, they could freeze under the enemy gaze of another. But now, those timid eyes were bright and wide open and shining; they were like brown marbles as she sat alone on the porch gazing over the paper at the beach and the figures there.

She had not seen either of them before. The girl had not been to any of the dances or buffets and the boy . . . he was very young.

After breakfast she put on her bathing suit and went down to the beach. She could not swim, for the water had always filled her with an unreasonable sort of terror, but she spent hours lying lazy in the sun. Now she opened her chair on an empty spot of sand and stretched out on it, her long animal limbs overspreading the narrow aluminum frame, her straight dark hair hanging neatly over the curve of her broad bare shoulders. She put lotion on her bamboo-colored skin and closed her eyes. But the voices of the two youngsters lifted now and then over the sand and she was forced to look at them. They were quite close to her and she lay as quiet and engrossed as a bird-watcher.

The boy was as beautiful as the girl. He was small and smooth-limbed and shone as if he were made of polished wood, his chest hard-nippled and drum-tight, and the muscles in his arms thin and long like half-filled stretched balloons. His eyes, pale blue with blond lashes, were petaled flowers growing in his dark skin. He was a silent boy; his mind fixed on the beautiful world of his little coral bank where there was no sound but only looking and touching; and his existence in the world was as hushed as the sea grass waving against those porous cliffs.

Margaret watched them go into the water and in twenty minutes come out again, unstrapping their little air tanks as they splashed up onto the dry sand. She watched them sit down, crossing their legs, one pair pale, the other dark, and she listened to the first words she had heard them say.

"It's too bad we haven't got a skiff," said Clover. "Then we could go out to the far reef where the big coral is."

"Who could give us a skiff?"

"I don't know anyone who could. I've never seen anyone but fishermen in them. I don't know any fishermen."

They were silent, looking out to the far ring of coral that divided the bay from the sea. White rolling waves broke against the rock that lifted its forehead an inch above the water line.

Margaret, too, looked out at the bank, her eyes almost glinting with her absorption in the two figures. Then she extricated her legs from the chair, unfolding them as a deer's legs unfold, and approached them across the sand.

"If you would like to go to the banks," she said in her deep quick voice, before she reached them, "I'll ride you out in my outboard."

Their faces were blank for a moment as they looked at her standing tall and square above them; then they accepted and thanked her in one gesture and leaped up to get the equipment.

The three of them walked down the beach toward the small pier at the end, Margaret striding a little ahead. And that is how they are remembered. People who come back to the hotel every season remember them clearly; they remember the threesome, always walking together. The tall one a mystery, especially her leaving so soon afterward. And the children, not telling a thing and the skipper as silent as any scared colored man ever was.

Margaret took them out and waited in the boat while they dove and dove again, shimmering bodies in the green sea. Then she brought them back.

"If you would like to go tomorrow, I'd be glad to take you again."

So they went the next day, too. And a third day. And it went on that way until it was no longer Joey and Clover. It was Joey and Clover and Margaret. The threesome.

They went many places together that summer. They rode bikes to nearby beaches, flying along narrow shore roads in their bathing suits, with blankets and shirts bundled over the back wheels. They drove in Margaret's open sports car to more distant towns, then left it and walked through the crowded smelly market streets, with Joey's white head bouncing along above the bright bandanna-bound skulls of the natives.

The gatherings at the hotel suffered from Margaret's absence. "Why don't you join us any more, Marg? Surely the two children can't keep you occupied all the time." But Margaret only answered with a shrug, impatient to be in the car, for they were start-

ing out on an overnight trip to a coral formation on the other side
of the island.

When Margaret finally bundled into the driver's seat, she jabbed
the gas pedal with her bare foot as if it were a spur into a horse's
flank, and they lurched off with Margaret's black flag of hair
flapping over the thick bundle of dust they dragged behind them.

The trip did not at first seem to be any different from others
they had taken together. The roads were the same—unpaved,
strewn with natives on foot and on bicycles and in donkey carts,
always inching along in the middle where it was dry and where
there were not so many mosquitoes. Margaret honked at them as
she always did and swore and stood up on the seat and yelled at
them until they sidled off into the ditches and let her pass. Clover
wore her same yellow scarf and Joey took his same position in the
back seat, gazing silently between the two girls, his dark arms
crossed on the seat in front, his chin on his folded hands. It was
just another trip where they would eat their sandwiches together
from wax-paper bags and sleep together on the car seats or on a
blanket on the beach; and Clover and Joey would go out together
in a rented boat to dive. That is how it had been, and this trip
would not be different.

They arrived at the edge of the long narrow beach at nightfall,
and Clover and Joey jumped over the doors of the car for the
water, stripping off their shirts as they ran. Margaret followed
slowly with the towels and prepared to sit on the sand.

"Margaret," Clover called, spreading her arms on the waist-deep
water, "come in tonight. It's perfect all right. No drops. No holes.
Just come in and float with us."

Margaret shook her head as always and spread out a towel. But
Joey was out of the water and beside her, touching her wrist with
a warm wet hand. "Margaret, you have no idea how wonderful it
is. Especially at night. Just once you must get more than your toes
wet." His voice was tense and eager. She laughed and bent to sit
down, but Clover was beside her. "Margaret, you must, you must,"
she coaxed, and the two took her by the arms and led her down
to the edge of the sea. She was laughing and afraid, pulling back
from their hands, but they led her straight in and up to her thighs.

"My shirt," she said, "wait, my shirt," turning to run back, but
Joey lifted his arms, glistening in the dark, and unbuttoned it. She

stood quietly and let him. He did it very delicately taking it off her shoulders and carrying it up to the beach. Then they took her in up to her waist.

"You must learn to float," Clover said. "Lie on your back and we'll hold you."

Margaret's face broke its crust and was terrified.

"Margaret, the water will hold you," Clover encouraged, her voice soft, her round delicate face saddened and touched by Margaret's fear. "You mustn't be afraid."

"You weigh nothing in the water," Joey said. "You can't sink."

Gently they bent her backward and reached their arms under her. Her feet rose, she slapped the water, her neck craned. But they held her firmly and soon she was quiet and floating in their arms. Their faces looking down at her were gentle and smiling. The curve of their shoulders and the roundness of their wet cheeks and the dark hollows of their shadowed eyes in the night were almost identical. They could have been twins, either boys or girls, but for the small round bosom of the one facing the flat hard breastplates of the other.

Margaret, spread long between them, was all pale head on the black water, hair out to one side, her throat arched. Her eyes were half closed and her face was no longer strained with fear. Her lips were smiling a smile so soft, so vulnerable, that both Joey and Clover in the same movement reached out their hands toward her head to touch her floating hair and the wet nape of her neck.

Later, after they had eaten, they built a fire of brown fronds from the palms and dried themselves around it, kneeling on the spread blanket side by side. Margaret was much the largest of the three, as tall as a man, her sleek arms glowing orange in the firelight as she lifted them to comb her hair. And when the light went down she seemed to loom up like the slender tree she sat against, and her voice as she talked came soft and deep, as comforting and strong in the still night as a distant thunder roll. Dancing had never loosened her nor wine brought flush to her cheeks, but leaning damp and sleepy against the tall tree she was curved and heavy and her face shone warm long after the firelight had faded from it.

Joey lay on his side next to her as she and Clover talked, slowly and softly, about nothing in particular. The two had fallen to talking like that often, saying nothing either could remember later, but

using the words like patches for a quilt, a quilt they made only
to have something warm to pull about themselves. And Joey lay
and listened to the sound and not the words, lay and listened and
never took his eyes off Margaret. He turned to her boldly, shielded
by the dark, and filled himself with looking at her as if he were
the coral and she were the sea. He studied her face with its timid
eyes and smooth square jaw; he looked long at her shoulders and
the full breasts that moved slightly and softly with her breathing,
that burned warm and half bare in the firelight. He watched her
hands flex and shift and flatten on her thighs as she talked, broad
and hard like the beautiful, calloused, long-used hands of a guitar-
ist or a wood-carver.

He lay close to these hands, and once when they became still
with the silence of an ended sentence, he reached over and
touched the ridge of the knuckles, withdrawing his arm, but only
halfway, so it lay against her thigh.

She looked down at him. His body lay curved and breathing
full, with his face hidden in his shoulder. She bent slowly over
him and tried to see his eyes.

"Are you asleep, Joey?" she said.

"Margaret," he whispered, as if he had not heard her, and his
voice was trembling.

"What's the matter, Joey?" she asked, encircling his shoulders
with her long arm.

"You're beautiful."

There was a hush, with Joey's words echoed in it, and Clover's
mouth opening in the shadows. Margaret looked across at the girl,
as though sensing the tiny twitch of the white cheek, then reached
down and took Joey up in her arms. His eyes were closed tight as
he pressed his face against her. She rubbed her hand lightly over
the white hair and the hill of his shoulder blade and the sharp cliff
of the hip and the downy slope of the flank. He trembled and
clung to her.

"You funny little boy," she whispered to him, "to tremble like
that," and there was awe and sweetness in her voice.

The next day Clover and Joey explored the reef and Margaret
waited, lying flat on the sand. Joey appeared on the surface before
Clover and waded up quietly to where the girl lay stretched out,

long and still. She had fallen asleep and her hand had slipped
down by the side of her head. He scooped up a little sand and
kneeled down to sprinkle it on her shoulder and wake her; but
his hand remained suspended holding back the grains, and he
crouched there with his long white forelock burning in the sun, the
flower eyes wide and still, as if even their blinking might waken
her. He crouched with his haunches raised, crouched in the sleeping heat of Margaret's body, bending close, locking his legs so the
muscle bands stood in ridges. He was suspended there when Margaret's mouse eyes opened and met his, and they looked at one
another. She lay, not speaking, as if in her sleep she had prepared
herself to find him there.

"I was going to wake you," he said softly, and his voice rippled
over her like fingers. "I was going to wake you with this sand,
but here you are already awake."

Margaret lay with the white-headed boy close above her, and did
not move even to blink when he spoke, and only closed her eyes
slowly, as if she were in pain, when he bent and softly, quickly
kissed her on the lips.

When their heads moved apart, Clover was there, her full pale
legs apart, her air tank dripping in the sand.

No one said anything. The sandwiches were brought out and
they ate. They talked about the reef. That is how it went for the
rest of the trip. They never spoke of the new thing that had slipped
in with them on that broad and deserted beach; but Joey never let
Margaret out of his sight, looking quickly behind him sometimes
to see if she was there, and Margaret only smiled, her face a little
sad, exchanging no looks with his ardent eyes, but glancing now
and then at Clover when her back was turned. And Clover had
become very silent. She followed closely in their footsteps, her eyes
quick and guarded, her face pinched and nearly blank. She no
longer kept alive the conversations with Margaret, but answered
questions quickly and in monotone like a morose and jealous serv-
ant girl.

Two days after they arrived back at the hotel they were prepar-
ing to leave again. Margaret had found a gentleman with a small
launch, and she had persuaded him to loan it to her with its native
skipper for the weekend. So on an airless, cloudless morning in

August, they filed aboard, the three of them in a line, with Margaret in the lead. The boat was old, with a stout varnished deck and a pilothouse that perched on the top of the squat cabin like a black top hat. There was a stove, a tiny sink-hole and four cotlike beds below. The skipper confined himself exclusively to his steerage, sleeping there and sitting unsmiling at the wheel with a bottle of rum and a grimy hunk of pork on the ledge beside him.

Clover, Joey and Margaret clustered at the broad stern the first day out, sunning themselves and gazing at the misty colorless horizon of the open sea. They spoke little, but the silence was not sleepy and languid as it had once been. It had a hard listening quality. It was a silence that had sat poised and pulsing, ready to leap out.

"When will you be going home, Margaret?" Joey asked, swinging his legs over the low sill of the stern.

Clover looked around to see her face when she answered.

"Oh, the beginning of September sometime. It's a long way off."

"Not so long," Clover mumbled, and turned her head away.

"Shall I be seeing you sometime?" he asked.

"You live across the country from each other," Clover broke in sharply.

"I can write, then," Joey said, a spot of anger on either cheek, his eyes frowning into the surging foam below.

Clover rose and without looking at either of them took her towel and disappeared to the bow of the boat.

"She's tiresome," Joey said. "Tiresome and bad-tempered. We never used to quarrel . . . before; on the beach in the mornings, she never gave me those looks. She's very peculiar." He brooded over it a few moments, then came and knelt beside Margaret, smiling shyly at her as she sat staring at the deck, her arms around her knees.

"Don't bother about her," he said. "She's just put out because I'd rather sit with you than take her diving."

Margaret nodded abstractedly.

"Margaret," he said with sudden timidity in his voice, "Margaret, you do like me, don't you?"

"Of course, Joey." Her voice was clear and expressionless.

"It's only . . . it's only you seem rather peeved with me at times, rather cold." There was a silence while he waited for her to say something. Then he blurted quickly and earnestly, "I'm almost seventeen, Margaret. Seventeen is getting on. Seventeen is not so young."

"Of course it isn't, Joey," she said and looked him in the eyes. He put his hand out to touch her face, but she was getting up and slowly tossing her dark hair back like a fisherman casting his net. "Come on, Joey," she said, looking down at him kneeling there. "Come on and I'll fix us some dinner if you'll light the stove."

The night was dark and moonless. The tiny stars gave no light, and the boat had electric sockets without bulbs. Everyone went to bed early, and the old vessel swayed and creaked gently at its anchor in the black, smooth-rolling sea. The sense of wakefulness in the cabin mixed with the smell of sleep. No bed curtain moved for many hours, but sometime in the early-morning blackness there was a rustle and a crack of cot slats, then in the inky closeness, the presence of someone in the middle of the floor. A lithe figure moved noiselessly to Margaret's far bunk and pulled back the mosquito netting. The hands folded back the sheet from the broad shadow of Margaret's form and the shadow raised up.

"Who's that!"

"Hush, Margaret . . ."

At the sound of the voice Margaret was very still, sinking slowly down again.

"It's you . . ." she said, and the sound was part of the boat's sounds, was part of the washing, dripping sighs of the wooden hull. And the voice, as it lived in the narrow space between their two faces, was another part of the night, a whisper of water and air.

"Margaret . . . tomorrow we dock."

"Yes."

"And soon you'll be going back home."

"Yes," and the voice was faint in the shadows.

"Margaret . . ." and the sound was a weeping sound. "I came to tell you . . . I may never be able to tell you . . ."

An arm went up from the bunk and silenced the voice.

"You don't need to tell me."

The sea sounds hid the long soft cry of "Margaret . . . Margaret," from a throat overflowing and breathless, and the darkness

hid the movement of the head and shoulders as they closed down
upon Margaret's breast.

When the dawn came gray into the cabin, three cots sagged under the weight of three outstretched forms. Two slept, but the
largest, tall as a man, lay awake. Her hair hung disheveled on her
forehead and she stared at the ceiling with fixed, unblinking eyes.
She lay until the rumble and scrape of the motors started and rat-
tled the floor under her. Then she rose, put on her suit and went
out onto the stern. The boat was turning toward shore and the
white carpet of foam had made almost a complete semicircle.
The skipper stood in the black steerage, fingering the sliding wheel
in his hands. Margaret looked up at him a full minute, but his
long black back remained motionless.

At seven o'clock, with the sun full in the dingy cabin, Joey
stretched and swung off his cot and noticed immediately that Margaret was not there. He went on deck and walked around it and
came back to look once more in Margaret's bed.

"Clover!" He jogged her roughly, his face fallen with astonishment. "Clover, Margaret's not on the boat." The girl wavered in
front of him, then slowly her body stiffened as she understood his
words.

"Not in bed?" she asked, staring at the empty cot. "Not in bed?"

"I've gone up and back," he shouted, trying to make her understand, pulling at her to take her out on deck with him, but she
broke away, heading for the cot. Joey caught her arm again and
then dragged her out of the cabin and once around the deck until
they stopped below the skipper. Without letting her go, he called,
"Hey, hey, up there! Stop the engine! Margaret's not on the boat.
She's fallen off the boat!"

The engine died abruptly and the black man came down the
ladder and all three of them went to the rail and stared over, four
white hands clutching till their knuckles threatened to burst the
skin, two huge black hands holding lightly, uncomprehending.

"Turn the boat around," Clover said, her voice small and rattling like a pebble being shaken in a can. The Negro's eyes popped
out at them, fearful, as if they might be crazy. But there had been
three of them yesterday and there were only two now; and he ran
back up the ladder and ground the engine. They swung slowly
around and started back through their foam path. Clover and

Joey hung onto the bow and for twenty-five minutes there was
nothing but chopped green sea and the heaving horizon with a low
smear of land on it. The two faces thrust over the rail were wet and
dripping with wave spray. They looked from one side of the water
to the other. Then, beside him, Clover let her arms fall and she
slid down on the deck.

"She can't swim, she can't swim at all. She'd have gone under—
she'd have drowned by now. She'd have drowned . . ." The bronze
head wavered and fell down on the varnished deck, and she
sobbed.

But Joey kept his body arched out in the spray, not hearing her,
not turning from the green sea; and he was the first to see the dark
thing in the water, bobbing off to the side like a log. A long dark
log rolling up and over the close waves, a log with two branches
sticking out on either side.

He wheeled around on the deck and raised his arms to signal,
but the skipper had seen already and had cut the engine and was
sidling the boat over.

Joey wrenched Clover up by the arm and took her over to the
rail as they puttered up gently. It was Margaret, lying on the waves,
her arms outstretched. Joey was weeping now, standing, his white
head bowed on his shiny chest, weeping for Margaret, who lay
dead like a log.

The skipper leaned over the side rail and looked, his pink-lipped
mouth open, his neck craned. Then slowly, loudly he declared,
"She's not dead. She's floatin'. She's floatin' out there."

He ran on rubbery legs and got a rope ladder and climbed over
the side, stretching far out for her. He grabbed her around the
waist with his arm and hoisted her against him, climbing the ladder
slowly, straining with her weight.

"Lawd, this is a big girl," he panted. "This is the biggest girl I
ever saw."

Speechless, the two children followed him down to the cabin,
where he put her on the bunk.

"She's not full awake, but she's not dead," he said, looking down
at her. "No water inside either, 'cause she's breathing easy." Then
he turned and went up to his little steerage and started the motors.
Joey and Clover did not leave Margaret once, but sat on the floor
and watched her chest rise and fall with her breathing, as if it

would stop if they took their eyes away. Clover moved once to cover the cold legs with an army blanket, then sat down again like a sleepwalker.

Margaret was the first of them to speak. She looked at them with washed, blank eyes as the boat finally slid up against the hotel dock. "I float too well," she said, her voice strangely calm and natural coming from the mouth that opened in her gray face like a small black hole. "I tried but I can't sink. I just float. I can't do anything but float and float. If you hadn't taught me to float, you'd be Clover and Joey again. You'd be on the beach again, Joey and Clover, in the morning before breakfast." She closed her eyes and was still.

Then the black man came down and lifted her up from the cot. Even against his tremendous chest she looked large. He carried her out, with Clover and Joey behind. Clover walked ahead of Joey, her eyes on the one arm and the two legs that hung down limp as the skipper stepped up with her onto the dock. People were walking curiously toward them. Two beach boys in white shorts, and a woman, and three men in bathing suits. Clover saw them coming. They would crowd around. They would lead the Negro off to the hotel and perhaps call an ambulance. Clover's eyes looked after the limp legs and the one dangling arm, looked after the wet head on the black shoulder; and after the pale, tightly closed lips that had soothed her when she had cried, "Margaret . . . Margaret," in the dark, whispering cabin.

JAMES TRAMMELL COX was born in Virginia and graduated from the University of North Carolina. He taught at Clemson College and the University of Iowa, where he was managing editor of the *Western Review,* and in 1957 moved to Florida State University where he taught courses in literature and creative writing until his death in the fall of 1962. Mr. Cox's short stories have won two Thomas Wolfe Memorial Awards and have appeared in *Cross Section, Contact, Perspective,* and *Epoch.* His critical essays have been printed in *Modern Fiction Studies* and *English Literary History.*

That Golden Crane

"Where's Junior?" asked Mr. Gillespie as he stood beside the car. He had changed the tire, and now he was ready to go. It was hot. Down the long flat stretch of road toward Tallahassee, heat waves writhed above the asphalt like flames. From the car Mama Lester's reply was "Praise the Lord."

Removing his glasses to wipe the perspiration off them, Mr. Gillespie stared myopically at the oilcloth banner on the roof of the car. The bald forehead, which seemed suddenly naked when Mr. Gillespie took off his glasses, was bright pink except for a sprinkle of liver spots where his hairline had been when he was younger. It was gentle and full like the forehead of an infant.

"Junior Lester," he said, climbing in, "boy evangelist. Our sign surely tells them who we are." Even though the car was like an oven, it was a relief to get in out of the sun. He turned and smiled fondly at Mama Lester. "Where's Junior?" he repeated.

"He went onto that there rise, Mr. Gillespie," said Mama, "to pray for a good meeting." As she nodded toward the knoll where Junior had gone, the perspiration on the soft white roll of flesh beneath her dimpled chin caught the light from outside and glistened like strings of pearls.

MSS 1961.

The knoll toward which Mama nodded was crowned with a huge live oak. From the vertiguous spread of its branches hung a dense canopy of Spanish moss. Within the canopy, the deep shade seemed curiously forbidding—not cool or inviting at all. Mr. Gillespie hoped, if that was where Junior was, he would come out of there. Wherever he was, he wished he would come on. After a bit Mr. Gillespie repeated that the sign surely told people who they were. He sighed.

Impulsively Mama Lester covered his hand with her own, pressing down upon the bony knuckles with sudden passion. But when Mr. Gillespie sought to remove his hand from the wheel and take hers she withdrew it and picked up the fan in her lap—a Sunday school fan from Supchoppy with a picture of Jesus on it praying at a rock in the Garden of Gethsemane. She whipped the air as if it were eggwhites and scowled when Mr. Gillespie pecked her on the cheek. If she was lucky—and she knew she was—to have a gentleman friend like Mr. Gillespie and a son like Junior, it was also true that the Lord had not yet seen fit to open Junior's heart to her and Mr. Gillespie's terrible loneliness. Until He did, Mr. Gillespie would just have to keep his hands to himself. Mama Lester worshipped that boy.

In fact it was this worship, really, that had made her reach for Mr. Gillespie's hand. She herself was peeved with Junior, him not being here so that they could go on now Mr. Gillespie had finished. It was hot. Beneath the wet curls that clung to the back of her neck, her prickly heat burned. Her flowered organdy was soaked. Heat did not agree with her. Nevertheless, Mama Lester could not bear disapproval of Junior, even her own, which she was likely to regard as some weakness in herself, and when Mr. Gillespie had only said again that their sign surely told people who they were he had shown her the way to patience. He had spared her an expression of resentment she would have regretted later. Besides, Mr. Gillespie sounded so genteel the way he said *surely*. Her heart filled.

A little reading from the Scriptures being always a great comfort to them both, Mr. Gillespie took up the Bible which lay on the seat between them. As usual he began reading wherever the Good Book fell open. That way, it seemed more like a special message, even if the message itself was often hidden from them. "Thus saith the Lord," read Mr. Gillespie from Isaiah. Mama loved to hear him read: he always sounded as if he had just waked up. The timbre of Mr. Gillespie's voice *was* good. While resonant and firm, it seemed to carry with it whispers of personal tragedy and shy kindness.

The labour of Egypt, and merchandise of Ethiopia and of the Sabeans, men of stature, shall come unto thee, and they shall be thine: they shall come after thee; in chains they shall come over, and they shall fall down unto thee, saying, Surely God is in thee; and there is none else, there is no other God.

Verily thou art a God that hidest thyself, O God of Israel, the Saviour . . .

Suddenly Mama burst into tears. And when Mr. Gillespie hastily put the Bible down she fell into his arms and wept like a child. "Oh, Mr. Gillespie! Oh!"

Mr. Gillespie held her close, patting the damp organdy on her back. Tears filled his own eyes, and he kissed the damp, plump flesh at the nape of her neck tenderly. Into her ear he whispered, "Praise the Lord!" Her answer came quick and muffled, "Praise the Lord!"

It was no more given to Mr. Gillespie to understand Mama than to understand the Word of the Lord. He accepted both without question, for the long thirst which he had gratified with liquor for so many years now found true refreshment in this late love, at once intensely physical for Mr. Gillespie and serenely spiritual. In the better part of a lifetime he had spent as a night clerk in Tallahassee at the Andrew Jackson, he had lived entirely without either of these essential realities, existing only in the ghostly oblivion of cheap whiskey. Whenever, in fact, he handed a guest a key he carefully tucked the key itself against the room tag so that it wouldn't dangle and held the key and the tag both by the tip end for fear he might accidentally touch someone. In these, his own contacts with people, he was that afraid. Now, if only for his incarnation into this wet and heavy world of physical reality, Mr. Gillespie was eternally grateful. Every day, after God, he thanked Mama Lester and Junior. Gently he moved his hand so as to touch the mole on the plump, sweating slope of Mama's shoulder.

The incarnation of Mr. Gillespie was indeed something of a

miracle. It began with the touch of Junior's forefinger when Junior
and Mama checked in at the Andrew Jackson last spring for a revival at the Filmore Road Tabernacle Pentecostal Church. Mr.
Gillespie was drunk. By twelve, when they came in, Mr. Gillespie
was always drunk, which meant simply that he moved a little more
slowly and deliberately than usual. Otherwise, he might have
avoided Junior's grab for the key as he held it out for the elevator
operator who doubled as night bellboy, but he didn't. And the
shock of this unfamiliar contact was enough to sober him momentarily so that he listened with a solemn show of interest as Mama
confided that she had been in hoe-tel work before Junior was
called. She was the sixth floor maid at the Gulfside in Panama
City ever since her husband left her when Junior was still a baby.
Only she didn't like it—the things she seen, oh! She ended by inviting him out to the meeting the next night to hear Junior preach.
Whether it was the idea of a boy preaching or simply his uneasy
desire to get rid of her before she smelled the whiskey he didn't
know, but anyway he found himself slowly and deliberately promising that he would be there.

"I declare I don't know what come over me, Mr. Gillespie," explained Mama Lester, as she withdrew from his embrace. It seemed
to her now that what had flitted through her mind could hardly
have explained such an outburst. "Always the same," she had
thought, "Egypt and Ethiopia and the Sabeans—never any message!" She dabbed at her eyes with her handkerchief and mopped
her wet cheeks. "Hallelulia," she whispered hoarsely. "Praise the
Lord. *Where's* that boy, Mr. Gillespie?"

"Heaven only knows," said Mr. Gillespie with a chuckle. That
boy was a mystery to Mr. Gillespie. He had come into Mr. Gillespie's life like the children of Joel: "And it shall come to pass
in the last days, saith God, I shall pour out of my Spirit upon all
flesh; and your sons and your daughters shall prophesy . . . !" Yet
at eleven he could not be trusted in a strange bed without his rubber sheeting. Sometimes Mr. Gillespie thought him a little willful
too. And jealous, terrible jealous.

"Junior!" cried Mama Lester. "*Junior Les-ter!*" She lowered a
single fat white leg to the ground and then heaved herself out,
emerging from the car like dough that has risen and spilled over
the lip of its bowl. "*Junior Lester!*" As she turned back to Mr.

Gillespie, who was still in the car, she was suddenly anxious. "You don't reckon anything has happened to him, Mr. Gillespie?"

Mr. Gillespie got out and called too, but there was no answer —only the still, foreboding tree with its airless shadows within the motionless beards of moss. Where could the boy have gone to? Reluctantly Mr. Gillespie descended into the drainage ditch at the side of the road and made his way through the wire grass and briars, the jack oak and sassafras, up the slope of the knoll. He eyed with care each fat, fallen stick that lay suspiciously undulant and spotted with spores of lichen in the long grass—this was snake country.

Once when he stepped on a stick he hadn't seen and it rolled under his foot like something alive, striking against his heel, he was so startled he jumped back into the enveloping branches of a small persimmon. Then as he extricated himself from this, pawing at the cobweb that had clung to the back of his neck, he thought he heard something that was almost as upsetting as the buzz of a rattler would've been: he could have sworn he heard a snicker. But he listened a moment and decided it was only the dry rustle of the leaves of the persimmon as its branches resettled. He pushed on, ashamed of himself for having thought, even for a moment, what he did.

At the tree he paused before the curtain of moss. He knew it was crawling with chiggers. He hated to even touch it. Remembering Mama, though, sitting out there in that hot car, he parted several of the thinner strands and ducked quickly inside. "Junior?" he called, in a voice that was hardly above a whisper, "Junior, are you in here?" In the sudden darkness he couldn't see, he could scarcely breathe. He was about to turn at once to go when he heard it again: somewhere above him Junior was hiding and laughing at him.

As the serpentine trunks, which are often separate and only twisted together at the base of the tree in live oaks, became gradually visible, Mr. Gillespie stalked to the base for a more comprehensive view of the massive, low-hanging limbs that spread out above him. "Junior!" he demanded, "where are you?" Another snicker told him.

There, out on the limb just above where he had been standing, sat Junior. From his chin hung a long grey beard of Spanish moss.

In his fist he clutched a bouquet of wilted foxglove. With uncertain bravery he began to swing his feet back and forth, and as Mr. Gillespie stared, speechless, he began then to scowl. "I seen you," he said, scowling down at Mr. Gillespie like some Blakean Jehovah, at once infantile and ancient, "you and her," he added, "a-lovin' each other up. I seen you."

"Junior Lester!" exploded Mr. Gillespie at last, "do you want them chiggers to eat you alive?" It seemed a foolish thing to say, even to Mr. Gillespie, but it was the only thing he could think of because his thoughts were entirely given over to the sudden realization that he needed a drink. Not once since he had been saved had he burned with such a thirst.

"I seen you," repeated Junior.

"That moss is crawling with chiggers, Junior! Take it off! Take it off right now and come down from there!" Mr. Gillespie had never spoken to Junior quite like this before. In some vague way it was the beard that made him so angry. "Come down from there, Junior Lester, right this minute!"

Now it was Junior who was speechless, surprised and a little frightened by the authority in Mr. Gillespie's voice. His scowl began to wilt, and then he began to cry.

"There's no need to cry," continued Mr. Gillespie firmly. "It won't do you any good at all." Even as he said this, Mr. Gillespie knew he had gone too far, because it wouldn't do to take him back to Mama crying. Mama wouldn't understand at all. "I'm only trying to get you to come down from there," he added.

"You're trying to make me fall off this limb," said Junior, as if sensing the direction of Mr. Gillespie's thoughts. "That's what you're trying to do!" He was standing up now, making his way back along the limb with his arms spread wide like wings for balance.

"Junior!" cried Mr. Gillespie, "how can you say that?" He begged the boy to stop where he was and to sit down and let himself down into "Mr. Gillespie's arms," speaking of himself in third person as he occasionally did in especially affectionate moments. And now, for some reason, he really did need a drink.

But Junior ignored him, walking the limb with his arms tipping perilously to first one side and then the other. At the base, Mr. Gillespie offered his hand, but Junior jumped, with his shirt tail bil-

lowing out behind him and his beard flying. He landed at Mr.
Gillespie's feet as nimble and surefooted as if he had floated down.
Quickly rearranging his beard, he stepped up to Mr. Gillespie
with flashing eyes and his hair awry. He was covered from head to
foot with bits of bark and flakes of lichen that were like ashes.
"'Let them be confounded,'" he said, wagging a vengeful finger,
"'and put to shame that seek after my soul: let them be turned
back and brought to confusion that devise my hurt!'"

Mr. Gillespie was not sure now at what point he had so completely lost that moment of new-found authority, but lost it he had
—he knew this. And now all he could think of was a drink. He was
afraid . . . He would've liked to ask Junior to pray with him. Now,
before it was too late. Here, in this place, he would make a new
covenant with the Lord. But how could he now? He had only to
look into Junior's eyes . . . "You're a sight," he managed to say to
Junior, but with a voice as hoarse and unsteady as a boy's. "Fix
yourself," he added, "you don't want Mama to see you like that."
He turned quickly away, but not before he had seen the furious
scowl on Junior's childish features become a strangely lidded,
frightening smile.

"Praise the Lord!" cried Mama from the roadside when they
emerged from the curtain of moss, "Glory Hallelulia!" She was so
relieved that nothing had happened to Junior she seemed to have
forgotten entirely her discomfort and resentment. "Lord have
mercy," she cried when she saw his beard, "ain't he something
now? Ain't that the cutest thing you ever seen, Mr. Gillespie? For
all the world," she said, "like a little old man!" She hugged him
happily to her and closed her eyes against any love greater than
this. "Praise the Lord," she moaned.

Mr. Gillespie ducked around to his side of the car and got in
without telling her that he had found Junior hiding from them up
in the tree. He even managed to return Mama's proud smile when
Junior assured her the Lord would give them a good meeting. He
thought about it though. All the way into Tallahassee the image of
Junior up on that limb in his beard kept coming back to Mr. Gillespie—this and the taste of whiskey.

As they approached the outskirts of Tallahassee from the south,
they passed a piano painted red and mounted up on posts in a
newly cleared lot where the stubs of cut pines were still yellow-

white and sharp as gator teeth. A tarpaper shack set back on the lot bore a sign MUSIC SCHOOL. After several miles of flat fields of jack oak and pine, black-water marshes scabbed with algae and sway-roofed shacks buried beneath green mounds of cudsue, they began to come to little frame houses with chartreuse window blinds and telephone wires that sagged from brown-glazed insulators attached to the side of the house. In a tiny yard of packed clay farther on stood two monumental boxwoods, dwarfing the unpainted Negro shack behind them. From a tub beside the porch steps leaned a cross of orange crating with WORMS crudely lettered on the cross piece. Fruit stands and country-store filling stations began to appear on either side of the road, along with frequent billboards advertising automobiles, gasoline, and eternity. When they had crossed a railroad siding they were in the city limits, where huge storage tanks of oil and gas gleamed mercilessly with fresh coats of aluminum paint. Second-hand furniture stores displayed beds, chests of drawers, rockers, and mirrors out front. Across the road from the Tabernacle, to which they came at last, was a field of rusting automobiles. Above it swung a towering crane arm with a scoop dangling from it by a slender cable. A man with some kind of helmet on sat in the closed mandibles of the scoop, looking down, as the cable swayed with the crane arm.

Mr. Gillespie turned into the parking lot between Teague's Welders and the Tabernacle, aching with a vague anxiety that had grown upon him with each mile closer to Tallahassee. It was more than wanting a drink and being afraid of what would happen if he took one, though this, God knows, was a part of it. He didn't know what was the matter. And even though this was the place where his new life in Christ had begun five months and three days ago today, when the Lord first sent His Holy Spirit to such as him, Mr. Gillespie could hardly persuade himself to get out of the car and shake hands with Mrs. Billy Jo Fain, who came out to welcome them. He even dreaded the thought of the meeting tonight. In fact he suddenly admitted to himself something he had avoided for weeks: The Holy Spirit had not really entered into him since one night in July, over a month ago. Lately his speech was only his own jabbering, in the *hope* the Spirit would come. "Praise the Lord," whispered Mr. Gillespie to himself.

"Praise the Lord!" cried Mrs. Billy Jo Fain, because Mama had just been telling her how proud she and Junior was to bring Mr. Gillespie back without a drop passed his lips all summer. "Glory Hallelulia!" Mrs. Fain wrung his hand with joy. She then turned to Junior, who allowed her to take his hand, but held himself stiffly apart and avoided looking at her when it appeared that she was about to embrace him. While she talked on about the souls Junior had brought to Christ, Junior fixed his gaze on Mr. Gillespie, permitting the suggestion of a smile to lift one corner of the pout that swelled his lower lip. Finally when she released his hand Junior looked at her and nodded and quickly looked away again. "Well," said Mrs. Billy Jo Fain, "no sense in us standing out here in the hot sun, is they?"

But this was the smile, Mr. Gillespie told himself, of one man to another at the way women carry on. He was sure of it, and his spirits lifted. "Don't reckon so," he said, with a chuckle the women wouldn't understand, "huh, Junior?"

Junior was watching the man up in the scoop across the road and didn't seem to hear at first. But then he turned around and nodded. As the women moved along the walk to the Tabernacle, he fell in behind with Mr. Gillespie. He wanted to know if Mr. Gillespie had seen the red piano and why the man was riding in the scoop. He was as full of questions as any twelve-year-old, thought Mr. Gillespie, and you wouldn't know a thing had happened this morning. "Well," said Mr. Gillespie, "when they lower it to the car they want that man will jump out, you see, and hook them chains around the car so as they can lift it."

Inside, Mrs. Fain explained why she was so anxious for them to see what they had done: with the new expenses she couldn't figure how her poor flock could offer Junior the same guarantee as before. Would keep and $25.00 do? At this point, Junior, who had been over admiring the red velveteen cushions on the new chancel chairs, rejoined them and said, yes, it was privilege enough for him just to be able to preach the gospel to his elders—he wasn't trying to get rich off his preaching. " 'It is easier for a camel to go through the eye of a needle than for a rich man to enter the kingdom of heaven,' " he added.

"Amen," said Mrs. Fain.

Mama stared in shocked disbelief.

"Junior," Mr. Gillespie pointed out gently, "if you want to

preach the gospel in Valdosta too, come Friday night, we'll have
to have money for new tires."

Then she and Mr. Gillespie both commenced to tell Mrs. Billy
Jo Fain how tight money was with them, their surprise at Junior's
butting in only adding fuel to the fire. So Mrs. Fain finally agreed
to $50.00 and took them out to the Old Nursery, which had been
newly partitioned off into two sleeping rooms, with a bath between, and a kitchen on the end.

They passed a young apple tree in the back yard and Junior
plucked one of the small green apples from its branches. "Boy!"
snapped Mrs. Fain, "leave them apples alone."

Junior made a face, having tasted it, and then with a major
league hop, skip and jump he threw the apple over the roof of the
Nursery.

"Ain't it nice?" asked Mrs. Fain, remaining outside when she
had opened the kitchen door for them. She smiled broadly.

"It's real nice," agreed Mama leading the way inside.

But as soon as Mrs. Fain was gone Mama turned on Junior and
demanded to know what on earth had possessed him to say a thing
like that. Junior only smiled and pouted and acted as if he didn't
know what she was talking about. Mama was furious. Mr. Gillespie, though, had already begun to reconsider, because, when you
stopped and thought about it, probably it was just the thing that
decided Mrs. Billy Jo Fain to agree to fifty. Only he couldn't believe Junior was *that* clever. He tried to catch Junior's eye again,
as man to man, but Junior only stalked away into the next room,
disgusted with them both. Wearily Mr. Gillespie returned to the
car to bring their things in.

When he got back Mama was standing before the brightly
lighted interior of the refrigerator. "Potato salid," she said, "it's always potato salid." She closed the door, and moving over to the
table she let herself down onto a chair where she sat staring va-
cantly at the dime store picture of Jesus hung, crooked, on the
wall before her.

When he had put the suitcases down Mr. Gillespie took the
chair beside hers and reached out to console her with a gentle pat
on the thigh, drawing comfort from the mere touch of the wrinkled
organdy and the warm dough of the flesh beneath. Mama seemed
to find contentment in the weight of his hand, sighing as she

turned to him to count his liver spots. She liked to do that. She would touch each one, then stroke his forehead. When she repeated "potato salid," they both smiled.

"Is there anything to drink in that box?" It was Junior scowling first at the refrigerator and then at Mr. Gillespie's hand in Mama's lap. "I'm thirsty," he added, "aren't *you*, Mr. Gillespie?"

Aren't YOU, Mr. Gillespie? What did Junior mean by that? Mr. Gillespie turned and stared at Junior, who then took a quick step toward Mama, putting his hand out to the other side of her chair, where he stood with his head to one side smiling as if for a publicity poster.

"Koolaid," said Mama, hoping it would sound inviting because she had already begun to accuse herself of meanness for having spoken to Junior the way she had about the money.

Mr. Gillespie could not believe Junior would tease about a thing like that, not about drinking. It was just *him* and him having only one thing on his mind made him think a thing like that. "Junior?" he asked, "why did Jesus say to the fig tree, 'Let no fruit grow on thee henceforward forever'?"

Junior frowned. His clear brown eyes clouded with suspicion. This was obviously not what he had expected from Mr. Gillespie. He went to the refrigerator where he lifted the Koolaid out before answering: "It's not for us to question the Lord, Mr. Gillespie."

"Amen," said Mama.

Mr. Gillespie sighed. Junior hadn't understood that he was only trying to put things right again.

"Ugh!" Junior spit the Koolaid into the sink and bent over it spluttering. Then he poured the rest of the glass into the sink, watching with satisfaction as it disappeared, gurgling, down the drain. Suddenly his face brightened. "Mama," he cried, "can Mr. Gillespie go get us some Doctor Pepper?"

Mama looked at Mr. Gillespie and shook her head. "Mr. Gillespie's tired, Junior."

"Please?" He went to her chair and put his arms around her neck, watching Mr. Gillespie as he leaned to kiss her on the cheek. "Please?"

Mr. Gillespie swallowed uneasily. All he would have to do for a fifth of liquor would be to keep on going, down to the Andrew Jackson, and he had no wish for such temptation to be put before

him. He avoided Mama's eyes as she turned to ask him if he
minded. "Surely," he said at last, "but why don't Junior come with
me?" Though Junior didn't want to go, Mama insisted, because
she was going to take a bath and lie down for a while.

As they went out Junior hung his head sulkily and kicked at the
sparse tufts of crabgrass, stirring up small clouds of dust that only
made Mr. Gillespie thirsty to look at. He also plucked another
apple and threw it over the Tabernacle. Recalling how friendly
Junior had seemed before, Mr. Gillespie couldn't understand what
had happened. This hurt Mr. Gillespie, because only thirty minutes ago he was thinking how they used to go cane fishing in June,
wondering if he and Junior couldn't slip off tomorrow morning
down to the Wacissa. He dropped his arm around the boy's shoulder. He would just tell Junior the truth about why he wanted him
along. But Junior shook off his arm.

"Junior, look—" the words died in his throat. He could see it was
no use. "Say, Junior, how would you like to go fishing tomorrow?"
In the way the back of Junior's curly head lifted, Mr. Gillespie
could see that he had surprised him. But then his head bent stubbornly forward again, and he wouldn't answer. "Junior?" Mr. Gillespie's voice dropped lower, "I want you to go with me after the
pop, son."

"I'm *not* your son!" cried Junior. "And I'm *not* going with you!"
He ran to the side door of the Tabernacle where he turned in the
doorway and explained angrily: "I need to meditate on Him for
tonight." As he stepped back, drawing the door after him, it seemed
to Mr. Gillespie for a moment that Junior smiled from within
the deep shadow of the Tabernacle—the same frightening, lidded
smile as before at the tree.

The darkened interior of Teague's Welders was lit with the spitting tongues of welders' torches as Mr. Gillespie pulled out into
the highway. Mr. Gillespie looked the other way: his own tongue
was fire enough. Then when he passed a store where he could
have bought Doctor Peppers, he kept going. On South Baptist
Avenue as he neared town he passed the fairgrounds where a ferris
wheel turned slowly in the sunlight, its seats rocking. Then at the
Andrew Jackson Mr. Gillespie pulled over to the curb across from
the hotel and sat a moment, still rigid, still holding tightly to the
wheel as if to his decision—for he had made up his mind exactly

what he would do. Back at the Tabernacle it had come to Mr. Gillespie like a revelation that Junior *wanted* him to go back to his bottle. It was a terrible thing to have to believe. But it was the truth. And on the way in Mr. Gillespie had thought it all out very carefully: he knew what he would do. Trance-like, he crossed the street and entered the Andrew Jackson.

For ten dollars, Doc Pugh, the hotel doctor with an "office" in his room, was glad to give Mr. Gillespie a couple of signed health certificates. In a wistful cracked voice he kept saying Mr. Gillespie was a "new man, a new man." Mr. Gillespie would've liked to stay and "witness" for his old friend, but he was afraid. He didn't feel safe until he was once again outside on the street.

At the Courthouse they didn't want to issue the license without Mama there to sign it too. He wouldn't leave, though, until finally they gave it to him to take out to her to sign. Walking back to the car, which was still parked across the street from the Andrew Jackson, he had his worst time.

With the license in one hand and a carton of Doctor Pepper in the other, Mr. Gillespie collapsed into a chair at the kitchen table, exhausted. After a while he got up and went to the wall and straightened the picture of Jesus. Then when he returned to his chair, he put his head down on the table to rest, the plastic top as cool as marble.

"Where's Junior?"

Mr. Gillespie lifted his head from the table and looked up: it was Mama, standing in the door into her room in her slip. He told her that Junior hadn't gone with him, he supposed he was still over at the Tabernacle meditating.

"Oh, Mr. Gillespie!" cried Mama, padding quick and weightless in her bare feet to where he sat. She seemed to know at once what he had been through. "Why didn't you tell me? Why didn't you tell me, Mr. Gillespie." She embraced him, pressing his head to her breasts, and Mr. Gillespie slipped his arm about her waist, thankful to the Good Lord who had gone with him into the very furnace of his fiery thirst and brought him safely out again. "Praise the Lord!" moaned Mama. "The Good Lord was with you, Mr. Gillespie."

"Mama," said Mr. Gillespie, "look what I brought you." He held up the license for her to see.

"Oh!" Mama gasped. Her eyes opened wide, and she stared at the little black rainbow of print that said MARRIAGE LICENSE as if it might be a summons of some kind. "Oh, Mr. Gillespie, you know you shouldn't have done that. I declare. Oh!" There were tears in her eyes as she clutched Mr. Gillespie's head to her bosom again and began to sway from side to side. Mr. Gillespie didn't know whether she was laughing or crying, and neither did Mama. "I declare," she said, "I declare."

Mr. Gillespie put his arms about her waist, happily allowing himself to be held like this until suddenly the image of Mama holding Junior just this way came back to him and he sought clumsily to stand up and take her in his arms.

But Mama stepped back. "No, Mr. Gillespie," she said, with a kind of frightened determination. "I just can't. Not less'n Junior will marry us. You know my heart is set on that."

"But Beulah,"—it was the first time he had ever called her by her given name—"he won't marry us. You know he won't."

"I can't help it, Mr. Gillespie, I just can't help it. My heart is set on that." Then abruptly she shushed him, eyes growing wide and fearful. "Psst! He's coming!" She slipped from his arms, snatched up the license, and disappeared into the bedroom.

Wearily Mr. Gillespie turned to the refrigerator to take out an ice tray for the Doctor Peppers. The trays were stuck, and he was still trying to pry one loose when Junior came in, behind him.

"Where's Mama?"

Mr. Gillespie nodded toward the other room without turning from the refrigerator.

"I thought I seen her in here."

He finally managed to shake a tray loose, carrying it to the sink where he ran water over it before he tried ejecting the cubes. Then he took down three glasses and dropped the ice cubes in, one by one, three to a glass. Turning around, he knew that now was no time to ask Junior, but he could not seem to help himself. "Junior," he asked, "when are you going to marry your mama and me? I want to know."

Junior scowled. His clear brown eyes clouded unhappily. "When the Lord tells me to," he mumbled.

"When is the Lord going to tell you to?" asked Mr. Gillespie almost angrily.

Junior's eyes cleared, bright and sparkling with sure indignation. "Shall he that contendeth with the Almighty instruct him? He that reproveth God, let him answer it!"

The ice in the glasses which Mr. Gillespie still held in his hands began to rattle noisily as his hands trembled now. Embarrassed, Mr. Gillespie stepped quickly to the table with the glasses. He sighed. There was no use to try and reason with Junior. He had known this before he asked. He put his hand to his mouth and sucked at the blood in his palm where he had skinned it messing with the ice tray. Then he opened the Doctor Peppers, somewhat calmer now.

Junior wasn't satisfied. "'It hath been said,'" he added, "'Whoever shall put away his wife, let him give her a writing of divorcement. But *Jesus* says, That whosoever shall put away his wife, saving for the cause of fornication, causeth her to commit adultery; and whosoever shall *marry* her that is divorced committeth adultery.'"

As Mr. Gillespie stared at the Doctor Pepper in his glass, his stomach all at once rose up against it and he could no more have drunk it than he could a full glass of 666. Queasy and exasperated, he put it down and walked out, having to go outside in order to get to his room on the end since he couldn't go through Mama's room. Here he took off his glasses and lay down on his unmade bed to think, praying that the Lord would not allow his heart to be filled with hate for any that were in His image. Then when he found that this was not to be given to him without a struggle, he got up, put his glasses on again, and opened his Bible, being careful to read at the first verse his eye fell upon:

At the same time came the disciples unto Jesus, saying, Who is the greatest in the kingdom of heaven?

And Jesus called a little child unto him, and set him in the midst of them,

And said, Verily I say unto you, Except ye be converted, and become as little children, ye shall not enter into the kingdom of heaven.

Whosoever therefore shall humble himself as this little child, the same is the greatest in the kingdom of heaven.

And whoso shall receive one such little child in my name receiveth me.

"Amen!" cried Mr. Gillespie aloud. "Praise the Lord!" He fell onto his knees and thanked the Lord for sending him a message in his pride and his wicked resentment of a little child. When he arose from his knees he would have rushed to tell Junior of this message the Lord had sent him, but all at once his knees were like water and he began to tremble again, violently. Besides he had just remembered the dry cleaning. Somebody would have to take that in.

At 7:00 the gooseneck over the REVIVAL sign in the yard went on, at 7:30 the lights in the crosses and the inside lights. The three fiery crosses of glass brick, set into the facade that rose in tiers like a child's block house at the front of the Tabernacle, glowed a blood red, for red bulbs were used in the cross lights. They cast a red light onto the faces of the crowd gathered about the stoop and even onto the three dead palms along the highway. Now the crowd began drifting in. Old women, moving slow, with their wrinkled necks out. Old men, shrivelled, but stiffly erect like prisoners in some vague battle they could not believe they had lost, never having fought it. A few young women, thin, looking around. Young girls with bad eyes or poor complexions, inclined to be stout. No boys over twelve. Few men, these few guarded and un-inquisitive, wanting only to get to a seat and not be seen. Some small children and infants, solemn-eyed, as if expecting a slap.

"It's a good crowd," said Mrs. Fain, turning around to Mama with a quick, muscular smile. She was at the lectern, which served as pulpit. Behind her were Mama, Junior, and Mr. Gillespie, seated on the platform in three throne-backed chairs of blond oak with bright red cushions. Everything was blond oak and new: the chairs, the Hammond organ, the lectern, the pew benches, and the wall plaques showing attendance and offering.

"Praise the Lord," said Mama. Then after a quick appraisal of Junior's handkerchief, bow tie, hair, and shoes, she leaned across in front of him to whisper to Mr. Gillespie that she was certainly glad he remembered the dry cleaning. (It had turned out that Mr. Gillespie had to make another trip into town to get their clothes pressed.) Mr. Gillespie nodded with slow, deliberate gravity.

First they sang "One Rose":

> Don't send me any flowers
> When I pass on
> Just one rose for Jesus
> When I pass on . . .

Then Mrs. Fain told them about what a successful revival they had last year when Junior preached and how she hoped this one would be a success too because she had promised Junior's mama a set of tires so as he might carry the Lord's Word on to Valdosty next week. When she was through she introduced Mama, who told them how Junior was called at camp meeting two years ago, with him only nine when Mr. Bingham from Supchoppy laid on his hands and declared Junior was a witness to the power and the glory of God's Holy Spirit. (*Amen! Praise the Lord!* came sprinkled cries from the assembly.) She told how it was all she could do to keep Junior in school on account of him wanting to go forth and preach the gospel in all the world like Jesus told the eleven. (*Amen! Praise the Lord!*) She followed him for two summers wherever the Lord called, and now—praise be to God!—Junior had a church of his own in Lynn Haven, and they travelled about only when they was specially invited like tonight. "And for you folks tonight," Mama concluded, "we have a special guest I am sure will open your hearts to the glorious power and the everlasting mercy of Our Savior Jesus Christ when he tells you what Our Savior done for him in this very Tabernacle last Spring. Tell the folks what He done for you, Mr. Gillespie!"

Glory Hallelulia! Praise the Lord! Oh yes, Lord!

As Mr. Gillespie rose and walked to the lectern with very slow and very solemn dignity, a hush fell over the assembly. He took hold of the stand with both hands, then half turning with a slight bow to Mama, he said, "Yes, I'll tell them what He's done for me, Mrs. Lester. Surely." He faced the assembly. He paused. Then in the whispering resonance of his best voice, which seemed charged tonight with a special tragedy, a special kindness, he spoke with slow and deliberate emphasis. "He *saved* me. He saved me, and privileged me to work for Him in the company of two of His finest servants. That's what he did for me!" Mr. Gillespie paused to reach back and scratch himself under the shoulder blade, his elbow protruding like a broken wing.

Amen! Praise the Lord! Glory Hallelulia!

Mr. Gillespie went on to tell them what a lonely life he had led until a kind word from Mama to a miserable drunken sinner like himself had brought him into that very door five months and three days ago today, drunk. So drunk he hardly knew where he was. (A young woman wailed, and gasps of surprise and pity stirred the assembly.) Mr. Gillespie pointed to the very bench in back where he had staggered to a seat. (Every head turned.) Then with a slow, awesome sweep of his arm, he pointed now at Junior. "But this boy," he cried, "this child before you now, preached like I'd never heard preaching before. Like Peter and John in Jerusalem, when the high priests told them they couldn't preach no more in Jerusalem, this boy was filled with the Holy Spirit and spoke the Word of God with boldness!" Mr. Gillespie dropped his arm now to scratch along the inside of his thigh.

Slowly and deliberately, with occasional pauses to scratch his chigger bites, Mr. Gillespie finished the story of how the Spirit had come to him also when he turned to embrace his neighbor as Junior had told them to and what a joy it was to discover God's mercy in sending His Holy Spirit to such as him. He told them about his return to the hotel where in the middle of his transcript he walked off and left his desk and his bottle under the desk, going up to Mrs. Lester and Junior's room to pray all that night and to make a covenant with the Lord to serve Him all the rest of the days of his life and never again to touch strong drink—

Praise the Lord! sounded one of the men's voices, deep and agonized. The women wailed afresh. *Praise the Lord!*

Mr. Gillespie himself seemed to choke up with emotion, visibly sagging as he stood there before them, holding onto the stand now with both hands. He paused. He moistened his lips. He turned first to one side and then to the other, slowly, as though suddenly he had forgotten where he was or was looking for some way out. He looked at his audience. He carefully moistened his lips with his tongue, to go on. He whispered, "But—"

A young woman on the front row seemed almost to scream.

There was another long pause in which Mr. Gillespie only stood there, holding onto the stand, looking at the young woman as if he had to decide why she had screamed before he could go on. He scratched at the place on his back. He moistened his lips. "The flesh," he whispered, "is weep." Again he paused. Something was wrong. He scratched himself. He thought very deeply for a moment, and then he knew: "Weak," he corrected himself in a whisper that trailed off into silence while Mr. Gillespie stood there, still facing his audience, holding onto the stand . . .

In the intense hush that had fallen over the assembly now Junior was heard to whisper to his mama: I *knew* it! Then suddenly he was there at the stand beside Mr. Gillespie, his eyes shining, as he cried, "Fall *down*, Sinner! Fall down on your knees before your God and confess your sins! *Pray!* Pray for His Forgiveness—you're *drunk*, Mr. Gillespie!"

The hush was shattered with a single explosion of cries and screams as though a child having tired of his block house had put his mouth to the door and shouted.

As Mr. Gillespie sank to his knees Junior seemed to descend upon him on some invisible ferris wheel, rocking in the lights as he came down with beard flying and his voice roaring in Mr. Gillespie's ears. Now he was floating off, up and away again with his long grey beard flying and a bouquet of foxglove in his hand. Mr. Gillespie cried out in confusion. It had all happened so quickly. He had simply run out of the strength to concentrate. He didn't understand. Junior's voice was close again.

"Do you confess your sins before Almighty God?"

"Yes, Lord," moaned Mr. Gillespie. Now Mama was there on her knees beside him, her arm around his shoulders, repeating after him, "Yes, Lord."

Yes, Lord! came a thundering echo from the wailing, still frightened assembly.

"Have you broken your covenant with the Lord?" shouted Junior, brushing the hair out of his eyes and jumping up and down in his excitement.

"Yes, Lord," said Mr. Gillespie.

"Yes, Lord," repeated Mama, "he has."

The assembly moaned.

"Have you defiled the lips that He gave you for His worship with the stink and fire of alcohol?"

"Yes, Lord," confessed Mr. Gillespie.

"Yes, Lord, he has—when he went after the dry cleaning."

"Is this the first time since you made your covenant with the Lord?"

"Yes, Lord."

"Yes, Lord, it is."

"Do you repent your sin, you miserable sinner?"

"Yes, Lord, he does." Mama's voice in his ear as she held him close was full with love and faith.

Praise the Lord! came the cries. *Glory Hallelulia!* shouted others. *Save him, Lord!*

"Save him, Lord!" shouted Junior, stepping forward to lay his hands on Mr. Gillespie's head. He looked up and cried again: "Save this miserable sinner, O Lord! He has confessed his sin and repents, O Lord!"

Praise the Lord! Glory Hallelulia!

"Send down your Holy Spirit to this flesh, O Lord, that his sins may be washed clean for Jesus Christ's sake!"

But it didn't come. Instead came the image of Junior sitting up on that limb of the live oak tree. And Mr. Gillespie cried out in the agony of his doubt. Mama clutched him to her, moaning.

"Sinner, do you believe?" shouted Junior wrathfully.

Mr. Gillespie lifted his eyes to the stage light overhead, blinded, in his plea for the mercy of belief. Then there again in the flood of light appeared Junior: the beard flying, eyes flashing. Mr. Gillespie closed his eyes. He bowed his head. "Yes, Lord," he whispered, "I believe." At once, as if his very blood were turned to light, Mr. Gillespie was filled with a glorious discovery of his own unworthiness: His resentment of Junior was only rage against his own sinful thirst; even his determination *not* to drink was pride; his love for Mama, an awful lusting after the flesh; sneaking back with that bottle to his room, the weakness of an unregenerate sinner. And trying, for Mama's sake, to go through with his testimonial was a dark hypocrisy God alone could forgive. While this light, this throbbing unbearable pulse of light brought tears to Mr. Gillespie's eyes that streamed down his cheeks, it also filled him with a frightening joy—a bright incredible realization that God in His unbounded mercy could forgive even him. "*Yes Lord!*" shouted Mr. Gillespie. "*I believe, O Lord!*"

"Yes Lord, he believes!"

O yes, Lord! Yes Lord! roared the assembly, moaning now in unison except for the intermittent screams of the young woman.

"Do you in your heart desire a new life in Christ?" shouted Junior. He bent over Mr. Gillespie now, bright brown eyes wide and shining, his lips spread in a proud and blissful smile. His eyes rolled heavenward as he dropped his hands dramatically to Mr. Gillespie's shoulders.

It was then that Mr. Gillespie knew the Holy Spirit was entering into him. It split his bones apart as he leaped to his feet, trembling. It set his tongue to dancing in an unknown language. After this he seemed to be in a dream as he turned to Mama with open arms, feeling the Spirit flow into her body from his own as she too began to tremble and to speak. He could hear Junior's voice as he preached a sermon about Jesus coming in a golden crane, but it was like a voice in a dream, disembodied and distant in the darkness. He couldn't seem to discover where it was coming from, and even though he was listening closely he knew that he didn't hear it all. The part he heard was glorious, glorious. Jesus, Junior said, would come again, riding in the golden scoop of a golden crane, riding high above everybody's head till He looked down and saw one that was saved. Then Jesus would give the signal and God would lower that crane, that golden crane, so Jesus could step forth and bind His loved one with that golden chain, binding His loved one around and around with that golden chain. And when His loved one was bound secure in that golden chain, dear Jesus would give the signal again, and away they would swing off to heaven in that golden crane, in that golden crane . . .

Mr. Gillespie wasn't sure when it was that the final pandemonium broke loose, with everyone surging forward to be saved by the touch of Junior's hand. He knew only that it was like something faraway, faraway. And it was the loving-sweet cry of Mama's fulfillment that was close in his ear as he awoke with her beneath the apple tree in the soft light of the scoop of a new moon, tipped high in the sky above them.

"Heavens!" cried Mama, "what have I done?"

JOYCE CAROL OATES and her husband currently live in Detroit, where she is an instructor at the University of Detroit. She has studied at Syracuse and the University of Wisconsin. Her stories have appeared in *Epoch*, the *Literary Review*, the *Arizona Quarterly*, and *Mademoiselle*, where she was co-winner of the *Mademoiselle* college fiction contest in 1959. She is the author of various critical pieces that have appeared in *Renascence* and *Texas Studies in Literature and Language*. She will have a book of short stories published early in 1963 by Vanguard Press, and is currently at work on a novel.

The Fine White Mist of Winter

Some time ago in Eden County the sheriff's best deputy, Rafe Murray, entered what he declared to the sheriff, Walpole, and to his own wife and man-grown sons, and to every person he encountered for a month, white or black, to be his second period—his new period, he would say queerly, sucking at his upper lip with a series of short, damp, deliberate noises. He was thirty-eight when he had the trouble with Bethl'em Aire, he would say, thirty-eight and with three man-grown sons behind him: but he only had his eyes open on that day, he was just born on that day, he meant to keep it fresh in his mind. When the long winter ended and the roads were thick and shapeless with mud, shot with sunlight, the Negro Bethl'em and his memory both went out of Eden County, and—to everyone's relief, especially his wife's—out of Murray's mind too, but up until then, in those thick, grey, mist-choked days he did keep whatever it was fresh in his mind; so that the fine driving snow of that year seemed to play back again and again Murray's great experience.

He and the Negro Bethl'em, whom he had arrested out in a field, had been caught in a snowstorm driving in to the sheriff's office. Murray had declared, muttering, he had never seen such snow; and every time he exploded into a brief, harsh, almost painful series of curses the snowstorm outside grew thicker. Murray was a big proud man, with eyes that jutted a little out of his head, as if with rage, and these he turned to the swirling world beyond his windshield while the Negro sat silent and shivering beside him, his own eyes narrowed, discreet, while Murray swore at the snow. Never had a man been so tricked by the weather, never so confused by his own country, as Murray thought himself to be; and it seemed to him too, though he pushed the idea right away, that he was lost and would never find his way back again.

Back in the sheriff's office they would be waiting for him, the windows warm and steamy, the men sitting around the stove with their legs outstretched smoking, surely talking of him—of this queer bad luck that had come to Murray, the best deputy, the only man beside Walpole himself good enough to bring in Bethl'em Aire. Murray grimaced to himself at the picture: he saw the men, and he saw their picture of him in turn—Murray with his proud big shoulders, his big hands, but no common farmer either, no common country farmer, Murray with his felt hat stuck tight on his head, the filthy band fitting right on his forehead as if it had grown there, his black felt hat like a symbol of something, or like a pot overturned upon his face. So his face would emerge beneath the hat broad and tanned, stung by the December wind, but raw-looking too, and his eyes blinking and squinting as if there were a glare. He would have his overcoat as great as any horse blanket, stiff and looking like wood, or iron, from a distance, always braced as if in a wind, or just emerging out of one, he would have his leather glove as fine and gleaming as new leather could be, his big boots dully gleaming with grease or melted snow; and these he would kick against the stove, ceremoniously, grunting, first the left foot and then the right, with his chin lowered so upon his chest, or down to where the big coat seemed to swell out from his body: no sheriff's deputy carried himself like Murray, no country son of them had his look, or his voice, could be trusted to bring in such a one as Bethl'em Aire. . . . But Murray, sitting in the cold car, felt the vision slip away. He was looking at the snow, the crazy whirling of flakes. Not that these seemed infinite, or even numerous—they looked instead just like a constant shuffling and reshuffling of the same flakes, the same specks which gleamed back at him like little eyes so white in the glare of the headlights. On either side they fell away into a mass of grey, like cloud. Murray grinned and swore, spitting, at the storm. Now and then he saw stiff, shocked trees alongside the road, bare things as naked in the cold as if someone had peeled all their bark off with a jack-knife, peeled it off and tossed it up to be sucked away by the wind. It was then that Murray noticed the Negro Bethl'em staring at the trees too. "This won't last long," Murray said. "It's just a freak storm, and a freak cold too, and you know it as well as me."

It was good to hear his voice again. He went on. "When I lived up north farther there were storms there! That's where they really were—snow up past the first floor windows of houses, there—and my father would have to dig his way out, to see about the stock. People ust to die, there, in storms like that! People who were alone. . . ." He wondered why he had taken that turn. His voice had just gone that way by itself. He waited for the prisoner to say something; but they only sat for a minute or two in silence, listening to the wind. Then he laughed, harshly and humorlessly, and found himself going on: "They wouldn't find them till maybe a month afterwards," he said, "old people who lived all alone, old men, frozen to death in their homes. There was one in a school house caught, one old man, he'd sleep there to save wood at home. He got caught in the schoolhouse when a storm come on and he couldn't get home, and burned all he could—books and desks and all— That old man, I remember him, I remember him coming around, asking to shoe horses in the summer—" Murray wondered at himself, at the odd sound of his voice. He went on, immediately, "That was then. A man caught so all alone in the winter, that would happen to him—then or now—up there or right here, any-where—a man is got to stick with others, doing how they do, their laws, obeying their laws, living with them—not off by himself—with his own laws— The ones that think different are the ones get kilt—or we bring them in to get—"

He quit; he drove on a while, silent, impressed with his own words, and also with the peculiar closeness of that old man's death. Then he shook his mind clear of the thought and decided they ought to stop. "We'll wait this goddam wind out," he said. The wind kept on. Before him the road reared out in broken, bare stretches, as if it had been torn out of the drifts of snow on either side. "Wait it out," Murray muttered. He had not glanced at his prisoner for some time; he did not do so now. He knew, and the prisoner knew, that he was talking to himself. But then he went on to say, "You know where we are now?"

The question hung in the air between them. Murray looked around in surprise, as if the Negro had spoken to him. The Negro Bethl'em, however, just sat there, as big a man as Murray, his puffed black face turned right to him, and his eyes, too, small and close together like Murray supposed a pig's eyes would be, these were staring right at Murray's face, or maybe at those queer words Murray had just heard himself say. Bethl'em, a well known country Negro, well known up and down the road, who worked for hire in the summertime, hay mowing and such, had come to Murray to look, now, not like himself any more, but like someone else, or a statue of someone else, all hard and cold and ageless, as if he had been staring at Murray or someone like him, so, with those pig's eyes, for centuries. Then he began to cough—not bothering to turn his head aside, coughing in a wracking, terrific, almost spiteful way.

"Ya, you wouldn't know, would you," Murray said. He felt his cold cheeks tighten. "Cough your goddam heart out, your black tonsils out then. Go on." Sitting near the edge of the seat, his knees apart and rubbing against the steering wheel, Murray stared at the storm, his face distorted with the effort of seeing. "There— something over there—" he said. The prisoner had stopped coughing. Murray pressed the car forward slowly. A ridge of land to his left seemed to fly right up out of the ground, a giant swelling of white like the side of a mountain. "There's a garage somewhere here—I'm damned if there ain't—I know it, I seen it enough times—" He spit out his words, as if he almost expected the garage to appear as soon as he spoke, as if his words had made it appear. "It must be here somewhere," he said, a little quieter. "Out here somewhere—" Next to Murray the Negro began coughing again. Murray stared at him for a moment; then he looked away. "Are you all right?" he said.

Bethl'em did not answer. "Most likely getting sick," Murray went on, harshly, even angrily, as if he were talking to the snow. "Running all that ways without a coat, like a goddam fool nigger. . . . Well, you cough all you like. I'm getting out here." He stopped the car, or allowed it to stop, or allowed the wind to stop it. "I'm going out to see what's here. I think there's a building here." He switched off the ignition but left the lights on. He could barely open the door, and when the first gust of wind hit his face he grunted with surprise, and looked back to Bethl'em. He saw the Negro sitting there, watching him.

Murray carried the picture of the man with him as he made his way, bent awkwardly against the wind, against the terrific on-slaught of snow, around the front of the car and off the frozen road. Now the snow seemed to mock Murray, Murray with all his pride, all his strength, stumbling first in one direction and then stopping, slyly, perhaps, and turning in another, now walking as if he had really caught sight of something. When he found himself looking at two shapes, oblong and upright with long narrow drifts extend-ing out behind them like angels' wings, he could only gape at them in confusion. Then he saw behind them the dim flicker of light, a light which grew stronger just as he stared at it, shielding his big face with his hands. Pulsing clouds of snow, like handfuls of fine hard sand, were flung against his face.

While helping Bethl'em out and to the building, Murray had to hold him once from falling—the ground underfoot was ice—and stood with his feet far apart, bracing both of them; the prisoner, with his wrists tied behind him, could not help himself. Murray put his arms right around the man's shoulders and in this way, panting, with both their heads bowed, the line of snow slashing at their foreheads as if they were no different from the gasoline pumps, they made their way through to the little wasteland of shelter before the garage. Murray slammed at the door with his foot. He bent to look through the glass of the door, to a blurred picture of two men, at the back of the garage, and a stove, and a lamp of some sort; he saw, muttering with impatience, that one of the men was advancing slowly and hesitantly toward the door.

When the door opened Murray pushed Bethl'em inside and then stepped in himself to a warm surge of air, and to the vision—how startling only Murray himself could have said, and yet it could not have been really a surprise to Murray, who knew this country so well—of the man in overalls, a Negro, a man with a black and red plaid shirt queerly clean, and, at the back, still another Negro, who sat up straight staring at them with the look of a rabbit or chip-munk or any small animal who believes himself not really seen, but disguised by the foliage around him, and whose belief gives him an air of absurdity. Murray, who was still a little shaken at this time, turned to close the door; and for an instant he stared at the frosted glass, and the sense of his isolation among these men welled up and subsided within him, leaving him a little weak. Then he turned back. "We only come to sit out this storm," he said.

The first Negro was staring at him and, past him, to Bethl'em, with a look of muffled recognition. "You c'n come in here," the Negro said slowly. "By the stove an' get warm . . . I was . . . I was scairt for a minute who was out there."

It was warmer at the back of the garage. The other Negro, a younger man, watched them. He was sitting in a swivel chair before a large office desk, an old-fashioned, ridiculous piece of furniture with scratches and initials on its surface. The older Negro went to the side of the desk and picked up a screwdriver, idly. He looked back at Murray over his shoulder.

"We thank you for this." Murray said, nodding brusquely. He had begun to feel oddly warm. Now, as if performing before these men—whom he believed he recognized, vaguely—but at the same time not really before them at all, but for his own satisfaction, his own delight, Murray began ceremoniously to unbutton his coat. One of his fine leather gloves he had taken off and this stuck, now, in his pocket, as if it were an ornament, and so with one glove on and one off he began to unbutton the big plastic buttons of the coat, frowning, his face distorted with concentration. The Negroes watched him. When he pushed the last button through the button-hole he sighed and straightened his shoulders and made a gesture— even Murray could not have said how he did it—so that the older Negro started, and went to take Murray's coat. Murray watched him take it gingerly in his arms and hang it on a peg, brushing snow off it, yet gingerly too, as if he knew he was being so closely watched. With his right hand Murray took hold of the red wool scarf his mother had knitted for him the first winter he was a deputy, and now he began to unwind it, again ceremoniously, while the others watched. This too he handed to the Negro, who hung it by the coat. Murray touched his hat, but only touched it; for some reason he thought it might look better on, though it was wet. Then he turned ceremoniously to Bethl'em and, while the others stared, began to brush some of the snow off him. "Stand by the stove," he said. Bethl'em turned blindly—the stove was an old one, made of iron, a large, squat, ancient stove that gave forth a low roaring murmur and glowed, in spots, a hard-looking yellow. Murray patted Bethl'em's shoulders and untied his wrists, and he saw now that the cord had cut into the man's flesh, that it had made raw red lines in his skin. "Look at that," Murray said in disgust. He held the cord at arm's length. "Never even told me it was too tight."

He faced the two Negroes boldly, as if they were somehow involved in this. They were watching him, looking at his uniform. They had been sitting at the desk, on either side of an opened drawer with a piece of stiff cardboard over it, playing cards—some of the cards were back against the inside of the desk, blown there when the door was opened. The fingerworn, soiled surfaces, the drunken glazed faces of the kings and queens and jacks seemed to be gazing idly at Murray. "Expect we could offer them some coffee," the young Negro said. "It's a purely cold night out."

Murray's mouth watered. But no one moved; and he caught his confusion quick enough to keep it from showing. The older Negro, who stood picking at the desk half-heartedly with the screwdriver, as if he thought he should look busy, said, "If there's trouble with the car we ain't any help. We ain't up to these new cars. We just give out gas, now."

"No trouble with the car," Murray said.

"That's luck for you," the other Negro said. He and the older man—Murray supposed they were brothers—laughed shortly. The young man leaned back in the swivel chair. He took a pack of cigarettes out of his pocket. "Ain't much luck for your friend you got there, though." Again he and his brother laughed. "Say, ain't goin' to tie us up with that, are you?"

Murray saw he was still holding the cord. He shrugged his shoulders and tossed it to the floor. The brothers were grinning identically. At the stove Bethl'em stood with his arms out as if to embrace the heat; his eyes were averted. "That had us purely scairt for a minute," the young Negro said. He was lighting a cigarette. Still moving slowly he got to his feet. "You, boy. I expect you'd like a cigarette too." He was grinning at Murray, showing his teeth; but when he extended the pack it was to Bethl'em. Murray saw, cautiously, out of the corner of his eye, the prisoner's fingers take a cigarette. "What's he done to get himself arrested so?" the young man said. "He hurt some white folks somewheres?"

His chest seemed swollen when he sat down again, leaning back precariously in the swivel chair; and now his brother had begun to smile too, looking up from the scratches he was making on the desk. Murray felt, alarmed, that they did not only look alike but seemed now to be sharing the same expression, a sly, knowing, inviting look. The young man smoked his cigarette. "Maybe you can't talk none," he said. Murray blinked at his words. "We got to let you in here, or anything you want, but you never need to talk to us. But I expect we already know what he done, anyhow. That Bethl'em Aire, there, there was talking all up an' down here about him. . . . He never left off fightin' too early. Ain't that right?"

Murray glanced at the prisoner, who stood with his eyes lowered as if he were listening to something forbidden. His face, though, looked as if it had thawed, and he held the burning cigarette in his hand like a weapon. "What they goin' to do to him?" the older Negro said suddenly.

Murray stiffened. "A matter of the law," he said.

"What they goin' to do?"

Murray stared. The brothers met his stare equally, easily, like burlesques of himself, or like negatives of himself mocking him.

"Seems that takin' a man in to somethin' like he's goin' to get, there, an' not even know for sure what it is—that ain't the way to do," the young man said seriously. "You, Bethl'em. You think that's the way to do? Takin' a man in, an' him sure to be kilt for it—"

"Wait," Murray said. His voice sounded quite young. But what most surprised him is that he felt whatever concern he did, whatever alarm, not for himself but for Bethl'em.

The word, however, came as a pleasant surprise to the young Negro, evidently, who now lounged in the chair with the cigarette in his teeth. "That sheriff Walpole knows me fine, an' he might of come through here an' tole me somethin'," he said. "Yes. He might of tole me somethin' about Bethl'em. An' I surely wouldn't want to trade no place with that boy there."

Murray glanced from the prisoner's strong back to the brothers. The brothers had drawn closer together; the older man, standing, leaned in against the desk, the younger sat up slowly in the creaking chair. He shook some ashes deliberately onto the concrete floor. "It ain't easy to consider a man that's alive right now," he said grandly, as if beginning a speech, "an' is goin' to be dead in a time. Why, that there blood goin' through him right now, only think—only think—how it'll get all cold an' hard like grease in the cold— How a man c'n go from alive to dead in such a time! Not just black but white too or any color. Ain't that so? A thing no moren that-there screwdriver, ust to puttin' in screws an' pickin' around here an' scratchin' the ice off the window, why, set up against any man's forehead an' pushed in only a bit—any man at all, why—"

Murray felt his face burn, and he felt something, at first quite small, like a pin-prick, touch coldly at his heart. When he looked around to the prisoner he saw the man was staring at something invisible on the top of the stove. Murray could no longer stand still, but began to shift his weight from one foot to the other grimacing as if in impatience with the storm. But when he spoke it was not of the storm. His words seemed to explode from him. "But I helped him," he said suddenly. "I did. I found him half a mile out in a field trying to run up a hill that was all drifted, and it was sundown, dark in a hour . . . and this storm coming. . . . He would have died there."

Now the young man laughed. "One place, here or there, another place; there ain't much diffrence." He and his brother laughed quietly. "You, Bethl'em. You see much diffrence?"

Bethl'em did not look around. "He would have got lost in the storm anyway," Murray said. "Lost and frozen, all alone, what good is it for a man all alone? By himself, thinking by himself. . . . He did that just to get away from me. That's what I can't get ust to," he said, strangely, "them always running away. Goddam fools, don't know what's for their own good, what's all thought up to help them! They don't understand anything but how hungry they are, they live by their stomach, you can't talk to them for five minutes explaining any law—about deer or bass or anything—without their eyes going all around to something else, something over your shoulder—a bird in a tree, or the tree itself, or the sky—"

"Hey, what's that?" the young man said. "What's that you're sayin'?"

Murray was breathing hard. He felt more words crowding and jumbling inside him.

"Somethin' about a bird in a tree," the older brother said.

"An' the sky too. Bethl'em, you hear that? You spose you're goin' to see much of a sky? Huh? Where you're goin'?"

When Bethl'em turned they all must have thought he was crying. Two almost even trickles of water had run down his face. But it was only from the snow in his hair, and he licked his lips and spat and glared at them. He held the cigarette without smoking it. "I got nothin' to say," he muttered.

"Got nothin'? Why, you better have!" the young man said gaily. "What you think they're bringin' you in for? Why, to talk, Bethl'em, to talk—you got to answer questions polite. You know that sheriff? Don't you spose he's got things to ask you? He'll hit right on that trouble with that-there man, at the saloon, you know, an' how you done somethin' with your knife you oughtn't of; an' you ain't goin' to like it, no, but you got to answer polite for him." The young man began gathering up the playing cards, which had been blown back into the desk. He picked them up one by one, nodding, clicking his tongue as if in agreement with something. "Yes," he said. "You got to answer polite. An' you know what, Bethl'em? You know what?"

The young man's expression was blank, serious, and knowing, all at once, and he sat nodding at the dirty cards, picking them up and inspecting them, putting them into a pile. "You know what?" He looked right past Murray to the prisoner. "There ain't goin' to be a person at that trial, later, only maybe the wife of the guy you cut, an' his kids or somethin', not a person, sheriff or judge or nobody, that ain't goin' to be glad for what you done. They'll all be pleased fine with it." He nodded again, turning back to the cards. Murray could see the glazed faces of the cards, sometimes a king or queen, whose eyes, like those of the Negroes, were turned toward him. "Ain't that right, mister deppity? You tell him. Ain't that right?"

Murray turned away; he walked blindly toward the front of the garage. "Ain't that right!" the young man cried; there was joy in his voice. "Ain't it! An' nobody here ain't explained the diffrence between lettin' a man die a good way, a clean way, by himself out in the snow, in his own land, an' bringin' him in so they c'n make a fuss out of it—a show out of it—" His words tumbled about themselves. "Yes," he said loudly, "that ain't been tole to me yet. Or to Bethl'em either. He ain't got much time to be tole it in. If you're goin' to take a man in to be kilt you better explain to him why. You—"

Murray calmed his wild eyes. He stared out the window; his hand was on his pistol. Most of all he was conscious of Bethl'em's eyes on him, on his back; and he could feel his heart cringing inside him, in shame, a shame that was all mixed up, that had no direction in which to go. The best deputy, Murray thought, the best one of them, as good almost as Walpole himself. . . . And he saw a picture of himself, suddenly: tall and proud with his hat stuck so tightly on his head, his broad face sick and pale, like uncooked dough, just a mockery of the old Murray, the one everyone along the road knew, Murray with his hard chin and his sun-burned, wind-blown good looks. . . . Outside the snowstorm had thinned a little, the wind had nearly stopped; there was a glaring moon somewhere that lit up everything with a delicate whiteness, a crystalline whiteness; it was so clean, so white, it would be painful to the touch, burning to the breath. . . . "A man let loose in all this cold wouldn't last," the young man said loudly, "he'd walk off by himself further an' further, all alone, an' never need for any white folks to do it to him. Any man is got a right. . . ."

Murray stared out at the great banks of white, toppled and slanted in the dark; he felt, beyond his surface paralysis, something else, something peculiar—a sense, maybe, of familiarity. Such scenes as this he had seen every night, just about, in the winters of his childhood farther north, when he would crouch at his bedroom window in the dark and stare out at the night, at the snow falling or the fine whirling mist which held no strangeness, he felt, except what people thought strange in it, the chaos of something not yet formed. . . . Outside the garage the earth seemed to roll out of sight, out of mind, too gigantic for Murray's mind to hold. And Murray felt again the isolation not only of himself but of the prisoner and the other Negroes as well; he felt their separate freedoms; and he felt too the time coming on him when he would have to do something—by himself—not with the sheriff behind him, or laws anywhere, but only by himself—

When Murray turned back **his** heart was pounding. Bethl'em

had straightened, he stood, now, taller than any of them, he was
sucking in his breath slowly, moving his eyes slowly about Murray's
face and behind his head as if it were all the same thing, doing
something with his hands—rubbing his wrists—he was grinding out
the cigarette on the floor. The brothers had not moved but grinned
toward Murray, their smiles fixed and expectant, and the younger
one went on, quietly, proddingly, "Now you, Bethl'em, you maybe
got your only chance now. We're behind you. We ain't goin' to
stand by to see such things happen—we ain't now, that's true—
An' that-there deppity what's-his-name, that I seen ridin' around
in the back seat of Walpole's old car enough times, he knows
what's good for him, he ain't goin' to interfere—he ain't—" The
young man's arms came loose. "You go on, now, Bethl'em!" he
said. "You go on! You are a man, an' you got your right to—"

Murray waited. Both he and the prisoner were breathing
strongly, almost at the same time, their big chests taut and falling,
stiff, rigid, waiting, their eyes tied up together as if they were counting the steps between each other. But Bethl'em's look was so un-
flinching, so intense, so knowing of what was right, what was just,
that Murray thought he could not bear it any longer—that look
pierced him like a sliver of glass—and he looked away. Now the
young Negro's chanting voice, even his words, which ought to have
been so terrible to Murray, seemed only familiar—only right—exactly what he had expected, almost what he should have said himself— "You are a man," he said, "an' there's no law here—not here,
not tonight— Where is there any law? Where is it? Or any one of
us better'n another? All of us caught here in a storm, a blizzard,
who's to say if there's anything left but us? Any laws? Any ol'
sheriff? You surely got a right to your own life. You got a right.
You got a right to—"

Neither Murray nor the prisoner had moved. They seemed
locked by their eyes, as if in an embrace, with the air swelling about
them, about their ears, so that Murray knew in a minute it would
explode in to him, crashing and deafening his brain. . . . Then he
saw something he did not, at first, believe. Then he saw it again,
the young Negro behind Bethl'em's shoulder, winking at Murray
himself— There he stood, nodding brightly, grinning incredibly,
with one eye shut tight and wrinkled. Murray gaped, he sucked at
the air, at its tremendous pressure. "You—you—" he stammered.

His fingers were so tight on the revolver handle that he could not move them. "You—what are you— What—"

Just as Bethl'em was about to move the young Negro and his brother began laughing. Even their teeth seemed to laugh, and Murray felt, just as he knew Bethl'em felt, their laughter tear through him. "Look at that Bethl'em, now!" the young man cried. His delight so shook him that he jerked, his arms loose, his shoulders rocking. "Just look! Here he thinks he's goin' somewhere! He ain't never goin' to get along with no white men—ain't one time goin' to learn—"

Bethl'em's shoulders relaxed just a little. His face stayed tight, like a mask, or a statue, staring right at Murray's shamed face. "Now, you, Bethl'em, now," the young man said, dancing around, "don't you get mad at *me*. I ain't done a thing. It ain't a fault of mine, you come to believe so much!"

Murray went to the prisoner and took his arm. He could not look at the man's face, so he looked at his collar, and at the wet hair that grew so long down his neck. Murray stood, so, for a minute. Then he said, "We're leaving now. The storm let up." Murray could hear nothing but the prisoner's slow, even breath, and the almost noiseless laughter of the brothers. "You, Bethl'em," he said. "You go on out to the car. You get in and wait." He waited a moment. "Go on," he said.

Bethl'em went to the door. Murray did not watch him, nor did he look at the brothers. At first he did not know what to do; he did not know where to look; he could not, for a minute or so, even think past the terrible shame he had seen, he felt weak and sickened before it. . . . Then he turned, briskly, he stiffened his shoulders, he took his red scarf very carefully off the peg and began winding it around his neck. It took him some time to dress. The young Negro kept on, a little louder now: "That Bethl'em's a big man, a good big man, I known him too long a time already. A big man up an' down this road! Hey!"

Murray finished buttoning his coat. He did not hurry. He watched himself, and then he watched himself putting on his gloves. When he was dressed he knew there was something left wrong, unfinished, but he could not think what; his mind still buzzed and crowded so. "An' you tell that sheriff, too," the young man was saying. "Will you? You tell him." The laughter had suddenly drained out of his face. "Mister deppity—wait— Wait a minute—"

Murray was staring at him. Then he saw the cord on the floor; then he bent, slowly, and picked it up and put it in his pocket. He went to the door. The young man hurried along behind him. He took hold of Murray's arm. "You, mister," he said. "You tell the sheriff how I did here. You tell him that. An' how you caught on to the game right away, an' played it too. You tell him. He'll like that. He will. I know that sheriff, he comes out here sometimes . . . he buys gas here sometimes. . . ." Murray stared at the man. "That black boy out there don't demand no more consideration than any other one. He is got to have it done to him too. Is he any different?" The young man spoke quickly and a little shrilly. "Why, there ain't a one of us ain't had it done to him," he said, proudly, "an' ain't a white man here don't know it— That's how it is. An' him too, him too, he is got to have it done to him too—"

He smiled shakily as Murray opened the door and the cold air fell upon them. Murray stepped out. "Wait, wait," the young Negro said, pulling at his arm. "Mister, you wait. You tell the sheriff, huh? Huh? Will you? You tell him how I did—he'll laugh—you say it was me, here, this garage— He knows me good— Why, look here, mister," he said, and he pulled one of his trouser legs up, so fast Murray hadn't time to look away, all the way up to the knee so that Murray had to look at the queer mottled scars, "they sic'd the dogs on me, once, had them chase me for fun down by the crick; I wasn't fifteen then; they chased me a long ways, I kept runnin' with them right on my legs an' somebody tole the sheriff an' he come to see me himself an' ast about it, an' looked sorry, but there couldn't be nothin' done. . . . Why, I never needed to knife no man first, did I? But I had it done, it's how it is, I never even thought much on it. So that black boy you got ain't no different. . . . You tell the sheriff. He'll remember which one I am, he'll remember me. . . ."

ELLEN DOUGLAS is the pen name of a new Southern writer whose first novel, A *Family's Affairs*, was published in 1962 by Houghton Mifflin, and was a Houghton Mifflin Fellowship Award winner.

On the Lake

Late summer in Philippi is a deadly time of year. Other parts of the United States are hot, it is true, but not like the lower Mississippi Valley. Here the shimmering heat—the thermometer standing day after day in the high nineties and the nights breathless and oppressive—is compounded, even in a drought, by the saturated air. Thunderheads, piling up miles high in the afternoon sky, dwarf the great jet planes that fly through them. The air is heavy with moisture, but for weeks in July and August there is no rain.

In July, Lake Okatukla begins to fall. The lake, named from a meandering bayou that flows into it on the Arkansas side, bounds the town of Philippi on the west. It was once a horseshoe-shaped bend of the Mississippi, but its northern arm is blocked off from the river now by the Nine-Mile Dike, built years ago when a cut-through was made to straighten the river's course. The southern arm of the lake is still a channel into the Mississippi, through which pass towboats pushing strings of barges loaded with gravel, sand, cotton, scrap iron, soybeans, fertilizer, or oil.

In August, the lake drops steadily lower, and at the foot of the levee mud flats begin to appear around the rusty barges that serve as Philippi's municipal terminal and around the old stern-wheeler moored just above them that has been converted into the Philippi Yacht Club. The surface of the mud, covered with discarded beer cans, broken bottles, and tangles of baling wire, cracks and scales like the skin of some scrofulous river beast, and a deathlike stench pervades the hot, still air. But the lake is deep and broad—more than a mile wide at the bend, close to the town—and fifty feet out from the lowest mud flat the steely surface water hides unplumbed black depths.

Late in August, if rain falls all along the course of the Mississippi, there will be a rise of the lake as the river backs into it. The mud flats are covered again. The trees put on pale spikes of new growth. The sandbars are washed clean. Mud runnels stream from the rain-heavy willow fronds, and the willows lift their heads. The fish begin to bite. For a week or two, from the crest of the rise, when the still water begins to clear, dropping the mud that the river has poured into the lake, until another drop has begun to expose the mud flats, Lake Okatukla is beautiful—a serene, broad wilderness of green trees and bright water, bounded at the horizon by the green range of levee sweeping in a slow curve against the sky. Looking down into the water, one can see through drifting forests of moss the quick flash of frightened bream, the shadowy threat of great saw-toothed gar. In the town, there has been little to do for weeks but wait out the heat. Only a few Negroes have braved the stench of the mud flats for the sake of a slimy catfish or a half-dead bream. After the rise, however, fishermen are out again in their skiffs, casting for bass around the trunks of the big willow trees or fishing with cane poles and minnows for white perch along the fringe willows. Family parties picnic here and there along the shore. The lake is big—twelve miles long, with dozens of curving inlets and white sandy islands. Hundreds of fishermen can spend their days trolling its shores and scarcely disturb one another.

One morning just after the August rise a few years ago, Anna Glover set out with two of her three sons, Ralph and Steve, and one of Ralph's friends, Murray McCrae, for a day on the lake. Her oldest son, who at fifteen considered himself too old for such family expeditions, and her husband, Richard, an architect, for whom summer was the busiest season of the year, had stayed behind. It was early, and the waterfront was deserted when Anna drove over the crest of the levee. She parked the car close to the Yacht Club mooring float, where the Glovers kept their fishing skiff tied up, and began to unload the gear—life jackets for the children, tackle box, bait, poles, gas can, and Skotch cooler full of beer, soft drinks, and sandwiches. She had hardly begun when she thought she heard someone shouting her name. "Miss Anna! Hey, Miss Anna!" She looked around, but, seeing the whole slope of the levee empty and no one on the deck of the Yacht Club except Gaines Williamson, the Negro bartender, she called the children back from the water's edge, toward which they had run as soon as the car stopped, and began to distribute the gear among them to carry down to the float.

Anna heaved the heavy cooler out of the car without much effort and untied the poles from the rack on the side of the car, talking as she worked. At thirty-six, she looked scarcely old enough to have three half-grown sons. Her high, round brow was unlined, her brown eyes were clear, and her strong, boyish figure in shorts and a tailored shirt looked almost like a child's. She wore her long sandy-brown hair drawn into a twist on the back of her head. Ralph and his friend Murray were ten; Steve was seven. Ralph's straight nose, solemn expression, and erect, sway-backed carriage made him look like a small preacher. Steve was gentler, with brown eyes like his mother's, fringed by a breathtaking sweep of dark lashes. They were beautiful children, or so Anna thought, for she regarded them with the most intense, subjective passion. Murray was a slender, dark boy with a closed face and a reserve that to Anna seemed impregnable. They were picking up the gear to move it down to the Yacht Club float when they all heard someone calling, and turned around.

"Ralph! Hey there, boys! Here I am, up here!" the voice cried.

"It's Estella, Mama," Ralph said. "There she is, over by the barges."

"Hi, Estella!" Steve shouted. He and Ralph put down the poles and cooler and ran along the rough, uneven slope of the levee, jumping over the iron rings set in the concrete to hold the mooring lines and over the rusty cables that held the terminal barges against the levee.

"Come on, Murray," Anna said. "Let's go speak to Estella. She's over there fishing off the ramp."

Sitting on the galvanized-iron walkway from the levee to the terminal, her legs dangling over the side of the walkway ten feet above the oily surface of the water, was Estella Moseby, a huge and beautiful Negro woman who had worked for the Glover family since the children were small. She had left them a few months before to have a child and had stayed home afterward, at James', her husband's, insistence, to raise her own family. It was the first time that Anna or the children had seen her since shortly after the child was born. Estella held a long cane pole in one hand and with the other waved toward Anna and the children. Her serene, round face was golden brown, the skin flawless even in the cruel light of the August sun, her black hair pulled severely back to a knot on her neck, her enormous dark eyes and wide mouth smiling with pleasure at the unexpected meeting. As the children approached, she drew her line out of the water and pulled herself up by the cable that served as a side rail for the walkway. The walk creaked under her shifting weight. She was fully five feet ten inches tall—at least seven inches taller than Anna—and loomed above the heads of the little group on the levee like an amiable golden giantess, her feet set wide apart to support the weight that fleshed her big frame. Her gaily flowered house dress, printed with daisies and morning-glories in shades of blue, green, and yellow, took on the very quality of her appearance, as if she were some tropical fertility goddess robed to receive her worshippers.

"Lord, Estella," Anna said. "Come on down. We haven't seen you in ages. How have you been?"

"You see me," Estella said. "Fat as ever." She carefully wrapped her line around her pole, secured the hook in the cork, and came down from her high perch to join the others on the levee. "Baby or no baby, I got to go fishing after such a fine rain," she said.

"We're going on a picnic," Steve said.

"Well, isn't that fine," Estella said. "Where is your brother?"

"Oh, he thinks he's too old to associate with us any more," Anna said. "He *scorns* us. How is the baby?"

The two women looked at each other with the shy pleasure of old friends long separated who have not yet fallen back into the easy ways of their friendship.

"Baby's fine," Estella said. "My cousin Bernice is nursing him. I said to myself this morning, 'I haven't been fishing since I got pregnant with Lee Roy. I *got* to go fishing.' So look at me. Here I am sitting on this ramp since seven this morning and no luck."

Steve threw his arms around her legs. "Estella, why don't you come *work* for us again?" he said. "We don't like *anybody* but you."

"I'm coming, honey," she said. "Let me get these kids up a little bit and I'll be back."

"Estella, why don't you go fishing with us today?" Ralph said. "We're going up to the north end of the lake and fish all day."

"Yes, come on," Anna said. "Come on and keep me company. You can't catch any fish around this old barge, and if you do they taste like fuel oil. I heard the bream are really biting in the upper lake—over on the other side, you know, in the willows."

Estella hesitated, looking out over the calm and shining dark water. "I ain't much on boats," she said. "Boats make me nervous."

"Oh, come on, Estella," Anna said. "You know you want to go."

"Well, it's the truth, I'm not catching any fish sitting here. I' got two little no-'count bream on my stringer." Estella paused, and then she said, "All y'all going to fish from the boat? I'll crowd you."

"We're going to find a good spot and fish off the bank," Anna said. "We're already too many to fish from the boat."

"Well, it'll be a pleasure," Estella said. "I'll just come along. Let me get my stuff." She went up on the walkway again and gathered up her tackle where it lay—a brown paper sack holding sinkers, floats, hooks, and line, and her pole and a coffee can full of worms and dirt.

"I brought my gig along," Ralph said as they all trudged across the levee toward the Yacht Club. "I'm going to gig one of those great big buffalo or a gar or something."

"Well, if you do, give it to me, honey," Estella said. "James is really crazy about buffalo the way I cook it." Pulling a coin purse out of her pocket, she turned to Anna. "You reckon you might get us some beer in the Yacht Club? A nice can of beer 'long about eleven o'clock would be good."

"I've got two cans in the cooler," Anna said, "but maybe we'd better get a couple more." She took the money and, while Murray and Ralph brought the skiff around from the far side of the Yacht Club, where it was tied up, went into the bar and bought two more cans of beer. Estella and Steve, meanwhile, carried the fishing gear down to the float.

Gaines Williamson, a short, powerfully built man in his forties, followed Anna out of the bar and helped stow their gear in the little boat. The children got in first and then he helped Estella in. "Lord, Miss Estella," he said, "you too big for this boat, and that's a fact." He stood back and looked down at her doubtfully, sweat shining on his face and standing in droplets on his shaven scalp.

"I must say it's none of your business," Estella said.

"We'll be all right, Gaines," Anna said. "The lake's smooth as glass."

The boys held the skiff against the float while Anna got in, and they set out, cruising slowly up the lake until they found a spot that Estella and Anna agreed looked promising. Here, on a long, clean sandbar fringed with willows, they beached the boat. The children stripped off their life jackets, pulled off the jeans they wore over their swimming trunks, and began to wade.

"You children wade here in the open water," Estella ordered. "Don't go over yonder on the other side of the bar, where the willows are growing. You'll bother the fish."

She and Anna stood looking around. Wilderness was all about them. As far as they could see on either side of the lake, not even a road ran down to the water's edge. While they watched, two white herons dragged themselves awkwardly into the air and flapped away, long legs trailing. The southern side of the sandbar, where they had beached the boat, had no trees growing on it, but the edge of the northern side, which curved in on itself and out again, was covered with willows. Here the land was higher. Beyond a low hummock crowned with cottonwood trees, Anna and Estella discovered a pool, twenty-five yards long and nearly as wide, that had been left behind by the last rise, a few days before. Fringe willows grew all around it, and the fallen trunk of a huge cottonwood lay with its roots exposed on the ground, its whole length stretched out into the still water of the pool.

"Here's the place," Estella said decidedly. "Shade for us, and fringe willows for the fish. And looka there." She pointed to the fallen tree. "If there aren't any fish under *there* . . ." They stood looking down at the pool, pleased with their find.

"I'll go get our things," Estella said. "You sit down and rest yourself, Miss Anna."

"I'll come help you."

The two women unloaded the boat, and Anna carried the cooler up the low hill and left it in the shade of one of the cottonwood trees. Then they gathered the fishing tackle and took it over to a shady spot by the pool. In a few minutes, the children joined them, and Anna passed out poles and bait. The bream were rising to crickets, and she had brought a wire cylinder basket full of them.

"You boys scatter out, now," Anna said. "There's plenty of room for everybody, and if you stay too close together you'll hook each other."

Estella helped Steve bait his hook, then baited her own and dropped it into the water as close as she could get it to the trunk of the fallen tree. Almost as soon as it reached the water, her float began to bob and quiver.

"Here we go," she said in a low voice. "Take it under, now. Take it under." She addressed herself to the business of fishing with such delight and concentration that Anna stopped in the middle of rigging a pole to watch her. Even the children, intent on finding places for themselves, turned back to see Estella catch a fish. She stood over the pool like a priestess at her altar, all expectation and willingness, holding the pole lightly, as if her fingers could read the intentions of the fish vibrating through line and pole. Her bare arms were tense, and she gazed down into the still water. A puff of wind made the leafy shadows waver and tremble on the pool, and the float rocked deceptively. Estella's arms quivered with a jerk begun and suppressed. Her flowery dress flapped around her legs, and her skin shone with sweat and oil where the sunlight struck through the leaves across her forehead and down one cheek.

"Not yet," she muttered. "*Take* it." The float bobbed and went under. "Aaah!" She gave her line a quick, short jerk to set the hook; the line tightened, the long pole bent, and she swung a big bream out onto the sand. The fish flopped off the hook and down the slope toward the water; she dropped the pole and dived at it, half falling. Ralph, who had been watching, was ahead of her, shouting with excitement, grabbing up the fish before it could flop back into the pool, and putting it into Estella's hands, careful to avoid the sharp dorsal fin.

"Look, boys, look!" she cried happily. "Just look at him!" She held out the big bream, as wide and thick as her hand, marked with blue around the gills and orange on its swollen belly. The fish twisted and gasped in her hand while she got the stringer. She slid the metal end of the stringer through one gill and out the mouth, secured the other end to an exposed root of the fallen tree, and dropped the fish into the water, far enough away so that the bream's thrashing would not disturb their fishing spot.

"Quick now, Miss Anna," she said. "Get your line in there. I bet this pool is full of bream. Come on, boys, we're going to catch some fish today."

Anna baited her hook and dropped it in. The children scattered around the pool to their own places. In an hour, the two women had caught a dozen bream and four small catfish, and the boys had caught six or seven more bream. Then for ten minutes no one got a bite, and the boys began to lose interest. A school of minnows flashed into the shallow water at Anna's feet, and she pointed them out to Estella. "Bream are gone," she said. "They've quit feeding, or we wouldn't see any minnows."

Anna laid down her pole and told the children they could swim. "Come on, Estella," she said. "We can sit in the shade and watch them and have a beer, and then in a little while we can move to another spot."

"You aren't going to let them swim in this old lake, are you, Miss Anna?" Estella said.

"Sure. The bottom's nice and sandy here," Anna said. "Murray, your mama said you've got to keep your life preserver on if you swim." She said to Estella in a low voice, "He's not much of a swimmer. He's the only one I would worry about."

The children splashed and tumbled fearlessly in the water, Ralph and Steve popping up and disappearing, sometimes for so long that Anna, in spite of what she had said, would begin to watch anxiously for their blond heads.

"I must say, I don't see how you stand it," Estella said. "That water scares me."

"Nothing to be scared of," Anna said. "They're both good swimmers, and so am I. I could swim across the lake and back, I bet you, old as I am."

She fished two beers out of the Skotch cooler, opened them, and gave one to Estella. Then she sat down with her back against a cottonwood tree, gave Estella a cigarette, took one herself, and leaned back with a sigh. Estella sat down on a fallen log, and the two women smoked and drank their beer in silence for a few minutes. The breeze ran through the cottonwoods, shaking the leaves against each other. "I love the sound of the wind in a cottonwood tree," Anna said. "Especially at night when you wake up and hear it outside your window. I remember there was one outside the window of my room when I was a little girl, so close to the house I could climb out the window and get into it." The breeze freshened and the leaves pattered against each other. "It sounds cool," Anna said, "even in August."

"It's nice," Estella said. "Like a nice, light rain."

"Well, tell me what you've been doing with yourself," Anna said. "When are you going to move into your new house?"

"James wants to keep renting it out another year," Estella said. "He wants us to get ahead a little bit. And you know, Miss Anna, if I can hang on where I am we'll be in a good shape. We can rent that house until we finish paying for it, and then when we move we can rent the one we're in, and, you know, we own that little one next door, too. With four children now, we got to think of the future. And I must say, with all his old man's ways, James is a good provider. He looks after his own. So I go along with him. But, Lord, I can't stand it much longer. We're falling all over each other in that little tiny place. Kids under my feet all day. No place to keep the baby quiet. And in rainy weather! It's worse than a circus. I've gotten so all I do is yell at the kids. It would be a rest to go back to work."

"I wish you *would* come back to work," Anna said.

"No use talking about it," Estella said. "James says I've got to stay home at least until Lee Roy gets up to school age. And you can see for yourself I'd be paying out half what I made to get somebody to keep mine. But I'll tell you, my nerves are tore up."

"It takes a while to get your strength back after a baby," Anna said.

"Oh, I'm strong enough," Estella said. "It's not that." She pulled a stalk of Johnson grass and began to chew it thoughtfully. "I've had something on my mind," she said, "something I've been meaning to tell you ever since the baby came, and I haven't seen you by yourself—"

Anna interrupted her. "Look at the fish, Estella," she said. "They're really kicking up a fuss."

There was a wild, thrashing commotion in the water by the roots of the cottonwood tree where Estella had tied the stringer.

Estella watched a minute. "Lord, Miss Anna," she said, "something's after those fish. A turtle or something." She got up and started toward the pool as a long, dark, whiplike shape flung itself out of the water, slapped the surface, and disappeared.

"Hey," Anna said, "it's a snake! A snake!"

Estella looked around for a weapon and hastily picked up a short, heavy stick and a rock from the ground. Moving lightly and easily in spite of her weight, she ran down to the edge of the water, calling over her shoulder, "I'll scare him off. I'll chunk him. Don't you worry." She threw the rock into the churning water, but it had no effect. "Go, snake. Leave our fish alone." She stood waving her stick threateningly over the water.

Anna came down to the pool now, and they both saw the whiplike form again. Fearlessly, Estella whacked at it with her stick.

"Keep back, Estella," Anna said. "He might bite you. Wait a minute and I'll get a longer stick."

"Go, snake!" Estella shouted furiously, confidently. "What's the matter with him? He won't go off. Go, you crazy snake!"

Now the children heard the excitement and came running across the beach and over the low hill where Estella and Anna had been sitting, to see what was happening.

"A snake, a snake!" Steve screamed. "He's after the fish. Come on, y'all! It's a big old snake after the fish."

The two older boys ran up. "Get 'em out of the water, Mama," Ralph said. "He's going to eat 'em."

"I'm scared he might bite me," Anna said. "Keep back. He'll go away in a minute." She struck at the water with the stick she had picked up.

Murray looked the situation over calmly. "Why don't we gig him?" he said to Ralph.

Ralph ran down to the boat and brought back the long, barb-pointed gig. "Move, Estella," he said. "I'm gonna gig him." He struck twice at the snake and missed.

"Estella," Anna said, "I saw his head. He can't go away. He's swallowed one of the fish. He's caught on the stringer." She shuddered with disgust. "What are we going to do?" she said. "Let's throw away the stringer. We'll never get him off."

"All them beautiful fish! No, *Ma'am*," Estella said. "Here, Ralph, he can't bite us if he's swallowed a fish. I'll untie the stringer and get him up on land, and then you gig him."

"I'm going away," Steve said. "I don't want to watch." He crossed the hill and went back to the beach, where he sat down alone and began to dig a hole in the sand.

Ralph, wild with excitement, danced impatiently around Estella while she untied the stringer.

"Be calm, child," she said. She pulled the stringer out of the water and dropped it on the ground. "Now!"

The snake had indeed tried to swallow one of the bream on the stringer. Its jaws were stretched so wide as to look dislocated; its body was distended behind the head with the half-swallowed meal, and the fish's head could still be seen protruding from its mouth. The snake, faintly banded with slaty black on a brown background, was a water moccasin.

"Lord, it's a cottonmouth!" Estella cried as soon as she had the stringer out on land, where she could see the snake.

A thrill of horror and disgust raised the hair on Anna's arms. The thought of the helpless fish on the stringer sensing its enemy's approach, and then of the snake, equally and even more grotesquely helpless, filled her with revulsion. "Throw it away," she commanded. And then the thought of the stringer with its living burden of fish and snake struggling and swimming away into the lake struck her as even worse. "No!" she said. "Go on. Kill the snake, Ralph."

Ralph paid no attention to his mother but stood with the long gig poised, looking up at Estella for instructions.

"Kill him," Estella said. "Now."

He drove the gig into the snake's body behind the head and pinned it to the ground, where it coiled and uncoiled convulsively, wrapping its tail around the gig and then unwrapping it and whipping it across the sand.

Anna mastered her horror as well as she could with a shake of her head. "Now what?" she said calmly.

Estella got a knife from the tackle box, held the dead but still writhing snake down with one big foot behind the gig on its body and the other on its tail, squatted, and deftly cut off the fish's head where it protruded from the gaping, fanged mouth. Then she worked the barbed point of the gig out of the body, picked the snake up on the point, and stood holding it away from her.

Ralph whirled around with excitement and circled Estella twice. "We've killed a snake," he chanted. "We've killed a snake. We've killed a snake."

"Look at it wiggle," Murray said. "It keeps on wiggling even after it's dead."

"Yeah, a snake'll wiggle like that for an hour sometimes, even with its head cut off," Estella said. "Look out, Ralph." She swept the gig forward through the air and threw the snake out into the pool, where it continued its aimless writhing on the surface of the water. She handed Ralph the gig and stood watching the snake for a few minutes, holding her hands away from her sides to keep the blood off her clothes. Then she bent down by the water's edge and washed the blood from her hands. She picked up the stringer, dropped the fish into the water, and tied the stringer to the root of the cottonwood. "There!" she said. "I didn't have no idea of throwing away all them—*those* beautiful fish. James would've skinned me if he ever heard about it."

Steve got up from the sand now and came over to his mother. He looked at the wiggling snake, and then he leaned against his mother without saying anything, put his arms around her, and laid his head against her side.

Anna stroked his hair with one hand and held him against her with the other. "It was a moccasin, honey," she said. "They're poison, you know. You have to kill them."

"I'm hungry," Ralph said. "Is it time to eat?"

Anna shook her head, gave Steve a pat, and released him. "Let me smoke a cigarette first and forget about that old snake. Then we'll eat."

Anna and Estella went back to the shade on the hill and settled themselves once more, each with a fresh can of beer and a cigarette. The children returned to the beach.

"I can do without snakes," Anna said. "Indefinitely."

Estella was still breathing hard. "I don't mind killing no snake," she said happily.

"I never saw anything like that before," Anna said. "A snake getting caught on a stringer, I mean. Did you?"

"Once or twice," Estella said. "And I've had 'em get after my stringer plenty of times."

"I don't see how you could stand to cut the fish's head off," Anna said, and shivered.

"Well, somebody had to."

"Yes, I suppose I would have done it if you hadn't been here." She laughed. "*Maybe*. I was mighty tempted to throw the whole thing away."

"I'm just as glad I wasn't pregnant," Estella said. "I'm glad it didn't happen while I was carrying Lee Roy. I would have been *helpless*."

"You might have had a miscarriage," Anna said. She laughed again, still nervous, wanting to stop talking about the snake but not yet able to, feeling somehow that there was more to be said. "Please don't have any miscarriages on fishing trips with me," she went on. "I can do without that, too."

"Miscarriage!" Estella said. "That's not what I'm talking about. And that reminds me, what I was getting ready to tell you when we saw the snake. You know, I said I had something on my mind?"

"Uh-huh."

"You remember last summer when you weren't home that day, and that kid fell out of the tree in the yard, and all?"

"How could I forget it?" Anna said.

"You remember you spoke to me so heavy about it? Why didn't I stay out in the yard with him until his mama got there, instead of leaving him laying on the ground like that, nobody with him but Ralph, and I told you I couldn't go out there to him—couldn't look at that kid with his leg broke, and all—and you didn't understand why?"

"Yes, I remember," Anna said.

"Well, I wanted to tell you I was *blameless*," Estella said. "I didn't want you to know it at the time, but I was pregnant. I *couldn't* go out there. It might have *marked* my child, don't you see? I might have bore a cripple."

"Oh, Estella! You don't believe that kind of foolishness, do you?" Anna said.

"*Believe* it? I've seen it happen," Estella said. "I know it's true." She was sitting on the fallen log, so that she towered above Anna, who had gone back to her place on the ground, leaning against the tree. Now Estella leaned forward with an expression of intense seriousness on her face. "My aunt looked on a two-headed calf when she was carrying a child," she said, "and her child had six fingers on one hand and seven on the other."

Anna hitched herself up higher, then got up and sat down on the log beside Estella. "But that was an accident," she said. "A coincidence. Looking at the calf didn't have anything to do with it."

Estella shook her head stubbornly. "This world is a mysterious place," she said. "Do you think you can understand everything in it?"

"No," Anna said. "Not everything. But I don't believe in magic."

"All this world is full of mystery," Estella repeated. "You got to have respect for what you don't understand. There are times to be brave and times when you go down helpless in spite of all. Like that snake. You were afraid of that snake."

"I thought he might bite me," Anna said. "And besides, it was so horrible the way he was caught."

But Estella went on as if she hadn't heard. "You see," she said, "there are things you overlook. Things, like I was telling you about my aunt, that are *true*. My mother in her day saw more wonders than that. She knew more than one that sickened and died of a spell. And this child with the fingers, I know about him for a fact. I lived with them when I was teaching school. I lived in the house with that kid. So I'm not taking any chances."

"But I thought you had lost your head and got scared because he was hurt," Anna said. "When the little boy broke his leg, I mean. I kept thinking it wasn't like you. That's what really happened, isn't it?"

"No," Estella said. "It was like I told you."

Anna said no more, but sat quiet a long time, lighting another cigarette and smoking calmly, her face expressionless. But her thoughts were in a tumult of exasperation, bafflement, and outrage. She tried unsuccessfully to deny, to block out, the overriding sense of the difference between herself and Estella, borne in on her by this strange conversation so foreign to their quiet, sensible friendship. She had often thought, with pride both in herself and in Estella, what an accomplishment their friendship was, knowing how much delicacy of feeling, how much consideration and understanding they had both brought to it. And now it seemed to her that it was this very friendship, so carefully nurtured for years, that Estella had unwittingly attacked. With a few words, she had put between them all that separated them, all the dark and terrible past. In the tumult of Anna's feelings there rose a queer, long-forgotten memory of a nurse she had once had as a child—the memory of a brown hand thrust out at her, holding a greasy black ball of hair combings. "You see, child, I saves my hair. I ain't never th'owed away a hair of my head."

"Why?" she had asked.

"Bad luck to th'ow away combings. Bad luck to lose any part of yourself in this old world. Fingernail parings, too. I gathers them up and carries them home and burns them. And I sits by the fire and watches until every last little bitty hair is turned plumb to smoke."

"But why?" she had asked again.

"Let your enemy possess one hair of your head and you will be in his power," the nurse had said. She had thrust the hair ball into her apron pocket, and now, in the memory, she seemed to be brushing Anna's hair, and Anna remembered standing restive under her hand, hating, as always, to have her hair brushed.

"Hurry up," she had said. "Hurry up. I got to go."

"All right, honey. I'm through." The nurse had given her head one last lick and then, bending toward her, still holding her arm while she struggled to be off and outdoors again, had thrust a dark, brooding face close to hers, had looked at her for a long, scary moment, and had laughed. "I saves your combings, too, honey. You in my power."

With an effort, Anna drew herself up short. She put out her cigarette, threw her beer can into the lake, and stood up. "I reckon we better fix some lunch," she said. "The children are starving."

By the time they had finished lunch, burned the discarded papers, thrown the bread crusts and crumbs of potato chips to the birds, and put the empty soft-drink bottles back in the cooler, it had begun to look like rain. Anna stood gazing thoughtfully into the sky. "Maybe we ought to start back," she said. "We don't want to get caught in the rain up here."

"We're not going to catch any more fish as long as the wind is blowing," Estella said.

"We want to swim some more," Ralph said.

"You can't go swimming right after lunch," Anna said. "You might get a cramp. And it won't be any fun to get caught in the rain. We'd better call it a day." She picked up one of the poles and began to wind the line around it. "Come on, kids," she said. "Let's load up."

They loaded their gear into the skiff and dropped the stringer full of fish in the bottom. Anna directed Murray and Steve to sit in the bow, facing the stern. Estella got in cautiously and took the middle seat. Anna and Ralph waded in together, pushed the skiff off the sandbar, and then got into the stern.

"You all got your life jackets on?" Anna said, glancing at the boys. "That's right."

Ralph pulled on the recoil-starter rope until he had got the little motor started, and they headed down the lake. The heavily loaded skiff showed no more than eight inches of freeboard, and as they cut through the choppy water, waves sprayed over the bow and sprinkled Murray and Steve. Anna moved the tiller and headed the skiff in closer to the shore. "We'll stay close in going down," she said. "Water's not so rough in here. And then we can cut across the lake right opposite the Yacht Club."

Estella sat still in the middle of the skiff, her back to Anna, a hand on each gunwale, as they moved steadily down the lake, rocking with the wind-rocked waves. "I don't like this old lake when it's windy," Estella said. "I don't like no windy water."

When they reached a point opposite the Yacht Club, where the lake was a little more than a mile wide, Anna headed the skiff into the rougher open water. The wind, however, was still no more than a stiff breeze, and the skiff was a quarter of the way across the lake before Anna began to be worried. Spray from the choppy waves was coming in more and more often over the bow; Murray and Steve were drenched, and an inch of water sloshed in the bottom of the skiff. Estella had not spoken since she had said "I don't like no windy water." She sat perfectly still, gripping the gunwales with both hands, her paper sack of tackle in her lap, her worm can on the seat beside her. Suddenly a gust of wind picked up the paper sack and blew it out of the boat. It struck the water and floated back to Anna, who reached out, picked it up, and dropped it by her own feet. Estella did not move, although the sack brushed against her face as it blew out. She made no attempt to catch it. She's scared, Anna thought. She's so scared she didn't even see it blow away. And Anna was frightened herself. She leaned forward, picked up the worm can from the seat beside Estella, dumped out the worms and dirt, and tapped Estella on the shoulder. "Here," she said. "Why don't you bail some of the water out of the bottom of the boat, so your feet won't get wet?"

Estella did not look around, but reached over her shoulder, took the can, and began to bail, still holding to the gunwale tightly with her left hand.

The wind freshened, the waves began to show white at their tips, the clouds in the south raced across the sky, darker and darker. But still, although they could see sheets of rain far away to the south, the sun shone on them brightly. They were now almost half-way across the lake. Anna looked over her shoulder toward the quieter water they had left behind. Along the shore of the lake, the willow trees tossed in the wind like a forest of green plumes. It's just as far one way as the other, she thought, and anyhow there's nothing to be afraid of. But while she looked back, the boat slipped off course, no longer quartering the waves, and immediately they took a big one over their bow.

"Bail, Estella," Anna said quietly, putting the boat back on course. "Get that water out of the boat." Her mind was filled with one paralyzing thought: She can't swim. My God, Estella can't swim.

Far off down the channel she saw the Gay Rosey Jane moving steadily toward the terminal, pushing a string of barges. She looked at Murray and Steve in the bow of the boat, drenched, hair plastered to their heads. "Just sit still, boys," she said. "There's nothing to worry about. We're almost there."

The wind was a gale now, and the black southern sky rushed toward them as if to engulf them. The boat took another wave over the bow, and then another. Estella bailed mechanically with the coffee can. They were still almost half a mile out from the Yacht Club. The boat's overloaded, and we're going to sink, Anna thought. My God, we're going to sink, and Estella can't swim.

"Estella," she said, "the boat will not sink. It may fill up with water, but it won't sink. Do you understand? It is all filled with cork, like a life preserver. It won't sink, do you hear me?" She repeated herself louder and louder above the wind. Estella sat with her back turned and bailed. She did not move or answer, or even nod her head. She went on bailing frantically, mechanically, dumping pint after pint of water over the side while they continued to ship waves over the bow. Murray and Steve sat in their places and stared at Anna. Ralph sat motionless by her side. No one said a word. I've got to take care of them all, Anna thought. Estella kept on bailing. The boat settled in the water and shipped another wave, wallowing now, hardly moving before the labored push of the motor. Estella gave a yell and started to rise, holding to the gunwales with both hands.

"Sit down, you fool!" Anna shouted. *"Sit down!"*

"We're gonna sink!" Estella yelled. "And I can't swim, Miss Anna! I can't swim!" For the first time, she turned, and stared at Anna with wild, blind eyes. She stood all the way up and clutched the air. "I'm gonna drown!" she yelled.

The boat rocked and settled, the motor drowned out, another wave washed in over the bow, and the boat tipped slowly up on its side. An instant later, they were all in the water and the boat was floating upside down beside them.

The children bobbed up immediately, buoyant in their life jackets. Anna glanced around once to see if they were all there. "Stay close to the boat, boys," she said.

And then Estella heaved out of the water, fighting frantically, eyes vacant, mouth open, the broad expanse of her golden face set in mindless desperation.

Anna got hold of one of the handgrips at the stern of the boat and, with her free hand, grabbed Estella's arm. "You're all right," she said. "Come on, I've got hold of the boat."

She tried to pull the huge bulk of the Negro woman toward her and guide her hand to the grip. Estella did not speak, but lunged forward in the water with a strangled yell and threw herself on Anna, flinging her arms across her shoulders. Anna felt herself sinking and scissors-kicked strongly to keep herself up, but she went down. Chin-deep in the water, she threw back her head and took a breath before Estella pushed her under. She hung on to the grip with all her strength, feeling herself battered against the boat and jerked away from it by Estella's struggle. This can't be happening, she thought. We can't be out here drowning. She felt a frantic hand brush across her face and snatch at her nose and hair. My glasses, she thought as she felt them torn away. I've lost my glasses.

Estella's weight slid away, and she, too, went under. Then both women came up and Anna got hold of Estella's arm again. "Come *on*," she gasped. "The *boat*."

Again Estella threw herself forward, the water streaming from her head and shoulders. This time Anna pulled her close enough to get hold of the grip, but Estella did not try to grasp it. Her hand slid, clawing, along Anna's wrist and arm; again she somehow rose up in the water and came down on Anna, and again the two women went under. This time, Estella's whole thrashing bulk was above Anna; she held with all her strength to the handgrip, but felt herself torn away from it. She came up behind Estella, who was now clawing frantically at the side of the skiff, which sank down on their side and tipped gently toward them as she pulled at it.

Anna ducked down and somehow got her shoulder against Estella's rump. Kicking and heaving with a strength she did not possess, she boosted Estella up and forward so that she fell sprawling across the boat. "*There!*" She came up as the rocking skiff began to submerge under Estella's weight. "*Stay* there!" she gasped. "*Stay* on it. For God's . . ."

But the boat was under a foot of water now, rocking and slipping away under Estella's shifting weight. Clutching and kicking crazily, mouth open in a soundless prolonged scream, eyes staring, she slipped off the other side, turned her face toward Anna, gave a strange, strangled grunt, and sank again. The water churned and foamed where she had been.

Anna swam around the boat toward her. As she swam, she realized that Ralph and Steve were screaming for help. Murray floated in the water with a queer, embarrassed smile on his face, as if he had been caught at something shameful. "I'm not here," he seemed to be saying. "This is all just an embarrassing mistake."

By the time Anna got to Estella, the boat was a couple of yards away—too far, she knew, for her to try to get Estella back to it. Estella broke the surface of the water directly in front of her and immediately flung both arms around her neck. Nothing Anna had ever learned in a lifesaving class seemed to have any bearing on this reasonless two hundred pounds of flesh with which she had to deal. They went down. This time they stayed under so long, deep in the softly yielding black water, that Anna thought she would not make it back up. Her very brain seemed ready to burst out of her ears and nostrils. She scissors-kicked again and again with all her strength—not trying to pull loose from Estella's clinging but now more passive weight—and they came up. Anna's head was thrust up and back, ready for a breath, and the instant she felt the air on her face, she took it, deep and gulping, swallowing some water at the same time, and they went down again. Estella's arms rested heavily—trustingly, it seemed—on her shoulders. She did not hug Anna or try to strangle her but simply kept holding on and pushing her down. This time, again deep in the dark water, when Anna raised her arms for a strong downstroke, she touched a foot. One of the boys was floating above their heads. She grabbed the foot without a thought and pulled with all her strength, scissors-kicking at the same time. She and Estella popped out of the water. Gasping in the life-giving air, Anna found herself staring into Steve's face as he floated beside her, weeping.

My God, I'll drown him if he doesn't get out of the way, she thought. I'll drown my own child. But she had no time to say even a word to warn him off before they went down again.

The next time up, she heard Ralph's voice, high and shrill and almost in her ear, and realized that he, too, was swimming close by, and was pounding on Estella's shoulder. "Estella, let go, let go!" he was crying. "Estella, you're drowning Mama!" Estella did not hear. She seemed not even to try to raise her head or breathe when their heads broke out of the water.

Once more they went under and came up before Anna thought, I've given out. There's no way to keep her up, and nobody is coming. And then, deep in the lake, the brassy taste of fear on her tongue, the yielding water pounding in her ears: *She's going to drown me. I've got to let her drown, or she will drown me.* She drew her knee up under her chin, planted her foot in the soft belly, still swollen from pregnancy, and shoved as hard as she could, pushing herself up and back and Estella down and away. Estella was not holding her tightly, and it was easy to push her away. The big arms slid off Anna's shoulders, the limp hands making no attempt to clutch or hold.

They had been together, close as lovers in the darkness or as twins in the womb of the lake, and now they were apart. Anna shot up into the air with the force of her shove and took a deep, gasping breath. Treading water, she waited for Estella to come up beside her, but nothing happened. The three children floated in a circle and looked at her. A vision passed through her mind of Estella's body drifting downward, downward through layers of increasing darkness, all her golden strength and flowery beauty mud-and-water-dimmed, still, aimless as a drifting log. I ought to surface-dive and look for her, she thought, and the thought of going down again turned her bowels to water.

Before she had to decide to dive, something nudged lightly against her hand, like an inquiring, curious fish. She grabbed at it and felt the inert mass of Estella's body, drained of struggle, floating below the surface of the water. She got hold of the belt of her dress and pulled. Estella's back broke the surface of the water, mounded and rocking in the dead man's float, and then sank gently down again. Anna held on to the belt. She moved her feet tiredly to keep herself afloat and looked around her. I can't even get her face out of the water, she thought. I haven't the strength to lift her head.

The boat was floating ten yards away. The Skotch cooler, bright red-and-black plaid, bobbed gaily in the water nearby. Far, far off she could see the levee. In the boat it had looked so near and the distance across the lake so little that she had said she could easily swim it, but now everything in the world except the boat, the children, and this lifeless body was unthinkably far away. Tiny black figures moved back and forth along the levee, people going about their business without a thought of tragedy. The whole sweep of the lake was empty, with not another boat in sight except the Gay Rosey Jane, still moving up the channel. All that had happened had happened so quickly that the towboat seemed no nearer than it had before the skiff overturned. Murray floated in the water a few yards off, still smiling his embarrassed smile. Steve and Ralph stared at their mother with stricken faces. The sun broke through the shifting blackness of the sky, and at the same time a light rain began to fall, pattering on the choppy surface of the lake and splashing into their faces.

All her senses dulled and muffled by shock and exhaustion, Anna moved her feet and worked her way toward the boat, dragging her burden.

"She's gone," Steve said. "Estella's drowned." Tears and rain streamed down his face.

"What shall we do, Mama?" Ralph said.

Dimly, Anna realized that he had sensed her exhaustion and was trying to rouse her.

"Yell," she said. "All three of you yell. Maybe somebody . . ."

The children screamed for help again and again, their thin, piping voices floating away in the wind. With her last strength, Anna continued to work her way toward the boat, pulling Estella after her. She swam on her back, frog-kicking, and feeling the inert bulk bump against her legs at every stroke. When she reached the boat, she took hold of the handgrip and concentrated on holding on to it.

"What shall we do?" Ralph said again. "They can't hear us."

Overcome with despair, Anna let her head droop toward the water. "No one is coming," she said. "It's too far. They can't hear you." And then, from somewhere, dim thoughts of artificial respiration, of snatching back the dead, came into her mind and she raised her head. Still time. I've got to get her out *now*, she thought. "Yell again," she said.

"I'm going to swim to shore and get help," Ralph said. He looked toward his mother for a decision, but his face clearly showed that he knew he could not expect one. He started swimming away, his blond head bobbing in the rough water. He did not look back.

"I don't know," Anna said. Then she remembered vaguely that in an accident you were supposed to stay with the boat. "She's dead," she said to herself. "My God, she's dead. My fault."

Ralph swam on, the beloved head smaller and smaller on the vast expanse of the lake. The Gay Rosey Jane moved steadily up the channel. They might run him down, Anna thought. They'd never see him. She opened her mouth to call him back.

"Somebody's coming!" Murray shouted. "They see us. Somebody's coming. Ralph!"

Ralph heard him and turned back, and now they saw two boats racing toward them, one from the Yacht Club and one from the far side of the lake, across from the terminal. In the nearer one they saw Gaines Williamson.

Thirty yards away, something happened to Gaines' engine; it raced, ground, and died. Standing in the stern of the rocking boat, he worked frantically over it while they floated and watched. It could not have been more than a minute or two before the other boat pulled up beside them, but every moment that passed, Anna knew, might be the moment of Estella's death. In the stern of the second boat they saw a wiry white man wearing a T shirt and jeans. He cut his engine when he was beside them, and, moving quickly to the side of the boat near Anna, bent over her in great excitement. "Are you all right?" he asked. He grabbed her arm with a hard, calloused hand and shook her as if he had seen that she was about to pass out. "Are you all right?" he asked again, his face close to hers.

Anna stared at him, scarcely understanding what the question meant. The children swam over to the boat, and he helped them in and then turned back to Anna. "Come on," he said, and took hold of her arm again. "You've got to help yourself. Can you make it?"

"Get this one first," she said.

"What?" He stared at her with a queer, concentrated gaze, and she realized that he had not even seen Estella.

She hauled on the belt, and Estella's back broke the surface of the water, rolling, rocking, and bumping against the side of the boat. "I've got somebody else here," she said.

He grunted as if someone had hit him in the stomach. Reaching down, he grabbed the back of Estella's dress, pulled her toward him, got one hand into her hair, raised her face out of the water, and, bracing himself against the gunwale, held her there. Estella's peaceful face turned slowly toward him. Her mouth and eyes were closed, her expression was one of deep repose. The man stared at her and then at Anna. "My God," he said.

"We've got to get her into the boat," Anna said. "If we can get her where we can give her artificial respiration . . ."

"It's Estella," Steve said. "Mama had her all the time." He began to cry again. "Let go of her hair," he said. "You're hurting her."

The three children shifted all at once to the side of the boat where the man was still holding Estella, and he turned on them sternly. "Get back," he said. "Sit *down*. And sit still."

The children scuttled back to their places. "You're hurting her," Steve said again.

"It's all right, son," the man said. "She can't feel a thing." To Anna, in a lower voice, he said, "She's dead."

"I'll push and you pull," Anna said. "Maybe we can get her into the boat."

He shifted his position, bracing himself as well as he could in the rocking boat, rested Estella's head on his own shoulder, and put both arms around her. They heaved and pushed at the limp body, but they could not get her into the boat. The man let her down into the water again, this time holding her under the arms. A hundred yards away, Gaines still struggled with his engine.

"Hurry up!" the man shouted. "Get on over here. We can't lift this woman by ourselves."

"Fishing lines tangled in the screw!" Gaines shouted back. His engine caught and died again.

"We're going to have to tow her in," the man said. "That fellow can't start his boat." He reached behind him and got a life jacket. "We'd better put this on her," he said. They worked Estella's arms into the life jacket and fastened the straps. "I've got a rope here somewhere," he said. "Hold her a minute. Wait." He handed Anna a life jacket. "You put one on, too." While he still held Estella by the hair, Anna struggled into the life jacket, and then took hold of the straps of Estella's. Just then, Gaines got his engine started, raced across the open water, and drew up beside them.

The two boats rocked in the rough water with Anna and Estella between them. Anna, with a hand on the gunwale of each, held them apart while the two men, straining and grunting, hauled Estella's body up out of the water and over the gunwale of Gaines' boat. Gaines heaved her legs in. She flopped, face down, across the seat and lay with one arm hanging over the side, the hand trailing in the water. Anna lifted the arm and put it in the boat. Then the white man pulled Anna into his boat. As he helped her over the side, she heard a smacking blow, and, looking back, saw that Gaines had raised and turned Estella's body and was pounding her in the belly. Water poured out of her mouth and, in reflex, air rushed in.

The boats roared off across the lake toward the Yacht Club. The white man's was much the faster of the two, and he quickly pulled away. As soon as they were within calling distance, he stood up in the boat and began to yell at the little group gathered on the Yacht Club mooring float. "Drowned! She's drowned!" he yelled. "Call an ambulance. Get a resuscitator down here. Hurry!"

They drew up to the float. He threw a rope to one of the Negroes standing there and jumped out. Anna dragged herself to a sitting position and stared stupidly at the crowd of Negroes. Gaines Williamson pulled up behind them in the other boat.

"Give us a hand," the white man said. "Let's get her out of there. My God, she's huge. Somebody lend a hand."

To Anna it seemed that all the rest of the scene on the float took place above and far away from her. She saw legs moving back and forth, heard voices and snatches of conversation, felt herself moved from one place to another, but nothing that happened interrupted her absorption in grief and guilt. For the time, nothing existed for her except the belief that Estella was dead.

Someone took her arm and helped her onto the float while the children climbed up by themselves. She sat down on the splintery boards, surrounded by legs, and no one paid any attention to her.

"I saw 'em." The voice of a Negro woman in the crowd. "I was setting on the levee and I saw 'em. You heard me. 'My Lord save us, some folks out there drowning,' I said. I was up on the levee and I run down to the Yacht Club . . ."

"Did somebody call an ambulance?" the white man asked.

"I run down here to the Yacht Club, like to killed myself running, and . . ."

"How . . ."

"Gay Rosey Jane swamped them. Never even seen them. Them towboats don't stop for nobody. See, there she goes. Never seen them at all."

"Still got a stitch in my side. My Lord, I like to killed myself running."

"Anybody around here know how to give artificial respiration?"

"I was sitting right yonder on the terminal fishing with her this morning. Would you believe that?"

"God have mercy on us."

"Oh, Lord. Oh, Lord God. Lord God."

"Have mercy on us."

A young Negro in Army khakis walked over to where the white man and Gaines Williamson were trying to get Estella out of the bulky jacket. "We'll cut it off," he said calmly. He pulled a straight razor from his pocket, slit one shoulder of the life jacket, pushed it out of the way, and straddled Estella's body. "I know how," he said. "I learned in the Army." He arranged her body in position— lying flat on her stomach, face turned to the side and arms above her head—and set to work, raising her arms and then her body rhythmically. When he lifted her body in the middle, her face dragged on the splintery planks of the float.

Anna crawled through the crowd to where Estella lay. Squatting down without a word, she put her hands under Estella's face to protect it from the splinters. It passed through her mind that she should do something about the children. Looking around, she saw them standing in a row at one side of the float, staring down at her and Estella—no longer crying, just standing and staring. Somebody ought to get them away from here, she thought vaguely, but the thought left her mind and she forgot them. She swayed, rocked back on her heels, sat down suddenly, and then lay on her stomach, her head against Estella's head, her hands cradling the sleeping face.

Who's going to tell James, she thought. Who's going to tell him she's dead? And then, I. I have to tell him. She began to talk to Estella. "Please, darling," she said. "Please, Estella, breathe." Tears of weakness rolled down her face, and she looked up above the forest of legs at the black faces in a circle around them. "She's got four babies," she said. "*Babies*. Who's going to tell her husband she's dead? Who's going to tell him?" And then, again, "Please, Estella, breathe. Please breathe."

No one answered. The young Negro soldier continued to raise the limp arms and body alternately, his motions deliberate and rhythmical, the sweat pouring off his face and dripping down on his sweat-soaked shirt. His thin face was intent and stern. The storm was over, the clouds to the west had blown away, and the sun had come out and beat down bright and hot, raising steamy air from the rain-soaked float.

A long time passed. The soldier giving Estella artificial respiration looked around at the crowd. "Anybody know how to do this? I'm about to give out." He did not pause or break the rhythm of his motions.

A man stepped out of the crowd. "I can do it," he said. "I know how."

"Come on, then," the soldier said. "Get down here by me and do it with me three times, and then, when I stop, you take over. Don't break it."

"Please, Estella," Anna said. "Please."

"One . . . Two . . ."

She felt someone pulling at her arm and looked up. A policeman was standing over her. "Here, lady," he said. "Get up off that dock. You ain't doing no good."

"But the splinters will get in her face," Anna said. "I'm holding her face off the boards."

"It ain't going to matter if her face is tore up if she's dead," the policeman said. "Get up."

Someone handed her a towel, and she folded it and put it under Estella's face. The policeman dragged her to her feet and took her over to a chair near the edge of the float and sat her down in it. He squatted beside her. "Now, who was in the boat?" he said. "I got to make a report."

Anna made a vague gesture. "We were," she said.

"Who is 'we,' lady?"

"Estella and I and the children."

"Lady, give me the names, please," the policeman said.

"Estella Moseby, the Negro woman. She used to work for me, and we *asked* her, we asked her—" She broke off.

"Come on, who else?"

Anna stared at him, a short, bald man with shining pink scalp, and drum belly buttoned tightly into his uniform. A wave of nausea overcame her, and she saw his head surrounded by the shimmering black spokes of a rimless wheel, a black halo. "I'm going to be sick," she said. Collapsing out of the chair onto the dock, she leaned her head over the edge and vomited into the lake.

He waited until she was through and then helped her back into her chair. "Who else was with you?" he said.

"My two children, Ralph and Steve," she said. "Murray McCrae. I am Mrs. Richard Glover."

"Where is this McCrae fellow? He all right?"

"He's a little *boy*," Anna said. "A child. He's over there somewhere."

"You sure there wasn't nobody else with you?"

"No. That's all," Anna said.

"Now, give me the addresses, please. Where did the nigger live?"

"For God's sake," Anna said. "What difference does it make? Go away and let me alone."

"I got to make my report, lady."

Ralph tugged at Anna's arm. "Mama, hadn't I better call Daddy?" he said.

"Yes," she said. "Yes, I guess you had." Oh, God, she thought, he has to find out. I can't put it off. Everybody has to find out that Estella is dead.

Anna heard a commotion on the levee. The steadily increasing crowd separated, and two white-jacketed men appeared and began to work over Estella. Behind them, a woman with a camera snapped pictures.

"What are they taking *pictures* of her for?" Anna asked.

Then she heard her husband's voice shouting, "Get off the damn raft, God damn it! Get off. You want to sink it? Get back there. You want to drown us all?"

The policeman stood up and went toward the crowd. "What the hell?" Anna heard him say.

"And put that camera up, if you don't want me to throw it in the lake." Anna's husband was in a fury of outrage, and concentrated it for the moment on the woman reporter from the local newspaper, who was snapping pictures of Estella.

"You all right, Anna?" Richard asked her.

The people on the float were scuttling back to the levee, and the reporter had disappeared. Anna, who was still sitting where the policeman had left her, nodded and opened her mouth to speak, but her husband was gone before she could say anything. She felt a wave of self-pity. He didn't even stay to help me, she thought.

Then, a moment or an hour later—she did not know how long—

she heard a strange high-pitched shriek from the other end of the float. What's that, she thought. It sounded again—a long, rasping rattle and then a shriek. Does the machine they brought make that queer noise?

"She's breathing," somebody said.

"No," Anna said aloud to nobody, for nobody was listening. "No. She's dead. I couldn't help it. I let her drown. Who's going to tell James?"

The float was cleared now. Besides Estella and Anna, only the two policemen, the two men from the ambulance, and Gaines Williamson were on it. The man who had rescued them was gone. The crowd stood quietly on the levee.

"Where is Richard?" Anna said. "Did he leave?"

No one answered.

The long, rasping rattle and shriek sounded again. Gaines Williamson came over to where Anna was sitting, and bent down to her, smiling kindly. "She's alive, Mrs. Glover," he said. "She's going to be all right."

Anna shook her head.

"Yes, Ma'am. She's moving and breathing, and yelling like crazy. She's going to be all right."

Anna got up shakily. She walked over to where the men were working Estella onto a stretcher.

"What's she doing?" she said. "What's the matter with her?"

Estella was thrashing her arms and legs furiously, mouth open, eyes staring, her face again the mask of mindless terror that Anna had seen in the lake. The rattle and shriek were her breathing and screaming.

"She must think she's still in the water," one of the men said. "Shock. But she's O.K. Look at her kick."

Anna sat down on the float, her knees buckling under her, and someone pulled her out of the way while four men carried the stretcher off the float and up the levee toward the ambulance.

Richard reappeared at the foot of the levee and crossed the walkway to the Yacht Club float. He bent down to help her up. "I'm sorry I had to leave you," he said. "I had to get the children away from here and find someone to take them home."

"My God," Anna said. "She's alive. They said she would be all right."

Later, in the car, she said to her husband, "She kept pushing me down, Richard. I tried to hold her up, I tried to make her take hold of the boat. But she kept pushing me down."

"It's all right now," he said. "Try not to think about it any more."

The next day, when Anna visited Estella in the hospital, she learned that Estella remembered almost nothing of what had happened. She recalled getting into the skiff for the trip home, but everything after that was gone.

"James says you saved my life," she said, in a hoarse whisper, "and I thank you."

Her husband stood at the head of her bed, gray-haired and dignified in his Sunday suit. He nodded. "The day won't come when we'll forget it, Miss Anna," he said. "God be my witness."

Anna shook her head. "I never should have taken you out without a life preserver," she said.

"Ain't she suppose to be a grown woman?" James said. "She suppose to know better herself."

"How do you feel?" Anna asked.

"Lord, not a square inch on my body don't ache," Estella said. She laid her hands on the mound of her body under the sheet. "My stomach!" she said, with a wry laugh. "Somebody must've jumped up and down on it."

"I reckon that's from the artificial respiration," Anna said. "I had never seen anyone do it that way before. They pick you up under the stomach and then put you down and lift your arms. And then, too, I kicked you. And we must have banged you up some getting you into the boat. Lord! The more I think about it, the worse it gets. Because Gaines hit you in the stomach, too, as soon as he got you into the boat. That's what really saved your life. As soon as he got you into the boat, he hit you in the stomach and got rid of a lot of the water in your lungs and let in some air. I believe that breath you took in Gaines' boat kept you alive until we got you to the dock."

"You kicked me?" Estella said.

"We were going down," Anna said, feeling that she must confess to Estella the enormity of what she had done, "and I finally knew I couldn't keep you up. I kicked you in the stomach hard, and got loose from you, and then when you came up I grabbed you and held on, and about that time they saw us and the boats came. You passed out just when I kicked you, or else the kick knocked you out, because you didn't struggle any more. I reckon that was lucky, too."

Estella shook her head. "I can't remember anything about it," she whispered. "Not anything." She pointed out the window toward the smokestack rising from the opposite wing of the hospital. "Seems like last night I got the idea there's a little man up there," she said. "He peeps out from behind that smokestack at me, and I'm afraid of him. He leans on the smokestack, and then he jumps away real quick, like it's hot, and one time he came right over here and stood on the window ledge and looked in at me. Lucky the window was shut. I said 'Boo!' and, you know, he fell off! It didn't hurt him; he came right back. He wants to tell me something, yes, but he can't get in." She closed her eyes.

Anna looked anxiously at James.

"They still giving her something to keep her quiet," he said. "Every so often she gets a notion somebody trying to get in here."

Estella opened her eyes. "I thank you, Miss Anna," she said. "James told me you saved my life." She smiled. "Seems like every once in a while I hear your voice," she said. "Way off. Way, way off. You're saying, 'I'll save you, Estella. Don't be afraid. I'll save you.' That's all I can remember."

MAGAZINES CONSULTED

THE ANTIOCH REVIEW — 212 Xenia Avenue, Yellow Springs, Ohio.

THE ARIZONA QUARTERLY — University of Arizona, Tucson, Arizona.

ARTESIAN — 2223 S. Main Road, Ann Arbor, Michigan.

THE ATLANTIC MONTHLY — 8 Arlington Street, Boston 16, Massachusetts.

AUDIENCE — 140 Mt. Auburn Street, Cambridge 38, Massachusetts.

AUDIT — Box 92, Hayes Hall, University of Buffalo, Buffalo 14, New York.

BETWEEN WORLDS — Inter American University, San Germán, Puerto Rico.

BIG TABLE — 1316 North Dearborn Street, Chicago 10, Illinois.

CARLETON MISCELLANY — Carleton College, Northfield, Minnesota.

THE CAROLINA QUARTERLY — Box 1117, Chapel Hill, North Carolina.

CHELSEA REVIEW — Box 247, Old Chelsea Station, New York 11, New York.

CHICAGO REVIEW — University of Chicago, Chicago 37, Illinois.

THE COLORADO QUARTERLY — Hellums 118, University of Colorado, Boulder, Colorado.

COMMENTARY — 165 East 56th Street, New York 22, New York.

CONTACT — Box 755, Sausalito, California.

COSMOPOLITAN — 57 Street and Eighth Avenue, New York 19, New York.

THE DIAL — 461 Park Avenue South, New York 16, New York.

ENCOUNTER — 25 Haymarket, London, S. W. 1, England.

EPOCH — 159 Goldwin Smith Hall, Cornell University, Ithaca, New York.

ESQUIRE — 488 Madison Avenue, New York 22, New York.

EVERGREEN REVIEW — 64 University Place, New York 3, New York.

FANTASY AND SCIENCE FICTION — 580 Fifth Avenue, New York 36, New York.

FIRST PERSON — Box 273, Boston, Massachusetts.

FOUR QUARTERS — La Salle College, Philadelphia 41, Pennsylvania.

GQ (GENTLEMEN'S QUARTERLY) — 488 Madison Avenue, New York 22, New York.

THE GEORGIA REVIEW — University of Georgia, Athens, Georgia.

HARPER'S BAZAAR — 572 Madison Avenue, New York 22, New York.

HARPER'S MAGAZINE — 49 East 33rd Street, New York 16, New York.

THE HUDSON REVIEW — 65 East 55th Street, New York 22, New York.

IDENTITY — Box 773, Boston 2, Massachusetts.

THE KENYON REVIEW — Kenyon College, Gambier, Ohio.

LADIES' HOME JOURNAL — 1270 Sixth Avenue, New York 20, New York.

THE LITERARY REVIEW — Fairleigh Dickinson University, Teaneck, New Jersey.

MADEMOISELLE — 575 Madison Avenue, New York 22, New York.

MAINSTREAM — 832 Broadway, New York 3, New York.

THE MASSACHUSETTS REVIEW — University of Massachusetts, Amherst, Massachusetts.

MIDSTREAM — 515 Park Avenue, New York 22, New York.

MINNESOTA REVIEW — Box 4068, University Station, Minneapolis, Minnesota.

MSS — 702 Madrone, Chico, California.

MUTINY — Box 278, Northport, New York.

NEW MEXICO QUARTERLY — University of New Mexico Press, Marron Hall, Albuquerque, New Mexico.

NEW WORLD WRITING — c/o J. B. Lippincott Company, 521 Fifth Avenue, New York 17, New York.

THE NEW YORKER — 25 West 43rd Street, New York 36, New York.

NIMROD — University of Tulsa, Tulsa, Oklahoma.

THE NOBLE SAVAGE — Meridian Books, 119 West 57th Street, New York 19, New York.

NORTHWEST REVIEW — Erb Memorial Student Union, University of Oregon, Eugene, Oregon.

THE PARIS REVIEW — 45–39 171 Place, Flushing 58, New York.

PARTISAN REVIEW — 22 East 17 Street, New York 3, New York.

PERSPECTIVE — Washington University Post Office, St. Louis 5, Missouri.

PLAYBOY — 232 East Ohio Street, Chicago 11, Illinois.

PRAIRIE SCHOONER — Andrews Hall, University of Nebraska, Lincoln 8, Nebraska.

QUARTERLY REVIEW OF LITERATURE — Box 287, Bard College, Annandale-on-Hudson, New York.

THE REPORTER — 660 Madison Avenue, New York 21, New York.

SAN FRANCISCO REVIEW — Box 671, San Francisco, California.

THE SATURDAY EVENING POST — 666 Fifth Avenue, New York 19, New York.

SECOND COMING — 200 West 107 Street, New York 25, New York.

SEQUOIA — Box 2167, Stanford University, Stanford, California.

THE SEWANEE REVIEW — University of the South, Sewanee, Tennessee.

SHENANDOAH — Box 722, Lexington, Virginia.

SOUTHWEST REVIEW — Southern Methodist University Press, Dallas 22, Texas.

STORY — 135 Central Park West, New York 23, New York.

TEXAS QUARTERLY — Box 7527, University of Texas, Austin 12, Texas.

THE TRANSATLANTIC REVIEW — 821 Second Avenue, New York 17, New York.

THE UNIVERSITY OF KANSAS CITY REVIEW — University of Kansas City, 51st and Rockhill Road, Kansas City, Missouri.

VENTURE — Box 228, Old Chelsea Station, New York 11, New York.

THE VIRGINIA QUARTERLY REVIEW — University of Virginia, 1 West Range, Charlottesville, Virginia.

VOGUE — 420 Lexington Avenue, New York 17, New York.

WOMAN'S DAY — 67 West 44 Street, New York 36, New York.

THE YALE REVIEW — 28 Hillhouse Avenue, New Haven, Connecticut.

Stories
Prize stories of
1963: O. Henry...

Stories
Prize stories of 1963: O. Henry